THE CONFRONTATION

"What do you see in the man?" Nick burst out, a dark tide of anger swamping his better judgment.

Lynn frowned in confusion. "What man?"

"You know who I mean—that idiot Werth."

"Conrad? I really don't understand."

"Cut the crap! It's obvious what's between you. Why else did he bring you here from Boston if it wasn't to be his spy?"

She gaped at him and after a moment opened the door and slid out. He slammed out of the car and caught her by the arm.

"You're not going anywhere until I get an answer," he snarled.

"I have nothing to say to you." Ice clung to every word.

He gripped her shoulders. "You're damn well going to!"

"Let me go!" she cried, struggling to get free.

Nick yanked her toward him, his hands holding her body tight against his. His mouth covered hers in a savage kiss.

Suddenly Lynn thrust her arms between them and wrenched loose. "I'll walk from here," she said, turning from him and striding briskly away.

DOCTORS
and Lovers

Jane Toombs

PINNACLE BOOKS

Windsor Publishing Corp.
475 Park Avenue South
New York, NY 10016

PINNACLE BOOKS
WINDSOR PUBLISHING CORP.

PINNACLE BOOKS

are published by

Windsor Publishing Corp.
475 Park Avenue South
New York, NY 10016

First printing: April, 1989

Printed in the United States of America

Chapter 1

Harper Hills Hospital.

The sun's heat struck Lynn Holley like a blow as she stood staring at the sign. What was she doing here? It had been a mistake to leave everything she knew in the hope of freeing herself. She'd left the cold and the snow behind in Boston, but the past was inescapable.

She took a deep breath and glanced quickly around. If not for the sign, she might believe she was about to enter a resort rather than a hospital. In the east hospitals were tall, multistoried, utilitarian buildings, and in February nothing brightened their winter grime.

Harper Hills' modest five floors sprawled picturesquely over landscaped grounds where palms and colorful splashes of flowers softened the building's outlines. Southern California, with its red-tiled roofs and exotic shrubbery, seemed as alien to Lynn as another planet.

Even though she'd been forced to carry the unwelcome baggage of her past life with her, she was a long way from Boston ... a long way from winter. Lynn smoothed her hair and moistened her lips with her tongue. Santa Ana weather, Californians called this hot dry wind blowing from desert to ocean. Hostile weather. The wind sucked all the moisture from her skin and the sunlight glinting off the upper windows of the hospital hurt her eyes.

Harper Hills. Had it been a mistake to come? Had she acted too hastily because she felt she owed Conrad a favor?

Never mind, she told herself. She was here, and she would see it through. She strode purposefully toward the entrance, pulled open the door, and walked into the lobby. Instantly she felt more at home. Harper Hills smelled like a hospital, with that distinctive blend of antiseptics, food, and a subtle tinge of something not quite identifiable but not unpleasant. A familiar, welcoming smell.

She started toward the information desk, intending to ask the way to the nursing director's office. Unreasonably, her stomach twisted into knots. Why should she be nervous about the interview? She was an experienced twenty-seven-year-old, not a green graduate intimidated by authority. Besides, she'd been invited to work at Harper Hills by the hospital administrator himself.

Lynn stopped abruptly when a tall dark-haired man in a green scrub suit cut in front of her. He paid no attention to their near-collision as he grasped the arm of a short, stout older woman who was hurrying to the door.

"So you thought you could sneak out without talking to me!" he snapped at the woman, who gazed up at him fearfully. "No such luck, Grandma."

Lynn frowned. Grandma? Another insensitive doctor who didn't bother to remember names, she thought smugly.

"You're trying to kill your daughter, is that it?" he went on. "You *want* her to die."

Lynn glared at him. What a cruel thing to say!

"No, no!" the woman cried, her hands clasped tightly.

6

The doctor dropped her arm and she backed away from him. "You know what convulsions are?" he demanded.

The woman, her dark eyes looking everywhere but at his angry face, nodded.

"She's going to have convulsions, your daughter. She's going to shake and shiver until it kills her." He bent threateningly toward the woman. "Do you understand, Grandma?"

Lynn couldn't stand any more. She marched over to them, put an arm around the woman, who was now weeping, and glared at the dark-haired doctor. "You have no right to be so cruel!" she cried.

His black eyes glittered with annoyance. "Who the hell are you, and what right do you have to interfere?"

She countered with her own question. "Why must you be so abusive? You've frightened her nearly to death."

"Good. Maybe she'll think twice the next time." Ignoring Lynn, he leaned down and caught the older woman's gaze. "You remember what I said, *comprende?*"

"*Si,*" the woman muttered, freeing herself from Lynn and scuttling for the door.

Wanting nothing further to do with him, Lynn started to turn away, but the doctor grabbed her wrist. "I have some advice for you." He waited until she looked at him. "Don't be so pushy when you have no idea of what's going on." He let her go, strode from the lobby and down a corridor, and disappeared from sight.

Lynn, conscious only now of the bystanders' stares, lifted her chin and walked quickly to the information desk. If he was an example of how doctors at Harper Hills behaved, then the medical staff here had a lot to learn about how to treat patients.

"That Dr. Dow," the pink-clad woman at the desk said

before Lynn could open her mouth. "He's really something, isn't he?"

Lynn blinked. The volunteer actually sounded admiring.

"Can I help you?" the woman asked before Lynn had thought of the best way to describe how *she* felt about the arrogant Dr. Dow.

"Where is Mrs. Morrin's office?" she asked finally.

Two phones sat on the director of nurses' desk, one white, one red. Mrs. Morrin, gray muting her carroty hair, waved Lynn to a chair while continuing to talk into the red phone. The DNS's pale blue eyes, magnified by oversized glasses, assessed Lynn with cool efficiency and she felt her stomach tighten into knots of tension once again.

Mrs. Morrin hung up the red phone. "We have an emergency situation, Ms. Holley," she said in lieu of any greeting, "and you're my solution." Her voice was firm, her words clipped. "I hope you'll be able to begin work by tomorrow morning. As day charge nurse on maternity."

Lynn stared at her, unable to answer. *Maternity.* The word hung in the air between them. A phone rang, the secretary buzzed, Mrs. Morrin picked up the white phone, but what Lynn heard and saw was without meaning. Desperately, she interlocked her fingers and clenched her jaw as the past washed over her in a tidal wave of grief.

"You're lucky, you know," Dr. Lourdes had said. "The high concentration of CO obviously damaged the embryo. You're fortunate to have aborted spontaneously so you didn't have to make the decision."

CO: carbon monoxide. A deadly, invisible killer.

"Extremely lucky," Dr. Lourdes went on, "to have no permanent damage whatsoever when you could have come out of this a gork, as you well know."

8

Mindless . . . a vegetable who didn't think or feel. She'd rather be dead. Her baby *was* dead . . . dead and gone from her body before it had a chance. Ray was dead, too. But somehow, against all odds, she'd survived to carry the guilty burden of remembering.

"Ms. Holley?"

Lynn stared at the graying woman who sat across the desk from her and for a moment couldn't place her. El Doblez, California, she told herself. Harper Hills Hospital. Mrs. Morrin. She took a deep breath, searching for words. Not maternity, she couldn't possibly work in maternity.

"I understood I was being hired as day charge nurse on the medical unit." Lynn was surprised at how even and reasonable her voice sounded while her insides churned in panic.

Mrs. Morrin's cool eyes grew chillier. "When our administrator, Mr. Werth, asked me to place you on medical, I told him I would . . . if possible. Last night my maternity charge nurse, Lois Johnson, was admitted to ICU at St. Vincent's in LA with a head injury following a freeway accident. Her condition's guarded; she may have a subdural hematoma."

"I'm sorry about the accident," Lynn managed to say.

"So you understand why I'm assigning you to maternity."

Did she detect the tiniest thread of satisfaction in Mrs. Morrin's voice? It suddenly occurred to Lynn that the DNS might resent Conrad Werth's invasion of her territory, might be annoyed at being told what nurse to hire and where to put her.

Obviously this really was an emergency. But Lynn wasn't ready to help deliver babies, to deal with happy mothers and their healthy newborns when she hadn't yet dealt with losing her own child. Maybe she would never be ready.

"It's been three years since I worked in maternity," Lynn pointed out. "I'm not up on current practice."

"Are you telling me you won't take the position?" Again Lynn caught a nuance in Mrs. Morrin's voice that suggested the DNS would just as soon see the last of her here and now. The woman was waiting to pounce on a reason not to hire her.

Lynn damn well wasn't going to oblige her. She stiffened and met those cold blue eyes. "As you say, this is an emergency. I'm willing to be assigned where I'm needed and I can begin tomorrow. I do hope, though, the injured nurse will be able to return to maternity as soon as she recovers."

Mrs. Morrin smiled without warmth. "Naturally, I hope so, too. When and if she does, I'll reevaluate your request for a medical unit."

It sounded to Lynn like a lie.

"I'll have my assistant take you around for a brief orientation today," the DNS continued. "Welcome to Harper Hills."

Lynn tried to convince herself that a begrudging welcome was better than none at all. For some reason Mrs. Morrin had made up her mind to dislike Lynn Holley before she'd ever set eyes on her.

Mrs. Morrin opened her office door and introduced Lynn to her assistant director. Ms. Elkins was about Lynn's age, an attractive black woman whose uniform fit her tall, slender body like a designer dress, the white setting off her brown skin.

"Call me Joyce," she told Lynn, who relaxed a little at the friendliness in her voice.

"Do all RNs at Harper Hills wear white?" Lynn asked as they entered an elevator.

"Yes, except for pediatrics, where no one wears white.

10

On maternity you're in green scrub gowns half the time, of course." Joyce paused, looking curiously at Lynn. "How do you feel about plunging in tomorrow with no orientation?"

Lynn smiled slightly. "Scared." She was more scared than Joyce could possibly know. "I've been a charge nurse before, but only on medical."

"Morrin wouldn't put you on maternity if she didn't think you could handle it—if that's any comfort. Take it from me. She has a good eye for quality."

It'd be nice to believe that cold-eyed woman saw *my* quality, Lynn thought, but I don't. She just wanted to get rid of me. I wonder if she knows how close she came?

"Have you heard exactly how badly injured Ms. Johnson is?" Lynn asked.

"Not really. You never know what's going to happen with head injuries."

The elevator door slid open and Joyce gestured to a sign as they got out. "Three West. This is maternity."

She led Lynn through double swinging doors and past the windows of the newborn nursery. Lynn turned her head to avoid seeing the long-legged bassinets looking like so many storks holding babies.

"The labor rooms are down there," Joyce pointed out, "next to delivery. Our operating room for Caesareans doubles as a second delivery room if we need it. These are two private rooms, sometimes used as labor rooms. The postpartum semi-private rooms start beyond them. We'll walk through and I'll introduce you to your staff."

Her staff. Lynn tried to fix names in her mind—Sheila Burns, acting charge nurse; Clovis Reilly, nursery nurse; Mary Rodrigues, Lisa, Jean, Helen—but knew she wouldn't remember them all. Familiar sights—a piggyback intravenous hung on a pole, infusing into a patient's arm, a

11

medication cart, a doctor scribbling on a chart—reassured her. She'd handled a unit before; she could handle one again, even if it was maternity.

The next morning Lynn arrived on Three West nearly forty-five minutes early. She was due in at seven, but charge nurses always came in at least a quarter-hour early. She didn't see the night charge, Ms. Garcia, so she decided while she waited for the change-of-shift report, she'd make rounds ... beginning with the labor rooms.

She felt both tired and nervously alert. Her biorhythms hadn't yet adjusted to west coast time and her night had been restless because of her apprehension about starting a new job. Maternity was the last service she wanted to be on. With the unresolved grief she carried for her lost child, how could she tolerate dealing with newborns? But she had to try.

Labor room one was empty. Lynn checked the card on the door of labor room two. Mrs. Derrick was a primipara, a woman having her first child. The patient's husband was with her, holding her hand and leaning over the bed, breathing with his wife in a pattern Lynn recognized as a natural childbirth technique. The monitor showed a normal fetal heart pattern.

"The baby's doing fine," Lynn assured the Derricks.

"So am I," the woman said. "So far, anyway."

Lynn managed a smile as she went out. The light was on in the delivery room. Ms. Garcia was probably helping with a birth. Lynn hesitated at the door and heard the muted squall of a newborn making its first protest. She tried to force herself to go in, but failed.

"Ms. Garcia," a voice called urgently and Lynn turned. The young nurse who'd spoken broke off and stared at her from the doorway of one of the private rooms.

"Sorry," the nurse apologized, walking toward Lynn.

"You're not Ms. Garcia. I don't know why I thought so—you're taller and your hair is lighter. Honestly, you don't look like her at all."

"I'm Lynn Holley, the new day charge."

"Carrie Maybanks." The woman's pin told Lynn she was an LVN, a licensed vocational nurse. In the east she'd have been an LPN, licensed practical nurse.

"You're younger than I expected," Carrie added. "Anyway, I'm glad you're here. I'm worried about Mrs. Miller." She nodded toward the room she'd just left. "I was going to ask Ms. Garcia to look at her. Mrs. Miller's thirty-five. Her husband works for Scripps and is on sea duty, so she's alone. She's a multipara—this is her third pregnancy and there's something wrong, but I'm not sure just what."

Lynn started toward Mrs. Miller's room with Carrie at her side. "Why do you think something's wrong?"

Carrie made a face. "You probably heard already from Ms. Garcia how I tend to overreact. Only this time I don't think it's that. Mrs. Miller's not actually hemorrhaging, but there's more blood than usual. I thought of a low placental implant, a placenta previa, but there's a sonogram report on her chart that says the placenta's in high normal position."

"Nurse," Mrs. Miller called as they entered the room. "Oh, Nurse, the pain's worse. It hurts terribly."

Lynn hurried to the bed. "We'll take a look," she said soothingly as she checked the monitors—one for the fetal heart rate, one to evaluate uterine contractions—before leaning over the patient. Mrs. Miller's face furrowed in pain and she clutched at Lynn's hand apprehensively.

"It isn't like labor contractions," she gasped. "This came on all of a sudden and it's awful ... I can't stand much more."

13

Abruptio placenta? Lynn had never seen a case, but she knew acute pain was a symptom of the placenta separating from the uterus prematurely, before the baby was born. Carrie had mentioned bleeding. Lynn lifted the sheet to check Mrs. Miller's pads. Bright red blood, not excessive—but more serious bleeding could be concealed inside the uterus.

She looked again at the monitors. The fetal heart rate was one hundred and twenty—normal. She put her hand on the patient's abdomen. The uterus felt board-hard in one place, soft in another, totally unlike a normal contraction. The monitor showed an unusual contraction wave.

Thoughts flicked with laser-like speed through her head as she urged Carrie ahead of her to the door. Should she risk a vaginal exam? Did she have time? This could be a real emergency. Abruptio placenta wasn't common, one in five hundred pregnancies at the most. What if she alerted the doctor for an emergency when there was none? It was not the best way to start off as charge nurse. But something was very wrong with Mrs. Miller.

If the sonogram report on her chart showed a normal, high site on the uterine wall for the implantation of the placenta, then Mrs. Miller couldn't have what Carrie tentatively diagnosed, a placenta so low the baby's head was damaging it as labor progressed, causing bleeding. What Lynn feared was even worse—the premature peeling off of a normally situated placenta inside the uterus, a condition that could kill both mother and baby.

Lynn made up her mind. "Get her doctor here as fast as you can," she ordered Carrie, keeping her voice low. "If any of the day shift nurses are here, tell one of them to come *stat.*"

"A Caesarean?" Carrie whispered.

"Probably. Get moving."

14

The fetal monitor beeped, alerting Lynn to a drop in the baby's heart rate, a sign of fetal distress. The beeps continued as Lynn hurried back to the bedside.

"What's that noise? What's happening?" Mrs. Miller cried. "I heard someone say 'a Caesarean.' Where's Dr. Linnett?"

"I'm going to wheel you into the operating room," Lynn said, speaking as calmly as she could. "We want to be all ready if your doctor decides to do a Caesarean. He'll be here soon."

"Is the baby all right?"

"The beeps mean the heart's beating," Lynn answered evasively as a short and attractive dark-haired RN came into the room. Lynn recognized Sheila Burns from yesterday.

"What's the matter?" Sheila asked.

"I'm moving Mrs. Miller into the C-section room. Help me with the monitors."

As they pushed the bed through the doorway, Lynn saw a man in a green scrub suit come out of the delivery room. "Doctor?" she said.

He turned and came toward them and Lynn, to her dismay, recognized the dark-haired, arrogant man she'd encountered in the lobby yesterday.

"Dr. Dow isn't Mrs. Miller's—" Sheila began.

Lynn cut her off. Never mind—he was a doctor and she needed one desperately. "Dr. Dow," she said crisply, "I believe this patient has an abruptio. The baby's in distress. Could you stand by until Dr. Linnett gets here?"

Dr. Dow raised his eyebrows in belated recognition, but didn't comment on their previous meeting. "You're sure it's abruptio?"

Lynn's nod was terse.

Dr. Dow looked down at the patient. "I can see you're

15

in pain," he said to Mrs. Miller, "and I'm going to find out why." He laid his hand on her abdomen and almost instantly removed it. "You have a problem," he told her, "but we're going to take care of it and get rid of that pain for you." He turned to Lynn. "Get her on the table," he ordered, rapidly pushing the bed into the operating room.

Carrie came running along the corridor. "Dr. Linnett is on his way."

"Is he in the hospital?" Dr. Dow snapped.

"No, at home."

"We can't wait. Set up for a C-section while I get the anesthesia cart."

While Lynn and Sheila slid Mrs. Miller onto the operating table, Lynn decided how to handle the emergency most efficiently. "You scrub," she told Sheila. "I'll circulate."

Sheila stared at her with mutinous brown eyes, opened her mouth and closed it without speaking, then nodded.

"Get the patient on her side for a spinal," Dr. Dow ordered. "Page any pediatrician in the house and get him up here stat. Try for an anesthesiologist, too. Draw blood for type and cross-match. Four pints at least, better ask for six."

"Carrie," Lynn said as she eased the groaning Mrs. Miller onto her side, "you do the paging and send someone in to take blood to the lab." She turned to Dr. Dow. "Shall I start a unit of dextran intravenously after I draw the blood?"

"Right."

Lynn grabbed the IV cart, threaded a needle into a vein in the patient's left forearm, withdrew blood, then connected IV tubing so dextran dripped into the vein. By the time she finished, Dr. Dow had given the spinal anesthetic.

A stocky blond man in a scrub suit pushed through the swinging doors.

"Problems, Nick?" he asked.

"Abruptio." Dr. Dow's voice was abrupt. "I imagine all the anesthesiologists are busy in the OR. Could you monitor the mother until Linnett gets here, Joe? Then we'll need you for the baby." Without waiting for an answer, he hurried off to scrub.

Joe must be a pediatrician, Lynn decided as she inserted a catheter into Mrs. Miller's bladder. Sheila returned masked, wearing a sterile gown and gloves. After Lynn painted Mrs. Miller's abdomen with antiseptic, Sheila laid sterile drapes around the patient.

Dr. Dow, in sterile gear, picked up a scalpel and cut through the skin, frowning in concentration. Lynn watched as he deftly incised the uterus. His height and dark coloring reminded her of Ray. Also his nerve. According to regulations, he should have waited until Dr. Linnett had arrived to scrub with him.

But was it worth it even if they lost Mrs. Miller while he waited? Lynn wondered.

"Her pressure's dropping," the pediatrician warned.

Blood welled up, poured over the operative field, trickled off the table and began to pool on the floor.

"Damn," Dr. Dow muttered.

"What's going on?" a voice demanded from behind Lynn. She turned and saw an flush-faced graying man in street clothes.

"Abruptio," Dr. Dow said without looking up, his gloved hands groping through the blood.

"You want to spell me, Dr. Linnett?" the pediatrician asked. "Or do you want to take the baby?"

Dr. Linnett hesitated. "Dr. King, is it? I'll monitor my patient." He emphasized the last two words.

Lynn found a gown for Dr. Linnett. He shrugged into it and replaced Dr. King at the head of the table. The pediatrician took the baby Dr. Dow lifted from the open uterus, sponged blood off its face with gauze, and aspirated the nose and mouth while Dr. Dow clamped and cut the cord.

When the pediatrician carried the baby to the warmed Isolette, his shoes left a trail of bloody footprints. Lynn hadn't heard the newborn cry and she bit her lip as she watched Dr. King insert an endotracheal tube into the baby's trachea to begin ventilating its lungs. She wouldn't believe the baby was dead, she couldn't bear the thought. It would be like losing her baby all over again.

"Where's the blood I ordered?" Dr. Dow's tense voice made her jump.

"I'll check." Lynn started for a phone and almost ran into the lab messenger carrying blood packets. As quickly as she could, Lynn checked the blood, the patient's name, and the type. She rushed back into the operating room and attached one unit of blood as a piggyback into the IV line in Mrs. Miller's vein.

"Bring the ventilator over," Dr. Linnett ordered. "She needs help breathing."

Lynn pushed the machine closer to the head of the table. Dr. Linnett grabbed the mask and slapped it over Mrs. Miller's face. A soft clicking began as the machine breathed for her.

"Couvelaire uterus," Dr. Dow announced. "It'll have to come out to stop the bleeding." He looked at Dr. Linnett. "Do you agree? She's your patient."

Couvelaire uterus. Lynn had read about it but she'd never seen one. It was caused by blood seeping into the uterine muscle until the uterus couldn't contract to shut off the bleeding vessels left by the peeled-away placenta.

Mrs. Miller would bleed to death unless they did a hysterectomy. *Stat.*

So why was Dr. Linnett hesitating? Lynn wondered. Was it because Dr. Dow had taken over his patient without his permission? But if he hadn't, Mrs. Miller would be dead.

"Nothing else to do," Dr. Linnett muttered finally.

"Joe, can you leave the baby?" Dr. Dow asked. "Dr. Linnett's going to scrub in."

"She's doing fine," the pediatrician said.

"What the hell are you talking about?" Dr. Dow demanded. "She's damn near exsanguinated; I'm standing in blood an inch deep."

"The baby's a girl," Lynn told him. "That's who Dr. King means."

Dr. Dow glanced at her and she could tell from the way his eyes crinkled that he was smiling behind the mask. "To tell the truth, I hadn't noticed." He handed a retractor to Sheila. "Hang onto this until Dr. Linnett's ready. We've got to save that little girl's mother for her."

To Lynn's surprise, Dr. Linnett assisted rather than taking over the surgery. When Dr. Dow at last began sewing up the skin, Lynn glanced at the door. Only eight-thirty! She felt like she'd been in this operating room for an entire eight-hour shift.

"Her pressure's back up a little," Dr. King announced. "I think the last unit of blood turned the tide."

Lynn exhaled slowly. Mrs. Miller stood a chance of making it. Clovis Reilly, the tall, thin redheaded nurse from the newborn nursery, worked over the baby in the isolette and the infant, who'd been coughing and mewing weakly, began to cry.

Mrs. Miller's eyelids fluttered and opened briefly. A faint smile touched her lips.

"I owe you thanks," Dr. Linnet said to Dr. Dow. Reluctantly, Lynn thought. Begrudgingly.

Dr. Dow shook his head. "Any thanks goes to Ms. Holley. She made the diagnosis and then commandeered me."

Both doctors looked at Lynn. Pulling his mask down, Dr. Dow grinned one-sidedly and said to her, "Sometimes it pays to be pushy."

Chapter 2

Lynn carried her lunch tray toward the cafeteria tables, looking for Joyce Elkins. In the two weeks she'd been working on Three West, the maternity unit staff hadn't warmed to her and all conversation stopped if she sat at a table with them. It puzzled and upset her, since up until now she'd always gotten on well with her fellow nurses.

Joyce was the only one who welcomed her as a lunch partner, and had even helped her find an apartment, something Lynn had rather expected Conrad might do. For some reason he hadn't contacted her once since she'd arrived in El Doblez. Did he have second thoughts about asking her to come here?

Joyce was nowhere in sight, so Lynn headed for an empty table. Sooner or later she was going to have to confront her staff and thrash things out, but the hospital cafeteria at noon wasn't the place for it.

"Hello there." Lynn looked up at Dr. King's smiling face. Instead of carrying his tray on to the special room reserved for doctors, he put it down on the nearest table and, with a sideways nod of his head, invited her to join him.

"How're things going?" he asked as she sat down.

"Fair."

He raised his eyebrows when she didn't elaborate. "Find it hard being the new girl in town?"

"Something like that."

"Well, you certainly impressed old Nick with the way you handled that abruptio. Me, too, for that matter—but then I'm easy to impress, or so my wife claims. Nick isn't."

Nick. Dr. Dow. Lynn hadn't seen him except in passing since Miss Miller's C-section, and those few times he hadn't given any indication of noticing her.

"Mrs. Miller took the baby home yesterday," Lynn said. "They're both doing fine."

"I like happy endings."

"You helped make it one, Dr. King." And so had she. Being partly responsible for saving another woman's baby had helped ease her own loss a little.

"Joe, okay?"

Lynn smiled and nodded. "I thought maybe Dr. Linnett would be angry with me because I didn't wait for him to get there that morning, but he hasn't said a word."

"He was a tad pissed off with Nick, but he knows damn well Nick saved mother and child, so he could hardly lodge a complaint."

Lynn's eyes widened. "I never meant to get Dr. Dow into trouble."

Joe King laughed. "He told me he knew the first time he saw you that you were a woman who went out of her way to look for trouble."

She was taken aback, then annoyed. Nick Dow had no right to pin such a label on her. She wasn't a trouble-maker. Did he expect her to do nothing when she saw someone treated abusively, to stand back and let a woman die instead of taking forceful action?

"Nancy and I are having a barbecue at our place this Saturday," Joe said. "I hope you can make it. Nancy can hardly wait to meet you. She said she didn't think the nurse existed who could knock Nick back on his heels."

"Oh? Does Dr. Dow have something against nurses?"

Joe's smile was wry. "Not when they stay in their place. Nick's a great guy, but a firm believer in nurses staying at the bedside."

"The doctor's handmaiden?"

"You've got it. About the party—"

"It's nice of you to invite me. I'd like to come."

Lynn watched Joe scribble directions, her pleasure muted by her mounting irritation at Nick Dow. He might be a capable doctor, but he was narrow-minded, egotistical, and cruel.

"How does his wife stand him?" she muttered, only half-aware she spoke aloud.

"Stand who?" Joe asked. "If you mean Nick, no problem. He isn't married."

Nicholas Dow stood in the cafeteria line, his eyes on Lynn Holley. No doubt about it, she was worth a second look. Not pretty, exactly, but disturbing with those huge green eyes that seemed to penetrate a man's defenses. Her chestnut curls gleamed beneath her white organdy cap. The rest of her was temptingly shaped—he'd give her legs alone a ten.

But she was trouble with a capital T. Attractively packaged trouble. He was sure of that even before Sheila Burns told him what she'd unearthed: Lynn Holley was a friend of Conrad Werth's . . . a close personal friend. And Conrad had arranged for Lynn to follow him from Boston and come to California to work at Harper Hills.

To have his mistress conveniently near? Or to plant a management spy? Both, he'd bet.

23

Nick gritted his teeth. She had a hell of a nerve reaming him out in the lobby when she'd come here under false pretenses. She had turned out to be one very sharp nurse, but so what? There was no excuse for spying on the side. Her personal life was her own business, but what she saw in the new hospital administrator was beyond him. In his opinion Werth was long on smarm and short on sex appeal.

Absently he chose a sandwich and set it on his tray, moving to the cashier. Lynn was a good-looking woman; why would she waste herself on Werth? Nick couldn't warm to the man—five feet ten inches of boyishly freckled affability concealing a heart of ice. Werth had been appointed administrator when Consolidated Medical Corporation, a management company, took over Harper Hills a few months ago. He was profit-centered, a home office man through and through, never mind what was best for the patients.

There'd been rumors that Werth planned ruthless cuts in all services. With Lynn his hatchetwoman for nursing? Nick grimaced in distaste. That's one gal to steer clear of, he told himself.

Ignoring his own advice, he threaded between the tables and set his tray down beside Joe.

"Yo, Nick," Joe said and Nick gave him a brief half-smile.

"Hello, Dr. Dow." Lynn's voice was cool.

He nodded without speaking and saw a flash of anger light up her green eyes. He'd riled her. *Good.*

"Lucky you're not married," Joe told him.

He glanced at Joe and raised his eyebrows.

"You're wearing your mess-with-me-and-you-get-wasted mask," Joe went on. "Lynn, here, figures a wife wouldn't be able to stand you and, man, she's right on. Wives don't go for dark moods."

Nick scowled at Lynn. She shrugged and put down her coffee cup. He saw she intended to leave, even though she'd barely touched her food. For some reason this made him even angrier.

"Don't let me scare you off," he said caustically.

Her back straightened. "Like you did 'Grandma'?" The question flicked out like a whip.

Nick leaned forward, his eyes narrowing. "I don't have to tell you how serious preeclampsia is, how it can escalate into eclampsia and terminate in fatal convulsions, killing both mother and baby. Well, Grandma almost did in her pregnant and preeclamptic daughter with *curandera* medicine. Not once—twice. If I didn't manage to scare her out of it, chances are she'll succeed the next time." Watching her brows draw together, he added, "A *curandera*'s a Mexican folk healer. Maybe Bostonians don't have to deal with them, but here in California we do."

"Did you ever think of reasoning with the woman instead of threatening her?" Lynn's voice quivered with suppressed anger.

Nick threw up his hands. "Reason!"

" 'Reason, which fifty times to one does err, Reason, an *ignis fatuus* of the mind." ' Joe finished his quote and beamed at both of them in turn. "John Wilmot, Earl of Rochester," he added. "Supposed to be one of my ancestors, but that's probably wishful thinking, an *ignis fatuus*, a will-of-the-wisp. I suspect I really come from lusty old peasant stock. I won't tell you my wife's opinion."

Nick's lips twitched in reluctant amusement. He could never hold onto his anger when Joe was around. He saw Lynn's tense expression ease, though she didn't smile. On impulse he reached his hand toward her across the table.

"Truce?" he said.

She hesitated, her gaze evaluating him. He was about to draw back his hand when she lifted hers and clasped his in a firm grip.

"Truce," she echoed.

"Any other games you'd like to play, children?" Joe asked.

At this, Lynn did smile. When she sought to draw back her hand, Nick realized he was still grasping it and let go abruptly.

"And how do you like Harper Hills so far, Ms. Holley?" he asked, using formality to cover having held her hand longer than necessary.

"I'm reserving judgment until I've been here longer, Dr. Dow."

Joe's sigh suggested he was sorely tried. He pointed at himself—"Me Joe," at Nick—"he Nick," at Lynn—"she Lynn. Okay?"

Lynn returned to Three West not quite sure how she felt about Nick Dow. His dark good looks attracted her, but his manner put her off. She didn't trust him, that she knew. Maybe it wasn't fair to compare him to Ray, but she couldn't help it because Nick reminded her so much of Ray. She'd thought she loved Ray. When they married it was a dream come true, but their life together had been a nightmare. She was damned if she'd involve herself with another unstable, moody doctor, no matter how attractive he was.

In fact, she didn't care to become involved with any man at the moment. Her main concern was succeeding in her new job—and that wasn't going to be easy. The work wasn't the problem, she'd mastered all the new procedures

26

quickly. No, the problem was the staff's attitude, and Lynn knew exactly who was influencing the others. Sheila Burns, who'd acted as charge during the few days after Lois Johnson's accident and before Lynn arrived, was doing her best to undermine Lynn's authority.

Lynn checked her watch. Yes, Sheila was late returning from lunch . . . again. Seven minutes so far—she was pushing her luck.

Sheila had started so subtly that Lynn hadn't realized at first she was carrying on an insidious campaign. One minute late from a break, two from lunch. Not enough to comment on. Then three, four, five. It didn't take long for the other employees to follow suit. If Lynn wasn't going to reprimand Sheila, then the others wouldn't knock themselves out to get back to work on time.

So far, only two remained uninfluenced by Sheila's behavior—the ward clerk, Mary Gabaldon, a competent older woman who did her work and minded her own business, and Clovis Reilly, in the nursery, a perfectionist if ever there was one. They were always prompt. Naturally Lynn took pains to be on time herself.

Sheila's tardiness seemed to be a minor irritant, but Lynn was certain she was doing it deliberately to test Lynn's reaction. If Lynn didn't confront her on this issue, Sheila would think of another sly challenge and, eventually, force all the employees to take sides, to stand either with her or with Lynn. No unit could run smoothly with such internecine warfare. Though she wasn't sure of Sheila's motive, she suspected it was anger at being passed over as charge nurse for an outsider from the east.

Sheila returned from lunch nine minutes late with LVN Lisa Fuentes, who'd gone with her. Lynn held her tongue. She'd get to Sheila before the shift was over, but in private.

Her chance came on a break, when she followed Sheila into the empty nurses' lounge.

Before she had a chance to say anything, Sheila spoke. "Hey, I hear you had lunch with the Harper Hills Heartbreaker."

Even if Joe King hadn't been married, Lynn would never cast him in the role of heartbreaker; she knew very well who Sheila meant, but she had no intention of slipping into a just-us-girls mode.

"I ate lunch with Dr. King and Dr. Dow," she said dismissively.

Sheila wasn't to be deterred so easily. "You don't mind a friendly warning, I hope. Keep any relationship with Nick Dow on the light side. He once told my husband that if he ever, God forbid, decided to get married, the last woman he'd choose would be a nurse."

Lynn tamped down her annoyance at Sheila's implication that Lynn was even mildly interested in Nick Dow, aware she had to remain calm.

"Thank you for your concern," she said crisply. "I wish you showed the same concern for being on time at work."

Sheila widened her eyes. "I've been late?"

"I'm sure you know you have. I expect it to stop. I don't give second warnings. I'd like us to cooperate in caring for—"

"Are you threatening me?" Sheila's brown eyes smoldered.

Lynn was taken aback to see what looked like real hatred in her co-worker's gaze but she concealed her reaction. "I'm simply pointing out that I, as charge nurse, and you, as a team leader, are responsible for setting standards for the other employees. Don't you agree?"

"Are you going to take this to the top?" Sheila challenged.

"To Mrs. Morrin? Why should I? It's no big deal, I'm sure you can manage to be prompt."

Sheila muttered something Lynn couldn't quite hear. It sounded like she'd said Morrin wasn't who she had in mind.

"Pardon?"

Sheila shrugged. "As you say—no big deal. I just didn't realize you counted seconds."

Lynn overlooked the sarcasm ... for the time being. "I appreciate your cooperation." She deliberately made her tone formal.

Without answering, Sheila headed for the door into the bathroom. As she opened it, Lynn sprang her question. "If not Mrs. Morrin, who did you think I'd report you to?"

Sheila turned enough to say over her shoulder, "You know as well as I do." She hurried through the door, shutting it behind her.

Lynn stared with dismay at the closed door, a light beginning to dawn: Conrad Werth. The hospital grapevine spread news with the speed of sound. By now all the employees must have heard how the administrator had arranged this job for her. How stupid she'd been ... no wonder her co-workers were standoffish. They weren't sure they could trust her.

Maybe it had been a mistake to come to Harper Hills, no matter how much she owed Conrad. He'd called her long distance on Christmas to wish her holiday greetings and ask how she was getting along, then spilled out his problems.

"It's my big chance, Lynn," he had said, "and I don't want to mess up. Two months ago my company, CMC, bought Harper Hills, a 275-bed community hospital in El Doblez—that's a coastal town between LA and San Diego—and sent me here as administrator. Naturally they expect miracles. Harper Hills has been losing money, and they want it on a paying basis by the end of my first year. Frankly, I need help. Your help."

Lynn wasn't interested. Since Ray's and the baby's deaths, her shroud of lethargy threaded with self-pity closed her off from everyone and everything. But Conrad persisted.

"I'm to correct the inefficiencies, raise the quality of medical care, weed out staff incompetents, and wind up the year in the black. Impossible! At least, without a friend in the ranks. You've always been a gal who knew what was going on—you're one sharp cookie, Lynn. If you were working at Harper Hills as a staff nurse, I'd have a friend where I need one."

She had protested, saying that if she couldn't bring herself to go back to work in Boston in familiar surroundings, she couldn't take on a new job in a strange place.

"If your father were alive he'd tell you the change is just what you need," Conrad pointed out.

The mention of her father was his master stroke. All through the long wearying months of her father's final illness, Conrad, who hadn't yet moved west, was a faithful visitor at the dying man's bedside. Furthermore, he'd helped Lynn when the end came when Ray refused.

She thought she could never repay Conrad for his kindness to both her and her father during that trying time. Now Conrad was hinting she could—by coming to work at Harper Hills in California. And in leaving Boston, maybe she'd be doing herself a favor as well.

She'd finally agreed and here she was.

Lynn took a deep breath and let it out slowly. She could have gotten this job on her own merit, her own references. She was a good nurse with excellent experience. Instead, she'd let Conrad pave the way. Now she'd have to prove her worth to her own staff as well as Mrs. Morrin.

Lynn squared her shoulders. That's exactly what she intended to do: show them all ... starting with Sheila Burns.

As she passed the bathroom door on her way out, she heard retching sounds from inside and hesitated. Her instinct was to knock and ask Sheila if she was all right, but as she was about to, the noise stopped and the toilet flushed. Lynn, aware Sheila would resent any inquiry from her, shrugged and left the lounge.

Shortly before six Lynn was eating a cold chicken leg and spinach salad in her kitchen when the phone rang. She wondered if it was another wrong number.

"How's the heroine of Three West?" Conrad asked.

"Villainness is more like it," she told him.

"Not from what I hear. Dr. Linnett tells me you're a remarkably capable nurse."

Dr. Linnett? She'd thought he was upset with her.

"I wish he'd told my staff instead of you," she said. "How's Pat feeling? I've been meaning to come by and see her but I've been busy."

While it was true she was busy, she and Conrad's wife had never become friends, mostly because Pat obviously didn't like her. Lynn was sure Pat would be perfectly happy never to set eyes on her again.

"Pat's arthritis isn't any better here than it was back east," Conrad said. "At the moment she's trying to lose enough weight to convince her orthopedist she's a good candidate for hip surgery, and you know how dieters are— cross and hungry."

31

In other words, visit Pat at your own risk. Okay, she'd been warned.

"I sympathize," she told him, leaving it fuzzy as to where her sympathy was directed.

"You and I have to get together. I want to pick your brains about Harper Hills—first impressions, any problems you've noticed, and so on. What about dinner tomorrow night?"

"Oh, I wouldn't want to put Pat to all that trouble when I know she's in pain."

"Shop talk bores Pat. I thought you and I would dine out. There happen to be a few passable restaurants around here, thank God."

Lynn held the phone away from her and stared at it. Was he crazy? "Uh, Conrad, we're friends, and I know you don't mean anything by suggesting a public tête-à-tête, but have you thought how it might look? To Harper Hills employees in particular? If you want to talk to me, you'd better come over here."

"You're right of course."

His reply had been a bit too quick and Lynn frowned, feeling he'd manipulated her into inviting him over. Still, there was nothing wrong with him coming to her apartment. Good grief, she'd known Conrad since she was fourteen and he was twenty-two. He'd been a protégé of her father's as well as a friend.

"Are you busy tonight?" he asked.

"Actually, no."

"Is it all right if I come over in about an hour?"

Push, push, that was Conrad. He'd sweep the ground with you if you didn't watch out. She was looking forward to seeing him, though. "Fine," she agreed.

Lynn didn't bother changing from her jeans and her

old blue T shirt with the Cape Cod logo. When Conrad rang her buzzer she went to the door barefoot.

He stepped inside and hugged her. "I've missed you, Lynn."

She smiled and stepped back. "It's good to see you."

He gestured at the T shirt. "That takes me back. There's nothing like the Cape."

"But now you have the Pacific at your disposal, isn't that compensation?"

"East is east and west is west."

"I can't argue with that. Pick a thrift store special and sit down." She indicated her sparsely furnished living room.

He glanced around. "You managed to find a fairly decent place. Sorry I wasn't more help, I thought I'd better keep a low profile."

Too late for low profiles, she felt like saying, but held her tongue. That had been as much her fault as his. She should have insisted on applying for the job without any help from him. On the other hand, she'd been too self-pitying to take any action on her own; if he *hadn't* arranged everything and pushed her into it, she'd still be moping in Boston.

Conrad eased into the one comfortable chair she'd been able to afford. "You're looking great."

Maybe she was. Lynn knew she felt better since she'd been in California. Maybe it was the sun and maybe it was being thousands of miles away from the places that brought back the nightmare memories. She'd never told Conrad or anyone except Dr. Lourdes what had really happened back there.

"So how're you doing at Harper Hills?" Conrad continued.

Lynn had already made up her mind not to make an

33

issue of being shifted to maternity. The less Conrad was involved in her work, the better. She certainly didn't want him complaining to Mrs. Morrin on her behalf.

"It's early yet to tell," she temporized. "I'm still getting oriented."

He nodded. "It takes time to sniff out the problems."

Lynn blinked, wondering what he was getting at. "I think I can handle anything that comes up."

"I'm well aware that you're efficient, Lynn. What I meant was problems you'll be reporting to me, deadwood on the staff, excessive use of supplies, things of that sort."

She stared at him. True, he'd mentioned she'd be his friend at court, so to speak, but she hadn't realized all the ramifications.

"Conrad, I'm not going to be your spy!"

He waved a hand dismissively. "Who suggested that? I'm after the big stuff, not piddling problems. All I expect is for you to let me know what's wrong at Harper Hills so I can put it right. For instance, if you hear any rumors about unionization."

"You mean among my nursing staff?"

He nodded. "CMC's clamped a temporary freeze on nurses' wages—just until the home office draws up a budget—and some hothead on the staff might take it into her head to start organizing a protest."

"I haven't heard of any such thing." That was the truth, but Lynn wondered what she'd have said if she'd known of rumors about a protest.

"I'm sure you want good medical care for your patients as much as I do," he said. "The bottom line *is* the patients. Any improvements will be for them."

Somewhat mollified, Lynn nodded. "You can trust me to do what I can along those lines. Oh, I forgot to ask— would you care for some coffee?"

He sighed and rose from the chair. "I'd love to stay and talk over old times, but Pat's a bit paranoid these days—better keep the peace. We'll get together for a good long talk next month."

Lynn had no trouble translating "paranoid" to "jealous." Pat was ten years older than her husband and chronically suspicious. If only she realized how little cause she has to be jealous of me, Lynn thought. Conrad was like the brother she'd never had.

At the door he put his hands on her shoulders and gazed at her affectionately. "I'm glad you're here."

She had one uneasy instant when she thought he was going to kiss her, but if he had the impulse, it passed and he let her go.

Impulsively she took his hand and squeezed. Trust Conrad to remember she didn't like being kissed in greeting or farewell. "I'm glad I'm here, too," she assured him. "Give my best to Pat."

The phone rang.

"Admirers already?" he asked, not quite jocularly.

"Probably a wrong number. Goodbye, Conrad."

She shut the door and walked to the phone, not hurrying, frowning over what she thought she'd heard in Conrad's voice. No, she was imagining things.

"Hello?"

"Lynn? This is Nick. Nick Dow."

Her eyes widened.

"Joe mentioned he'd invited you to the barbecue on Saturday."

"He did ask me," she said warily.

"And you're coming?" He sounded as though he wished she'd say no.

"I planned to, yes."

"Well, since you're a newcomer to El Doblez and Joe's place is hard to find, I could pick you up, if you like."

Lynn hesitated, unsure if she wanted to go anywhere with Nick. On the other hand, she didn't know the area and Joe's sketchy map left a lot to be desired. Nick's offer was downright reluctant. But if he didn't want to take her, why ask her? It wasn't like her to be indecisive but she couldn't make up her mind whether to accept or refuse.

"Hey, you still there?" he asked.

"I'm trying to decide whether to go with you or not," she snapped.

He laughed. "Scared?"

In truth, she was ... not that she'd ever admit it to him. He wouldn't understand, how could he—he'd never known Ray. She certainly wasn't afraid of him in the way he meant. Oh, the hell with it, she was making too much out of nothing. He didn't want to take her, she didn't want to go, so what could go wrong?

"What time will you be picking me up?" she asked.

Chapter 3

When Lynn got home from Harper Hills on Saturday, she hurriedly changed into a denim skirt and white shirt so she'd be ready when Nick came by to pick her up for the barbecue at the Kings'. She supposed he'd be driving a sports car, he was the type—a Porsche, at the very least.

He pulled up in a metallic blue Kharmann Ghia.

"I didn't know they still made these cars," she commented as she settled into the passenger seat, feeling uncharacteristically lighthearted. She was going to her first California party, in fact, her first party in more months than she cared to count. And no matter what reservations she had about Nick, she couldn't help enjoying being escorted by a handsome man.

"This was an old junker before I restored her." He patted the steering wheel affectionately as he started the car. "She's taught me a few hard lessons, but I wouldn't part with her for anything."

Well, Lynn told herself, she wasn't altogether wrong. The Kharmann Ghia was technically a sports car, even if it was an ancient one he'd resurrected.

"El Doblez isn't your ordinary southern California coastal community," Nick observed as he turned onto a spiraling drive winding up a steep hill. "First of all—no ancient Spanish mission. Second—no great surfing beaches. Third—"

"But I've been to a lovely beach," she protested.

"The coastal configuration here's no good for surfing, though. Nor can we claim seaquariums, or ramshackle but historic piers. No ex- or current presidents have homes here, there's no racetrack, no colorful California old town. On the positive side, if you're partial to atomic reactors, we're not too far from San Onofre."

"You're some civic booster."

He slanted her a grin. "Don't get me wrong. I like living in El Doblez. The weather's the best in the U.S., but luckily we don't have anything else to attract tourists—a definite plus."

"You sound like an isolationist."

"What's wrong with wanting to keep my home turf uncrowded?"

"Are you a native?"

His smile faded, replaced by a scowl. "No, I was raised in Michigan."

And touchy about it for some reason, she decided, studying him covertly. He wore jeans with a blue polo shirt, open at the neck, the casual garb suiting his lean, athletic build. She could understand why Sheila dubbed him the Harper Hills Heartbreaker. His smile alone would devastate the susceptible. Fortunately, she wasn't that. Another Ray was the last thing she needed in her life.

Nick swung into a turnout at the hill's summit, shut off the motor, and waved a hand westward. "There's the best of what El Doblez has to offer."

Lynn gazed down at the Pacific. Lazy waves curled onto the sand beach below, the sun-spangled water darkening to a deeper and deeper blue as her eyes swept to the horizon where a fog bank hovered. Because she was accustomed to the dune barriers of Cape Cod intervening between land and sea, it seemed to her this western ocean went on forever.

"El Doblez's best makes me wonder why anyone stays in Boston during the winter," she said.

"Or any other season. Admit it, you're already hooked on sunshine and good weather."

"It *is* addictive." But she wasn't ready to give up the east; she'd been born and raised there, it was home. Although she was working here and not simply lazing in the sun, it was hard to think of California as more than just a vacation spot.

Nick restarted the car and they wound down the hill between attractively landscaped red-tiled homes. Expensive homes, most with that fantastic ocean view.

"Someday I'm going to live up here," he said.

"With a Lamborghini replacing the Kharmann Ghia?" She hadn't meant to say it aloud, but the words slipped out before she realized what had happened.

He stared at her, eyebrows raised.

"Forget it," she told him. "What I said has nothing to do with you." Because he reminded her of Ray, she'd projected Ray's desire for a Lamborghini onto Nick. Ray hated not having enough money to buy what he wanted. He didn't like to wait, always demanding immediate gratification.

Forget Ray, too, she warned herself. He belongs to the past. Leave him there or you'll never be free.

Thinking of the past vanquished her party mood and she wished she'd had sense enough to stay in her apartment. She didn't have anything in common with a bunch of strangers having a good time. When she got out of the car at Nancy and Joe King's ranch-style home in a new development near the beach, Lynn had to force herself to smile.

Whisked through the house by her jovial host to a fenced-in backyard, she found she was wrong about strangers. She knew many of the people—Joyce Elkins, Clovis Reilly, Sheila Burns and her pharmacist husband, Justin, Conrad and Pat Werth. Joe's outgoing red-haired wife, Nancy, made Lynn feel genuinely welcome.

Joe handed her a drink. "I prescribe a San Onofre Special—it rearranges your atoms."

She'd relaxed enough so her grin was genuine. "You think they need rearranging?"

He cocked his head and pretended to study her. "Not need, exactly—but take the risk anyway. The result's bound to be interesting."

"Good to see you, Lynn," Conrad said, coming up on her right. "How do you like El Doblez?" His manner was unusually formal.

She turned to him, wondering if she was supposed to respond as though they hadn't met since she'd come to California. Surely Pat knew he'd been to her apartment the other night. But Pat wasn't with him, she remained in her chair by the pool.

"It seems to be a pleasant little city," she said noncommittally.

"I noticed Nicholas Dow drove you here." Conrad's brows drew together. "I didn't realize you were friends." The tone of his voice suggested friendship with Nick was a bad idea.

Why did people feel obligated to warn her to steer clear of Nick? She had no intention of involving herself with

40

him, but it certainly was neither Sheila's nor Conrad's business what she did.

"I didn't know how to find Joe and Nancy's house." Despite her attempt to control her irritation, her tone was crisp.

"You should have called me. Pat and I would have been happy to bring you with us."

Involuntarily, Lynn glanced toward Pat and caught her glaring at them. Knowing what she had to do next, Lynn took a long swallow of her drink to fortify herself.

"I must say hello to your wife," she told Conrad, moving toward the pool as he kept pace with her.

Up close, Lynn was shocked by Pat's appearance. In Boston, Pat had kept her hair tinted an attractive ash blond, and though she was on the heavy side, she hadn't been fat. But she was now, and for some reason, she hadn't bothered to find the right clothes for her increased girth. She wore no makeup and had let her hair go, so gray strands mixed with growing-out blond as well as her original brown color. She looked older than forty-five.

"Hello, Pat." Lynn couldn't force enthusiasm into her greeting but she managed a smile. "How nice to see you again."

"Is it?" Pat snapped.

Lynn blinked.

"Now, Pat," Conrad said mildly.

Lynn searched for something to say, finally coming up with, "I understand you're going to have a hip replacement. I have a friend who had it done and it's really remarkable how—"

"When did you tell her that?" Pat asked Conrad. "You've hardly had time to say two words to her here, so you've been with her some other time, don't try to deny it."

41

She should have kept her mouth shut, Lynn realized. Now what was she going to do? She couldn't just walk away.

Conrad shrugged, remaining silent.

Pat drained her glass, then fixed a malevolent gaze on Lynn. "Why didn't you stay in Boston?" she demanded, her words slurring slightly.

Lynn looked nervously around, hoping no one had overheard. Pat'd always disliked Lynn, but she'd never made a scene as she now threatened to do. To Lynn's dismay, she spied Nick no more than three feet away, watching them. How long had he been there?

Maybe she could make use of him. "Nick," she called, "have you met Mrs. Werth?" Without waiting for his answer, she added, "Pat, this is Dr. Dow."

"I believe we were introduced once before." Pat spoke slowly and carefully as Nick came up to her.

"It's always a pleasure to see you, Mrs. Werth," he said.

As Lynn had hoped, Nick's smile charmed Pat, and for the moment she ignored everyone else.

Conrad extended a hand to his wife. "We'd better be going, Dear, if we want to make the concert."

As Pat batted his hand away none too gently, she dropped her plastic glass onto the concrete of the pool apron. "You just don't want me to talk to Dr. Dow," she said. "Why should you have all the fun?"

"I'd be happy to escort you to your car." Nick offered his hand. "Please allow me to."

With a gracious smile, Pat accepted and he helped her to her feet. Conrad retrieved her cane and tucked it under his arm.

As she watched the three of them walk toward the house, Lynn felt sorry for Pat, wishing Conrad's wife would re-

42

alize she had no basis for jealousy. Jealous people were unreasonable and the only thing Lynn could do was try to keep away from Pat in the future. And from Conrad, too, for that matter.

Lynn started toward Joyce but Sheila, wearing a bright red jumpsuit, intercepted her. "I see you've met the charming Mrs. Werth. But then you knew her before, didn't you?"

"Mr. Werth was a friend of my father's," Lynn said, angry at herself for explaining, but feeling she had to. She wished she hadn't let Conrad put her in such a position.

Sheila's eyebrows rose slightly. "But Mrs. Werth is no one's friend?"

Certain Sheila would deliberately misconstrue anything she said, Lynn merely shrugged and sipped her drink. Justin sauntered over to them and handed a drink to his wife. She took a swallow, made a face, and poured the rest of the liquid onto the grass.

Justin scowled. "What the hell, Sheil."

"Joe's atomic cocktails *are* on the strong side," Lynn put in.

Justin, his angry attention fixed on his wife, didn't so much as glance her way.

"I told you I'm off alcohol," Sheila said to him, "and I meant it. You deliberately brought me that drink when you knew damned well I wanted lemonade."

Lynn, not wanting to be drawn into a marital tiff, began to edge unobtrusively away from the pool.

"You're getting to be a real bitch, you know?" Justin said to his wife.

"I suppose you think you're Mr. Sunshine!" Sheila's voice was shrill.

Lynn turned her back on them and, seeing Joyce engrossed in conversation with a sandy-haired man, headed for Nancy King, who was setting out more dip and crudités. "Can I help you with anything?" Lynn asked.

"Thanks, but we've got it under control," Nancy said.

A shriek followed by a splash startled both women. Lynn stared toward the pool, where Sheila floundered in the water, sputtering and staring up at her husband.

"You bastard!" she cried.

Nancy shook her head. "Someone always seems to get dunked at our parties!"

If Justin had been laughing, Lynn might have dismissed the incident, too. She didn't know Justin well and he could have a twisted sense of humor. But as he watched his wife's attempts to climb out of the pool, his rage-distorted face implied he was capable of holding her head under the water until she drowned. Alarmed, Lynn hurried to the pool and reached out a hand to Sheila.

When Sheila, her soaked jumpsuit clinging to her like a second skin, was out of the water, Lynn stood between her and Justin, eyeing him warily.

"Someday you're going to go too far," Sheila snarled at him.

"It'll be your own damned fault," he muttered.

"That's right, blame me like you always do." Tears mingled with the drops of water on Sheila's face. She hugged herself, shivering.

"Let's get you dried off," Lynn suggested, her hand on Sheila's back urging her toward the house.

Nancy came toward them with a beach towel and Lynn helped her wrap it around the shuddering Sheila. The sopping jumpsuit molded itself to Sheila's lush, full-breasted figure and Lynn couldn't help noticing the small rounded bulge in Sheila's lower abdomen. She was pregnant. It would explain her vomiting in the nurses' bathroom earlier this week and the fact that she refused to

44

touch alcohol. But surely Justin, a pharmacist, knew the dangers of alcohol to a developing embryo, so why would he offer it to his pregnant wife?

Inside the house, Nancy left them in the bathroom while she went off to find clothes she thought would fit Sheila.

"How far along are you?" Lynn asked, then could have kicked herself.

Her baby was dead. Why couldn't she let herself accept that instead of probing a still-hurting wound by a morbid curiosity about another woman's pregnancy?

Sheila grimaced. "Oh, shit, I hoped no one would notice. I should have known *you* would. Do you think anyone else did?"

Lynn shrugged. "You don't show ordinarily—it was that wet jumpsuit."

Sheila's eyes narrowed appraisingly, then she gripped Lynn's wrist. "For God's sake don't tell anyone."

"I won't."

"Not *anyone,*" Sheila reiterated, still holding her.

"I said I wouldn't."

Sheila's brown eyes bored into Lynn. "I might as well tell you—there's a problem."

Before she could say anything more, Nancy reappeared with a colorful cotton muumuu. Sheila dropped Lynn's arm and shut up. Going out of the bathroom with Nancy, leaving Sheila to shower and dress, Lynn thought she'd caught on to what the problem was. Sheila hadn't told Justin she was pregnant.

A shiver of dread curled along Lynn's spine as her own past rose to haunt her. She and Sheila weren't friends and at work Sheila was a problem she could do without. At this moment, though, Lynn couldn't have felt closer to her if they'd been sisters. Somehow she had to break through Sheila's barrier of dislike and mistrust because Sheila was making a bad mistake and, whether she wanted it or not, she needed Lynn's advice.

"I don't think much of Justin's idea of fun," Nancy said. "Pushing his wife, in her condition, into the pool. What's the matter with him?"

Lynn turned to her. "Does everyone know? I mean about Sheila's, uh, condition?"

"I certainly didn't before I saw her sopping wet."

"Nancy, Sheila wants it kept a secret."

"Sure. I won't mention it to a soul."

Lynn eyed her. She liked Nancy, but she didn't know her well. Maybe she could be trusted. But there was an old saying that had a lot of truth to it—"Two can keep a secret only if one of them is dead."

Despite Pat's mini-scene and Sheila's dunking, by the time the barbecued ribs were ready, the constant buzz of talk interlaced with laughter signaled a successful party. When she saw Sheila and Justin had made up, Lynn set aside her worry about Sheila and began to enjoy herself.

Phil Vance, the psychiatrist she'd noticed talking to Joyce earlier, brought out his guitar. The sandy-haired doctor knew more folk songs than she imagined existed. Sitting between Joyce and Clovis, Lynn sang along with the others when he played tunes she recognized.

Requests from the group kept him going until he pleaded exhaustion. "The finale's my own favorite," he said.

The haunting strains of "Beyond the Reef" drifted into the cool evening. Only Phil knew the words, and his reedy tenor mingled with the chords, giving voice to the longing of someone left behind.

"That has to be the saddest of folk songs," Joe commented into the silence when Phil finished. "You told it like it was, Phil."

Nick, who'd been withdrawn much of the evening, broke into the chorus of compliments for the guitarist.

"No arguments about how great you play, Phil, but I disagree with Joe. I know a sadder folk song."

"Prove it," Joe told him. "Put up or shut up."

Nick shrugged. "I'm no singer."

"Do I know the song?" Phil asked. When Nick shook his head, he offered Nick his guitar. "I happen to know you can handle this thing, so why not show us? I'm always looking for new stuff."

Nick hesitated, but finally accepted the guitar. "The song's meant for a flute, and you can't get the flavor without understanding the words," he muttered, looking down at the guitar. He didn't move for so long that Lynn wondered if he'd decided not to play. Finally he slid the instrument into position.

His first chords rose plaintively, almost eerily into the night. Lynn was reminded of Asian music, yet this was different.

Nick raised his head, looking into the dark sky and, to her surprise, began to half-chant, half-sing:

Wah-yaw-burn-maud-e
Anishinabe quainee-un-e
We-maw-jaw-need-e.

He repeated the strange words, and then, continuing to play, lowered his gaze to his listeners, but Lynn was certain he looked beyond them all to his own private world. He began to speak in a low, rhythmic tone, his voice twisting in and out of the melody:

"The Chippewa maiden weeps as she watches her lover

47

paddle away. His canoe takes him far from her, far across the sea of sweet water. She'll never forget him, but she knows he's lost to her forever. He'll forget her, he'll find a new love, and he'll never return."

A few final chords and the song was over. Nick sat without moving.

Lynn had never heard anything quite like what he'd played and sang. It had made the hair on her nape rise.

"Jesus, what a performance," Joe exclaimed, breaking the spell.

"I've got to tape that," Phil said. "I don't have a Chippewa song, they're hard to come by."

Nick looked up with a half-smile. "Depends on who you are, white man."

"Come off it, Big Chief," Joe put in. "Those few Indian genes of yours are outnumbered by all the others your ancestors threw into the pot."

"Next thing I know you'll be hiding my tomahawk," Nick complained good-naturedly, handing the guitar back to Phil and rising.

He was pretty sure no one realized how hard it had been to come back from where the Chippewa song had taken him, a place he didn't visit often. Sometimes he wished he could forget his past entirely.

He caught Lynn's green gaze and read a question in her eyes. He'd been avoiding her ever since he'd taken Pat Werth to the car, his intervention aborting the mess-in-the-making caused by Werth parading his mistress's youth and health in front of his middle-aged, arthritic wife. Of course Pat had exploded and Werth and Lynn should have known better. Nick had felt like grabbing Lynn by the shoulders and shaking some sense into her. He still did.

Smiling at those gathering round to praise his singing,

Nick eased past them to confront Lynn. She'd put a blue jacket over the white shirt she wore and, in the flare of Joe's torches, her eyes looked as green and deep as Lake Michigan.

"Joe could be wrong," she told him as he came up to her. "It had to be those Chippewa genes that gave you the ability to project the pain and longing of the song. I was impressed."

"I've noticed how Indians seem to turn women on." He was deliberately insolent, intent on angering her as much as she had him.

She turned away, withdrawing, something she did very well, as though she'd had a lot of practice. "It's time I was getting home, if you don't mind."

He watched her as she stalked off to say her good-byes to the Kings. The short denim skirt she wore showed enough of her long, shapely legs to whet a man's appetite for seeing the rest. Easy to want her, hard to resist her.

He nodded to Phil, who was putting his guitar back into its case, and ambled after Lynn. He'd take her home and forget about her. Permanently. She was definitely not on his future agenda. He'd made a big mistake in bringing her to Joe and Nancy's party. Why the hell he'd done it was beyond him, but he wouldn't make the same mistake twice.

Nick opened the passenger door of his car, waited until Lynn had seated herself, and closed it. He'd been nasty. Now he'd stay polite but remote until he left her at her apartment.

The night was California wonderful—cool, no fog, a half-moon sharing the sky with the stars, the breeze hinting of the sea. He could think of a number of better things to be doing on a night like this with a woman like Lynn.

He snapped on the radio to break the silence as they drove. A golden oldie was playing—the Beatles' "All You Need Is Love." Yeah, sure. Forget money, a career, pride in your work, the whole schmeer. He wasn't sure he even believed in love. Lust he understood. And felt. At this very moment.

He slanted a look at Lynn, who was moving slightly in rhythm to the song. Women tended to believe in love. Was love what she thought she felt for Conrad? He snorted. She turned her head to glance curiously at him.

"Not one of my favorites," he muttered.

"Don't you like the Beatles?"

"Sure, who doesn't? It's the song."

"So it's love you don't believe in."

Damn, she was quick. "Do you?" he demanded.

He felt her withdraw again and thought she wasn't going to answer.

"Some people manage love," she said finally.

"Manage love? You make it sound like it was an animal."

"A wild animal," she agreed. "Dangerous."

Because he couldn't think of Werth as being anything but smarmy, he decided her odd comment had nothing to do with Conrad but came from her past. Someone, sometime had hurt her badly.

"Others don't manage it well," she went on. "Justin Burns, for example. He pushed his wife in the pool tonight. Not in fun, either. Yet for all I know, he loves her and she loves him."

"Justin's got a mean temper. Goes out of his gourd when he gets mad. It's going to get him in a real jam one of these days.

50

"I don't envy Sheila."

Nick shrugged. "She married him."

Lynn turned as far toward him as her seat belt would allow. "What a terrible thing to say! You don't know a man when you marry him—only afterward."

"California makes it easy to get unmarried."

"It's never easy." Her words were etched with bitterness.

Probing might annoy her, but he had nothing to lose since he didn't intend to see her again. "You sound as though you're speaking from experience. Been through a divorce?"

"No." Her voice was so low he barely heard her. "My husband is dead."

He'd really put his foot in it this time. "Sorry," he muttered. "Maybe we'd better stick to shop talk."

She made a ragged sound that might have been a laugh, but certainly had no humor in it. After a minute she asked, "How's your preeclamptic patient with the mother who believes in *curandera* medicine?"

"Doing pretty well. It's possible I scared Grandma into behaving, but I'm not taking any bets. How about you? Diagnosed any more abruptios?"

"No, maternity's quiet—all the births normal, not even twins."

"Ah, that's the quiet before the storm. Watch out, all hell's ready to break loose. I foresee a shoulder presentation, premature triplets, and two C-sections at the same time."

He saw she was smiling. "Thanks, HHH, for your prediction of chaos on maternity. For sure it'll keep me from slacking off."

"HHH?"

Her smile stretched to a grin. "If you don't know what

they call you at the hospital, I'm not going to be the one to spill the beans."

Seeing that they were in a quiet residential district, he swerved to the curb under a street light and cut the engine. "This car goes no farther until you tell me."

She shook her head. "I'm no stoolie." Glancing out the window, she added, "Besides, I can walk home from here, so you can't scare me, HHH."

Nick's playful mood turned sour at her use of the word "stoolie." She was describing herself. That's exactly what she was ... a stoolie for Werth. A dark tide of anger swamped his better judgment.

"What the hell do you see in the man?" he burst out.

Lynn frowned in confusion. "What man?"

"You know who I mean—that bastard Werth."

"Conrad? I really don't understand."

"Cut the crap! It's obvious what's between you. Why else did he bring you here from Boston if it wasn't to be his spy?"

She gaped at him and after a moment unbuckled her seat belt, opened the door, and slid out. He slammed out of the car, caught her by the arm, and swung her around to face him.

"You're not going anywhere until I get an answer," he snarled.

"I have nothing to say to you." Ice clung to each word.

He gripped her shoulders. "You're damned well going to!"

"Let me go!" she cried, struggling to get free.

Without knowing he meant to, Nick yanked her toward him, his hands sliding from her shoulders to hold her body tight against his. His mouth covered hers in a savage kiss. She yielded limply for an instant, then began to fight.

Trapped by his violent arousal from the feel of her, he was oblivious.

He never knew exactly when she started to respond rather than fight, but he sure as hell knew the difference when her lips parted beneath his. Her erotic invitation flamed through him.

Suddenly Lynn thrust her arms between them and wrenched free. She backed away, her eyes wide with apprehension.

His first reaction was to capture her again. Without her in his arms, though, reason quickly returned. He shook his head, trying to rid himself of the remnants of his lust. When he made a mistake, he went first-class, that was for sure. Touching Lynn had been like pouring lighter fluid on blazing charcoal and he'd gotten burned.

So had she. For a minute or two, anyway. He stared at her.

"I'll walk from here," she said, turning from him and striding briskly away.

He couldn't blame her for not wanting to get back in the car. He'd scared her. Scared himself, too.

"Let's compromise," he suggested, catching up to her. He was careful to keep safe inches between them. "I'll walk with you."

"There's no need. It's only a few blocks."

"I'm going with you. Don't argue, just think of me as a stubborn Indian and leave it at that."

He thought he saw her lips twitch with brief amusement. They walked a block in silence.

"I'd say I was sorry, but I'd be lying," he said finally. "I'll admit to being out of line. Would you believe me if I told you it surprised me as much as it did you?"

She shook her head.

He shrugged. "Happens to be true. I don't force myself on women. That is, not before tonight."

"I'll accept that. But I'm not going out with you again, Nick. That's final." She didn't look at him as she spoke.

Since he'd already crossed Lynn off his agenda, he should have been happy. The trouble was, he'd changed his mind against his will, against his better judgment. And too late.

She'd made up her mind not to see him again. Besides, Werth still stood between them.

He didn't know how he was going to get her to reconsider, he only knew he'd make it happen. Somehow. Zapping Werth the hell out of her life posed a massive problem, too.

His ancestors had a simple solution in the old days— take off in the old canoe, pluck the maiden from her lodge, and paddle away with her into the sunset.

Lynn locked the door behind her and leaned against it, sorting through her feelings. Joe's drink may not have rearranged her atoms, but Nick's kiss had come close. Never again. At least she'd had the sense to solve that problem by refusing to see him again outside of the hospital.

What he'd said about her and Conrad being lovers had shocked her. Is that what others believed? Certainly Pat did. How could she convince people it wasn't true? Perhaps she ought to resign and return to Boston. Lynn shook her head. She'd never been a quitter and didn't intend to start now.

The phone rang. She picked it up and heard the soft hum that signaled a long-distance call.

"Hello?"

"I don't want you to leave me," a man's voice said.

Lynn froze in shock, her heart racing in panic.

Ray's voice!

It can't possibly be Ray, you know it can't be, she tried to tell herself. Summoning all her strength, she managed to gasp, "Who is this?"

The only answer was a click, then the buzz of disconnection.

Chapter 4

When a week passed with no repeat of that awful phone call and the horror she'd felt began to fade, Lynn told herself it had only been her imagination that the voice sounded like Ray's. The dead don't call the living—at least not on the telephone. Either it had been a wrong number, or some weirdo with a perverted sense of humor had dialed her at random.

She went to work the following Sunday cautiously optimistic, both about herself and about her unit. She'd made it this far. Even Sheila had stopped her disruptive behavior since the Kings' party. A real improvement, although they still weren't friends. Three West was almost peaceful this past week. So much for Nick's prediction of disaster on maternity—premie triplets, a shoulder presentation, and two C-sections all at the same time. If it came true, a fitting punishment would be making all the mothers Nick's patients.

When she got off the elevator, Lynn was smiling at her mental picture of Nick trying to cope with such chaos. Serve him right. As she pushed through the double doors and heard a man shouting, her smile faded.

"I don't care where the hell you get it, I need an ampule of magnesium sulfate, *stat.*" The doors of the delivery room stood open, the voice came from inside.

Nick's voice.

Lynn hurried toward the uproar, noted the lighted windows in the closed doors to the C-section room and hoped there'd be no problems with the patient who was being sectioned. If Nick needed mag sulfate something was terribly wrong with his patient and one change-of-shift emergency was more than enough to cope with.

She almost collided with Carrie Maybanks as the LVN came flying out of the delivery room. Lynn stopped her. "We have magnesium sulfate in the emergency medical box."

"It's outdated," Carrie wailed.

"Call the ER," Lynn ordered. "If they have an ampule, run down and get it. That's quicker than finding someone to open the pharmacy."

Carrie plunged back inside, grabbing the wall phone. Lynn headed for the delivery table where Nick and a staff pediatrician, Dr. Salvador, struggled with a thrashing, moaning patient in the throes of a grand mal seizure. Epilepsy? No, it must be eclampsia if Nick needed mag sulfate.

Eclampsia was a complication of pregnancy with coma and convulsive seizures and was fatal if not treated. Magnesium sulfate, if given in time, usually controlled the seizures. It was imperative to get the baby out quickly, but it was also impossible with the mother convulsing.

"The ER's got two ampules," Carrie called. "I'll be right back with them." She rushed from the room.

"The magnesium sulfate will be here in a few minutes, Dr. Dow," Lynn said to make certain he'd heard.

Nick glanced up briefly, keeping his attention on the

convulsing woman. "I need a line for the mag sulf," he told Lynn. "Get a big bore needle in and start some Ringer's Solution with dextrose."

As Dr. Salvador exerted himself to hold an arm steady so Lynn could insert a needle into the patient's vein, the thought crossed her mind that the sealed emergency box had come back from the pharmacy last Friday. The pharmacist's job was to check and replace all used or outdated medications. Personnel on the unit weren't supposed to break the box's seal and open it unless an emergency medicine was needed and Lynn wondered if the seal had already been broken when Carrie opened the box.

Whether it was or not, no medication in that box should be outdated. Maybe Carrie had made a mistake and if she hadn't, the pharmacist was at fault ... Justin Burns, Sheila's bad-tempered husband. She would have to check later, there wasn't time now.

As Lynn secured the IV line to the patient's arm, she remembered what Nick had told her about his problems with folk healers.

"Is this the woman whose mother feeds her *curandera* potions?" she asked.

He nodded, then indicated the pediatrician with a jerk of his head. "Paul's the expert on those concoctions."

"Many *curandera* medicines are harmless, some are even effective," Dr. Salvador said. "Unfortunately a lot of them contain diuretics. Not good for Elena here."

"Whatever she got, it's messed up her electrolytes," Nick agreed. "Her blood pressure must be through the roof."

Because of the woman's continuous convulsions, they weren't able to hook up the monitors, it was all they could do to keep the patient on the delivery table with Lynn doing her best to steady the arm with the IV line.

"Where the hell are those ampules?" Nick demanded.

A breathless Carrie hurried through the open door and over to the table. "Fifty percent magnesium sulfate," she told Nick and showed him the syringe containing the medication before readying the needle for injection into the IV line. Handing Lynn the syringe, she took her place steadying the patient's arm.

"Give four grams," Nick ordered. "And inject it slowly, take three minutes."

Lynn timed the injection of the solution by the second hand on the delivery room wall clock. By the time she'd finished, the patient's convulsing had eased.

"She's still hyperreflexic," Nick observed. "I'd like a pump connected to the IV to deliver a gram of mag sulf every hour until her blood pressure drops to 150/100. We'll get the baby out as soon as she stabilizes. She's at least a month from term, but she was in active labor and ready to deliver when she came in. I hope we don't have to section her." He connected monitors to the woman, who now lay fairly quietly, twitching now and then. She seemed unaware of her surroundings.

"What's the patient's name?" Lynn asked Carrie.

"Elena Diaz. She's nineteen, a primipara."

Having her first baby. Lynn looked over Nick's shoulder to check the fetal monitor and drew in her breath at the flat line. No fetal heartbeat. Nick grabbed a fetoscope and bent to listen to Ms. Diaz's distended abdomen.

After long moments, he looked up and shook his head at Dr. Salvador.

The pediatrician, checking the flat line on the fetal monitor, sighed and clapped Nick on the shoulder. "I'll be in the hospital for the next hour," he said, heading for the door. "Call me if you need me."

Nick wouldn't need him. Elena Diaz's baby had no

heartbeat. Neither Dr. Salvador nor any other pediatrician could bring a dead baby back to life. Lynn tried to take a deep breath but was unable to. Her throat closed and she felt the hot sting of tears as she met Nick's angry gaze.

"Why the hell didn't your unit have usable mag sulf on hand?" he demanded.

"I intend to find out." Lynn forced the words past the lump in her throat.

"A little late for that." Nick turned his back to her to check his patient's vital signs.

Lynn swallowed, unable to defend herself, unable to speak at all. The baby was dead. Dead before being born, like hers. Not her fault this time, it couldn't be. Spots danced before her eyes and her ears rang. Carrie's voice, asking her a question, seemed to come from very far away.

You can't pass out, she told herself. Not here . . . not now. She leaned against the delivery table and, making an effort, focused on Carrie.

"I can stay overtime if you need me," Carrie offered.

Lynn, feeling as though she couldn't possibly make it through the next five minutes, much less an entire shift, struggled to pull herself together. No way could she allow herself to fall apart in front of Carrie or Nick Dow. Especially Nick. But she couldn't assist Nick in the delivery of a dead baby and keep control of herself. That wasn't an appropriate reason to keep Carrie overtime, though. She'd tell Carrie to send Sheila in. Let Sheila help Nick.

"Thanks," she said to Carrie, "but you've already done your share. Do me a favor on your way out and ask—" Lynn paused. Sheila wouldn't think it unusual to take over for her. Nick wouldn't either. After all, Lynn Holley was the charge nurse and her job was to run the unit. But having Sheila take her place would be admitting defeat, even if Lynn would be the only one who knew it. If she gave in now she'd never regain her confidence. Whatever happened to her, she had to meet it on her own.

Lynn took a deep breath and pushed herself free of the table's support. "Ask Sheila to take charge at the desk until I'm through in here," she said to Carrie before turning to check to see if the patient's contractions had resumed.

The delivery was an hour-long nightmare that seemed to last a lifetime—the unresponsive, moaning patient, Nick's curt orders as he fought to keep Ms. Diaz from convulsing again, Lynn's dread anticipation of what would emerge from the woman's uterus, then the stab of anguish when a premature but perfectly formed boy was pushed out into a world he'd never know.

Clovis, who'd come in from the nursery, took the tiny, limp form from Nick's hands and laid it in the waiting Isolette, covering the dead baby with a receiving blanket. Lynn turned away.

Dr. Lourdes hadn't permitted Lynn to see her dead baby. "Dead embryo," he'd insisted on calling it, because unlike this child, the baby was too small to have survived even if it had been alive when she miscarried. He claimed he hadn't noticed whether it was a boy or a girl. Later Lynn searched out and read the lab report. The words were etched in her brain: "Macerated male fetus of eighteen to twenty weeks...."

Elena Diaz opened her eyes and stared up at Lynn, her face creased into apprehensive confusion.

"Your patient is awake, Doctor," Lynn said, at the same time trying to project reassurance at Ms. Diaz.

Nick, delivering the placenta, glanced at her, then at Clovis, who was rolling the isolette toward the door. "Leave it," he ordered. "She's beginning to respond and she'll want to see her baby."

62

Lynn thought she saw the corners of Ms. Diaz's mouth lift and her heart contracted. She glared at Nick. How dare he hold out hope to the poor woman?

"Elena?" Nick said. "Do you hear me, Elena?"

"Yes." The word was a whisper.

"You've had a bad time of it, but you're going to be all right. Understand?"

Again the faint whisper.

"The baby—" Nick paused. He rose from the stool at the foot of the table and walked around to where Elena could see him. "I tried to save your baby." His voice held an angry sadness. "I tried but I couldn't."

"My baby?" Fear glinted in her sunken dark eyes.

"Your baby is dead." Nick peeled off his bloody gloves to release the restraining straps that held Elena's arms and took her hand in his. "Do you want to see him?" He motioned to Clovis to bring over the Isolette.

An indescribable sound of anguish burst from Elena's throat. "I killed him," she cried.

"No!" Lynn's protest was involuntary, as much for herself as for Elena. She ignored the glance Nick shot at her. "It wasn't your fault. *Not your fault.*"

Nick turned his attention back to his patient and smoothed a strand of hair from her forehead. "These things happen, Elena. You can't blame yourself. Would you like to look at him?"

Elena nodded.

As Nick lifted the baby from the Isolette, Lynn saw that Clovis had prepared for this by wrapping the blanket around the tiny form and cleaning the face of blood and birth fluids. The child almost looked as if he were asleep.

Elena reached a trembling hand to touch her son's cheek. *"Pobrecito,"* she whispered. "Poor little baby."

After a moment, Nick returned the baby to the Isolette

and Clovis wheeled it from the room. Sobs shook Elena as tears streaked her face. Lynn wept with her, not caring what Nick or anyone else might think.

"She'll have to be monitored carefully." Nick's voice plowed ruthlessly through Lynn's grief, jolting her to awareness. She wasn't here to indulge her emotions but to take care of Elena and the other patients on the maternity unit.

"See to it you have sufficient—and usable—mag sulfate on hand," he continued.

A hot surge of annoyance dried her flow of tears. She hadn't been responsible for the outdated ampules in the locked emergency box, but he was blaming her for it without even trying to find out who might be. She opened her mouth to defend herself and closed it without speaking. To hell with what he thought. To hell with him.

Yanking a tissue from her pocket, she wiped her wet face, then raised her chin. The anger within her chilled her voice. "Your orders will be followed exactly, Dr. Dow."

He raised an eyebrow and waited, but when she didn't react in any way, he said, in a low tone, "Above all, don't let Grandma slip Elena any of her potions when she comes to visit. I'll put the devil's own fear in both of them, but I want all of you here to be on guard. Elena's not out of the woods yet, and a few swigs of Grandma's brew might well finish her off."

"I'll alert all personnel to the problem." Her words were as cold as liquid nitrogen.

"Damn it, Lynn," he began, but broke off when Blanche Wells, a nurse assistant, pushed open the delivery room door.

"Ms. Reilly said she thought you were ready to transfer the patient to her room."

"Yes, Blanche. Go ahead, I'll help you with the IV

64

equipment." Lynn turned away from Nick to assist Blanche. A few minutes later, she noticed he'd left the room.

Once Blanche had everything under control, Lynn headed for the nurses' station. Because it was a Sunday, the ward clerk was off. Sheila sat at the front desk, talking on the phone. To Lynn's surprise, she wore dark glasses, incongruous with her white uniform and black-banded white cap.

"Everything all right?" she asked when Sheila hung up.

Sheila turned the dark lenses toward her. "Mrs. Lawrence had a C-section, she's back in her room wide awake and thrilled with having a twin of each gender. No one in labor, all postpartums doing fine, two going home with their babies."

Lynn listened, wondering if she ought to mention the sunglasses or not. She certainly would if it were anyone besides touchy Sheila. Before she decided, Sheila winced and hunched over, folding her arms across her lower abdomen.

"What's the matter?" As she spoke, Lynn hurried around the desk and crouched beside Sheila.

"Just—a—cramp."

If Sheila, pregnant, was cramping. . . . Lynn's heart sank. "Any bleeding?" she asked as calmly as she could.

"Spotting, that's all. Nothing serious." Sheila's words were at odds with the tremor of panic threading through them.

"Have you called your doctor?"

When Sheila shook her head, the dark glasses slipped down her nose. Before she shoved them back into place, Lynn saw that her right eye was swollen and bruised.

"My God, did you fall?" Lynn asked.

Sheila's only answer was to hunch over farther, clutching at her abdomen.

Lynn straightened from her crouch and quickly scanned the unit census sheet. Room 309, a private room, was still empty. "You need to lie down," she said. "I'll help you across the hall."

Sheila stood up. "Oh my God," she cried, grabbing Lynn's arm. "Now I really am bleeding. It feels like it's gushing out."

"Hang on, I'll get a wheelchair." Lynn hurried toward the storage cubicle. Room 309 was no place for Sheila if she was actively bleeding. Housekeeping wouldn't have had time to clean the delivery room, but maybe one of the labor rooms was ready.

Deciding in favor of the latter, Lynn wheeled Sheila along the hall just as Nick Dow, changed from his scrub suit into street clothes, emerged from the doctors' lounge.

"Sheila's pregnant and she's cramping and bleeding," Lynn said to him before he could ask any questions. "Could you take a quick look at her?"

As she helped Sheila undress in the labor room, Lynn drew in her breath when she saw the massive bruise across Sheila's abdomen. If it was a fall, it must have been a bad one. But was it that? Nick's words when he was driving back from the Kings' party came back to Lynn: "Justin's got a mean temper. Goes right out of his gourd when he gets mad."

Maybe Sheila's husband had hurt her like this. Lynn shook her head, appalled at the thought.

As though reading her mind, Sheila muttered, "Bastard. You bastard, see what you've done." She began to cry.

With Sheila in position for his exam, Nick took one glance and told her, "You've aborted the baby. The embryo's at the introitus. With luck you'll push out the placenta, too, and won't need a D&C."

With luck? Lynn thought. What a way to phrase it. Yet he was right. Better to avoid dilatation and curettage of the uterus, better to have it over with quickly if the baby was already lost.

A few minutes later, Nick grunted in satisfaction as the placenta slid into view. Sheila's bleeding immediately slowed.

"Looks like everything came out," Nick told her. "I want you to call your doctor, though, and have him follow up on this. Okay?"

"Okay." Sheila's voice was blurred with tears.

"Hell of an ugly bruise you've got here," Nick said.

"He found out about the baby. Got mad cause he didn't want it. I hate the bastard." Sheila clenched her fists. "I'd like to kill him the same way he—" Sobs cut off her words.

"No!" Lynn said before she could control herself. "There's been too much killing."

Nick stared at her.

She couldn't explain, she wouldn't try. Let him think whatever he wanted.

Sheila grasped Lynn's hand. "I can't go home," she cried. "I'm afraid of him."

Lynn pressed the cold fingers reassuringly. "Don't worry, you can move in with me for the time being."

"You ought to press charges against Justin." Anger roughened Nick's voice.

Sheila gasped. "Never! He'd kill me."

Nick shrugged. "It's your business." He glanced at Lynn. "Maybe I owe you an apology."

She raised her eyebrows.

"The outdated mag sulf," he went on. "It came out of

the unit emergency box, as I recall. When was the box last checked at the pharmacy?"

"On Friday," Lynn said.

Nick grimaced. "Then I definitely apologize. Must've been Justin who fouled up. Doesn't surprise me. Any man who'd beat his pregnant wife has got a few clogged cylinders. Find me those outdated ampules, Lynn, and I'll check. If Justin did make the error I'll alert the chief of staff. The sooner Harper Hills starts looking for a new pharmacist, the better."

Once Sheila was comfortable, Lynn left her resting in the labor room and looked in on Elena Diaz, who was sleeping, her vital signs not only stable but near normal. She retrieved the mag sulf ampules from the medicine cart and returned to the desk where Nick was writing on Elena Diaz's chart.

"Everything under control?" he asked, looking up.

"Sheila's fine and so is Elena." Lynn handed him the ampules. "I checked the emergency box. It was restocked by the pharmacy on Friday and returned to the unit with Justin's signature okaying it. The seal was intact until Carrie broke it earlier this morning to get those." She nodded at what he held.

"This is one morning I don't care to relive," he said. "It'll take a lot of jogging to work it off. You ever jog?"

"Not here, not yet, but I'm thinking about it."

"I recommend the beach. You can't beat—" The operator's intercom page cut off his words.

"Thirty-three, number thirty-three."

"They're playing my song," he said, reaching for the phone.

Lynn left him talking to the operator and when she came back he was gone.

68

By the time the shift was over, Sheila felt strong enough to walk to Lynn's car with her.

"You've got the next two days off," Lynn said as she slid behind the wheel. "Maybe you'd better take a couple more."

Sheila shook her head. "I'll be okay, I'm better off working. The problem is all my stuff's at home and so is Justin. I won't be able to collect anything until he goes to work tomorrow. Except he has our car." She hugged her arms to her chest. "I'm afraid of the bastard. You know?"

"I'll find something you can wear tonight and if you'll drive me to work in the morning, you can use my car to pick up what you need. Provided you feel up to it."

"I'm pretty damned tough." Sheila's laugh was harsh. "You must be wondering why the hell I married Justin."

Lynn shook her head. She knew only too well how blinding an infatuation could be. She'd learned the hard way that a woman never really knew a man until she lived with him.

"He's world-class in bed," Sheila said. "I guess I thought that was enough. Never again." She glanced at Lynn. "Some nerve I've got, dumping on you. You must be pretty damn fed up with me, considering."

Lynn shrugged. What could she say? She couldn't deny that Sheila had deliberately made trouble for her on the unit. Nor could she explain her feeling of kinship with Sheila without revealing more than she wanted to of the past, more than she ever intended to tell anyone.

"Now I'm moving in with you, putting you out when the last person in the world you really want for a roomie is me."

Lynn gave her a one-sided grin. "Not quite the last. I'm no martyr. If I hadn't meant it, I wouldn't have in-

69

vited you. And the apartment has two bedrooms, so you're not putting me out."

Sheila's look was skeptical. "I bet you were the kind of kid who brought home every stray animal you ran across."

"You're wrong . . . just cats. I never took much to dogs or birds, I don't know why."

"That sure classifies me. Okay, but don't be surprised if I scratch and bite. I'm not the purring type."

Sheila dropped Lynn off at Harper Hills the next morning. She wore the dark glasses to hide her black eye and affected a jaunty manner to conceal the grief and fear Lynn knew she had to be feeling.

Lynn would never understand why women were drawn to obnoxious men. There had to be more to it than sex. In her own case, among other things, she'd believed Ray needed her. . . .

"See you at three-thirty." Sheila waved and drove away.

Three West was quiet, the census down. Elena Diaz hadn't had any more convulsions, the Lawrence twins were alert and active. When Mrs. Morrin's secretary called to ask Lynn to come to the director's office when she had a free moment, there was nothing on the unit to prevent her from leaving immediately.

"I'm sure you'll be pleased to hear Ms. Johnson's head injury wasn't as serious as her doctor feared," Mrs. Morrin said, her pale eyes alert for Lynn's reaction.

For an instant Lynn's mind went blank and she couldn't place the name. Before she panicked, it came to her . . . Lois Johnson, the maternity charge nurse who'd been injured in a freeway accident.

"That's good news," she said.

"In fact, she's doing so well, her doctor says she can return to work. Half-time for two weeks, then full-time."

To Lynn's surprise, she felt a pang at the thought of leaving Three West. She'd established herself as charge nurse there and she'd survived what she'd once thought she'd never be able to face. On the other hand, she did prefer a medical unit, and she wouldn't want to stand in the way of Ms. Johnson's returning to maternity.

Not that Mrs. Morrin would let her.

"I must say you've proved to be competent," the director of nurses went on. "Also, Ms. Elkins reports you have a talent for problem solving and I trust her judgment. So I'm placing you in charge of Five East, starting next Monday." Again the pale eyes probed.

Five East? Mrs. Morrin couldn't be serious. No one in her right mind would want to be assigned there.

"You may not be familiar with that unit," the DNS went on smoothly. "Harper Hills utilizes Five East for overflow of both medical and surgical patients."

"So I've heard," Lynn managed to say.

"I admit the unit has had problems, but I feel certain you'll be able to cope."

She's waiting for me to refuse, Lynn thought. She's deliberately putting me in charge of the worst unit in the hospital in the hopes I'll resign and she'll be rid of me. If I point out that she more or less promised me a medical unit once Ms. Johnson returned, she'll only tell me there *are* medical patients on Five East.

Though Lynn had been tempted to give up when she first met the DNS and had been assigned to Maternity against her will, she felt very differently now. She'd struggled to prove herself capable in her own eyes as well as in the eyes of those she worked with. She meant to stay

71

no matter what Morrin threw at her but she wasn't going to meekly accept this assignment without having her say.

"I understand Five East is understaffed." Lynn's voice was crisp. Understaffed, disorganized, demoralized, you name the problem, Five East had it. "The first step in problem solving is adequate help."

"Because it's an overflow unit, the patient census fluctuates—sometimes Five East is full, other times the unit has very few patients. I'm reluctant to hire personnel who aren't needed," Mrs. Morrin explained.

"Understaffing hurts the patient. If and when the census is down, couldn't excess help on Five East float where they're needed? I know there've been days on maternity when an LVN or RN float would have been a godsend."

Lynn's words fell into a silence. Finally Mrs. Morrin said, "I'll consider your request, but I can promise nothing."

Lynn pushed a little more, using what she'd learned of the paper flow between departments. "Would you like me to put it in writing?"

The blue eyes frosted. "That won't be necessary."

Lynn met the cold gaze calmly. They both knew without saying it that Mrs. Morrin didn't want a written request from Lynn to wind up on the hospital administrator's desk. Actually, neither did Lynn. She had no intention of using her friendship with Conrad to defy the DNS, but the director had no way of knowing that.

Morrin was aware Five East needed at least one more nurse. It certainly wasn't unfair to push for what they both knew was right.

When Sheila picked her up at three-thirty, Lynn told her about the impending transfer.

"It's great Lois is able to come back to work," Sheila said, "but my God, Morrin must have it in for you. Don't you have more pull than that? I mean with Werth."

Lynn tried to squelch her annoyance, aware Sheila was only saying aloud what others whispered behind her back. "He did recruit me, but I don't expect favors," she said as evenly as she could. "I don't *want* favors."

Sheila's eyebrows rose in disbelief, but she dropped the subject of Conrad.

"You know Five East gets all the reject patients from the med and surg units, don't you?" she asked. "Complainers, pains-in-the-ass, weirdos ... and worse. They sometimes shove real nut cases up there, too, if the four psych beds are filled. The unit has no facilities for crazies but they don't care. Did you hear about the RN who got her jaw broken trying to sedate some schizo? They acted like it was her fault. If the Five East staff can't cope, why, it's the staff's fault, that's their attitude. I sure don't envy you. I'd quit before I'd work in that madhouse. You're out of your mind taking it on."

Lynn gritted her teeth. If Sheila wasn't the last person in the world she'd chosen for an apartment-mate, she was coming closer all the time.

On the other hand, if the phone rang some night and it was Ray's voice again, at least she wouldn't be alone.

Chapter 5

Nick jogged along the shoreline, disturbing long-legged shore birds feeding on ocean delicacies left behind by the ebbing tide. Hills to the east hid the rising sun that tinted the clouds a pale peach. Sunrise was his favorite time.

Had been, ever since he was ten and got picked off the streets of Flint and sent to the Upper Peninsula of Michigan to live with his Aunt Grace, the only relative the social worker could locate. That summer and every summer in the years he spent with her, Aunt Grace took him to a shack in the woods and left him with old John Greatcloud, a full-blooded Chippewa. At eight he might have been scared of the ancient, crazy-acting Greatcloud, but a lot had happened in the two years before he turned ten and none of it had been good. On guard with everyone, Nick had been more afraid of being left to face the world by himself than he was of any old Indian.

On the first morning after Nick's arrival, Greatcloud rose before dawn. The wary ten-year-old woke when he did and crept out behind him, determined not to be stranded alone in the woods. In the gray pre-dawn, he followed Greatcloud to the top of a ridge overlooking Lake Superior and watched with uncomprehending fascination as the old man raised his arms to the sky, chanting as the sun rose.

In the three years before Greatcloud died, Nick learned from him the most important lesson of his life—how to feel a part of the earth and everything in it. The realization helped him understand he belonged somewhere and Greatcloud's teachings enabled him to survive the bad times later. He was no Indian mystic who raised his arms and chanted, but he tried his best to be awake and outside at dawn. Sunrise renewed him.

The ocean waves lapping at Nick's feet turned from dull pewter to blue as they reflected the brightening of the sky. A gray-brown pelican swooped low offshore, rose with a fish crosswise in his beak, jerked his head to position the fish, and gulped it down.

Up the beach another jogger ran toward him. Seagulls fled from the woman's path, flying ahead of her in a squawking vanguard. The sun rose over the hills, turning her hair to flame, and he recognized Lynn Holley.

Two minutes later he was jogging beside her.

"Weren't you going the other way?" she commented.

He grinned at her. "I think I'm headed in the right direction." He wasn't sure of this by any means, but it felt good to run with her in the morning sunlight. It felt right.

She wore red satin jogging shorts and a loose, faded red T-shirt. The shorts affirmed that her legs above the knee were as sexy as below. He enjoyed looking at her, he'd like to see more of her—in all ways. Wise or unwise, who cared?

"You take jogging seriously," he said when she made no other attempt at conversation.

"I'm no fanatic who has to get X amount of miles in every day or die, if that's what you mean."

Was she always this defensive or was it just with him because he'd kissed her the night of Joe's party? Or because she'd kissed him back? Remembering how she'd felt in his arms brought a surge of desire that didn't mix well with jogging.

"Hear the latest about Justin Burns?" he asked.

"No."

"I had my conference with Lloyd Linnett—you know he's chief of staff?—and Lloyd talked to Werth about Burns. Seems Werth has had other complaints about the pharmacy. This latest error puts Burns out on his can."

She slowed and stopped, so he did, too.

"I can never forgive him for what he did to Sheila." She looked out over the water instead of at him.

"No excuse for it."

"Because of him two babies are dead."

"Sheila's, anyway. I don't know if we'd have saved Elena's even if the mag sulf had been okay." He touched her shoulder. "I tend to yell at people when things get hairy. Sorry you were on the receiving end that morning."

She turned to face him. "I didn't like being blamed. I'm not perfect, I can and have made mistakes, but I'm not careless."

He looked into her green, fathomless eyes. "I'll try to remember that the next time we're in the delivery room together."

Her eyes widened. "You mean you haven't heard? Lois Johnson's coming back to maternity and I'm being transferred to Five East."

His disappointment surprised him. Lynn was one damned good nurse, but why should he care what nurse assisted with his deliveries as long as she was competent?

"I rarely have any of my post-ops on the overflow unit,"

he said, "I guess if I feel the urge to yell at you, we'll have to keep meeting like this."

Her smile brought a glow to her eyes, but she said nothing as they started up again, walking instead of jogging.

"A lot of problems on that unit," he said. "They don't call it East Hell for nothing."

"Mrs. Morrin expects me to solve all the problems."

"She must think you're a miracle worker. Are you?"

"Ha. I don't even know if I'll get the additional nurse I asked her to hire."

Werth would get her the nurse—if she asked him. Come to think of it, she could have pulled Werth's string to avoid being sent to Five East in the first place. Werth could easily put pressure on Morrin. What was the relationship between Werth and Lynn, anyway? Nick didn't like to think of Lynn struggling with the chaos of Five East, and presumably Werth was a hell of lot more involved with her than Nick Dow. Didn't Werth care?

"So you let Morrin steamroller you into accepting the transfer." Anger colored his words. He wasn't sure who he was the most annoyed with—Werth, Morrin, or Lynn.

He heard her sharp intake of breath. "Accept or resign seemed to be the options," she said after a moment. "I came here to work at Harper Hills and I don't give up easily."

He'd never met a woman who confused him more. He'd been certain Werth had brought her here because he needed a spy at the hospital he could trust, and who better than his lover. Yet everything Lynn said and did contradicted that. She could be faking and yet he'd swear she wasn't. It wouldn't bother him so much one way or the other if he wasn't so damned attracted to her.

78

"Time I went back to the apartment," she said, her voice devoid of any emotion. She turned around.

She'd had enough of him. Every time they were together he seemed to say or do the wrong thing. Nick grasped her arm, stopping her.

"I don't give up easily, either," he said. "How do you feel about Komodo dragons?"

Lynn stared at him. Nick always kept her off balance. "I've never met one," she replied, conscious of how close he stood, very much aware of his hand on her arm. His scent, active male and provocative, mingled with the sea breeze.

"I'll arrange an introduction. What're your days off next week?"

"Unlike maternity, the Five East charge gets every weekend off."

He grinned, his dark eyes holding hers. "So being sent to hell has its compensations, after all. How about a week from this Saturday, then?"

"What about it?"

"For meeting a dragon face-to-face. Pick you up about three that afternoon."

Whatever this nonsense about dragons was, she shouldn't go anywhere with Nick. Now that she wouldn't be seeing him almost every day as she had on maternity, his disturbing presence would gradually fade from her mind entirely.

And she'd miss it. Miss him. Besides, she wasn't sure when she'd get another chance to meet a dragon.

She smiled and nodded. His hand dropped from her arm and she jogged away. She might be making a mistake, and probably was, but for the moment she didn't care. The sun's caress warmed her and the bright day welcomed her. She'd been right to leave the cold darkness of the east behind, right to begin a new life in California.

A life that included Nick Dow? She wasn't ready to answer that question. One dragon at a time.

She was still smiling when she reached the apartment.

Sheila, barefoot and wearing only a long T-shirt, sat over coffee in the kitchen. "Mr. Werth called," she said. "I wasn't going to answer the phone at first because I figured it might be Justin and I'm not talking to that bastard, but then I decided I could disguise my voice and pretend to be you. It must have worked, because Mr. Werth thought I *was* you."

Lynn put a foot on the chair to begin her cooling-down exercises. "Oh?"

"You don't sound very excited."

Lynn shrugged. Sheila couldn't be convinced there was nothing but friendship between her and Conrad, so why bother to comment?

"He was kind of upset when he found out who I really was and that I'm living here." Sheila's brown eyes probed Lynn's.

"Any message?"

"He said he'd be in touch."

As she twisted and stretched, Lynn wondered what Conrad had wanted. It couldn't be important if he hadn't asked her to call back. Since they lived in the same apartment, there was no reason Sheila shouldn't have taken Conrad's call, but it bothered Lynn that she had, especially since Sheila had pretended to be her. She'd grown used to her privacy.

"I'd been thinking about getting an answering machine before you moved in," Lynn said. "If we had one, you could avoid any call from Justin by letting the phone ring and listening to the message later."

"And I wouldn't take *your* calls." Sheila's smile was sly.

"That, too." Lynn kept her voice neutral. Sheila enjoyed needling her and she'd be damned if she'd react. "Had you heard Justin lost his job?"

Sheila shook her head. "Serves him right. He'll blame me for it like he does everything else, but at least I'm not around for him to take it out on. I hope to hell he leaves town." She finished her coffee and stood up. "Just who did you run into jogging to hear about Justin?"

"Nick Dow."

Sheila raised an eyebrow. "After it's over, remember I was the first to warn you to watch your step."

You and everyone else, including my own conscience, Lynn thought.

The note clipped to Lynn's time card on Monday told her to stop by the DNS's office before reporting to Five East.

"I've hired a second RN for your unit," Mrs. Morrin told her.

Lynn, who'd expected an LVN, if she got another nurse at all, smiled in relief. "Thanks. I'm certain the extra help will solve some of the unit's problems. What's her name?"

"His name is Rolfe Watson."

Lynn's heart sank. All her experiences working with male nurses had been negative. But she'd gotten the extra nurse she'd requested and she'd have to make the best of it.

Delayed by her stop at the director's office, Lynn arrived on Five East only fifteen minutes early instead of the thirty she'd planned on, since this was her first day. Both her RNs were already there, and she introduced herself before taking the report from the night shift.

Rolfe Watson was tall and slim and looked to be in his thirties. Standing next to Beth Yadon, the other Five East RN, his height made her appear even shorter than she was, while his dark brown skin made her fairness paler by comparison. Beth greeted her nervously. Rolfe's lips, under his neat moustache, had a cynical twist as he said hello, almost as though he knew Lynn had reservations. But if he thought it was because he was black he was completely wrong.

Two nurse assistants completed her staff—Connie Machino and Nai Pham, a Vietnamese RN who was working as an aide while trying to qualify for a California license. Connie was short and stocky, Nai Pham about Lynn's height and bony. Both had dark hair and brown eyes. Connie had been on the unit for six months, Nai Pham a week, Beth Yadon two weeks.

Five East, with beds for twenty-eight, had a current census of twenty. Without a ward clerk, Lynn would be tied to the desk much of the time, but once she got things sorted out, she'd work on getting a clerk.

At Harper Hills RNs did primary care, taking care of assigned patients, from bed baths, if necessary, to IVs. The nurse assistants did only patient care, and the medications and treatments of patients assigned to them would be split between the two RNs. Listening to the night report, Lynn made a list of the sickest patients so as not to assign too many to any one nurse. She noticed with dismay that all but two patients had moderate to severe problems. Her staff would certainly be kept busy.

As she drew up the assignment, Lynn glanced evaluatingly at Rolfe Watson. One male nurse she'd worked with in Boston had insisted it was discriminatory for him to be assigned primarily to male patients. Another had objected being assigned to women patients who needed bed baths.

She wondered what quirks Rolfe might have, not that she intended to indulge any of them.

"I have no objection to you calling me Lynn when there are no patients or doctors present," she told the staff, "but in front of doctors, patients, or relatives, I'm Ms. Holley. I'll do the same with you, unless you'd prefer I didn't use your first name at all." She gazed from one to the other. No one objected, but Rolfe seemed amused.

I'm going to have trouble with him, she thought, just as I figured.

But it was Beth, her blue eyes wide and apprehensive, who objected to the way Lynn assigned the patients.

"Mrs. Lanigan's got an ileostomy," she said. "She's too sick to take care of it herself, and I've never done one."

"I'll show you," Rolfe offered before Lynn could open her mouth. "Come and get me when you're ready."

Beth smiled at him. "Oh, thank you."

A knight errant, Lynn wondered, or a man who needed to prove his superiority to others? To women?

"I hope you don't think I'm dumb," Beth said, as much to Rolfe as to Lynn. "I just graduated a month ago and I'm finding out there's a lot they don't teach you."

At least Beth admitted she didn't know, a point in her favor. Still, having an inexperienced RN on an already problem-plagued unit was a minus.

Nai Pham lingered after the other three left the nurses' station. "Please?" she said to Lynn. "I no know."

It took Lynn a few minutes to find out what Nai Pham was getting at. The cadence of her speech as much as her accent made her difficult to understand. She'd never been assigned these particular patients before and wanted to know something about them.

"Do you read English?" Lynn asked, thinking Nai Pham could check the patients' care plans.

"I read. Take long time. No have."

Lynn, who'd hoped to be free to orient herself to the unit, prepared to help the Vietnamese woman. She'd learn about the patients, too, in the process, but having a nurse assistant who was far from fluent in English was another minus.

Well, she hadn't expected a bed of roses. Beth would do okay if she was supervised carefully. Nai Pham might prove to be a problem if she, like some other foreign nurses Lynn had worked with, became too embarrassed to keep asking when she didn't understand. She'd remember to treat the Vietnamese woman with special courtesy to try to avoid that situation.

Beth and Nai Pham, she decided, she could handle. Rolfe was another matter, but there was no use worrying about him until he gave her cause.

When she finished with Nai Pham, Lynn, the unit cardex in her hand, began visiting each patient, keeping an ear out for the phone since she was the only one free to answer it. The first room she walked into had the call light on. A quick check of the cardex showed her that the patient, Leonard Franklin, 48, had carcinoma of the pancreas. She saw he had a subclavian intravenous line in place.

"I want my shot and I want it now," Mr. Franklin demanded before Lynn could open her mouth. "I told that black guy who said he was my nurse, I told him I got a lot of pain and he had the nerve to say it wasn't time for the shot, I had a half hour to go. I asked him what did he expect—I should tell the pain to wait? Listen, you got to help me, I can't stand it."

"I'll check with Mr. Watson," Lynn said, then introduced herself briefly. "We'll be working together to keep you comfortable."

The skeptical twist of Mr. Franklin's mouth told her he didn't believe her for a minute.

Back at the desk, she pulled Leonard Franklin's chart. His doctor had ordered 75 milligrams of merperidine to be given into the IV line every three hours for intractable pain.

"I don't give medications ahead of schedule," Rolfe said when she asked him about his patient. "Or behind schedule, either." He glanced at his watch. "Franklin's got ten minutes to go. I took a look at his past history. He's been on merperidine for years. We're shooting up an addict here."

Lynn quelled her surge of annoyance at Rolfe's snap diagnosis. It wouldn't help to get angry. "Let's not make any premature judgments about Mr. Franklin. He says he's in severe pain, and neither you nor I nor anyone else can disprove it. I'm not suggesting you go against his doctor's orders, what I do suggest is that you come up with a care plan for the patient to keep him free of pain."

"If that's what you want." Rolfe's tone was not quite insolent, nothing she could really object to.

"It's what I expect." Lynn couldn't help the chill in her voice. "We'll discuss Mr. Franklin at our first staff conference."

By the time her shift had finished, Lynn's nerves were as tattered as a toddler's favorite blanket. Intent on Five East's problems, she passed Joyce Elkins in the corridor without even seeing her.

"Hey," Joyce protested, "I'm not exactly the invisible woman. Something the matter?"

"Sorry. It's just—" Lynn paused, uncertain where to begin. She hated to be a complainer.

Joyce's smile was understanding. "We never did make that date to have dinner together. How about tonight?"

"You said the magic words. Dinner out sounds great." Then Lynn remembered her apartment-mate. "I do have Sheila Burns living with me now, though."

"And you're Siamese twins?"

Lynn grinned at Joyce, wishing she had the same disarming ability to put things in perspective. She felt sorry for Sheila, but she wasn't her keeper. Each of them needed a life of her own. "About six?" she asked.

"Let me pick you up," Joyce said. "I finally broke down and bought that Porsche I've been debating about, and the more people I get to admire it, the more convinced I'll be I made the right choice."

The Porsche turned out to be sea blue. Joyce leaned casually against one front fender, deliberately striking a pose as Lynn looked the car over.

"I don't believe it!" Lynn cried. "You found a dress to match the Porsche. The dealer ought to use you for an ad, you and the car make a stunning combination."

Joyce smiled, obviously pleased. "You know, I dreamed of being a model when I was a skinny little kid, but Mama's 'You never see a nurse out of work' finally got to me."

"Are you sorry?"

Joyce shrugged. "I like what I do which, I guess, is more than *you* can say at the moment. But, hey, we aren't going to waste time talking shop, we're on our way to dine fine, we two."

The blue Porsche purred along the coast highway, finally stopping at The Divine Shrimp, a seafood restaurant perched on a pier. Conscious of second looks from the male customers as they followed the hostess toward their table, Lynn credited the stares to admiration for Joyce's svelte figure and exotic face.

"You've got to watch California males," Joyce said after they were seated. "The men in Boston may have inhibitions, but no man here has heard the word, as you've probably discovered by now. And don't shake your head at me, I've been noticing Nick Dow noticing you."

"Sheila's warned me he gives all the new nurses a whirl. I don't get dizzy easily."

Joyce's glance appraised her. "Anyone who survives a day as Five East charge nurse without coming off duty in hysterics is one strong woman. At long last Dr. Dow may have met his match."

Lynn, recalling her own reaction to Nick's kiss, wasn't so sure. On the other hand, she was damned if she'd allow herself to become seriously involved with another arrogant, insensitive doctor like her husband had been. Except Nick didn't seem to have Ray's insecurities and he really wasn't insensitive ... she brought herself up short. No! She wasn't ready for a deep relationship with any man—let alone the Harper Hills Heartbreaker.

When Joyce discovered Lynn had never eaten abalone, she made the shellfish sound so fantastically delicious that Lynn felt she had to order it or miss the taste treat of the century.

"You didn't exaggerate," she told Joyce after the first mouthful. "This is wonderful! I'm certainly coming back here again."

"The Divine Shrimp is definitely in with the Harper Hills crowd." Joyce nodded to their left.

Lynn, risking a casual glance in that direction, saw Pat and Conrad Werth at a table against the wall.

"I never know whether to stop by and speak when I see

him outside the hospital," Joyce said. "Mrs. Werth doesn't seem to like me."

"You're too attractive." As soon as the words were out of her mouth, Lynn could have bitten her tongue. She liked Joyce, she trusted her not to gossip, but because everyone at the hospital knew about Lynn's previous acquaintance with Conrad, it wasn't wise to say anything personal about the Werths.

"At the Kings' party I gathered *you* weren't exactly her favorite person."

Lynn couldn't leave the comment hanging. "I'd be her friend if she'd let me, but Pat misconstrues things."

"It's a bad habit that afflicts a lot of people."

Meaning Harper Hills thought like Pat did? That Conrad and Lynn were more than friends? Denials, she knew, were useless.

She only hoped Conrad didn't come over to their table, and that they got nothing more than a nod at the most. She'd prefer if he ignored her presence completely. But maybe that would make it seem like there *was* something between them. She hated being put on the spot like this.

Neither Conrad nor Pat gave the slightest hint they'd noticed either Joyce or Lynn and finally Lynn relaxed and began to enjoy her dinner again.

"Is Sheila still agitating for unionization?" Joyce asked.

Lynn looked up in surprise. "If she is, she hasn't mentioned it to me. In fact, she's never mentioned a union to me at all."

Joyce shrugged. "She's mentioned it to a lot of other people since Consolidated Medical took over Harper Hills, that's for sure."

Lynn remembering what Conrad had said about unionization asked, "What's CMC have to do with a nurses union?"

Joyce's eyes flickered. "Who knows? Shame on me for talking shop when I promised you we wouldn't."

She doesn't quite trust me, Lynn realized, unable to blame Joyce. Especially with Conrad sitting in the same room to remind her who'd brought Lynn to Harper Hills to begin with.

When she went to the ladies' room, Lynn saw the Werths were ready to leave so she lingered inside, reapplying her lipstick and brushing her hair to give them time to get out of the restaurant.

When she came out, to Lynn's dismay, Conrad was using the telephone in the tiny corridor leading to the bathrooms and there was no way to pass him without him seeing her.

He hung up and turned to her, frowning. "We need to talk."

"Here?" She was incredulous.

"No, Pat's waiting in the car. And you've got a Harper Hills nurse in your apartment these days, so that's out as a place to meet. We'll make it the library, that's safe enough. I'll have to check my calendar for the best time, then I'll call your place without mentioning my name, giving the date and the time to meet me. I expect you to be there."

Lynn stood staring after him as he left the corridor. He *expected* her to be there! What gave him the right to order her around? And what did they have to talk about? It was true he'd asked her to report any gross mismanagement to him, but she had no evidence of that . . . except Five East, and *she* was the one trying to manage that unit at the moment. Maybe it was about the unionization movement. She shook her head and started to leave the corridor, almost colliding with a man.

"Nick!" she cried, surprised to see him and not pleased at the burst of excitement she felt.

He stared down at her, unsmiling. "Old home week at the johns?" he said.

So he'd seen Conrad and put the worst interpretation on it. Lynn scowled. It was none of Nick's business even if what he thought was true and she was having an affair with Conrad. Since she wasn't, Nick had a lot of nerve condemning her. He was more like Ray than she'd admitted. He might even become dangerous if she allowed herself to deepen their relationship. As she'd known from the beginning, she couldn't take any chances with Nick Dow. She had to cut off anything between them immediately.

"About Saturday," she began.

"Three o'clock," he cut in. Without giving her a chance to say another word, he disappeared into the men's room, leaving her with the choice of hanging around waiting outside or returning to her table.

She'd make it a point to see him at the hospital before Saturday, she told herself as she walked back to join Joyce. She'd tell him then that she couldn't go with him on Saturday or any other day. As for Conrad, she would have a few choice words for him when he called.

"Pardon me for mentioning it, but you do seem a bit upset," Joyce told her after she sat down. "A touch of vertigo?"

It took Lynn a moment to recall her boast that she didn't get dizzy easily. "The next man I have anything to do with," she burst out, "will be sweet and understanding."

Joyce laughed. "Girl, that kind of man doesn't exist. And if he did, you'd be fed up with him in a week."

Chapter 6

Lynn stood staring in disbelief. She'd seen pictures of iguanas and other giant lizards, but coming eyeball-to-eyeball with a ten-foot-long Komodo dragon was something else. Its tongue flicked out as it appraised her, as though anticipating how she'd taste, and she was glad of the barrier the San Diego Zoo had placed between her and the reptile.

If she could only find a way to erect as effective a barrier between her and Nick. She'd meant to cancel their Saturday date, but somehow the chance hadn't come. So then she'd made up her mind to spend the day being polite but cool. That worked for the first few miles out of town, but by the time they passed Oceanside they were in the midst of a hot argument about nurse practitioners, she pro, Nick con. By then it was too late to retreat to being distant.

"Beautiful, isn't he?" Nick asked, intent on the lizard.

"Fantastic, yes," she countered, "beautiful, no."

"Women never appreciate reptiles."

"I went through the snake house with you, didn't I?"

"Reluctantly. I imagine the dislike goes back to Eve being tempted by the serpent and what came of all that."

"I'd never be seduced into sin by a snake. I prefer warm and cuddly to scaly and cold-blooded."

"I belong to the first group, honest." He grinned at her. "I'll even let you draw a blood sample to check." He drew the collar of his blue polo shirt away from his neck and angled his head to expose his carotid vein.

She couldn't suppress her smile. "Vampira, I'm not. I'll take your word for it. If I'm ever forced to choose between a reptile and you, consider yourself my first pick."

He was too damn attractive, the blue of his shirt enhancing his dark good looks, the snug-fitting well-worn jeans emphasizing his athletic build. Any woman would notice Nick, so she couldn't blame herself for that. The trouble was she was increasingly drawn to the inner Nick.

"That's the best offer I've had so far today," he said. "I'll keep it in mind. I was going to suggest we visit the tropical bird forest, but birds are distant cousins of reptiles, as I recall. How are you on feathers?"

"I can take them or leave them."

"On to the koalas, then, the cuddliest critters in the zoo ... present company excepted."

As they walked between flowering oleanders and hibiscus bushes from one display of animals to the next, bantam chickens scurrying from under their feet, Lynn relaxed. She hadn't been in a zoo since she was a child and something of the wonder she'd felt then came back to her as she gazed at nature's marvelous variety. Impulsively, she grasped Nick's hand, exclaiming, "This is fun!"

After that it seemed natural to stroll hand-in-hand like so many other couples on this sunny California afternoon.

As they headed for the primate display, Lynn thought of Boston, still in winter's grip. Though there might be tentative signs of spring, you'd have to search to find them. Any snow that remained would be mushy and ugly with filth, the wind would be chilly, and more than likely it would be raining. A cold, dreary rain.

"You've retreated again," Nick said, stopping and turning her to face him.

Without thinking, she said, "I was remembering the line a Harvard poet once wrote: 'The day is cold and dark and dreary.' "

" 'It rains and the wind is never weary.' " Nick glanced up at the blue sky, then raised an eyebrow at her.

Lynn withdrew her hand from his, controlling her impulse to wrap her arms around herself. "I didn't think anybody outside of Massachusetts and maybe Maine could quote Longfellow once they passed the age of twelve."

Nick, hearing the brittleness in her voice, took a deep breath. She was trying to turn attention away from herself as she always did. He understood, he wasn't one to share his own past. But if he let her glimpse a small part of his, maybe she'd reveal some of hers. He wanted to know what made her tick, he needed to know. What she hid was more than grief for a dead husband. And if he didn't jar her free of whatever was bothering her, she'd retreat farther from him.

"My Aunt Grace," he said slowly, "had a grudge against Longfellow for substituting an Iroquois hero, Hiawatha, for the Chippewa hero Manabozo—an insult, since the Iroquois were ancient traditional enemies. Aunt Grace used to read 'The Song of Hiawatha' to me, substituting Manabozo's name and correcting everything else she felt was a mistake.

"There were other poems in her book, and I secretly read them all under the impression I was doing something forbidden. The older I get, the more I suspect my aunt's motives. She was a damned crafty Indian to hook a smart-assed eleven-year-old on poetry."

Lynn's clear green eyes reflected her surprise and interest. He'd thrown her off balance with his confession. Now he'd strike like a reptile.

" 'My life is cold and dark and dreary,' " he quoted from the end of the poem she'd begun. "Is that what you meant to say, Lynn?"

Shock darkened her eyes.

"It's warm in California," he said quickly, wanting to add that he'd be warm, too, if she'd give him the chance. But he'd better not. It was neither the time nor the place. " 'Be still, sad heart, and cease repining,' " he quoted, then parodied Longfellow's last line, 'Look, no clouds, the sun is shining."

Her lips curved slightly. "You did learn something from your aunt, I see—how to revise Longfellow."

At least he had made her smile, he thought. Though he'd gotten no glimpse of her past, he'd lightened her mood and he'd have to be satisfied with that for now. "What I want to know," he demanded, "is your position on primates. Where do you draw the warm-and-cuddly line? Monkeys? Or somewhere among the great apes? Before you answer, I have to warn you that one of the gorillas here has a unique way of expressing his contempt for humans."

"How?"

"He stockpiles his own feces and has a pitching talent the Red Sox could have used last year."

Her brief frown faded as comprehension dawned and she laughed. "You're making that up."

"Cross my heart. His aim is especially good when the target wears white."

Lynn glanced at her white shirt and grimaced. "I never

had the urge to be friends with King Kong. Or an enemy of his either. Let's go see the big cats instead."

Later, he watched her as she stood before the lion's enclosure, intent on a cub stalking its mother's twitching tail. She wore a full white skirt that emphasized her small waist. Though otherwise plain, the shirt she wore had a ruffle along the edge of the stand-up collar framing her face. Nothing elaborate, but she didn't need frills, she'd be beautiful wearing a paper sack. Or nothing. His pulse rate increased markedly at that image.

Watch yourself, Dow, he thought. Stop pawing the ground or you'll scare this one off for good. He had to remember to take it slow and easy, to try for the romantic. Wasn't that what all women wanted? He had to be careful, though, that he didn't go overboard, to keep her laughing. And guessing.

"Since you've gone ape for abalone," he said, "I thought we'd have dinner at Anthony's Star of the Sea. They're abalone experts and there's a great harbor view."

Pleasant surroundings, soft lighting, good service, fine food, and a bottle or two of wine. Maybe even live background music. Enough to warm the coldest heart. He hadn't been able to forget the way she'd once responded to his kiss, brief though that response had been. He wouldn't go so far as to expect total capitulation, but he did look forward to a few successful preliminary maneuvers. In his experience, once the preliminaries began, the fortress was as good as breached.

The Star of the Sea Room produced a decent California pinot blanc and conversation at dinner, whether due to the wine or to their own high spirits, was light and breezy.

"Do you like practicing alone?" she asked him after dinner as they sipped the last of the wine.

"It has disadvantages," he admitted. "Paul Salvador

95

wants me to come in with him and set up a clinic for mothers and babies who can't afford quality medical care. He plans to run it on a pay-what-you-can, free-when-you-can't system. I like the idea and I just might go that route."

He was tempted. He liked Paul and he knew from bitter experience how those with no money fared in today's world. In a way, he owed them. On the other hand, he wasn't certain he was in tune with what Paul envisioned them doing.

"I had no idea." Lynn's eyes held a warmth he'd never before seen. For him. "I'm really impressed, Nick. From what I saw when I was on Maternity, I think Paul's a fine pediatrician, and I don't have to tell you how good you are in your specialty."

Nick's grin was wry. "Thanks. I think."

She smiled. "I'm judging on performance."

"In that case, many thanks." He was more pleased by Lynn's words than he wanted to show. She was one nurse who knew good medicine from bad.

She lifted her wineglass. "To the future partnership of Salvador and Dow. May it flourish." When they'd taken a drink, she set down her glass. "I knew you cared about your patients but I didn't realize you were a—a—well, an idealist."

Nick snorted. "No way. I want my share like everyone else. It wasn't easy getting where I am. That's why I understand how it can be for those the odds are against. Not everyone has an Aunt Grace. She never told the authorities, but she wasn't really my aunt, not a true relation at all. It was enough for her that we shared the blood. She took me in hand and had an old shaman set me on what she believed to be the true path."

"The Chippewa path?"

He nodded. "But not exclusively. Most tribes have similar beliefs."

She leaned forward, eyes wide, obviously fascinated. "Do you still follow that path?"

"No, but I know where it is."

Lynn sighed and shadows clouded her eyes.

"You don't strike me as a woman who's lost her way," he ventured when the silence between them grew, then he was sorry he'd spoken when he heard her quick, pained intake of breath. Hell. It was too late to make amends. He might as well forge on.

"I know you were married and your husband died." He chose his next words with care. "From a remark you once made, I also gather there was trouble between you. If that's what's festering inside you, remember incision and drainage is usually the best treatment."

A series of expressions flitted across her face. Shock, anger, the urge to kill him, then a hopeless sadness as she averted her gaze and stared down at her hands.

"Talk about it, Lynn," he ordered. "Let the poison out."

For long moments he thought he'd failed and that this would be the end for them. But then she straightened up in her chair and looked at him.

"I never should have married Ray," she said in a voice so low he could scarcely hear her. She looked away, reached for her wineglass, and took a sip. "We were all wrong for each other."

When she didn't continue, he tried to prime her by echoing, "Ray?"

"Graham. Dr. Graham."

He had to keep her talking. "You kept your maiden name when you got married, then."

"I took it back afterward. After they—after he died. I

97

didn't want any reminder of Ray.'' She looked at Nick again, but he had the feeling she didn't really see him. "I couldn't stand to be a Graham any longer, I shouldn't have tried to be a Graham in the first place. I wasn't what he expected, I couldn't be what he wanted. Renee warned me Ray wasn't easy to understand. Renee's his sister, his twin. She was shattered by what happened—by his death.''

"It was sudden and unexpected, I gather. An accident?''

Tears glittered in her eyes. "If you call suicide an accident.''

Nick cursed under his breath. The abscess went far deeper than he'd suspected. Reaching across the table, he grasped her hand. "I'm sorry.''

She blinked back the tears and tried to withdraw her hand. He held on. "Sorry for the hurt you had to endure,'' he said. "Sorry because my clumsy probing has hurt you all over again.''

Lynn's attempt to smile wrenched his heart. "I'll survive,'' she said. "And it's not your fault. You're probably right when you say I should talk about what happened. I never have. Not even this much.''

So there *was* more. It warmed him that she'd trusted him enough to tell him as much as she had. He wanted to take her in his arms, hold her gently and soothe her by murmuring that everything would be all right, wanted to assure her he'd never hurt her, that he'd protect her against all further harm.

His impulse shook him. He'd never in his life felt this way about a woman. Even the fact that he could was completely unsettling. The idea was ridiculous. No one could protect another against life's blows, no matter how hard they tried.

"Maybe the wine made me babble,'' she said. "My

head's spinning. If you don't mind, I'd rather not go to the theater."

The light-headedness may or may not be an excuse, but he preferred to think she'd wanted to tell him. As for the play—he couldn't care less about missing it. He had no intention, though, of driving back to El Doblez until things were straightened out between them. "A walk along the water will clear your head," he advised, reaching for the check.

The beach at La Jolla was all but deserted in the night chill. A half-moon rode the sky and the waves washed onto the sand in their eternal soothing rhythm as he walked barefoot with Lynn along the waterline.

"Mudway aushka," Lynn murmured, the first she'd spoken since they left the restaurant. "I don't remember much of 'Hiawatha,' but mudway aushka *is* what the waves say, if you listen. Are they really Chippewa words?"

"Aunt Grace never bothered to correct them, so Longfellow must have come close."

"Since he *did* teach at Harvard, he could hardly have been wrong all the time."

Is Harvard where Ray Graham went? he wanted to ask, but knew better than to remind her of the unpleasant past. Nick thought he'd long ago gotten rid of his resentment of those who could afford establishment schools like Harvard—he'd gone to Michigan State on a scholarship—but he realized with dismay some of the envy remained.

"My father was a Harvard man," she said after a moment. "I guess I'm reflecting his prejudice." She stopped walking and raised her head to look at the sky. "California nights are wonderful, California is wonderful, I don't ever want to go back."

To hell with Harvard. What did it have to do with him,

with here and now? The place was right, it might still be the wrong time but Lynn's face, faintly silvered by moonlight, was upturned to his. He caught her in his arms and kissed her.

Everything around him went out of focus. He no longer heard the waves, the dog barking somewhere close, the low voices of others on the beach. He was conscious only of the woman he held, the urgency of her response, and his own need for her.

Nick's arms, his lips, the long hard length of his body were part of the night's magic. Lynn clung to him, prolonging the embrace. She never wanted to think again, only to continue feeling as wonderfully alive as she did at this moment. Desire washed over her in a lazy wave, speeding her pulses, stealing her breath, creating a languorous heat deep within.

"Lynn?" Nick's warm breath caressed her ear. Yes, every part of her agreed. Yes, yes, yes. She wanted what he wanted, needed what he needed ... now. No matter what came later.

He held her away from him and she gave an involuntary moan of protest as she opened her eyes to look at him. The cool ocean breeze carried the faint sound of laughter, reminding her that they were on a public beach. She took a deep breath.

"Don't retreat," he said softly.

If only he knew how dangerous this felt to her—his touch, her own response. She wanted what she didn't dare risk, wanted him. She was afraid, not of her desire but of the consequences. After Ray, how could she ever trust another man?

"I can't help it," she blurted.

They both were quiet on the ride back to El Doblez.

"I'm not going to ask you in," she said when he parked in front of her apartment complex.

The questioning eyebrow rose—always his left, she'd noticed—but he didn't protest. Before she could escape from the car, he pulled her to him and kissed her, a soft, lingering kiss that teased and promised. She couldn't help winding her arms around his neck and returning the pressure of his lips.

"I'm still not inviting you in," she said breathlessly when he let her go.

"I've never cared much for chaperones, anyway."

Sheila . . . she'd forgotten all about her. "The day was wonderful," she told him. "I can't think when I've enjoyed myself as much."

"And the night?"

Lynn reached for the door, but he leaned over and put a preventive hand over hers. "Afraid to answer?" he asked.

She shook her head. "The night had its moments."

Despite her protest, he saw her to her apartment. She'd made up her mind not to let him kiss her again, but he didn't try. When he traced the curve of her mouth with his finger, her knees went weak. "Goodnight, Nick," she said hastily, fitting the key into the lock.

"May all your dreams be warm and cuddly," he replied as she opened her door.

Lynn was smiling as she walked into the apartment.

Sheila, sprawled on the couch watching TV, glanced at Lynn. "I can't believe it. You're home before midnight on a Saturday night when you don't have to work Sunday. Don't tell me you have a Cinderella complex. Or could it be the great lover is losing his touch?"

"I wouldn't know." Lynn's tone was curt, more because

she'd let herself be provoked into an answer than because of what Sheila had said.

"Now *that* I don't believe. Unless the man's been castrated." When Lynn didn't reply, Sheila said, "Guess who called me while you were out."

"I thought you were going to let the machine do the answering," Lynn said.

"I did, but when I heard his voice, I thought what the hell and picked up the phone." Sheila propped herself on an elbow. "He was crying, Lynn. He's really upset over me leaving."

"You're not thinking of going back to Justin!"

"I don't know, I really don't. I mean, he's sorry, he didn't mean to hurt me or the baby."

"Is he going for therapy?"

Sheila shook her head. "Nothing like that. But he's found another job. In Oceanside. And he begged me to come back. He says it will never happen again."

"Do you believe him?"

Sheila bit her lip. "Justin's like a little boy in some ways—he wants what he wants when he wants it. But he's not a bad guy, really he isn't."

Lynn raised her eyebrows.

"You just don't know him very well," Sheila protested.

And I don't want to, Lynn thought but didn't say it. She'd be glad to have her apartment to herself again, but she hated to see Sheila return to a precarious and possibly dangerous situation.

"He can be so sweet." Sheila smiled. "And he's a real sex fiend. God, I miss him."

"Don't do anything in a hurry."

"I won't. But—" Sheila eased down flat again, her smile dreamy.

If Sheila didn't insist Justin go for therapy first, she

could be setting herself up for a repeat of what had happened. Lynn doubted it would do any good to warn her, but she had to try. She opened her mouth to begin when Sheila sat up abruptly.

"Hey, I almost forget. You got a really strange message on the machine. Didn't make any sense to me. I would've figured it was some weirdo dialing at random, except he called you by name. Otherwise I would have wiped it off."

Lynn's eyes widened and her heart began to pound. "Did—did he say who he was?"

"No."

Lynn turned to look apprehensively at the answering machine. It couldn't be . . . not again.

"It wasn't a good connection," Sheila said, "he sounded like he was faraway, you know?"

Lynn forced herself to take a step toward the machine. Another and another. She pressed the button and held her breath, waiting.

"You know what the problem is?" Ray's voice came faintly to her, as from a distance. "You're the problem, Lynn." He laughed, his laugh trailing off into nothingness. The machine whirred on but there was no more.

Lynn stood frozen, unable to move.

"Aren't you going to shut it off?" Sheila's voice registered with Lynn, but not the sense of her words. "Lynn?"

The machine clicked off, Sheila's finger on the button. "You look like you've seen a ghost," she said. "Or maybe heard one, is that it?"

Lynn, still in shock, was unable to answer. It wasn't a misdialed number that first time, not a random one, either. It had been meant for her, as this one was. Reason told her it couldn't be Ray, but she shivered, the hair rising on her nape. It was unmistakably his voice, she'd know his voice anywhere. The words—had he ever said those words to her? Similar ones, certainly, but those exact words? She couldn't remember.

"Take it easy," Sheila said, urging her toward the couch.

So much for putting the past behind her. It had followed her, it was here in California, on her answering machine. Lynn sat down without resisting. " . . . The dead leaves fall," echoed in her mind, part of the poem she'd quoted earlier. Dead leaves fall. And the dead are buried. New leaves grow in the spring, but the dead never return.

Without comprehension, she watched Sheila fiddle with the answering machine. "Should've wiped the fucking thing off in the first place," Sheila muttered.

Too late, Lynn realized what Sheila was doing. Her "No!" came too late. Ray's message was gone forever.

At three in the morning, Lynn gave up on sleep. She wouldn't get any tonight. Rising, she walked quietly into the living room without turning on a light—no need to disturb Sheila. She prowled around the room, looking out the windows. All was quiet, the moon had disappeared. With a sigh she sat on the couch, lifting one of the throw pillows Sheila had piled underneath her head. The pillow might not be warm, but it was cuddly and she needed to hug something for comfort.

Something slid from the couch to thud on the rug. Lynn bent over and picked it up: a spiral notebook, by its feel. Sheila's.

Later, when she decided to return to bed with a book and try to put herself to sleep by reading, Lynn found she'd absentmindedly carried the notebook into her bedroom. It was Sheila's and none of her business. Too tired to return it to the couch, she set it on her nightstand.

The book, a shoot-'em-up spy story, failed to engross her, make her drowsy, or keep her mind from drifting back to the message on the machine. In exasperation, she thumped the fat paperback onto the nightstand, knocking the red notebook off. When it hit the floor, it flew open. As Lynn leaned over the edge of the bed to retrieve the notebook, words seemed to leap off its lined pages at her.

" . . . medication error, unreported." She frowned, involuntarily reading on. Holding the red notebook, she sat Indian-fashion on the bed, going through it with increasing disbelief.

A record of nursing and other medical errors on Maternity were listed by date and patient name in Sheila's handwriting. Some of the errors were trivial and others potentially dangerous. It dated back a month, so the list had been started when Lynn was in charge of the service. But the latest entries were current, and Lynn was no longer on Maternity, so it wasn't aimed just at her, but at Lois Johnson as well. Did Sheila hope to present sufficient evidence to Mrs. Morrin to get both Lynn and Lois Johnson in trouble?

But the first question Mrs. Morrin would ask was why Sheila hadn't reported each incident as it occurred. It was a question *she* certainly meant to ask her apartment-mate, and she meant to ask it now. She flung herself off the bed, marched into Sheila's room, threw open the door, and switched on the overhead light.

Sheila sat up, blinking. "You scared me half to death!" she accused. Then she saw the red spiral notebook in Lynn's hands. "Oh."

"What did you have in mind?" Lynn demanded. "Getting rid of both Lois Johnson and me in the hopes you'd become charge nurse on maternity?"

"No, no, nothing personal. It's because of the union

your dear friend Mr. Werth is so against us nurses joining. I'm going to use it as an example of how unionization will improve patient care."

Lynn stared at her. "And just how can joining a union prevent nursing errors?"

Sheila shrugged. "Maybe it won't, but it'll sure get the freeze off our salaries."

"The freeze is temporary, you know that. Until Harper Hills get integrated into the system."

"Ha. You may fall for Werth's crap, but there's plenty of us who know better. No union, no raises. You give me back that notebook, you had no right to snoop in my things."

"I wasn't snooping, not that it makes any difference. What I don't understand is how you could endanger patients by not reporting errors immediately. You certainly never told me about any of these, and I'll bet Lois Johnson doesn't know of the later ones, either." Lynn tossed the notebook at Sheila. "What kind of a nurse are you not to care about the welfare of your patients? Either you tell Lois Johnson about these last few, or I will."

Sheila glared at her. "I knew all along Werth had you hired as his stoolie. Well, you can tell your bastard of a lover that the nurses are damned well going to have a union at Harper Hills, and he hasn't a chance in hell of stopping us."

Chapter 7

Joyce Elkins studied Lynn. "What exactly do you mean by a diary of unreported medication and treatment errors?"

"A list with dates," Lynn said. "In a notebook."

Joyce glanced around her office as if for guidance. "Why would Sheila do that?"

"She thinks it'll push the nurses into unionizing. Or she'll threaten management. I'm not too sure of the way her mind works. I warned Sheila she'd be in trouble if she didn't alert Lois Johnson on Maternity to the recent errors, but I don't trust her to do it. I can't trust her at all anymore. How could she risk harming the patients by not reporting errors? We're lucky nothing awful happened because of her secrecy."

"Who else knows about this?"

"I came to you first."

Joyce gave her a brief smile. "So Mr. Werth isn't aware."

Lynn shook her head.

Joyce frowned in thought, rolling a pen in her fingers.

Finally she tossed the pen on her desk. "I think you ought to let him in on this."

Lynn stared at her.

"Don't worry," Joyce said, "I'll corner Sheila and do my damnedest to put an end to what she's doing. And I'll warn Lois about her. I'll also try to scare the shit out of Sheila by threatening to bring her conduct before the state professional ethics committee. Those lovely ladies—and the token gent—have the power to jerk your license so fast you don't realize it's gone until you look for it.

"The problem is we don't have the notebook. Without the damned notebook, I'd sure as hell hesitate to take this to Morrin. She's a stickler for documentation. *I* believe you because I know you and I know Sheila. But look at this as a stranger would—it's only your word against hers. My bet is that Sheila will deny up and down she ever wrote a single word in a notebook. Not l'il ole sweet her. And why is nasty mean troublemaker Lynn persecuting her?"

"But I saw—"

Joyce held up a hand. "The notebook exists, I have no doubt. Sheila can deny it as much as she wants and I'll never believe her. But my power is limited to threatening her—without witnesses, I might add, since I have to cover my own ass. The administrator of the hospital, on the other hand, has what amounts to unlimited power. And I'm sure Mr. Werth will take your word against Sheila's. That's why I advise you to tell him. I don't know what he'll do, but he'll sure do something."

Lynn, who'd taken her Monday morning break time to talk to Joyce, returned to Five East. Conrad had left a message for her to meet him tomorrow night at eight. At the library. She didn't know if she should tell him. Sheila might well lose her job if she did. Still, any nurse who

108

deliberately endangered a patient didn't deserve to be a nurse.

Mr. Franklin's call light was still on. It had been on when she left. Hadn't Rolfe answered the light in those fifteen minutes? Rather than go to the desk and ask Mr. Franklin what he wanted over the intercom, Lynn entered his room.

The minute he saw her, Mr. Franklin began shouting over the noise of his TV. "I want a bath and a shave. Here it is almost noon and he hasn't given me a bath yet. He's got it in for me on account've I told on him."

Lynn clicked off the call light. "I believe Mr. Watson discussed your care plan with you. Isn't that true, Mr. Franklin?"

"He marched in here and told me I gotta shape up—that's a care plan?"

"I can see there's some misunderstanding here. I'll speak to Mr. Watson."

"Tell him to hurry up with that pain shot while you're at it."

Rolfe's care plan, Lynn noted, called for a contract with Mr. Franklin wherein he agreed to assume gradually as many ADLs—activities of daily living—as possible. This week, according to Rolfe's plan, Mr. Franklin had agreed to try to shave himself with his electric razor.

"We went over the shaving bit and he agreed," Rolfe insisted when she asked him what was going on. "So after breakfast I set out his razor and the mirror. I told him I'd give him his bath when he finished shaving. He started in on needing his pain shot first, and I explained his doctor's pain orders all over again. So then he claimed he couldn't shave. I suggested he rest awhile and give it a try."

"His call light was on for about fifteen minutes."

Rolfe's eyes narrowed. "I was busy with one of my patients who's a hell of a lot sicker than Franklin. I knew what he wanted—the pain shot—and it isn't time yet. If we don't set up some rules for Franklin, he's going to keep bugging us all the time."

"Setting limits is fine, but you can't refuse to answer a call light to punish a patient."

"It wasn't punishment." Rolfe's tone was sullen.

"Maybe you should contact the doctor and discuss Mr. Franklin's pain problem with him," Lynn suggested.

"I thought that was your job."

His voice held a tinge of insolence. But she wouldn't react. She'd wait until they'd worked together longer before she made any value judgments about how he talked to her, she decided. For now she'd stick to Mr. Franklin and his problems.

"I believe the primary care nurse should call patients' doctors directly," Lynn said. "I do expect to be notified ahead of time, though."

"If that's the way you want it."

Lynn's control frayed. "My concern is for the patient," she said tartly. "You and Mr. Franklin obviously don't see eye to eye and the problem is yours to solve, with his help and his doctor's help. Mine, too, if you need it. Be firm, certainly, but be on his side, not against him. If you can't see the difference in improving his welfare and his attitude by working with him instead of getting into an adversary position, you don't belong in nursing."

Rolfe didn't reply and she walked back toward the desk, wondering if she'd said too much. Mr. Franklin *was* a nursing problem, every shift had their go-round with him. Whatever Rolfe tried wasn't going to work overnight. Maybe she expected too much from him too soon.

"Pardon, Ms. Holley?" Nai Pham stood in the doorway of Mrs. Phillips' room.

"What is it?" Lynn asked.

"The urine. Blood. You see?" Nai Pham gestured toward the patient's bathroom.

Lynn followed her into the bathroom where the Vietnamese nurse uncovered a bedpan. The urine was definitely a smoky red. "Save a sample for the lab," Lynn told her, making certain she was understood.

Back at the desk Lynn checked Mrs. Phillips' chart between phone interruptions. The patient, a white female, forty years old, wasn't on any medication that should change the color of her urine. She'd been admitted over the weekend because of severe abdominal pain—Dr. Brandon's patient, with Dr. Marlin scheduled to do a surgical consult. There was no mention in the history or the nurses notes of bloody urine.

Lynn was lifting the phone to call Dr. Brandon when she saw Nai Pham standing on the other side of the desk politely waiting to be noticed.

"Yes?" Lynn said.

"I ask her what be in family. Mrs. Phillips think, then she open eyes big and she say mother of her mother, she have same like this." Nai Pham held up a specimen bottle containing the red urine. "She forget until I ask. She scared, say her mother's mother be—she be—" Nai Pham searched for the word, finally touching her head. "Bad in head."

"Confused?"

"No, no."

"Psychotic?"

"Yes. Psychotic."

"Thank you, Nai Pham, you're very observant. I'll talk to Mrs. Phillips before I call her doctor."

Lynn found the patient huddled on the edge of the bed crying. Handing her the box of tissues, she put an arm around Mrs. Phillips' shoulders.

"You're worried about what's happening to you," she said. "Is it because your grandmother had red urine?"

Mrs. Phillips wiped her eyes and nodded.

"Would you tell me about her?" Lynn asked.

"She—my grandmother—lived with us because my mother and father both worked and she took care of me and my two brothers. Most of the time she was fine, she really spoiled us." Mrs. Phillips managed a watery smile. "Every once in a while, though, she'd act real strange for a few days, then she'd start talking to herself and she wouldn't fix meals or anything. My parents would lock her in her room so she couldn't wander off and my mother would feed her and all. The reason I know about her urine being red is that my mother had trouble washing it out of Grandma's clothes. After a month or so, maybe, Grandma would be all right again, just like she was before."

"She never saw a doctor?"

Mrs. Phillips shook her head. "My folks were old-fashioned about keeping things like that in the family. But the last time Grandma began acting odd, she—" tears filled Mrs. Phillips's eyes again—"she fell down and had a terrible fit right in the middle of the kitchen floor. No one was home but us kids. I was eleven, the oldest, and I didn't know what to do. By the time I ran across the street and got a neighbor to come back with me, Grandma's face was all purple. She—she died."

Lynn patted her shoulder. "I can understand how frightened you must have been. No wonder you blocked out the memory."

Mrs. Phillips clutched at her hand. "I remember

112

Grandma used to say her stomach hurt, too. Do you think I have what she had?''

"I'm going to call your doctor and tell him about your grandmother. He'll be ordering tests before he decides what this is all about." She squeezed Mrs. Phillips' hand. "Remember, whatever the doctor finds, you're under his care, you won't go untreated as your grandmother did."

Mrs. Phillips dried her eyes again. "That's true. I have complete faith in Dr. Brandon. He's such a good doctor and such a nice man. Don't you think so?''

Lynn smiled. "I'm sure he is." She'd only met Dr. Brandon once, too limited a contact to give her an opinion of his medical abilities. He'd seemed pleasant enough, even attractive, in a fortyish sort of way. She'd heard his wife had been killed in an accident.

At the desk, as she dialed Dr. Brandon's office number, Lynn wondered if the doctor would confirm her own tentative diagnosis. The red urine might not contain blood but porphyrins. Mrs. Phillips could have a rare metabolic anomaly, porphyria. King George III of England, the so-called mad king, had suffered from the disease. He'd been shut away in a tower during the psychotic episodes that can occur with porphyria ... not unlike Mrs. Phillip's grandmother being locked in her room.

The office receptionist transferred her call to the doctor and Lynn quickly ran through her observation of the urine and what Mrs. Phillips had said about her maternal grandmother. Unless she knew a doctor well or was asked, Lynn had learned very early in her nursing career not to venture an opinion about a patient's diagnosis. Doctors tended to be jealous of what they saw as their prerogative.

There was short silence when she finished, then Dr. Brandon said, "I'll lay odds you've already guessed what lab work I intend to order. Right?''

113

He'd asked. Okay, she'd tell him. "Urine, ALA, and PBG," she said. "Blood—"

His chuckle interrupted her. "I win my bet. Porphyria is a serious possibility. You're very acute to have put together the red urine and the grandmother's illness."

"I'm afraid I can't take the credit, doctor. One of my team members brought Mrs. Phillips' problem to my attention: When I was in school I did a term paper on metabolic anomalies, so I recognized the possible connection."

"I'm glad Five East has finally acquired a charge nurse with something in her head besides sawdust. What's your name? Holley? Thank you, Ms. Holley, and please tell Mrs. Phillips I'll be over to see her after lunch."

After Dr. Brandon visited his patient, Lynn introduced him to Nai Pham, who was so flustered by the doctor's praise she lost what fragile command of English she possessed.

"If you ever need a recommendation for your California license," he told Nai Pham, "all you have to do is ask me."

"I—I thanking you," the Vietnamese woman stammered.

Timothy Brandon, MD, *was* a nice guy, Lynn decided, watching him enter the elevator. And he cared about his patients. Mrs. Phillips was right ... he wasn't as spectacularly attractive as Nick Dow, but his prematurely gray hair contrasted agreeably with his deep tan and he had a pleasant smile. The circles under his blue eyes spoke of overwork—possibly an attempt to fill otherwise lonely hours.

She liked him. He was a doctor she could trust.

His only flaw so far was asking Dr. Marlin to do the surgical consult on Mrs. Phillips. Barry Marlin was one doctor Lynn didn't like *or* trust. Handsome, no argument there, Beth Yadon all but swooned every time he came on the unit. Dr. Marlin, well aware of Beth's palpitations, flirted with the pretty blonde nurse, rendering Beth useless when the surgeon was anywhere around.

Rolfe, who'd appointed himself Beth's protector, seemed amused by her crush on Dr. Marlin and Lynn suspected Rolfe covered Beth's lapses, giving meds to her patients and doing treatments for them. Lynn hadn't yet been able to prove it but when she did, the three of them would have a discussion about responsibility. If she couldn't trust Beth to do her own work, she didn't want her on Five East.

On Tuesday evening Lynn arrived at the library still not happy about meeting Conrad there. Even though the library was certainly an innocuous spot to rendezvous, this kind of meeting smacked of the furtive.

"We'll take a drive," he told her after casually drifting up to her as she stood glancing over the new books. "Meet me in the parking lot in five minutes—my car's way in the back. Blue Mercedes."

Liking it less and less, Lynn strode briskly across the paved lot, determined not to give in to the urge to glance around to see if anyone she knew was watching.

"I loathe being clandestine," she told Conrad as she slid into the plush blue front seat of the Mercedes.

He shrugged. "Name another way for us to meet without starting rumors."

About to say, "Your office," she stopped. No, she couldn't afford to be seen there without setting off more rumors at Harper Hills. She wasn't about to tell him she'd come home the night before to discover Sheila had moved out, bag and baggage. Her apartment was hardly the right place, either.

"We'd be better off talking in Pat's presence," she said. "Maybe in time she'll come around to accepting me."

"Not as long as she believes we're having an affair."

Lynn bit her lip, wishing he hadn't put his wife's suspicion into words.

"I'm sorry we're not," he added as he drove out of the parking lot.

She slanted a wary look at him. Deciding to keep it light, she said, "What, and ruin a beautiful friendship? Never!"

"It'd be worth the loss."

Allowing such talk to go on was dangerous. "Actually," she said, "I'm glad for the chance to talk with you because a problem's come up. It concerns Sheila Burns." She went on to tell him about the notebook.

"She intends to use this to promote unionization?" Anger simmered in his voice.

"One way or another."

"Out she goes! Just like her husband." He looked at Lynn. "You don't seem happy about getting rid of her."

"She could be a good nurse if it wasn't for her attitude. I wish there was a way to salvage Sheila, but I'll admit I don't see any."

"Might be a backlash," Conrad mused.

"What?"

"From firing her. She could use that damned notebook anyway. Why didn't you keep the evidence when you had your hands on it?"

"The notebook didn't belong to me." Lynn's words were stiff.

"A damn peculiar time for such nicey-nice courtesy."

Lynn didn't reply. Conrad was saying what Joyce had hinted—that she was a fool for giving the notebook back to Sheila.

"Well, it can't be helped," he said, "but much as I'd like to get rid of her once and for all, I'd better be careful not to compound the problem. The more I think about it, the more I'm convinced Harper Hills is stuck with Sheila. I can't leave her on Maternity, though."

Lynn shifted in her seat to face him, a prickle of apprehension raising her hackles. Conrad spoke before she could.

"Five East."

"No! How could you think of doing that to me?" she demanded.

"Face it, Lynn. You know her propensity for trouble better than anyone else and can keep an eye on her. Hell, you might even make her into the good nurse you claim she could be."

"Five East has enough problems. I don't need Sheila to contend with along with everything else."

"Morrin claims you can handle anything. Morrin and I may not always see eye-to-eye, but I trust her judgment implicitly. Besides, I know you."

Lynn glared at him. "I thought we were friends. Apparently I was wrong. Or do you shaft all your friends like this?"

He reached over and patted her jean-covered thigh, his hand lingering until she pulled away. "Take it easy," he urged. "It's the best solution for the moment. Harper Hills is stuck with Sheila, and you're the only one I can fully trust to keep an eye on her. I need your help in this."

Conrad had always been stubborn and Lynn realized nothing she could say was going to shift him one inch. Sheila would be sent to Five East. Just what the unit needed—more trouble. Lynn tamped down her anger and thought furiously.

"Okay," she said, finally, "if I have no choice, I have

117

no choice. But I want assurance I'll keep every one of the team members I have now and also that I can train one of the nurse assistants, Connie Machino, as my ward clerk."

"I'll speak to Morrin. You'll get what you want." He stopped the car.

Lynn saw they were parked at an overlook with the vast darkness of the ocean spread out below, rimmed by lights along the curve of the shoreline, a spot for lovers if she'd ever seen one. She stiffened.

"Lynn," he said, a hand on her shoulder. "I—"

She shrugged away from his touch. "Conrad," she warned. "I told you how I feel. We've been friends for years and I want it to stay that way."

"Come on, we both know the job wasn't the only reason you came here. Not the job or getting away from what happened back in Boston. Admit it. You're here because you want to be where I am."

She stared at him, unable to believe what he was saying.

"Maybe I'm wrong, maybe you haven't faced your real feelings," he said. "Your scruples about Pat—"

"Never mind my scruples about Pat," she said tartly. "If I had any subconscious reason to come here, it was because I thought you were my friend and I needed a friend. I don't need a lover. And if I did, it wouldn't be you."

He grasped her shoulder, turning her forcefully toward him. "I wish to hell I'd waited and married you." His voice was hoarse. "We both would have been a hell of a lot better off."

Lynn's body stiffened in rejection. "Don't talk to me about my marriage!" she cried. "Or about yours, either."

"I want you," he said. "I don't think you realize how good it would be for both of us."

"It'd be the mistake of the century," she said emphatically. "Under no circumstances would I *ever* have an affair with you. Is that clear?"

For a long moment he stared at her. She heard his ragged breathing and feared he was going to kiss her. She wrenched sideways, turning her face away from him. "Conrad, let me go!" she cried.

He released her and started the Mercedes. "One of these days," he muttered.

There'd never come a day when she'd accept Conrad as a lover. Why didn't he realize that? Didn't he understand the meaning of no? She'd be damned careful not to be alone with him again. If they ever had to meet, it would be in a public place with others around.

On the way back to the library she remembered she'd meant to tell Conrad, who'd known Ray, about the two strange phone calls. She shook her head. It was just as well she'd forgotten, because she never wanted to share anything personal with him again.

Sheila showed up for work on Five East on Thursday morning, blasting Lynn's hopes that she'd resign when she discovered she was being transferred off Maternity. Sheila's smug smile and the lazy droop of her eyes suggested she'd enjoyed her return to Justin—in bed, at least. But Sheila didn't reveal anything else by word or expression, and Lynn treated her as she would any new RN assigned to the unit. Since it was Beth's day off, Lynn assigned Sheila to Beth's section.

Rolfe, either having heard a rumor on the grapevine or more tuned into nuances than the average person, eyed both of them alternately, the trace of a smile on his lips.

Waiting to profit by whatever happens, Lynn thought

119

sourly, feeling surrounded by people who wished her ill, though she supposed she could count on neutrality from Nai Pham and Connie. The only good to emerge from Sheila coming to Five East was shifting Connie to ward clerk, but even that seemed an inadequate exchange.

Though nothing untoward happened, Lynn was frazzled by the end of the day. Changing into her jogging clothes, she left the apartment, heading for the beach. The last person she expected to see running along the sand late on a Thursday afternoon was Nick. The leap of her pulse when she recognized him told her how much she'd hoped she would.

"No office hours today?" she asked as she came up behind him.

He slowed, looking back smiling as she pulled even with him. "You could scare a guy to death sneaking up like that."

"If I look like I feel at the moment, I don't doubt it."

"In that case, I'd say you're feeling great. I was going to call and ask if you'd like to have dinner with me tonight. I'm tied up this weekend."

"Then I'll be waiting to hear from you." She grinned at him. "You didn't tell me why you aren't working."

"Been taking call for Lloyd Linnett, now he's back so I let him return the favor and took the afternoon off."

Lynn was surprised. Dr. Linnett's practice was strictly among the well-to-do. He refused to take welfare patients while Nick's practice was eclectic, come one, come all.

"Don't look so startled," Nick protested. "On the delivery table, I've discovered, a rich mother has the same anatomical layout as a poor one. The babies slide out in the same old way. Haven't you noticed?"

"Don't be vulgar."

He laughed. "The truth is, Dr. Linnett has decided he

120

needs a partner. To do his surgery, mostly, I think. I'm being auditioned."

It was Lynn's turn to laugh. Considering his enthusiasm when he'd talked to her about going in with Paul Salvador to treat the disadvantaged, she couldn't imagine Nick wanting to restrict himself to wealthy patients.

"You don't think I'm capable?" He sounded offended.

Taken aback, Lynn slowed and stopped. "I'm not surprised Dr. Linnett recognized what a fine surgeon you are," she said. "Everyone knows that. I was thinking about you and Paul Salvador. I know that's what you really want to do, not hold the hands of Dr. Linnett's patients."

He stared at her. "I said I was considering Paul's offer, I didn't tell you I'd made up my mind."

Lynn's face flushed. "I misunderstood you, then."

"Yes, you did." His voice was clipped.

To Lynn, his words implied he was sorry he'd ever mentioned anything personal to her because what he did with his life was none of her business. His words, on top of her day of tension and frustration, blew her control completely.

"If making money means more to you than helping those who need care, it's your privilege," she snapped. "Your business. If you hadn't raved to me about Dr. Salvador's plans for his clinic and how you really believed in his idea, I wouldn't have said a word. As it is, I can't help but think you're a shallow hypocrite." She turned on her heel to jog off in the opposite direction.

Nick grabbed her arm and whirled her around to face him again.

"Oh no you don't," he growled. "You're staying right here while I unload a few things that've been on my mind. You claim to care about the patients at the hospital, I've heard you go on about their welfare being more important

121

than anything else. Tell me this—are they more important than what Werth brought you here to do?"

Lynn tried to twist free and failed.

"I'm not through," Nick said. "Your private life is your own business but, shallow hypocrite though I am, I don't have much respect for a woman who encourages a man to cheat on his wife."

He released her so suddenly she staggered, almost falling. Regaining her balance, she began to run, tears blinding her so she couldn't see where she was going. But it didn't make any difference in which direction she went, as long as it was away from him.

Lynn had stopped crying by the time she reached her apartment. After a long shower, she pulled on one of the long T-shirts she wore to bed and padded barefoot into the kitchen. She should be relieved to have the decision taken from off her hands. This was the end between her and Nick, and a good thing it was. Another disaster avoided.

Certain he wouldn't be calling her for dinner, she fixed a salad and picked at it, her appetite gone. I won't let Nick upset me, she told herself firmly while she tried to swallow the salad. I know what he said about me isn't true, so why should I care what he thinks?

Though she'd never been more tired, she wasn't sleepy. She turned on the TV, hoping to find a program both interesting enough to distract her and unexciting enough to lull her into drowsiness. Around ten-thirty she thought she might possibly be reaching a point where she could try going to bed, so she switched off the set. Before she rose from the couch, the phone rang. Lynn hesitated, knowing the machine was off. What if she picked it up and Ray's voice spoke to her again? After the fifth ring, tense with apprehension, she reluctantly lifted the phone to her ear.

"This is Conrad."

Lynn sighed both in relief and in renewed anxiety. What now?

"I know Sheila's moved out," he said. "I have to see you. I'm coming over." His voice was slurred.

"No!" she cried. "Absolutely not."

"Either you let me in or you'll be sorry you didn't." He'd definitely been drinking, which was not like Conrad at all.

Drunk or sober, she wanted no part of him. "I'm not answering the door. Good-bye." She slammed down the phone and clicked on the answering machine.

Chapter 8

The doorbell rang. Lynn, propped on the couch, unable to sleep and trying to read, glared at the door. Conrad, she was certain. She swung her feet to the floor and waited. Maybe he'd go away.

The bell rang again. She tensed. Would he leave or stay and create a fuss, as he'd threatened? He was a man accustomed to having his way but usually in firm control of himself.

"I've never seen anyone so protective of his image," her father had remarked once.

But that was a Conrad who didn't overindulge in anything—certainly not alcohol. The Conrad on the phone tonight had been drunk.

"Lynn!" a man's voice called.

She frowned. It didn't sound like Conrad. Getting up, she walked to the door. "Who is it?" she demanded.

"Nick. Let me in."

Nick? What was he doing here? If she was smart, she'd tell him no, tell him to leave and not come back. Instead, she found herself opening the door.

"I came here instead of calling," he said once he was

125

inside and the door closed. "I wasn't sure you'd talk to me on the phone. I'll admit it's a tad late for dinner, but how about getting dressed and coming out with me for a midnight snack?"

Lynn stared at him. Did he seriously believe she'd forgive and forget his accusations?

"I overreacted," he went on. "I don't like anyone invading my private space. I forgot I'd invited you in. That gave you the right to say what you thought. I had no right to dump on you."

It was an apology of sorts, actually more of an admission he was in the wrong than she'd expected from Nick. But his earlier condemnation of her had cut too deep for her to smile graciously and accept his offer of a truce.

"It's late, Nick, and I have to work tomorrow," she began. "The way I feel, I think you'd better—"

In two strides, he closed the space between them. Before she could protest she was in his arms. *"This* is how *I* feel," he murmured before his mouth covered hers.

Nick's kiss triggered a rush of desire Lynn couldn't control. Her body tuned out all messages from her mind as she pressed closer to him, her lips parting at his urgent demand. His hands slid under her robe, touching, caressing. Her resistance waned from her wanting him so desperately. Nothing existed except Nick, nothing mattered but being in his arms.

What felt so right couldn't be wrong for her. He was here, they were together, united in their need for one another. That was enough.

Nick, swept along by his overwhelming desire for the maddening green-eyed woman in his arms, couldn't quite believe her ardent response. She kept her passionate nature so well hidden under that cool touch-me-not exterior that he was surprised anew each time he kissed her.

He hadn't been certain she'd open the door for him tonight, much less accept his apology. No way had he expected to be making love to her. God knows he wanted to. The thought of her long, lovely legs opening to him made him groan and cup her buttocks, rocking her against his need. She wore nothing under the long T-shirt and the feel of her softness excited him almost beyond endurance. If he didn't get her into the bedroom soon, he'd wind up taking her right here on the floor.

A bell pealed, loud and demanding. Again. The hell with it, all the bells in the world could ring their heads off as far as he was concerned, he had better things to do than answer them.

Lynn murmured something, pulling away from him. He resisted releasing her.

"They'll go away," he said hoarsely.

There was loud knocking, and someone banging a fist against the door. A man's voice shouted Lynn's name.

"It's Conrad," she said, wriggling free. "I told him he couldn't come here. He's drunk."

Her words were as effective as a bucket of cold water dashed over him. Lynn's eyes flicked to the door and back to him.

"I don't care what you believe," she said defiantly. "Or Pat, either. Conrad may want to be my lover, but he's not. He never has been, never will be."

"Damn it, Lynn, you let me in!" Conrad Werth shouted through the door.

Nick, hearing the slurred words, shook his head. Drunk as a skunk. Werth didn't seem the type. Had he been driven to it by Lynn?

"He threatened he'd make a scene if I didn't let him in," she said, folding her arms to make it obvious she had no intention of opening the door.

"He's pretty loud," Nick said. "Someone's sure to call the cops. I don't care about Werth but I'd hate to see Harper Hills splashed all over the papers. Getting rid of him will be a pleasure." He strode toward the door and flung it open.

Nick stopped short, shocked speechless by what he saw. Werth, apparently unaware of the danger lurking behind him, glared into Nick's face.

"You son-of-a-bitch," he muttered.

"Look out!" Nick cried and lunged at him, both of them slamming against the door frame and sprawling half-in, half-out of the open door.

A gun cracked. Lynn screamed.

Struggling free of Werth, Nick leaped to his feet and grabbed Pat Werth's wrist, twisting, so the gun aimed at Lynn clattered onto the threshold. He scooped it up, slid on the safety and jammed the pistol into his pocket.

"Are you hurt?" he asked Lynn.

She shook her head. He let out his breath, he'd been afraid the first shot hit her. He turned back to the Werths—Conrad climbing to his feet, Pat slumped against the side of the building. Doors opened around the complex, curious neighbors gawking.

"Take care of your wife," Nick ordered Werth. "Get her away from here as fast as you can."

Werth shuddered.

"Shape up, man!" Nick urged. "Get going. *Stat.*"

Werth grasped Pat's arm and, pulling her with him, stumbled away. As soon as they were gone, Nick stepped back into Lynn's apartment and closed the door.

"Okay, let's coordinate our stories," he said.

"Coordinate?" she echoed blankly.

He took her by the shoulders and shook her none to gently before he let her go. "You don't have time to go into shock. Someone's sure to have heard the shot and called the cops."

Lynn lifted a hand to her mouth. "Pat tried to kill me," she whispered. "She actually shot at me."

"Pat's a desperate woman. Jealousy does that to some people. She's probably been following her husband every time he left the house. I think she was aiming at him the first time. No question, though, that you were next. We can hardly tell the cops the truth."

"No." Her lips trembled as she spoke. Nick took her arm and steered her to the couch. Sitting beside her, he pulled her against him, stroking her back. "Take it easy. Pat's aim was bad. No one got hurt."

"If—if you hadn't been here—" A tremor shook her.

"But I *was* here. Now all we have to do is convince the cops neither of us recognized the man and woman who came to your door. Mistaken identity, that's our story. Unless somebody in this apartment complex works at Harper Hills, no one's likely to have recognized the Werths."

"I don't know many people here, there could be someone from Harper Hills."

"We'll take the chance. What other choice is there?"

Lynn bit her lip. "You're right. We can't let the truth get into the papers."

He wished he knew the real truth, he thought. What were Lynn and Werth to each other? He knew what she had told him and he'd like to believe it even though Pat clearly didn't.

He heard a siren approaching in the distance. Just as he'd figured, one of the onlookers had called the cops.

Lynn sat up, moving away from him. "While there's still time," she said, "we'd better rehearse what we're going to tell the police."

"And everyone else."

"I can hardly believe Pat really tried to kill me."

Nick rose. "I couldn't find a bullet hole anywhere, but here's the proof." He pulled the gun from his pocket. "I'll go stash this in the car until I can return it to Werth."

Lynn winced away from the pistol. "I could use a jolt of caffeine. I'll make coffee."

She was setting out the coffee mugs when the police knocked at the door. Whether or not the police believed the story, they didn't stay long.

"Time for me to go, too," Nick told Lynn, noting her wan face and the dark circles under her eyes. "Get some sleep."

She half-smiled. "Sleep? What's that?"

He wanted to comfort her, to take her in his arms and hold her for the rest of the night. But if he touched her he knew comforting would be the last thing on his mind and this wasn't the time to make love to her. They both needed time apart to recover from what had happened, from what could have been a god-awful tragedy. He grimaced as a possible headline flashed across his mind:

"Hospital Love Nest Shooting."

Lynn arrived on Five East on Friday morning aware that her equilibrium was as fragile as fine crystal—even a tiny jarring might shatter it into a million pieces. Intellectually she knew she was suffering from shock and from sleep deprivation, but that didn't help her jagged nerves.

Beth was still off so Sheila again took her patients.

"You look kind of frazzled," Sheila commented to Lynn after the change-of-shift report. "Hard night?"

Not trusting herself to say anything about the night, Lynn shook her head. "Are you having any problems so

130

far?" she asked, determined to keep away from the personal with Sheila.

"No problems. Justin's so glad to have me back he's being an angel."

Lynn had been speaking about the unit and she was sure Sheila knew it. Don't let her rile you, she warned herself.

"He took me to dinner last night and to a disco later." Sheila went on. "We had a ball. And guess who we saw dancing up a storm?"

Lynn shrugged.

"Lover Boy—" Sheila nodded toward Rolfe, who was walking down the hall away from them—"and this cute little blonde who looked about twelve. Very cosy, the two of them. He introduced her as Beth, so I assume she's my alter ego on the unit."

So Rolfe was dating Beth. Lynn didn't know why she was surprised. They were a perfect couple—he protected her and she provided the admiration and gratitude he needed. Except Rolfe, clever and manipulative, had been around a lot longer than Beth. He'd use her as long as it suited his purpose and then drop her. Poor little Beth wouldn't understand, she'd fall apart.

She'd find some way to warn Beth, Lynn thought. She probably wouldn't listen but Lynn had to try.

"I'm glad you and Justin are getting along," she told Sheila.

"But you don't think it'll last." Sheila eyed her defiantly.

"I hope it does." Lynn picked up a chart off the desk. "About the new orders on Mrs. Rollins—" she said, firmly switching the subject to where it belonged.

The morning passed without incident. At lunch, when Lynn sat down at a table with Lois Johnson and Clovis

Reilly from Maternity, she had the impression a silence fell, but conversation quickly resumed and she decided her fatigue might be making her a bit paranoid.

She returned to Five East a few minutes early and looked for Rolfe to tell him she was back so he could take his lunch break. She found him in the utility room, his back to her, chewing out Nai Pham.

"Don't give me any more of that 'Yes, Missel Wasson' crap." His mimic of her accent was cruelly sarcastic. "You don't understand what I tell you, you damn well say so. You hear, girl?"

Nai Pham ducked her head, whether from fright or in agreement, Lynn couldn't tell. Before she could open her mouth, Rolfe whirled around. His eyes widened briefly, then narrowed.

"She's a real problem," he said to Lynn, speaking as though Nai Pham weren't there. "She can't understand or speak English worth a damn—that wouldn't bug me so much if she didn't lie. We just lost another stool specimen on Mr. O'Hara because she lied to me."

"Please leave the room," Lynn said to Nai Pham, nodding her head toward the door. After Nai Pham exited, Lynn looked at Rolfe. "We'll discuss this after you get back from lunch."

He shrugged and left.

Lynn found herself trembling with fury. First he'd frightened the Vietnamese woman, then he'd humiliated Nai Pham by ignoring her presence. Nai Pham did present a problem, granted, but Rolfe's approach was no solution. In the first place, he should have brought his difficulties with her to Lynn as charge nurse. Rolfe seemed determined to go his own way, to handle everything as he saw fit and to hell with Lynn.

She'd been putting off discussing his attitude with him

because he'd never defied her openly. Considering how exhausted she was, today was the worst possible time to get into it. She wasn't sure she had enough control to rein in her anger at his subtle defiance, to keep her dislike of him from showing. Yet she hated to postpone their confrontation any longer.

Dr. Brandon was at the desk and smiled when he noticed Lynn. She felt her spirits lift. He had one of the most pleasant smiles she'd ever seen.

"Your diagnosis of Mrs. Phillips was accurate," he told her. "Acute intermittent hepatic porphyria. We'll hope her symptoms continue to remain mild. Any other insights about my patients?"

Lynn smiled at him. "I limit myself to one a month per doctor. You've had your quota for the time being, Dr. Brandon."

"I look forward to your next revelation."

Lynn's reply was lost as the intercom blared, "Dr. Brandon, call the operator. Dr. Timothy Brandon."

He picked up the phone and dialed. Lynn, watching him, saw the color drain from his face. "I'll be right there," he said, dropping the phone so it fell onto the counter rather than into its cradle. He ran toward the elevator.

Connie, stolid as always, hung up the phone without comment. The intercom message hadn't been an emergency code and Lynn briefly wondered what the operator had said to upset him so. But she had too many problems of her own to worry about his.

She still didn't know how she was going to handle the problem with Rolfe. The more she thought about it, the more she wondered if it wouldn't be better to wait until both Beth and Rolfe were on duty. Lynn had no real objection to one nurse helping another, but Beth and Rolfe

133

went too far. For one thing, this business of Rolfe covering for Beth so she could trail Dr. Marlin around the unit had to stop. Beth had to be made to realize she was responsible for her patients, not Rolfe.

Since this involved Beth as well as Rolfe, they both should be present when Lynn discussed the matter with them. She'd then ask Beth to leave and have the rest of it out with Rolfe in private. Lynn sighed. Okay, so she was putting it off, but she just didn't feel she could survive a session with Rolfe today.

Mr. Franklin's call light went on and she sighed. Connie looked at her. "I don't know if I'm up to Mr. Franklin at the moment," Lynn said.

"When he was my patient," Connie said, "what I used to do when I wasn't too busy was give him a back rub. He'd say he got this pain and what else could I do?"

"Did it help?"

"Sure. Everybody likes having their back rubbed."

I could use a back rub myself, Lynn thought as she left the nurses' station. Come to think of it, I haven't rubbed a patient's back in—how long? Years.

"I need my pain shot," Mr. Franklin said the moment she walked in the door.

"Mr. Watson hasn't forgotten you," Lynn told him. "He'll bring the shot as soon as it's due. In the meantime, why don't you turn over on your side?"

Mr. Franklin shot her a suspicious look. "Why should I?"

"Because I can't give you a back rub if you don't."

Either he was too surprised to refuse or he really did enjoy back rubs, because he obeyed her without another word. She dusted cornstarch onto her hands and began. Across the shoulders, down the sides of the back, across and up along the spine to the neck, then repeated the procedure, over and over. As Lynn slipped into the soothing rhythm of the strokes, she felt Mr. Franklin gradually relax.

She should have known earlier that Mr. Franklin liked his back rubbed, but she had never thought to ask Connie and he was too stubborn or too shy to say so. She was sure it hadn't crossed Rolfe's mind, either.

She decided, then, to hold brief, frequent patient conferences. Everyone on the unit would attend—even the patient's doctor, if possible. The conferences would result in better patient care and maybe even help weld all of them into a cohesive unit. She hoped she wasn't being too optimistic.

Lynn finished the back rub and retied Mr. Franklin's gown. When she reached the door, he muttered, "Thanks," in his usual gruff tone. She smiled. As far as she knew, Mr. Franklin never thanked anybody for anything.

Sheila was waiting for her at the desk. "Mrs. Lanigan insists on seeing you," she said.

"Do you know why?"

"She told me at great length. No one except 'that nice young man' knows how to take care of her ileostomy right. Or so she thinks." Sheila raised an eyebrow. "I take it that's Lover Boy, but I was under the impression Mrs. Lanigan was Beth's patient."

"I'll speak to Mrs. Lanigan." Lynn tried to control her fury as she walked down the hall. Damn it, Rolfe was supposed to be teaching Beth how to care for that ileostomy, not take over completely. This had to stop. Now.

It took time for Lynn to convince Mrs. Lanigan tactfully that Sheila was capable of changing her ileostomy bag. By the time she left the room, she felt that she might be only moments away from shattering into a million pieces.

135

"Mrs. Lanigan will cooperate," Lynn told Sheila, who was waiting in the hall.

"I heard a weird rumor at lunch," Sheila said. "The talk is you had a couple of visitors last night. One with a gun."

Lynn took a deep breath and let it out slowly. "Oh, really?"

"Names are being tossed around. Like a certain man we all know. And his jealous wife."

"Some people will say anything."

Lynn brushed past Sheila and strode toward the desk, devoutly wishing the shift was over. So much for keeping things quiet. Last night's trouble wasn't in the papers, but the hospital grapevine tendrils obviously extended to her apartment complex.

Somehow the shift ended without an explosion.

Lynn fell into bed the minute she got home and slept until the next morning. Saturday. She had two days off, thank heaven. She jogged on the beach before breakfast, but Nick wasn't there. Though she tried to tell herself it was just as well, she was disappointed. He'd said he was tied up all weekend, so he probably wouldn't call. If he ever intended to call her again after Thursday night's mess.

And a mess it had been. She didn't know when or if she'd ever be able to speak to Conrad again—she'd lost a friend as surely as if Conrad had died. And Nick. Was he a friend? Yes, with the potential to be a great deal more, if she dared. If he still wanted her.

Lynn washed her hair and did all the have-to-be-done-sooner-or-later chores she'd been putting off. She called Joyce twice, thinking they might go to dinner together, but got the answering machine each time. Finally she settled for a takeout pizza.

136

She spent most of Sunday walking on the beach and around the town, getting better acquainted with El Doblez. As she climbed into bed Sunday night, she told herself she hadn't expected Nick to call her, but she knew she lied.

By Monday morning she was more than ready to go back to work and was determined to confront Rolfe.

"Have you heard?" Beth asked Lynn the moment she stepped out of the elevator.

"Heard what?" Lynn asked.

"About Dr. Brandon's little girl, Carol."

Lynn remembering the phone call on Friday, tensed. "Has something happened to her?"

"Her school nurse brought her to the ER with massive bruising. You know what *that* means."

Lynn stared at Beth. "Did she fall at school?"

Beth shook her head. "Child abuse."

"I don't believe it!" Lynn said sharply.

"Rolfe says everyone knows Dr. Brandon's been on something ever since his wife died six months ago. Drugs, Rolfe thinks, because no one's ever smelled liquor. Now Dr. Brandon's abusing that poor little girl."

"And just how does Rolfe know all this?" Lynn heard the anger in her voice but didn't care.

"Hey, everybody's talking about Brandon." Rolfe had come up behind Lynn without her seeing him. "It's all over Harper Hills what he's been doing."

Lynn swung around and glared at him. "You don't *know* that it's so, you're just repeating gossip."

His eyes narrowed. "Hey, don't blame me. I don't beat up little kids."

Lynn controlled herself. Snapping at Rolfe wouldn't help Dr. Brandon. Nor would it help the already rotten relationship between her and Rolfe.

Rolfe's half-smile implied he knew all about her, too. Lynn was sure he'd heard the stories about the Thursday night fiasco. As he'd said about Dr. Brandon—"Everyone's talking." There was nothing she could do to stop the rumors about her. Unfortunately, they were based on the truth. The gossip about Dr. Brandon was different. At least she could try to shut Rolfe and Beth up when they had their conference with her later today.

She straightened. "Before you leave Five East after work, I'd like to see you both."

Rolfe and Beth exchanged a glance, leaving Lynn to wonder what they thought of her. Not that it made any difference . . . she was in charge on Five East and she was determined to run it properly.

Rolfe's condemnation of Dr. Brandon on no evidence but word of mouth unsettled Lynn, bothering her so much that when the doctor arrived on the unit near noon, Lynn decided she had to speak to him. Steeling herself, she took him aside into the seldom-used treatment room.

"Dr. Brandon, this is none of my business, but I feel I have to say something," she began.

He looked at her in bewilderment, his blue eyes bloodshot, his face sagging with exhaustion, and she realized he was all but out on his feet. She'd picked a terrible time to bring this up.

She forced herself on. "Harper Hills has the usual hospital grapevine—rumors, true and false, zip like laser beams from floor to floor. I think you ought to know what's being said about you."

Oh, God, how could she put this tactfully? What were the right words?

"They say you're on drugs," she finally said, hating her bluntness but unable to find any other way to put it. "And that you're abusing your daughter."

His mouth dropped open. He closed it abruptly, his eyes darkening. "You believe this? You believe I—?" He turned away from her, fumbling for the door.

"Wait," she pleaded. "I don't—"

He opened the door, pushed through and was gone. Lynn hurried after him, just in time to see the elevator door closing behind him.

Damn! She'd handled it all wrong. She'd have been better off saying nothing, minding her own business. She liked Dr. Brandon and now he'd never trust her again. Feeling too upset to face anyone, she went into the nurses' lounge for a few mintues.

"Mrs. Morrin left a message," Connie said when Lynn came back to the desk. "She wants to see you in her office right away."

Now what? Lynn wondered. Was it going to be one of those whatever-can-go-wrong-will days?

"Sit down, Ms. Holley," the DNS ordered. She folded her hands, placing them on the desk. Her pale blue eyes were chilly behind the oversized glasses.

Lynn perched on the edge of the straight chair by the desk.

"A very serious situation has been called to my attention," Mrs. Morrin told her.

"By whom?" Lynn asked. Mrs. Morrin's frown told Lynn she was expected to keep her mouth shut.

"Dr. Brandon has informed me you accused him of taking drugs and of abusing his daughter."

"No!"

"I haven't finished." Mrs. Morrin snapped. "I do not understand what reason you could possibly have for insulting one of our staff physicians."

"I didn't mean to insult him," Lynn said. "What I—"

"Do you deny you spoke to him? He says you took him into the treatment room on Five East."

"We were in the room. For privacy. Because I thought he should know—"

The red phone rang. Mrs. Morrin held up one hand to halt Lynn and answered the phone with the other.

"Salmonella?" Mrs. Morrin said into the phone. "We may have to quarantine the unit, I'll consult with the health department immediately. In the meantime—" She paused, remembering Lynn. Placing her hand over the mouthpiece, she said to Lynn, "We'll discuss this further. I want you back here in an hour."

Dismissed, Lynn eased from the office. Mrs. Morrin hadn't listened to her. She had her mind made up ahead of time that Lynn was in the wrong.

Lynn didn't blame Dr. Brandon. He was fatigued, no doubt worried about his daughter, and she'd shocked him with what she'd said. But why would either the doctor or Mrs. Morrin believe she was the kind of person who'd make such accusations? To her dismay, uncontrollable tears filled Lynn's eyes. Not wanting to be seen crying, she ducked into the medical records anteroom, the place where the doctors recorded notes for patients' charts. Most doctors were in their offices at this hour, so she hoped to find the room empty.

It was. She slumped into a chair, covered her face with her hands, and sobbed.

Chapter 9

Lynn couldn't stop crying. Her body shuddered with sobs as she mopped her wet cheeks with a damp and wadded tissue. It wasn't only because of Mrs. Morrin she wept, but because of Conrad's betrayal, Pat's trying to shoot her, Nick's not calling her, and beneath everything else, the past she hadn't quite left behind.

A hand touched her shoulder and she jumped, her tears stopping in shock.

"I'm sorry I startled you," Dr. Linnett said. "Ms. Holley, isn't it?" He picked up a chair, positioned it in front of her, sat down, reached into his pocket, and proffered a clean handkerchief. "Anything else I can do to help?"

She wiped her face and her eyes. "No one listens to what I tell them," she blurted.

"I understand the feeling." His blue eyes were sympathetic. With his graying brown hair and small mustache, he reminded her a little of her father. He was probably in his early sixties, about the age her father had been when he died.

Dr. Linnett leaned back in the chair. "*I'll* listen," he promised.

How she longed to talk to someone neutral, someone who wouldn't prejudge her. Without giving herself time to think, Lynn took a deep breath and plunged in.

"It started with the rumors about Dr. Brandon," she began, going on to tell him the story of how one misunderstanding had led to another. "I really don't believe Dr. Brandon would harm anyone," she finished.

Dr. Linnett nodded thoughtfully but said nothing for so long that Lynn grew tense. "Here's what we'll do," he said finally. "You stay right where you are. I'll round up Tim Brandon and bring him in here and we'll straighten this out among the three of us."

"Mrs. Morrin—" she began.

He waved a hand. "Mrs. Morrin can wait until we've talked."

After he went out, Lynn folded the handkerchief he'd lent her and tucked it into a pocket. She rose and smoothed her uniform skirt, also making certain her cap hadn't been knocked askew. She was about to sit down again when the door opened. She turned, surprised at how quickly Dr. Linnett had returned.

Nick stood in the doorway. "Lloyd—Dr. Linnett—said you needed me," he told her, coming inside the room and putting an arm around her shoulders. "What's the matter, Lynn?"

She leaned against Nick, so glad to see him she didn't care why he was here. "I'm in trouble," she said.

Quickly, she explained.

"Little Ms. Fix-It errs again," Nick observed.

His sardonic comment irritated her but also wiped away her self-pity. She had warned herself to leave well enough alone. Pulling away from Nick, she sat down.

"I won't make the same mistake twice."

He grinned. "This from the gal who accosted me a

142

month or so ago in the lobby and accused me of terrorizing little old ladies? You were born with the urge to set things straight and it'll get you into trouble all your life. So what's wrong with that? It keeps life interesting."

She smiled uncertainly. "I could use a little dullness."

He shook his head. "Impossible for anyone with red hair, green eyes, great legs, and an insistent instinct for order. Living is chaos, but you refuse to acknowledge that. You'll fight to make sense of things until the day you die."

She was never quite sure when Nick's cynicism shifted to seriousness, or if it did. Every time she thought she was beginning to understand him, he confused her.

Dr. Linnett's return with Dr. Brandon shifted her attention back to the problem at hand.

"I've explained to Tim that he misunderstood what you said to him," Dr. Linnett told Lynn. "I'd like you to explain to him, as you did to me, exactly what happened." He smiled encouragingly. "Tim will listen, we'll all listen. You can count on it."

She started with the rumors, as reported by Rolfe, and when she finished, Dr. Brandon shook his head. "I guess I heard what I'd been afraid of hearing, that's why I didn't take in what you were really telling me." He looked earnestly at her. "I'm off drugs now, thanks to Phil Vance and his unorthodox psychotherapy. But after my wife died, I got hooked for a while, no doubt about it. I'm sure some of the hospital personnel must have noticed. So that rumor had a basis in fact. What hurts is how anyone could believe I'd harm my daughter."

"I didn't believe it," Lynn said softly.

"Tim's little girl has a hereditary hemmorrhagic disorder," Dr. Linnet put in. "Fortunately mild. An insignificant injury, at times causes superficial hemorrhaging into

143

her skin. The widespread bruising often looks worse than it is. Carol fell going up the stairs at school. No one noticed, the bump to her shins wasn't hard enough to break the skin or even make her cry, but she soon developed so much local hemorrhage her teacher sent her to the school nurse. The nurse took one look and got frightened. Carol's had this happen before, so she wasn't too upset and she tried to talk the nurse into just calling Dr. Brandon, but the alarmed nurse rushed her to the ER.''

"Is Carol all right?" Lynn looked at Dr. Brandon.

His smile transformed his tired face. "Carol's doing fine since we gave her the prothrombin complex concentrate. I'm taking her home tonight."

"I'm sorry I added to your worries by upsetting you," Lynn said.

"I'm the one who should apologize. I wasn't thinking straight or I'd have realized you aren't that kind of person. I'll stop by Mrs. Morrin's office and tell her it was a mistake on my part." Dr. Brandon rose and extended his hand to Lynn, who stood up and clasped it. The other two men rose.

"Carol sounds like a brave little girl," she said. "I'd like to meet her sometime."

"I'll see that you do." Dr. Brandon pressed her hand and released it. Glancing at Dr. Linnett, he said, "Thanks, Lloyd." He nodded at Nick and went out.

"Tim's going to keel over if he doesn't get to bed soon," Dr. Linnett observed. "No wonder he misunderstood—he's so tired I don't see how he can function."

"Reserve energy," Nick said. "As interns we all learn how to tap the tank."

"Wait'll you turn forty," Dr. Linnett cautioned. "That reserve tank holds damn little by then. At sixty—forget it."

Nick raised his eyebrows.

Lynn turned to Dr. Linnett. "I can't thank you enough for helping me. How can I ever repay you?"

"Easily." He nodded toward Nick. "All you have to do is convince him to come in with me." He smiled at them both and went out.

Lynn stared at Nick. "What brought that on?"

"I told him you didn't approve of his partnership offer, that you thought I should be more idealistic."

Her hand flew to her mouth. "No! Why would you do that?"

"Isn't it the truth?"

"Well, yes but I—but you—I mean, why did you bring me into it?"

"Beats me."

She glared at him. Nick could be so infuriating.

He leaned over and, without otherwise touching her, kissed her, a quick and fleeting brush of his lips she felt down to the tips of her toes.

"That has to last for ten days," he said. "I'm flying to Mexico with Paul—he has a twin-engine Piper Navajo. We planned the trip some time ago, it's part of a fly-in clinic that brings modern medicine to the remote areas of Baja. We have about twenty doctors and dentists who take turns treating isolated communities."

"For free?"

"What else? The people we see don't have one peso to rub against another."

Lynn sighed. "I'm sorry I called you a shallow hypocrite. I speak before I think sometimes. I knew you'd never turn your back on people who needed help."

Resentment flared in his dark eyes. "Don't start planning my life. I'm still seriously considering Lloyd's offer."

145

She stiffened. They stood eyeing one another warily until he shook his head.

"Have to wait a couple of weeks to take this up where we left off," he muttered. *"Adios."*

Lynn watched him leave. Their relationship never seemed to run smoothly. If she was smart she'd take it as a warning not to go on with Nick.

As she left the anteroom she glanced at her watch. The hour Mrs. Morrin stipulated wasn't quite up yet, so she hurried toward the elevator, worrying about what might have happened on Five East while she was gone.

Rolfe wasn't on the unit.

"Mrs. Morrin called him to her office," Connie told her. "That's where I thought you were."

"I have to go back in a few minutes. I thought I'd check with you first. Any problems?"

"Two calls for you to return, that's all."

Lynn took care of the calls before going back down to the DNS's office. On the way, she speculated on why Mrs. Morrin wanted to see Rolfe. Had Dr. Brandon mentioned his name? Lynn hoped so. She wanted to see something, somebody wipe that insolent smile of Rolfe's face. If anyone could, it was the DNS.

The secretary motioned for Lynn to go in. Rolfe was seated in the chair by the desk and Lynn, at Mrs. Morrin's nod, took another, farther back.

"I have told Mr. Watson about Dr. Brandon's daughter," Mrs. Morrin said. "I assume you're aware of the girl's diagnosis."

"Yes," Lynn said.

"Then I shan't have to repeat myself. In the future I trust neither of you will repeat whatever harmful gossip you may hear."

Since there was no point in arguing that she never re-

146

peated gossip, Lynn simply agreed. Rolfe also agreed. Mrs. Morrin dismissed them without another word. There was little choice but to walk with Rolfe to the elevator and she braced herself but he neither looked at her nor spoke to her. His uncharacteristic silence made her sure Mrs. Morrin had done more than merely tell him about Carol's diagnosis. Well, it served him right if he got blasted.

Lynn gave up the planned conference with Rolfe and Beth, rescheduling it for Thursday because Rolfe was off for the next two days. The remainder of the shift passed without incident. Once she got home, Lynn pulled on her sweats and jogged. When she got back, she tried to call Joyce but there was no answer. She'd have to eat alone.

The next two days were fairly quiet for Five East, possibly because Rolfe had them off. On Tuesday Sheila, assigned to Rolfe's section, refused to help Beth with Mrs. Lanigan's ileostomy, forcing Beth to go to Lynn for help. Lynn talked Beth through a successful cleanup and change of the bag despite Beth's and Mrs. Lanigan's obvious misgivings.

Lynn reassured the patient by pointing out that the more nurses who could do the procedure the better, because Mrs. Lanigan could count on one of them always being there.

She took Beth aside, "You need to develop more confidence," she told her. "You did very well with the ileostomy."

"It wasn't as hard as I thought," Beth admitted.

"The more you do, the more confidence you'll acquire. You depend on Rolfe too much."

"I suppose. But he knows everything and he's so good at treatments. Better than I'll ever be."

147

"How do you know if you don't try to do them?"

Beth lowered her eyes. "I never was good with my hands. He is, though." A secret smile wafted over her face, suggesting that what Rolfe did with his hands in private was very good indeed, giving Lynn an unwanted glimpse into their relationship. This might be the chance, though, for her to warn Beth.

"Rolfe's quite a few years older than you."

"Only ten. That's about right, don't you think?"

"That depends."

"I think he's just wonderful." Again the smile. "And so handsome."

"You seem to find Dr. Marlin good-looking, too," Lynn observed dryly.

"Oh, wow, he's a dream ... only he's married. I mean, that eliminates him, doesn't it?"

"For anyone with any sense, yes. Back to Rolfe. You do realize he's been around a lot longer than you."

"I know. Isn't that great? He's teaching me so much."

Lynn gave up. Beth was too naive for hints to get through to her and, after all, it *was* Beth's affair, not Lynn's. She'd gotten in enough trouble from not minding her own business. Perhaps she was wrong and the Rolfe-Beth coupling would turn out fine, if only Rolfe could be trusted. She couldn't shake the uneasy feeling that Beth was riding for a terrible fall.

On Wednesday, to Lynn's surprise, Dr. Brandon came by her table in the cafeteria. Joyce had just left, so Lynn was alone. "You don't mind if I join you?" he asked.

"Please do, Dr. Brandon."

"Tim," he said, setting down his tray. She noticed that his eyes were clear, the dark circles under them gone.

"How long have you been working at Harper Hills, Lynn?" he asked when he'd settled at the table.

"Two months."

"Do I detect a touch of New England in your voice?"

"I grew up on Cape Cod."

"You're a long way from home."

His words echoed in her mind. *Home.* Lynn forced a smile. "California is my new home."

"Good." His smile was genuine. "I'm glad our misunderstanding was cleared up. My fault entirely, fatigue makes me paranoid, I'm afraid." He set down his coffee cup. "I'd like to ask you something."

Lynn looked at him expectantly.

"You can assure Nick I'm not interfering."

Her eyes widened. "Interfering?"

He shifted in the chair, obviously uncomfortable. "What I mean is, I'm not asking you for a date," he said finally. "But I'd like to invite you to come for a boat ride with my daughter and me sometime this weekend. Carol wants to be a nurse, or maybe a doctor, she hasn't quite made up her mind. I told her how you helped me with one of my patients and she wants to meet you. I wondered if you might be free Saturday afternoon?"

Lynn recovered from her surprise enough to say, "As it happens, I am. I'd love to meet Carol. The boat ride sounds like fun. What kind of boat do you have?"

"A forty-foot inboard. We'll tool around the bay for an hour or so, then have something to eat at one of the restaurants near the marina. Carol loves abalone."

"She and I have something in common—so do I." How fond he was of his daughter, Lynn thought, remembering how much closer she and her father had grown after her mother's death.

"That's great. What time would you like me to pick you up?"

"Why don't I meet you at the marina?" Lynn said. "Is two o'clock about right?"

"Couldn't be better. I can't wait to tell Carol. I'm warning you, she'll ask a million questions. You never saw such an inquisitive kid. Bright, too." Pride threaded through his words. "She knows as much about her blood disorder as I do. If the school nurse had listened to Carol...."

"Dr. Linnett said her case was mild."

"Thank God." He finished drinking his coffee. "I'm looking forward to Saturday."

"So am I."

Lynn left the cafeteria smiling. Her feelings for Dr. Brandon—Tim—were uncomplicated. She liked and respected him. The Saturday boat ride would be free of the treacherous undercurrents that always threatened to sweep her away when she and Nick were together. Even thinking of Nick made her apprehensive and, she had to admit, excited.

How careful Tim had been to make it clear he was inviting her for Carol, not for himself. No doubt everyone at Harper Hills knew she and Nick were—well, what were they? Not lovers, whatever the grapevine might imply. Not yet lovers. They would be, though, if she kept seeing him and unless her common sense took over.

Thursday Rolfe and Beth were on duty and Sheila was off. Lynn, aware she'd put off the discussion far too long, asked Rolfe and Beth into the treatment room before the change-of-shift report.

"I'll keep this brief," she said. "Rolfe, you've been doing too much of Beth's work for her. Beth, you've been allowing Rolfe to assume responsibilities for your patients, responsibilities that are yours. As your supervisor, I can't condone this. Beth, I expect you to take care of the patients assigned to you without Rolfe's assistance. And Rolfe, I realize you're competent and able to handle the extra work, but I want you to consider how you're undermining Beth's self-confidence when you do her work for her."

Lynn looked from one to the other. "Have I made myself clear?"

Beth gave her a subdued "Yes."

After dismissing Beth, Lynn then outlined for Rolfe that he was to be more understanding of Nai Pham's language problem and more sensitive to her feelings.

Rolfe nodded with no trace of an insolent smile or even a lifted eyebrow. Was it because of what Mrs. Morrin said to him last Friday? Whatever that had been.

Both Rolfe and Beth had taken what she had to say well, better than Lynn had expected, but whether they did as she'd asked remained to be seen. Beth's hardest challenge would come when Dr. Marlin made rounds—he had three patients on Five East. And Rolfe's test would come in working with Nai Pham.

At ten a new patient was admitted to one of their two private rooms. Thinking there was no time like the present to see how Rolfe had taken her admonitions, Lynn assigned the patient to Nai Pham, with Rolfe to take care of any medications or treatments. Lynn, who always made the final check of each new patient, reviewed the chart before she went to lunch.

Mr. Pietro, 50, pale and wheezing, with a history of hemoptysis, coughing up blood, had a tentative diagnosis of atypical pneumonia. His temperature on admission had been 99 degrees orally, his pulse 90, his respirations 26.

151

Blood pressure 150/90. He was receiving oxygen by nasal catheter. A series of lab tests had been ordered, blood cultures among them. His chest X ray showed infiltration in the apex of the right lung.

Lynn decided she'd better take a look at Mr. Pietro on her way to lunch. Outside his door, Nai Pham, her back to the corridor wall, her hands clutched together, stared up at Rolfe, who loomed over her.

"What's the problem?" Lynn asked crisply, thinking Rolfe hadn't listened to her at all.

"She claims the new patient has crabs." Rolfe nodded toward Mr. Pietro's closed door. "She's crazy—I examined the pubic area and he's clean. No lice."

"Crabs," Nai Pham squeaked nervously. "Come from crabs."

"What comes from crabs?" Lynn asked.

"In my country. We eat crabs. Crabs got Paragonimus, we can get." Nai Pham clenched her fist and beat on her chest. "In here. Cough, blood come. Like Mr. Pietro."

What, Lynn wondered, was Paragonimus? "Mr. Pietro lives in California," she pointed out.

"I ask. He take trip. To China. Same like there."

"What's Paragonimus?" she asked Nai Pham.

"Same like worm."

"Fluke," Rolfe said suddenly. "She means flukes—you know, they cause schistosomiasis when they get swallowed. Dysentery and that bit. Does she mean a fluke gets into the lungs?" He stared at Nai Pham. "You know what you're talking about, girl?"

Nai Pham braced herself against the wall. "Paragonimus go in here." Again she touched her chest.

"You may be right," Lynn said to her.

Rolfe scowled at both of them, obviously pained to hear Nai Pham might be right about anything. "Hell, they got a lot of weird diseases where she comes from," he muttered.

"I'll call Mr. Pietro's doctor and run it past him," Lynn said. "In the meantime, we'd better take precautions with Mr. Pietro's sputum and stool and red-bag his dirty linen."

Before she notified the doctor, Lynn looked up Paragonimus in the medical dictionary and found it was an Oriental lung fluke transmitted to humans by eating infected crayfish or crabs. Just in case Dr. Haskins wasn't up on his flukes any more than she'd been, Lynn managed to transmit her newly acquired information along with what Nai Pham had told her.

"She's a nurse from Vietnam, doctor," Lynn finished by saying, "and apparently this disease is common there."

"Well, if the guy's been to China recently, we can't take any chances," Dr. Haskins said.

Lynn took down his orders for stool and blood work and room isolation of Mr. Pietro. Luckily the patient was already in a private room. Even if he did carry this lung fluke, he wouldn't be highly contagious, since only his sputum or stool would carry the eggs.

Thursday afternoon was uneventful. Even Mr. Franklin's light went on only twice, a record. Beth cast longing glances toward Dr. Marlin when he appeared to see his patients, but didn't leave her work to trail after him. But Dr. Marlin seemed preoccupied and apparently didn't notice the difference.

Rolfe seemed preoccupied, too. He was so curt with Beth that she pouted for the last hour they were on duty. Lynn wondered what he was thinking. She knew he'd been galled by the possibility Nai Pham might be right about Mr. Pietro.

Just before the change of shift he came up to her. "Thought you'd be glad to hear I'm going to ask Mrs.

Morrin for a transfer to another unit," Rolfe said, striding away before she had a chance to say a word. Since he managed to go off duty without her seeing him leave, she wasn't able to talk to him.

Not that it mattered, she told herself on the way home. He couldn't have been more right about her being glad he wanted to leave Five East. He was hell-bent on ignoring her requests. She only hoped Mrs. Morrin agreed to transfer him somewhere else. Maybe he'd quit if the DNS refused. That'd be okay, too. She wouldn't miss Rolfe Watson at all. The sooner he left, the better.

That night Lynn couldn't sleep. She tossed and turned for two hours before getting up and turning on the TV. None of the talk shows held her interest. The old movie she finally chose, "Dial M For Murder," soon reminded her of her own horrible phone calls and her heart began to pound. She clicked off the set.

Calm down, she admonished herself. You haven't had any more calls. Whoever was trying to upset you, to frighten you, has given it up.

She had no doubt the voice she'd heard was Ray's. But he was dead, she reminded herself. The voice had to be a recording—even if the words he spoke on the phone were things he had said to her in Boston before he died.

She didn't understand how anyone could have recorded those words, but someone must have. Ray couldn't come back from the dead, it wasn't him talking on the phone, it had to be a tape of his voice. Tape or not, hearing his voice terrified her

Shape up, Holley, she admonished herself. *Ray is dead.*

Lynn stood up abruptly and went into the kitchen for a glass of milk. If she didn't stop going back over the past, she'd never get to sleep.

The problem was the present was equally tension-producing. Only last week Pat Werth had tried to kill her. Lynn shivered as she sipped the milk. She'd searched for a bullet hole in the outside wall and in her apartment but hadn't been any more successful than Nick in finding one. Where had the bullet gone? And what was Pat up to now?

Certainly not standing outside her door with a gun. Conrad would see to that. He had to protect the old image. Letting his wife shoot the woman she suspected of being his lover wasn't acceptable.

She had to stop mulling over the Werths, to stop thinking negatively.

Maybe when she got to work tomorrow, Rolfe would be permanently gone from Five East. Now *that* was positive.

Lynn frowned. He'd be leaving without the differences between them resolved. She'd never know if they could have come to terms, reached a successful working partnership. The next time she had differences with some other nurse, she'd be that much more insecure because of Rolfe, because he'd left before they'd truly confronted one another and tried to reach an understanding. Because she'd *let* him leave rather than tried to work with him.

Lynn set her empty glass onto the counter with a thunk. Maybe that was why she couldn't sleep. Because she was taking the easy way out for a change. She grimaced, knowing what she'd have to do in the morning, and not liking the idea one bit.

But nowhere was it written you had to like what you had to do.

Chapter 10

After the change-of-shift report on Friday, Lynn told Rolfe to come into the treatment room.

"Have you asked for a transfer yet?" she asked.

He shook his head. "I'm seeing Mrs. Morrin today."

Lynn took a deep breath. "Transferring off Five East's a cop-out. For you and for me, too."

He stared at her. "Why? You don't want me here, you never did."

Lynn opened her mouth to deny his accusation, but closed it again with out speaking. He was right.

"I'd sure as hell rather be *anyplace* else," he added.

"You've been hostile ever since you started on the unit," Lynn said. "Why?"

Rolfe's eyes narrowed. "Lady, you've been chilling me out from day one. What'd you expect in return? You were against me before you knew anything about me except I was male and black. I see you and Elkins together. I figure it can't be my color, so it must be my sex. Then I watch you with men and I see you're no man-hater. I finally got it—you don't like male nurses." His gaze was defiant. "What am I supposed to do about that? About you prowling around waiting for me to make a mistake you can call me on?"

"You've deliberately tried to provoke me with your insolence," she countered.

Anger twisted his features. "I'm supposed to kiss ass to you when I know you hate my guts?"

Did she hate him? Lynn asked herself. If she was honest, she'd admit she came close. Okay, her hostility might have provoked his. But what had Nai Pham ever done to deserve his cruelty? She had told him how she had expected him to treat the Vietnamese nurse. Now it was time to learn why he had defied her.

"I don't condone it," she said, "but I can understand how you might feel justified in your behavior toward me. What about Nai Pham, though? Why pick on her?"

He clenched his fists. "She's a fucking Vietnamese."

"You don't like Vietnamese. Were you over there?"

"No."

She regarded him warily, sensing she was treading on a thin crust stretched over a raging volcano. Because she wasn't sure of the right words, she remained silent.

"They killed him," Rolfe muttered.

"Who did they kill?"

"My brother. My twin. We got college scholarships, but they drafted him. Not me, just him."

Did Rolfe feel guilty because he hadn't gone? Because he was alive? She could point out that Nai Pham had nothing to do with his twin's death, but Rolfe already knew that—intellectually, anyway. Her words wouldn't reach his irrational anger. His rage was at himself as much as at anyone else, she suspected.

This confrontation was turning out to be far more complicated than she'd envisioned, they'd passed far beyond a courteous "We'll both try to do better" stage. Yet she was determined not to give up.

"You've hit on my weak point," she told him. "In the past I've had bad experiences working with male nurses. I shouldn't have brought that baggage with me, I shouldn't have allowed it to infect my relationship with you. I've been wrong and I apologize."

Surprise replaced his brooding anger.

"I can't promise the past won't ever influence me again," she went on, "but I'll try being fair to you. I'll give it my best shot."

His eyebrow raised.

"You and that damned eyebrow!" she snapped.

Rolfe chuckled, and after a moment she ruefully joined in.

"Okay, so it won't be easy," she admitted. "I still want to try. You're an excellent nurse, I'd hate to lose you."

Rolfe blinked, his eyes shifting from hers. He took a deep breath, and slowly released the air. "I'm not much for running. Like you say, it sure ain't going to be easy, but if you want me here, I'll stay."

Lynn held out her hand. Rolfe hesitated, then reached and clasped it briefly. He turned toward the door. Hand on the knob, he looked over his shoulder and said, "The unit's getting into shape. You're due some of the credit."

Lynn shook her head as he exited—she'd be helpless without his cooperation and that of the rest of the Five East team.

Still, if anyone had told her two days ago that she'd be happy because Rolfe Watson was remaining on her unit, she never would've believed it.

Saturday morning, under an overcast sky, Lynn jogged on the beach. A fog bank hovered offshore, sending misty tendrils curling over the sand. She wondered if Tim Brandon would have to cancel the boat ride and was surprised at how much she hoped not. She wasn't interested in Tim in the male–female mode, but more as a companion, like she and her father had been.

When the sun broke through the clouds shortly after noon, Lynn rejoiced. Because the breeze was cool, she put on blue cords, a blue T-shirt, and a navy hooded jacket. Tim was waiting in the marina parking lot.

"Carol's on the boat," he said, leading Lynn along a plank walk past a bait shop and a marine supply store. Narrow wooden piers extended into the water with boats docked to either side—some with sails, others without. Lynn followed Tim onto one of the piers.

"Daddy!" A young girl, her blond hair held back with a red ribbon, waved from the deck of a gleaming white boat with trim as red as the ribbon.

"Carol looks like you," Lynn said as they came up to the boat.

"Do you think so?" Tim seemed pleased.

"Daddy calls you Lynn," Carol said after they were introduced, "is it all right if I do?"

"Sure," Lynn said. "No one calls me Ms. Holley except when I'm on duty at the hospital."

"Not even Daddy?"

"No—just as I say Dr. Brandon, not Tim."

Carol's deep blue eyes fixed on Lynn. "Because of the patients, I suppose you have to."

Her voice was so solemn Lynn suppressed a smile.

"Where's my first mate?" Tim asked.

Carol grinned at Lynn. "That's me."

Lynn helped Carol cast off the lines as Tim backed the boat away from the mooring dock. "What's the boat's name?" she asked Carol.

"It's sort of a dumb name. Daddy bought the boat four years ago when I was only a little girl. He named the boat after something I used to ask all the time then. 'Why?' "

"I swear it was the first word she ever said," Tim put in as he guided the boat into the channel leading to the bay.

The fog bank grayed the horizon, but in the bay bright blue water shimmered in the sunlight. Lynn turned her face up to the warmth of the sun, luxuriating in the smell of the salt water and the rush of the cool breeze through her hair. Watching Tim maneuver the *Why* to avoid sailboats reminded her of being a child herself, with her father off the Cape in their old motorboat.

Tim couldn't be more than forty, so he didn't really remind her of her father. It was the ocean, the boat and his obvious fondness for his daughter that evoked her happy childhood memories.

"Is it hard to take care of sick people, Lynn?" Carol asked.

Lynn took a minute to think about the question. "Nurses are trained to know what to do when people are sick," she said, choosing her words carefully. "The easy part of nursing care is applying what you've learned. The hard part is seeing people every day who are hurt or in pain."

"Daddy says the hardest for him is when babies get sick."

"Sick babies are the hardest for all of us. The best part is when someone gets well and goes home." She smiled at Carol. "Like you did."

"Yeah, but I wasn't really sick. I didn't have to be in the hospital, Daddy could have given me the prothrombin.

161

But Ms. Innes wouldn't listen to me. She's the school nurse and she got scared. I wasn't scared."

"Getting scared makes everything worse. It's too bad the nurse didn't know more about your blood condition."

"Daddy explained it to her so she does now. I told her exactly the same thing, but grown-ups never pay attention to kids. Except my dad . . . he does. He listens."

"And she talks my ear off." Tim reached over and tugged Carol's ponytail.

The warmth and ease between father and daughter touched Lynn's heart but also made her feel a bit lonely. She had no family. Both her parents had been only children, so she had no aunts, uncles, or cousins. When she'd married Ray, she'd hoped to establish a new family with him, a happy family. Instead. . . .

"Oh, look!" Carol cried, pointing toward the bow, where sleek gray bodies surfaced and dived, circling the boat.

Lynn smiled in delight at the antics of the pod of porpoises. Now *there's* one big happy family, she told herself.

The afternoon passed all too quickly. After an early dinner at the Fisherman's Rest, Tim returned the boat to the marina. He bundled Carol into his car and walked Lynn to hers.

"I had a wonderful time," she told him when they reached her car.

"So did Carol and I," he said. "She really took to you."

"She's a sweet child."

He grinned. "Sometimes."

"The two of you have a great relationship." She opened the door.

"Thanks for coming today, Lynn. I hope—" he paused.

She waited but he didn't continue, so she slid onto the seat. He held the door, preventing her from closing it.

162

"What I mean is, I'd like to—that is, Carol has a birthday next week. Would you be part of the celebration?"

She smiled up at him. "How nice of you to ask me. I'd like to come to Carol's birthday party."

"On Wednesday evening at seven. I'll stop by for you if you'll give me your address."

She did, he shut the door and waved at her as she drove off. She felt good to think he wanted her at Carol's party. If she couldn't have a family of her own, it was nice to now and then be a part of someone else's. But he had been nervous asking her. Was it because he was afraid she'd think he was coming on to her?

Lynn laughed . . . no danger of that. Tim was friendly, but no more. She was certain all he wanted was a woman friend for Carol. No matter how fond she was of her father, Carol was a girl, and Tim knew girls sometimes needed a woman to talk to, a woman who'd listen. It pleased her Tim had chosen her to be Carol's friend.

On Monday it rained. Sheila was late, finally arriving at seven-thirty. Lynn, busy transferring Mrs. Phillips to the ICU with a possible coronary, told Sheila to take Rolfe's section. Once Mrs. Phillips was on her way, Lynn looked for Sheila, to hear her excuse for being late.

Beth stopped her in the hall. "Sheila took an awful fall," she said. "Did you see those bruises on her arm?"

Lynn shook her head and went on. A fall? More likely Justin. But she had no intention of getting involved with Sheila's personal life again.

Sheila eyed Lynn defiantly. "I slipped and fell down the apartment stairs this morning," she said. "That's why I was late."

Since the bruise on Sheila's forearm was already turn-

163

ing green, whatever had caused it had happened more than a hour or so ago. Sheila knew that as well as she did. Lynn held her tongue, accepting the excuse. She returned to the desk, wondering why women stayed with men who abused them.

But how could she condemn Sheila when she'd done it herself? Ray had never hit her, but his verbal abuse had hurt as much as physical violence. Get out, she wanted to tell Sheila. Leave Justin before it's too late. But Sheila wouldn't listen any more than she would have if someone had advised her to leave Ray.

Tim Brandon arrived on Five East at shortly after nine. Lynn, who knew he'd been in the ICU with his patient, asked, "How's Mrs. Phillips?"

He shook his head. "She's gone."

Lynn bit her lip. "Did the porphyria cause the infarction?"

"Possibly." He sighed, picked up a chart, and began to leaf through it.

She knew how he felt . . . as if there ought to have been a way to prevent it. When a patient died unexpectedly she always wondered if she shouldn't have noticed some symptom that would have alerted her in time.

After a few moments he put down the chart and looked at her. "I hear you're at it again."

She arched her eyebrows.

"Henry Haskins says you diagnosed some rare Oriental lung fluke in one of his patients and hit the bull's-eye."

"It was really Nai Pham again. She's a marvel. I can't wait for her to get her license."

"Don't give away all the credit. You listened to Nai Pham, you evaluated the patient, you called Henry. Like you called me about Mrs. Phillips." He smiled. "You're as much of a marvel as Nai Pham."

Lynn flushed with embarrassed pleasure. A compliment like that made up for the way some of the doctors ignored any suggestions from a nurse. Dr. Marlin was one of the worst. Lynn couldn't understand why Beth was so fascinated with the man.

At lunch, Lynn sat with Joyce.

"How're things on Five East this rainy Monday?" Joyce asked.

"So far, so good. I feel like crossing all my fingers and toes."

"Last week you claimed Monday went all right only because Rolfe Watson wasn't on duty."

Lynn grimaced. "He's okay. I may never like him, but I have to admit he's a damned good nurse. He's not crazy about me, either, but he credits me with being a fair-to-middling charge nurse."

Joyce grinned. "Sounds like the two of you had a go-round."

"Past time for it. My fault, not his. And that's enough of Rolfe. When are we going to dinner together again?"

"Wednesday's good for me."

"I've been invited to a birthday party that evening. Which reminds me—what's a good gift for an about-to-be-nine year-old girl?

"Clothes. Or a fancy pillow for her bed." Joyce eyed Lynn speculatively. "Couldn't be a certain doctor's daughter, by any chance?"

Smiling wryly, Lynn nodded. "The grapevine doesn't miss a thing."

"Dr. Brandon always uses the doctors' dining room. To my knowledge, he's never once eaten in the main room, much less with a nurse. You expect no one to notice?"

"It's because of Carol. I mean, she's interested in nursing and asked to meet me. Besides, I think he wants her to have a woman friend."

"Sure." Joyce gave the word two syllables—both disbelieving.

"Joyce—"

"How about Thursday night for dinner? Then you can tell me I'm right."

"Thursday's fine, but I'll be telling you how wrong you are."

"Honey, you go home and take a long look in your mirror. Dr. Brandon may dote on his daughter, but he's no different than any other red-blooded man. He wants you for himself—the rest is bullshit."

When Tim picked her up in his white Cadillac on Wednesday, Lynn, recalling Joyce's prediction, found herself tense. In an effort to ease it, she began asking questions. "Who stays with Carol when you're not home?"

"I have a full-time housekeeper, Mrs. Morales. She doesn't speak much English, but we're lucky to have found such a warm and caring person. One added benefit is that my Spanish and Carol's has improved a hundred percent."

"What grade is Carol in? Does she like school?"

Her questions and his answers lasted until they reached a tiled-roof ranch house nestled into a hillside overlooking the ocean. Azaleas and bougainvillea splashed brilliant colors against the tan adobe walls.

Tim ushered her in to the dining room where balloons festooned the gold and crystal chandelier above the table. Lynn, who'd expected there'd be others at the party, was surprised to see place settings for only three.

Apparently Tim caught her look, for he said, "Carol's

taking some of her girlfriends to a movie on Saturday, with ice-cream at Farrell's afterward. But today is really her birthday and I thought we should celebrate."

Joyce's comments surfaced in Lynn's mind, but she pushed them away again. Whatever Tim's reasons, this was Carol's day and Lynn was determined to do everything she could to make it a happy one for the little girl.

Seeing a small mound of presents at the end of the table, Lynn added hers. After a lot of thought, she'd taken Joyce's suggestion and bought a completely frivolous pillow—a ballerina whose long pink legs extended below the square of the pillow.

Carol had chosen the menu—fried chicken with refried rice and tortillas. After they'd eaten, Mrs. Morales, a dark, smiling woman who spoke, as far as Lynn could determine, no English, brought in a chocolate cake decorated with white rosettes and nine flaming candles.

Lynn and Tim sang "Happy Birthday" and Carol blew out the candles on her first try.

"I get my wish!" she cried. "I'm not going to tell anyone, even you, Daddy, or it won't come true." She was pleased with her presents and hugged the pillow Lynn had given her. "Thank you, thank you," she said. "And *muchas gracias, Señora Morales.*"

Carol insisted on viewing one of her gifts right away, a videotape cassette of "Sleeping Beauty." After she settled in the den with the VCR, Tim led Lynn onto a glassed-in patio overlooking the ocean. Plants and flowers hung from the beams and clustered on stands—begonias, fuschias, creeping charlie—making Lynn feel she was in a greenhouse. A string of tiny lights glided across the darkness of the ocean. A ship passing.

"I'd never tire of a view like this," she said.

"In December we can see the gray whales heading for

Baja," he told her. "Carol once counted thirteen in one day."

"You have a lovely home. I've enjoyed the evening." She turned to smile at him and found he was standing closer than she'd thought.

"Your coming made the party a success."

His gaze was intent. Too intent? "It's not every day a girl turns nine," she said lightly. "I had fun watching Carol and remembering when I was young."

He smiled. "You're still young."

She thought for a moment he meant to say more, but instead he turned away and reached for a decanter on a bamboo stand.

"Care for an after-dinner drink?" he asked.

She shook her head. "The coffee was enough, thanks."

He poured himself a tiny glass of a clear liqueur and the scent of peppermint drifted to her. "It's a great service—what Nick and the others are doing in Baja," he said.

She blinked at the abrupt change in subject.

"Going to Baja saved me," he went on. "You know Phil Vance?"

Lynn nodded, remembering the folksinging psychiatrist she'd met at Joe King's party.

"He loaded me on a plane and flew me down to Baja four months ago. 'You think you've got troubles,' he said, and turned me loose with the patients who'd gathered to be treated. Some of the adults were sad cases, but my God, Lynn, you should have seen the kids. There were defects— cleft palate, congenital dislocation of the hip, clubfoot— that should have been fixed when these kids were babies. There were—" he threw up his hands. "I can't begin to tell you the pathology I saw.

"I'm an internist, not a surgeon or a bone man, so I

couldn't help those kids directly. Once I got back, though, I stopped popping pills and started working on getting the kids to the States for surgery. You wouldn't believe the red tape. My first success is Ramos Ramirez, twelve, who has a cleft lip and palate. He's coming to stay with us while he waits to have corrective surgery. I don't know who's more excited—Carol or Mrs. Morales . . . or me."

Impulsively, she placed her hand on his arm. "I think you've done a wonderful job—and opening your house to Ramos, that's really special."

He covered her hand with his. "That was Carol's idea, I can't take the credit."

His hand was warm, it was pleasant to have him touch her. But she felt nothing else, no electric tingling, no breathless anticipation. Not that she'd expected to . . . or wanted to. She liked being with Tim, she wished to have him as her friend, with no added complications.

"I have to work tomorrow," she said. "Much as I've enjoyed this evening, it's time I was getting home."

The following evening at Smoky Joe's, Joyce raised her glass of white wine and asked Lynn, "Do we drink to me being right or not?"

Lynn shook her head. "I still think Tim invited me mostly for Carol's sake."

"Aha! I didn't hear any 'mostly' when you protested before. You admit, then, he's interested in you for himself as well as for Carol."

"I'm not sure."

"Come on, girl, you didn't get to be twenty-seven without learning when a guy's getting ready to put the moves on you."

"He's nowhere near that point. I don't think he ever will unless I encourage him."

"And?"

"Joyce, he's a nice guy, but—"

"Never mind, you said the magic words that tell me you couldn't care less about him. No woman calls a man she's hot for a 'nice guy.'"

"But he is. I wish I were more interested."

"Forget it. That's something you can't force. I know what you mean, though, I've been there myself. Somehow, though, I only fall for the not-so-nice ones." She sipped her wine. "How're you getting on with Sheila?"

"No complaints. She's a good nurse when she sticks to business."

"I've heard a rumor she's trying to set up a meeting of Harper Hills RNs and LVNs with the idea of organizing a protest movement about salaries."

Lynn stared at Joyce. "I don't know anything about that. I thought the salary freeze was supposed to end next month, anyway. Why is Sheila bothering?"

"She doesn't believe the company will lift the freeze. Who knows? She could be right." From the way Joyce looked at her, Lynn realized her friend was waiting for her either to agree or dispute the point.

Lynn shook her head. "What do I know? If you think I have a direct line to the administrator's office—forget it."

"I thought you might be able to find out whether or not CMC really plans to end the freeze. Harper Hills is going to have some angry nurses if the company stalls on this. They'll be fighting to join Sheila's protest group."

The last thing in the world Lynn wanted to do was talk to Conrad, but after all Joyce had done for her, how could she not make an effort? If anyone knew what CMC meant

170

to do, Conrad must. Whether he'd tell her or not was another story.

"If I learn anything, I'll tell you," she promised.

"I'd appreciate it. Otherwise, I don't see how I can counter Sheila's efforts."

On Friday, Lynn waited until her morning break to call Conrad's office and give her name to his secretary. Maybe he'd find an excuse not to talk to her, but at least she'd try. He came on the line almost immediately, to her surprise.

"I'd like to speak to you," she said. "In your office. Either now or at a time convenient for both of us."

"I have fifteen minutes now," he said, his tone as carefully neutral as hers.

"I'll be right down."

In the elevator, Lynn scolded herself for feeling tense. She'd done nothing wrong. If the meeting should make anyone nervous, it ought to be Conrad.

"Good to see you, Lynn," he said as he offered her a chair.

If he wanted to pretend nothing had happened, that was all right with her. "I'm concerned about CMC's freeze of the nurses' salaries," she said, coming immediately to the point. "I've heard talk that the company might renege on lifting the freeze next month."

Conrad leaned across the desk. "Who's doing the talking?"

Did he seriously think she'd tell him? Lynn looked him in the eye. "I really can't recall, you know how rumors float around the place."

"You know better than to pay attention to rumors."

"I've discovered most of them, no matter how distorted, have a basis in fact."

Did he wince ever so slightly? She wasn't sure.

171

"Lynn, all I can tell you is what CMC tells me. And I haven't heard a word from them about the salary freeze since the memo setting the date for the lifting—the fifteenth of next month."

Lynn measured his statement against what she knew of Conrad and decided he wasn't being completely honest. "If I were you," she said, "I'd make certain CMC intends to honor that date."

"Sounds like a veiled threat."

"What I mean is, the nursing staff is getting restless. We're professionals, we expect to be treated as such. If nothing happens on the fifteenth, I'm afraid there'll be trouble. And that's a fact, not a threat."

Chapter 11

Nick was thinking about his patient when he got on the elevator to go up to Five East—Shaleen McGuire, fifteen, admitted with severe pelvic inflammation and infection following a back-room abortion. Why she hadn't gone to a doctor in this age of legalized abortions he didn't know. He only hoped the girl wouldn't abscess and rupture into the peritoneal cavity. He'd worry about scarred fallopian tubes later.

Before the elevator door opened, he remembered Lynn was charge nurse on Five East now and his pulse quickened. He hadn't called her or seen her since his return from Baja two days ago.

He'd thought about her every day he was in Mexico and where they were headed. He wasn't ready for any long-term commitment, much less marriage, and when he was ready he had no intention of marrying a nurse. He'd marry a woman with money when the time came, if it ever did.

Yet the longer he knew Lynn, the more certain he became that, for him, she'd be no one-night, one-week, one-month stand. He didn't like not being able to control his need for her, didn't like the feeling that this woman played for keeps.

In Baja, it'd seemed simple to assure himself he could quit cold turkey, ignore his increasing need for her and get on with his life without Lynn. But in a moment or two he'd be face-to-face with her and, with his pulse rate already zooming in anticipation, it didn't take a genius to see it wasn't going to be as simple as that.

Keep your mind on the patient, Dow, he advised himself, not on the charge nurse.

Lynn wasn't at the nurses' station, wasn't anywhere in sight. He found her in the room with Shaleen McGuire.

"Her temp's 103 orally, Dr. Dow." Lynn's voice was crisp. "Up a degree since we admitted her. The right lower quadrant of her abdomen is extremely tender to touch."

After he'd been away from Lynn for any length of time, her beauty always surprised him anew, as though he was seeing her for the first time. He forced his attention from her to what she was saying about his patient.

"Has a specimen for culture and sensitivity gone to the lab?" he asked.

"The ward clerk took it down at half hour ago. She made certain the lab noticed the *stat* order on the C&S."

He checked the intravenous line and the piggyback of penicillin. If she was lucky, Shaleen's infection would be from a bug sensitive to penicillin, not one of the gram-negative baccilli resistant to the antibiotic. He'd keep on the lab until they reported on the C&S. The sooner he hit on the right antibiotic to kill whatever organism had invaded her pelvis, the better. The longer she had to fight the infection on her own, the greater the possibility of life-threatening complications. Peritonitis . . . paralytic ileus . . . tubal abscess.

"Right lower quadrant?" he asked Lynn.

She nodded.

Nick let down the side rail and folded back the sheet covering Shaleen's abdomen. He began to palpate her abdomen with gentle fingers. When he reached the right lower quadrant, the patient moaned and reached down with her hand to thrust his away.

"Don't," she protested, her voice thick. "Hurts."

"Sorry, Shaleen," he said. "I'm Dr. Dow. Remember me?"

She tried to focus on him. "Dr. Dow," she mumbled, closing her eyes. He wasn't sure whether she knew him or not. This was one very sick girl.

Lynn's eyes met his. He knew she'd made the same diagnosis he had. Right salpingitis, inflammation of the fallopian tube. The tube was undoubtedly filled with pus. Had an abscess formed?

He motioned with his head for Lynn to follow him from the room. After pulling the door shut, he said, "Keep close watch on her, she could go sour fast."

"I've been monitoring her myself," she assured him. Her steady green gaze reassured him as much as anything could. Lynn would surely be aware of any change and would alert him to it.

"She's only fifteen, just a kid. I'd like to strangle whoever did this to her. In the ER I put a speculum in to take a look—God, what a mess. For all I can tell the bastard used a bent coat hanger. Whatever it was, I wish he'd at least had the sense to boil it first."

"Where are her parents?" Lynn asked.

He shook his head. "No information. I'm her doctor only because I happened to be in the ER checking one of my patients when Shaleen got dumped in the waiting room by some guy who took off in a hurry. She either couldn't or wouldn't give the names of any next of kin—of *anyone*.

She had no purse, no ID. The admitting office is checking with the county, but I'll bet she's not on the welfare list."

Lynn nodded. "Her clothes are expensive—a cashmere sweater, designer labels in the skirt and shirt. Are you sure she gave her real name?"

"Who knows? I think the Shaleen's right because, sick as she is, she responds when you say the name."

"She must have been desperate," Lynn said. "What would make a fifteen-year-old afraid to go to a doctor?"

"Anything from her own wild imagination to a real threat."

"She must have parents. When she doesn't come home, won't they be upset? Report her to the police as a missing person?"

"I'm sure the admitting office will try the police, if they haven't already. They'll exhaust every possibility—if only to find someone to cover Shaleen's hospital expenses."

She frowned, then smiled wryly. "You're right. If the admitting office can't locate a responsible party, no one can."

"I've got a patient in labor, so I'll be on Maternity. Don't hesitate to call me, tell them to get word to me even if I'm in the delivery room. Okay?"

"I don't give up easily. If I need you, I'll get through to you."

He grinned at her choice of words. They worked well together, he and Lynn. He trusted her as a nurse as much as he'd ever trusted anyone. When he wasn't around her, he missed her. When he was with her, he wanted her. How the hell could he be expected to give her up?

After Nick left, Lynn returned to Shaleen's bedside and pushed a strand of blond hair, dank and greasy because of her illness, from the teenager's forehead. Taking the girl's hot, dry hand in hers, she softly called her name. Shaleen opened her eyes.

"Would you like me to call anyone for you?" Lynn asked.

Shaleen slowly shook her head.

"If you change her mind, let me know," Lynn told her. As she released the girl's hand, she noticed a pale strip on Shaleen's otherwise tanned left wrist. From a watch? Yet Shaleen had no watch on admission.

No rings, no jewelry at all. No bag, which meant no hairbrush or cosmetics. Unusual for a teenager not to be carrying a shoulder bag ... Shaleen must own at least one. Where was it? Where was her watch?

Who'd brought her into the ER waiting room and fled before he could be questioned? The man who botched the abortion? The father of the baby?

Lynn sighed. None of that concerned her at the moment ... her job was to try to prevent Shaleen's condition from deteriorating, to keep her alive, if she could.

Lynn remembered when she was a student back in Boston and an older nurse, near retirement, had told her how it was before abortions were legal.

"I know it's hard to believe, but the hospital needed one entire ward for infected OB cases. Most of the patients had gone to a back-street butcher for an illegal abortion. Some were kids, some were older, some weren't married, some were. They all were very, very sick. A lot of them died, even though we had penicillin by then. You ever hear of gas gangrene? It's what soldiers sometimes get from infected bullet wounds. Some of the patients had gas gangrene of the uterus. It was horrible. I hope to God those days never return."

"It hurts," Shaleen moaned. "Please don't ..." her words trailed off into a mumble.

177

Lynn bent over her, checking. Blood pressure stable. Pulse rapid, respirations up. Temperature still 103. Abdomen tender but not rigid, a good sign. One complication she knew Nick worried about was a tubal abscess. When it ruptured, the pus could drain through the uterus or even the colon without too many problems. But if the abscess broke through into the peritoneal cavity, it would cause fulminating shock. In such a case, unless Nick operated, Shaleen might be dead within an hour. A rigid abdomen would mean peritonitis and would indicate a surgical emergency.

"Don't let him," Shaleen cried suddenly. "Please don't let him find me."

"Who?" Lynn asked, keeping her voice low and unobtrusive.

"My daddy. Please, please—" Shaleen tried to sit up but was too weak and fell back.

"I'm the only one here," Lynn soothed her.

"Don't let him in." Shaleen didn't seem aware of her surroundings or of what Lynn was saying. "It's *my* bedroom." Tears rolled down the girl's cheeks. "Don't let him touch me," she begged.

"You're safe," Lynn told her. "Safe."

"You don't believe me!" Shaleen stared up at Lynn but her blue eyes were focused somewhere else, she didn't see Lynn or the hospital room. "No one believes me. Just because he's a judge. Oh, please, please—"

Shaleen's head thrashed from side to side. "No," she sobbed, "don't, Daddy, you're hurting me. Please. Oh, it hurts, it hurts!"

Shaleen's delirious pleading made the hair rise on Lynn's nape as she tried without success to quiet the girl. Shaleen's father was a judge. He came to her bedroom, he hurt her. Child abuse ... sexual abuse. Shaleen had

178

gotten pregnant. Is that why she was afraid to tell anyone, why she stayed away from doctors? Was she trying, despite everything, to shield her father? Had she risked death to save a man who deserved, as far as Lynn was concerned, to be put to death himself?

"I won't let you die," Lynn whispered as she wiped Shaleen's face with a cool cloth.

Connie stuck her head in the door. "Dr. Marlin's on the phone," she said. "I tried to get him to talk to Mr. Watson, but he insists on talking to the charge nurse."

"Tell him to go to—" Lynn caught herself. Dr. Marlin was an arrogant bastard, but he had nothing to do with her anger at Shaleen's father. If Dr. Marlin insisted on the charge nurse, she'd have to talk to him. "Connie, you stay with the patient. If she looks worse in any way, put on the call light, understand?"

"Yes, Ms. Holley."

Lynn seethed as she took down the order Dr. Marlin gave for one of his patients, a routine order Rolfe could have handled with no problem. Or Sheila. Even Beth. But Dr. Marlin always got his way or made things unpleasant for everyone.

As Lynn hung up, the call light for Shaleen's room went on. She ran.

"Her eyes rolled up," Connie said as Lynn hurried toward the bed. "She don't look so good."

Shaleen was unconscious. Lynn gently palpated her abdomen, then turned to Connie. "Dr. Dow's on Maternity—possibly in the delivery room. If you can't reach him directly, give whoever answers the phone this message from me. 'Tell Dr. Dow, *stat*, there's a surgical emergency: Shaleen McGuire.' Then call the lab and ask them if they have anything at all on that C&S from Shaleen you took down to them earlier. Tell them it's an emergency. Oh, and ask

179

Rolfe to take over if anything comes up while I'm with this patient. That includes Dr. Marlin."

Nick arrived, agreed with Lynn that Sheila had a rupture of an abscess into the peritoneal cavity, and made arrangements to take the girl to the OR. After Shaleen was off the unit, Nick with her, Lynn collapsed onto a chair at the desk. Shaleen might not survive the surgery—her next-of-kin should be notified. Slowly she reached for the phone and dialed the admitting office.

"Lynn Holley, Five East. About Shaleen McGuire—she's in surgery, condition critical. Have you located her parents?"

The admitting office was still trying.

If it came to testifying in court she was going to make certain everyone knew what Shaleen's father did to her, Lynn vowed. How could a man behave like that to his own child? What twisted kind of reasoning would permit a man to pass judgment on others when he was guilty of such an atrocity? If Shaleen lived, she'd need intensive therapy before she'd stand a chance of leading a normal life.

What kind of father would violate his daughter, harm her for life?

Lynn thought of Tim and Carol and the healthy love between them and sighed. Thank God every father wasn't like Shaleen's.

By the time she went off duty, Shaleen still hadn't returned to Five East, so Lynn stopped by the recovery room.

"How's she doing?" she asked the gray-haired nurse, Mrs. Wright.

"She's stabilized," Mrs. Wright said. "Dr. Dow wanted her sent to ICU, but when they heard the lab found penicillin-resistant staph on her culture, they wouldn't take her. The way ICU's set up, it's impossible for them to isolate a contaminated case."

"So we'll be getting her back on Five East."

"Looks that way. I'll keep her here for another hour and if she remains stable, she goes to you. Housekeeping's none to happy about having to disinfect the OR. Wait until I call and tell them the recovery room has to have the same treatment."

Staphylococcus, a gram-positive bacteria once quickly killed by penicillin, had adapted. Now some strains of the organism were resistant not only to penicillin but to other antibiotics as well. In a hospital, staph could spread from one patient to another if precautions weren't taken to isolate the affected patient and everything she used, including dishes and dirty linen. The nurses who took care of the patient had to observe isolation techniques to protect themselves and their other patients.

A patient with staph was a headache on any unit, Lynn thought. No wonder ICU refused Shaleen. They were harried enough without the additional stress of coping with staph.

Lynn called the evening charge nurse on Five East to alert her to the problem, adding. "We'll have to put Shaleen in a private room and have housekeeping clean the other one."

It wasn't until she reached home, changed clothes, and stretched out on the couch with a tall glass of cran-raspberry drink that Lynn allowed herself to think about Nick. She'd rather work with him than with any doctor she'd ever met, they made an excellent team. He trusted her judgment, depended on her observations, and used her skills to augment his own. Professionally, she and Nick meshed beautifully.

Privately? She shook her head. He hadn't called her since his return from Baja, hadn't made the slightest effort to see her. Why? Too busy catching up? She might buy that, except a phone call took only a couple of minutes.

Still, they hadn't exchanged any promises. Each was free to go his separate way. If she'd thought there'd been an implicit promise in the way he kissed her, she obviously was wrong. At the hospital today he'd been all business, she hadn't expected anything else, given the circumstances. But he could have dropped a hint he'd be in touch with her.

The phone rang and she almost spilled her drink in her hurry to answer it. She stifled her disappointment when she heard Joyce's voice.

"Hear any more from your front office contact about the salary freeze?" Joyce asked.

"No. I'm not sure I will, even if the CMC does send him a memo changing the date."

"The nurses are meeting tonight—Sheila's group. I thought I'd go. Want to come with me?"

I refuse to hang around waiting for Nick to call, Lynn told herself.

"Sure, Joyce. Shall I pick you up?"

"Maybe you'd better. Tonight may not be the best time to flaunt my Porsche."

The meeting was at Sheila's apartment, on the second floor of a new complex in the hills east of El Doblez. Outside and in, stark modern was the theme. Justin wasn't home.

If Sheila was surprised to see Joyce and Lynn, she didn't let on. Though the living room was crowded, Lynn recognized only a few of the nurses present. Neither Rolfe nor Beth was there.

Sheila spoke clearly and concisely, the gist of her argument being that if they didn't band together, they'd have no clout. "We must be prepared ahead of time, must

182

have our group organized and ready to fight for our rights," she concluded, "otherwise we'll get nothing. No salary raises, no increase in benefits."

Lynn, impressed with the short and effective speech, still wasn't convinced a group effort was necessary. After all, CMC had promised to lift the freeze. Why did Sheila think the company wouldn't stand by its promise?

Later, driving Joyce home, Lynn asked her how she felt about Sheila.

Joyce shrugged. "Sheila's determined to be a leader even if she has to scratch to dig up a cause. She'll find something else if CMC comes through on the salaries. If they don't, she's sitting pretty. Me, I'm waiting to see."

When she returned to her apartment, Lynn found a message on her answering machine. "This is the lonesome jogger," Nick's voice said. "Meet you on the beach at sunrise."

Another order. Not even a please. Lynn didn't usually run before work. She reserved her morning jogging for her days off, and she wasn't going to alter her schedule for him. He'd have to go on being lonesome.

She woke before the alarm went off the next morning, early enough to run before breakfast. No, she told herself firmly, she was not giving in. She got up, showered, and took her time putting on her uniform.

Her doorbell rang as she poured herself a second mug of coffee. "Who is it?" she called.

"The lonesome and stood-up jogger."

She couldn't control the leap of her heart when she opened the door and saw him on her doorstep in black shorts and a faded blue sweatshirt, but she did her best to hide her reaction.

"Coffee?" she asked, standing aside so he could enter.

He nodded and followed her into the kitchen. "Given

183

up jogging?'' he asked as he accepted the mug she handed him.

"No. When I work I run in the evening."

"And you damn well won't change for anyone."

Her lips tightened. "At the hospital you're Dr. Dow, and Ms. Holley, RN, obeys your every order. Outside the hospital Lynn might consider a request, but she doesn't take orders from Nick."

His dark eyes gleamed with mischief. "She makes great coffee, though."

"Compliments will get you no further than orders."

Setting down the mug, Nick swept her a bow. "Will she consider meeting Nick on the beach tomorrow morning?"

"Since tomorrow's Saturday and she doesn't have to work, she'll consider it."

"Lynn—"

"I really have to hurry." She started past him and he caught her arm.

"Please," he said.

One touch, one single touch, was all she needed from Nick and her knees grew weak. Pulling away, she said, "Saturday. The beach at sunrise. Got it."

Only when they went out her door together and she saw his face in the morning brightness did she realize how tired he looked.

"How's Shaleen?" she asked.

"Touch-and-go." He indicated the beeper hooked onto the band of his shorts. "They haven't called me, so she's still in there fighting."

"I think her father might have gotten her pregnant," Lynn said. "In her delirium Shaleen talked enough so that I'm pretty sure he's been abusing her sexually."

"I saw your notes on the chart." Nick shook his head. "Hell of a thing."

She got into her car and he waved as he jogged off. She'd see him again later today on Five East, but that would be different, that wouldn't be Nick and Lynn. She could hardly wait for tomorrow morning.

He'd made the first move, he'd admitted he was lonesome without her. It was up to her now. As long as they jogged, she didn't have to worry, but she'd be lying to herself if she pretended not to know what Nick really wanted, what she herself wanted. Her apartment was only a few blocks from the beach. If she invited him there after they jogged, she knew very well what would happen.

Ray's death and the trauma surrounding it had nothing to do with her and Nick. Ray was death, Nick was life. Ray was the past, Nick was the present. She lived in the here-and-now, not in yesterday. If there proved to be no future with Nick, so what? Let the future take care of itself.

As soon as she reached the unit, Lynn went into Shaleen's room. The girl was semi-conscious, not really aware of her surroundings. She was hooked to monitors, had a naso/gastric tube in, an IV line, a Foley catheter, and an abdominal drain. Lynn wished the judge could stand beside her at this moment, staring down at Shaleen as she fought for her life. If he didn't realize his daughter's precarious condition was his fault, she'd be more than happy to tell him.

Noting that at least Shaleen's vital signs were stable, Lynn returned to the desk, ready for the change-of-shift report.

Later, checking with Admissions, she found the office hadn't been able to locate Shaleen's parents. Nor did the girl fit any police description of a missing person.

"You told us she referred to her father as a judge, but there's no Judge McGuire in the county," Nadine Yates, the office manager, told Lynn. "Either she's not from the immediate area or she's given us a false name—or both. It's a real problem, especially since we're short-handed at the moment. Our social worker will talk to her when Shaleen's well enough to answer questions and maybe we'll get some answers then."

Mrs. Morrin arrived on the unit shortly before ten to check on how Lynn was handling the staph situation.

"We don't want an invasion of staph at Harper Hills," Mrs. Morrin told Lynn. "I expect you to be certain every person who enters that room is aware of the problem and has been fully trained in isolation procedures."

All Lynn could say was that she'd do her best. She wasn't on duty twenty-four hours a day to monitor everyone who went into Shaleen's room. She would, though, pass Mrs. Morrin's message on to the other shifts and stress the importance of proper techniques. She'd also conduct a brief brush-up of isolation procedures with her own staff.

Shaleen was still alive, still holding her own when Lynn went off duty.

Sunrise on Saturday arrived before Lynn had come to a decision about Nick. In her new rose jogging shorts and shirt, she headed for the beach. Seeing his silhouette against the brightening sky when she was still a block away, she realized she'd made up her mind without knowing it.

"Which way first?" he asked when she came up to him.

"North," she said, choosing at random.

"Facing up to the worst first? That's like you."

"Why is north worse than south?" she asked as they began to run side-by-side at the water's edge.

186

"To the Chippewas *Giwaydinnoong,* north, means cold and death, while south, *Zhawanoong,* is warmth and beginnings."

That's what Nick was to her—warmth and a chance to begin again. She smiled at him. "It gives me something to look forward to, anyway."

They jogged for a half hour, seldom speaking. She felt they didn't need words. If he was as aware of her as she was of him, that was more than enough.

"Would you like to have coffee at my place?" she asked when they slowed to a walk.

"How can I refuse? You know how I feel about your coffee." His glance told her he didn't just mean the coffee.

They walked the several blocks to her apartment. Though they didn't touch, his nearness and the anticipation of what was to come made her breathe faster.

"I'm going to take a quick shower while the coffee's brewing," she said.

"How big is your shower?" he asked.

Deliberately misunderstanding him, she said, "Man-sized, I'm sure."

His arm brushed against hers as he reached for her hand. "You could help me check it out," he said.

The vision of Nick, stripped, in her shower, kept her from answering.

In her kitchen, Lynn felt all thumbs as she set up the coffee maker. One part of her wanted to delay, another part urged her to forget the coffee entirely.

Nick took her hand again after she finished pouring in the water. "It's time we headed south, Lynn," he said softly and urged her from the kitchen.

Time for them to begin.

The phone rang. She hesitated, but the answering machine was on, so there was no need to pick up the phone.

They were in the hall when she heard a woman's voice leaving a message. It was a voice she'd hoped never to hear again.

"Lynn, it's Renee," the caller said.

"Oh my God, no!" Lynn cried. She pulled her hand free, plunged into the living room, and lifted the phone to her ear, clicking off the machine.

"Where are you?" she asked.

"I'm at the bus station," Renee said.

"What bus station?"

"Why, right here in El Doblez." Renee's high, childish voice grated on Lynn's nerves as it always had.

"What in hell are you doing here?" Lynn demanded.

"Is that any way to talk to your sister-in-law?" Renee asked plaintively. "I know how much you miss Ray and how guilty you feel about what happened, so I've come to California to help you."

Chapter 12

Lynn hung up the phone and stood staring down at it.

"Bad news?" Nick asked, and she started. Discovering Renee was in El Doblez upset her so, she'd forgotten about Nick. "My—my husband's sister, his twin. I was—surprised to hear from Renee. To find out she's in town. I have to pick her up at the bus station."

"She'll be staying with you?"

God forbid, Lynn thought. "I suppose so," she said. "Overnight, anyway."

"You mentioned Renee to me once. I got the impression then that you didn't care for her. It came out even stronger when you talked to her just now. What's wrong with Renee?"

She blinked at him. "I didn't say there was anything wrong with her."

"It's obvious you're not too happy about her coming. I must say, her timing couldn't have been worse." He crossed to Lynn and put his arms around her. "Do you suppose we're fated never to make love?" He kissed the tip of her nose.

Lynn managed a grin. "Maybe someone's trying to tell us it's a bad idea."

His arms tightened. "No way."

For a moment she yielded to her need to melt against him, but before she lost herself in his embrace she pulled away. "I do have to get Renee."

Nick released her. "I meant to ask you to dinner tonight. If I want you to come, I guess I'll have to invite Renee, too. And I do want you. I don't think you know how much." He cupped her face with his hands, leaned down, and kissed her.

As Lynn drove toward the fast-food restaurant that also served as the El Doblez bus station, she relived the moments with Nick, putting off thinking about Renee. The sight of her sister-in-law standing with an overnight bag by the curb forced her to face what she was up against.

Renee, at the moment talking animatedly to a man in black jeans and a black leather jacket, had been a problem from the beginning. There was no reason to think she'd changed. Who the man was, Lynn didn't know. She pulled the car up to the curb. Renee paid no attention to her and so, after a minute, Lynn tapped the horn.

Renee turned, saw her, waved, and went on talking to the man in black. Finally he nodded and strode to a motorcycle parked by a telephone booth. Renee opened the passenger door and slid in next to Lynn.

"Great to see you," she said.

"Yes." Try as she might, Lynn couldn't lie about how glad she was Renee was here. She wasn't and she couldn't force herself to be. "Is that all your luggage?"

Renee laughed. Her laugh was the one thing she shared with Ray. Despite the fact they were twins, they looked nothing alike. Ray had been dark, slim, and tall, and Renee was fair and tiny, with voluptuous curves.

"Hey, I'm here to stay," Renee said. "I brought everything I own, but when I changed planes in Chicago, I guess my luggage didn't make the LA plane. The airline said they'd be sending my things as soon as they found them."

Lynn's heart sank. "Do you mean you're not going back to Massachusetts?"

"Never." Renee smiled. "I said to myself, Lynn's moved to California, why shouldn't I?" Her smile faded. "With Ray gone, I have no one else."

Renee had made it clear from the first that she didn't like Lynn. Why was she pretending now?

Renee sighed. "Poor Ray. It's too bad you never understood him. If you'd tried harder—" She paused and shook her head. "Well, it's too late, isn't it? You don't have a second chance."

Lynn gritted her teeth. She'd tried in every way she knew to understand her husband. She would not let Renee bait her.

"I assume before you left Worcester you applied for a job in this area." Lynn said.

"No." Renee waved a hand. "Why should I worry about that? Everybody needs secretaries."

If she didn't set a limit, Renee might be with her indefinitely. "I'll put you up until you get a job." Inspiration struck. "In fact, I think I know where you can find one. Harper Hills needs someone in the admissions office."

"That's the hospital where you work?"

Lynn nodded.

"How handy."

Maybe she was being paranoid, seeing Renee as noth-

191

ing but trouble. Maybe Renee actually was lonely—she'd been very close to Ray—and wanted to be friends.

They'd never been friends, no matter how hard Lynn had tried. She'd badly wanted Ray's twin to like her, to be the sister she'd never had. Perhaps it might be possible yet if they both were willing to try.

Lynn couldn't make herself believe it. For one thing, Renee had an alarming tendency to pick up men, perfect strangers, and bring them home or to wherever she happened to be staying. Every time she'd visited Ray and Lynn in Boston, Renee had done this, infuriating Ray.

"If you want to be raped and strangled, go for it," he'd snarled at his twin the last time. "But don't include me in your mad schemes. Keep those weirdos away from my house."

To be fair, none of the men had behaved like weirdos. But who knew about a stranger? Lynn remembered the biker dressed in black and sighed. If Renee ran true to form, the biker, undoubtedly someone Renee had met while waiting by the curb, would soon be camped on Lynn's doorstep.

Lynn didn't want strangers in her apartment. She had to admit she didn't even want Renee there, constantly telling her how she, as Ray's wife, had failed him. Renee blamed her for everything that had happened, she'd told her that in no uncertain terms after Ray's death. And she'd already started in again.

"It's lucky you weren't working today," Renee said. "I took a chance."

"You might have let me know you were coming." Lynn couldn't help her tart tone.

Renee slanted her hazel eyes at Lynn. "Maybe I was afraid."

"What of?"

"That you didn't want me and you'd say so."

"I certainly would've advised you to be certain you had a job waiting for you."

"Oh, Lynn, you have no sense of adventure. That's what Ray used to say and he was right."

It *was* what Ray used to say, and hearing it from his twin hurt. But Renee wouldn't have known that. It wouldn't do to be upset by such things if they had to live together. All the same, Lynn felt a strong need to be by herself, if only for a few minutes.

Quickly showing Renee through the apartment, Lynn left her in the guest bedroom with relief. But she soon wandered back into the kitchen, where Lynn was making coffee.

"Would you like something to eat?" Lynn asked.

Renee shook her head. "A drink, maybe."

"If you don't want coffee, I've got cran-raspberry and orange juice."

"Could you stiffen the orange juice with a little vodka?"

"Sorry, the only alcohol I have is wine."

"White, I suppose. It'll do."

Without thinking, Lynn glanced at the clock.

"Is there something wrong with having a glass of wine at nine-thirty in the morning?" Renee snapped. "I happen to need it after such a harrowing trip, losing my luggage and searching for a bus to take me to El Doblez. You've no idea."

Lynn poured the wine for her, saying nothing.

"I haven't turned into an alcoholic, if that's what you're thinking. We Grahams aren't the type." Renee sipped the wine and made a face. "God, this is dry. Speaking of Graham, why didn't you keep Ray's name?"

"I prefer to use my maiden name."

193

"It's because you don't want to be reminded of him . . . of your failure."

Lynn took a deep breath and changed the subject. "I'm going to dinner this evening with one of the doctors I work with. He's invited you, too."

Renee gave her a long look before putting her hand to her mouth. "Oh, God, I don't have anything to wear. And nothing of yours would fit me, that's for sure. I can't count on my luggage arriving—it may take weeks." She peered out the window. "Isn't there a shopping mall around here somewhere?"

Lynn, who'd hoped Renee might decide to stay at the apartment this evening and get some rest, decided she should have known better. "The closest mall's five miles south," she said resignedly. "I'll drive you over."

By the time Nick arrived to pick them up, Lynn's nerves were stretched to the breaking point. It didn't help to watch Renee, in a new curve-hugging gold dress, flutter her eyelashes at Nick.

"Dear Lynn's told me so much about you," she cooed. "I just know we'll be good friends."

If Nick had raised an eyebrow or glanced her way, Lynn could have passed it off, but instead, he gave Renee his charming smile and held the hand she offered him longer than necessary.

"Lynn, as I'm sure you know, was married to my brother," Renee told Nick. "Ray was a doctor, too, and a wonderful man. He can never be replaced."

Nick did look over Renee's head at Lynn then. She met his gaze coolly, hiding her increasing tension, she hoped. The evening, she suspected, would be a total disaster as far as she was concerned.

"It's been difficult for Lynn, I know," Renee went on. "I'm happy she's found an understanding friend so soon."

Nick took them to Alice's Palace, a new restaurant festooned inside with so much greenery that Lynn felt half-suffocated. When she heard Renee order a vodka martini, Lynn decided she needed one. Nick raised an eyebrow when she said so. He ordered wine.

"Lynn's so sweet," Renee said. "She's already found me a job at the Harper Hills admitting office."

"I'm not sure—" Lynn began.

"Oh, they'll hire me." Renee smiled at Nick. "I've had lots of experience."

Nick was looking at Renee like she was a ripe apple he was dying to pick. What about this morning? Lynn asked herself. Did the attraction between her and Nick mean so little? Mean nothing?

"How's Shaleen?" she asked abruptly.

"Doing better than I expected." At last he focused on Lynn. "I think she's over the hump. But I wish we could locate her relatives."

"I think Lynn's apartment is really cute," Renee said. "Do you live in an apartment, too, Nick?"

"I have a condo. Nothing fancy."

Renee turned to Lynn. "He's being modest, isn't he? I'll bet he has a fascinating place. Am I right?"

Since Lynn had never been to Nick's condo, she had no idea. And that, she realized, was exactly what Renee was trying to determine.

"If I were you I wouldn't believe everything any man has to say," she advised Renee.

"How cynical." Renee picked up her martini and took a swallow. "But I guess a woman has to be. I know I'm far too trusting."

Lynn couldn't deny that Renee was attractive, sexy. The

expensive gold dress fit her like a second skin, yet didn't make her appear cheap. The soft restaurant lighting turned her eyes to mysterious amber and made her hair a blond halo. She'd softened the high pitch of her voice so it became appealingly childlike. Any man would be drawn to her, so Lynn shouldn't be surprised that Nick was.

But he's mine! Nick belongs to me, not to her! The words exploded in Lynn's head like firecrackers, focusing her attention inward.

What nonsense that was! No one owned Nick or ever could. People didn't belong to anyone except themselves. She had railed at Ray for his insistence that she have no life other than being his wife. He considered her a possession, his possession. Graham owned and Graham operated, and permitted no thought or opinion he didn't approve of.

No, she didn't own Nick. Even so, she couldn't bear to stay and watch him with Renee. Part of the reason might be jealousy, but what hurt most was the feeling that Nick had deserted her, had taken Renee's side, the two of them were against her.

"Excuse me," Lynn said, rising from her chair, the vodka making her head buzz. She walked away from the table, through the entry, stopping only to ask if the hostess would call her a taxi.

Back at the apartment Lynn shut herself in her bedroom. She'd given Renee the key she'd had made for Sheila, so there'd be no reason to come out. She undressed, pulled on her nightshirt, and crawled into bed, where she curled into a ball.

She'd been a fool for believing the past had lost its grip, a worse fool for trusting in Nick. He wasn't called the Harper Hills Heartbreaker for nothing. Joyce had warned her, so had Sheila.

What she'd feared from the moment she met him had happened. Her mistakes with Ray hadn't been warning enough; she'd invited more pain by falling for another man who, like Ray, would do nothing but maker her miserable, was making her miserable even now.

Let Renee have him.

No! Tears welled in Lynn's eyes and rolled down her cheeks. She didn't want to cry, hadn't meant to, but she couldn't help herself.

The phone rang. She tensed, but didn't move. The machine was on, she couldn't talk to anyone at the moment, certainly not Nick. For all she knew it might not *be* Nick, he might not care enough to call.

It might be Ray. Oh, God, she was really in bad shape to think like this.

Abruptly Lynn sat up. It wasn't Ray, she knew that. But she also knew now without question who had made those other three calls. There was only one possibility, only one person who could have taped his voice and played it over the phone to Lynn ... only one person who knew exactly how upset and distraught Lynn would be. Ray's twin, Renee.

Lynn shuddered. She'd known Renee didn't like her, but only hatred bordering on the pathological would drive anyone to do such a horrible thing. Why had Renee come to California? What did she plan to do next?

Anything she can to punish me, Lynn decided. She had started already—with Nick. Doing her best to charm him, to take him for herself, and there was nothing Lynn could do about it.

Nick was an adult, able to choose for himself. If he wanted Renee, let him have her. Lynn clenched her teeth. She was damned if she'd cry over him.

But there was one thing Lynn could do. She wouldn't

let Renee stay with her. She wasn't going to nourish a viper. Renee could check into a motel until she found an apartment and Lynn intended to tell her that. Tomorrow.

She heard Renee return about an hour later, heard her footsteps approach, heard the tap of her fingers on the bedroom door. Lynn remained silent, even when Renee pushed the door open and looked in.

"Asleep?" Renee asked.

She knows damn well I'm not, Lynn thought, but still refused to answer. The door closed, Renee's footsteps retreated. Lynn, straining her ears, heard the front door close. Had she left again?

Minutes later the bathroom was in use, then rustling sounds convinced Lynn that Renee was going to bed. The door closing must have been Nick leaving. After being reassured Lynn was safe at home? Why should he care? She blinked back tears. She would *not* cry.

For Lynn, it was a long, sleepless night. She rose early and pulled on her sweats. This morning's jog wouldn't be on the beach, that was for sure. She didn't want to meet Nick. Before she left the apartment, she checked the phone messages. Nick, asking her to call him. She erased the tape.

Renee rose at noon. Lynn, in the living room catching up on articles in her nursing journals, made no move to go into the kitchen.

"No coffee?" Renee asked plaintively.

"I'm afraid I'm out," Lynn said, keeping her tone even with difficulty. It happened to be true, she'd forgotten to buy coffee the last time she shopped. She could've stopped by the 7-Eleven and picked up a pound while she was jogging, but she'd decided not to . . . not for Renee.

"I suppose I can make some tea," Renee said.

"If you like. While you're waiting for the water to boil, we can talk."

Renee sauntered into the living room. She was barefoot and wore a cerise satin sleep-top that came to mid-thigh.

"I don't think it's a good idea for you to stay with me," Lynn said. "There are several motels not too far from the hospital and you can—"

"I've got exactly ten dollars to my name." Renee's voice was flat.

"And a credit card," Lynn said, remembering the shopping trip yesterday.

"I'm way over my limit. I was surprised the mall boutique didn't discover that and refuse to sell me the gold dress. A motel certainly would check."

Lynn stared at her, wondering if Renee was lying.

As if reading her mind, Renee smiled thinly. "I really am broke. And, yes, I left bills behind in Worcester. So I'm profligate, so sue me."

A Graham characteristic. Ray was always spending money he didn't have.

"I don't see why I should be the one to rescue you," Lynn said sharply.

Renee shrugged. "I told you why. I don't have anyone else. You know Ray would expect you to help me."

The old guilt trip. Lynn bit back a tart rejoinder. It wouldn't do any good to snap at Renee. It didn't change the fact she had no money. Now she couldn't order Renee to leave when she couldn't pay for a place to stay. Lynn shook her head. She was stuck with Renee for the time being.

"To be honest, I don't want you here," Lynn said. "But I'll let you stay until you find a job." She shuffled through the stack of newspapers on the coffee table and handed

199

Renee the classified section of the Sunday paper. "Here, you can start looking."

"You don't want me at the hospital?"

"You can apply at Harper Hills tomorrow, but you may find a better-paying position elsewhere."

"With me, money isn't everything."

"That's all too obvious." Lynn's voice was grim.

For the first time since she'd arrived, Renee's facade of friendliness crumbled. Her hazel eyes seethed with hatred as she glanced at Lynn, then looked quickly away.

If looks could kill, Lynn told herself, I'd be stone cold dead.

Monday morning ordinarily wasn't her favorite time of the week, but considering the problem at home, Lynn greeted Monday eagerly. Five East and its headaches were nothing compared to Renee.

She drove Renee to the hospital and told her to wait in the lobby or the cafeteria until the offices opened at eight. "Buses stop in front of the hospital, a number five will take you within two blocks of the apartment," she told Renee. "Get off at Oleander and Fourth. If you want to follow up other job leads, call the bus company to find out which bus goes where."

"I'm quite capable of taking care of myself," Renee informed her.

"I'm glad to hear that."

Lynn left her without another word. She desperately wanted Renee to find a job and move out, but she hoped the job would be somewhere else besides Harper Hills so she could avoid Renee completely. If only she hadn't mentioned the admissions office possibility. If only Renee had remained in Massachusetts.

On the unit, Lynn found herself so busy coping with the usual backlog that she didn't have time to worry about anything else. Connie didn't arrive until eight, and Lynn had to cover the phone until she got there. Today it seemed to ring continuously.

She'd just hung up after talking to Dr. Marlin about the patient he had going to surgery at eleven when Tim Brandon's voice said, "Don't I rate a smile this morning?"

Lynn looked up quickly, her lips curving. "I didn't see you."

Tim sat on the edge of the desk. "If I'm out of line, say so. What I'd like to do is ask you to dinner ... just the two of us."

Lynn drew in her breath. Nick's behavior Saturday night had certainly freed her to say yes if she chose. "I'd enjoy having dinner with you," she told him, wondering if Joyce had been right all along about Tim. It certainly seemed so.

He smiled. "Tuesday. I'll pick you up around seven."

Ready to agree that was fine, Lynn started when Nick's voice jolted through her.

"If I'm not interrupting," he said coldly, "I'd like a little help with my patient."

Nick must have heard every word. Tim nodded curtly to him, turned away, and picked up a chart.

Lynn rose. "Which patient, Dr. Dow?" she asked crisply, hoping he wouldn't notice the flush staining her cheeks. Nick had made it clear enough he didn't consider himself bound to her in any way. Why should she feel guilty? She had a perfect right to date Tim, or any other man.

"Shaleen McGuire," he said. "I'll be changing her dressing, so I'll need four-by-fours and—"

"I checked her when I came on duty, doctor. She has sterile dressings at her bedside. I'll be happy to assist you." Lynn walked briskly toward Shaleen's room, stopping briefly to ask Sheila to answer the phone until Connie arrived.

Because of Shaleen's staph infection, the door to her room was closed and a red isolation card was posted there. Once she and Nick were inside, Lynn shut the door and reached for an isolation gown to pull over her. He caught her hand.

"You didn't tell me you were going out with Brandon." His voice was low, but anger sizzled in the words.

As far as she was concerned, the other times Tim had invited her, she'd gone because of Carol, but if Nick thought she meant to excuse herself to him, he was badly mistaken.

"Why should I?" she hissed.

He glared at her. "I suppose you have an explanation for abandoning me and Renee on Saturday night?"

He actually had the gall to ask her to explain!

"I'm here to help you with your patient, Dr. Dow, and for no other reason." She pulled away from him. For a long moment she thought he meant to grab her. And shake her? Kiss her? She couldn't move, mesmerized by his fury and the tension crackling between them.

"Dr. Dow?" Shaleen's voice was weak and frightened.

"I'm here, Shaleen," he said, slipping into an isolation gown and stepping around the half-pulled curtain screening her bed from the door.

"I'm glad it's you." She sounded relieved.

Lynn, also gowned, walked to the far side of the bed and smiled down at the girl. "I'm Lynn Holley," she said. "I took care of you before your surgery, but you might not remember."

"I sort of do," Shaleen said shyly. "I remember a nurse holding my hand. I think it was you."

Lynn concentrated on the girl, doing her utmost to blot out her acute awareness of Nick. "I can see you're a lot better," she said to Shaleen.

"Dr. Dow says maybe I can leave the hospital in a week."

Lynn noticed Shaleen hadn't said, "Go home." She'd checked the chart earlier and saw there was still no next-of-kin listed.

"I'm going to have a look at your incision," Nick told the girl. "Okay?"

Shaleen gazed up at him with such trust in her eyes that Lynn's heart turned over. Though pale and drawn, the girl was still pretty, with big blue eyes dominating her elfin face. How could any man violate her vulnerability and harm her? Lynn felt an urge to take Shaleen home with her and keep her safe. Which was foolish. She'd learned the hard way that no one could keep another person safe forever. If that was possible, Ray would still be alive.

She handed Nick what he needed as he changed the dressing covering the sutured right rectus incision. A tube still oozed purulent drainage.

"At least a week, Shaleen," Nick said, "but you're doing very well—keep it up."

Lynn deliberately delayed leaving the room until Nick shrugged off the gown and left. As she was removing her gown, Shaleen said, "Ms. Holley?"

"Yes." Lynn turned back to her.

"I do remember you. You were the one who was here when I said all those things."

Lynn nodded.

"How much did I say?"

Lynn decided the girl deserved the truth. "Not enough to tell me what your real name is, but pretty much everything else."

Shaleen bit her lip. "But Shaleen McGuire *is* my real name."

"I won't argue that point or question you."

"Somehow I knew that, knew you understood. Dr. Dow's been talking to me about how I might not be able to have babies because of what happened. He says it's too early to be certain, but it's possible. I guess he thought I'd be upset."

"You're not upset?" Lynn asked.

Shaleen shook her head. "I never want to have any babies!" The bitterness Lynn heard didn't belong in a child's voice. "What if they were girls?" Her voice broke. "The most terrible thing in the world is to be a girl."

Chapter 13

Arriving home Monday after work, Lynn saw a motorcycle parked near her apartment. She wasn't too surprised to find the biker, still wearing black, inside with Renee, and both were watching an old Kung Fu movie on TV.

"This is Tex," Renee told her.

Tex lifted the hand not holding a beer. "Yo."

Lynn nodded at him. "Did you get a job?" she asked Renee.

"At Harper Hills. I start Wednesday. Luckily the airline found my luggage. They're sending someone down from LA with it in the morning."

By the time Lynn, changed into sweats, emerged from her bedroom, Renee and Tex were gone. So was the motorcycle. When she returned from running, Renee wasn't back yet, so Lynn had the apartment to herself all evening. At ten she went to bed.

Roused by Renee coming in, Lynn checked the time. Three in the morning. She rose and opened her door.

"Relax," Renee said. "I'm alone." The roar of Tex's departing motorcycle punctuated her words.

"Good. I don't want strange men in my apartment overnight."

"I never sleep with a guy on the first date. First I find out if he shoots himself up or swings both ways. Those I get rid of—who wants AIDS? Next I have to decide if I think he'll be any good in bed. Tex—"

"I don't care whether or not Tex passes all your criteria, or if you sleep with him. Just don't invite him to stay overnight as long as you're living with me."

Renee shrugged. "Like I said, you have no sense of adventure. I'll bet you haven't even slept with Nick yet."

Lynn flushed. "Goodnight," she said abruptly. She returned to bed, certain she'd be awake for the rest of the night. Sleep came unexpectedly fast and with it, dreams. . . .

She was naked in a strange place, something like a vast operating room, except that she was outside at the same time. Renee was there, too, winding a rope around Lynn, binding her to a surgical table.

"It's for your own good," Renee said, smiling. "You're only getting what you deserve."

She giggled as she bound Lynn with the rope, each turn tighter than the last. A man wearing a black surgical mask and black cap that hid everything but his eyes roared in on a motorcycle, riding in wide circles around Lynn. Fear surged through Lynn every time he passed in front of her.

When Renee had finished tying the rope, she beckoned to the rider and he leaped off the bike, letting it roar into the darkness. He grasped Renee's hands and they began a slow, courtly dance, their attention fixed on one another, a terrifying sight to Lynn, though she didn't know why.

Suddenly twisting, the man in the mask flung Renee away from him. She sprawled on the tiled floor, blood seeping from her head. He stared at Lynn, darkness where

206

his eyes should be, and took a step toward her. She writhed in vain against her bonds, panic-stricken as he slowly advanced step by step. When he was close enough to touch her, he lifted his hand and she cringed. He ripped off his mask.

Lynn screamed.

She woke with the echo of the scream ringing in her ears. Sitting up, she wrapped her arms around herself, shivering. It was dawn. She was in her own bed, she was safe. But shreds of the nightmare clung, the skull she'd seen under the mask grinned obscenely in her mind.

When she arrived on Five East, she was still thinking about the dream. She put it firmly from her as she began her daily routine by making a quick tour of the unit before the report. Shaleen was still sleeping. Mr. Franklin, as usual, grumbled to her about the night shift. Mrs. Lanigan, due to be discharged, was worrying about how she was going to manage at home.

As Lynn passed the empty private room, she noticed the door was closed. The policy was to leave doors of unused rooms open. She'd glanced at the log and there'd been no new admissions or transfers, so there couldn't be a patient in the room. Curious, she pushed open the door and stepped inside. She froze.

Close to the wall a man and woman stood entwined in a passionate embrace. She recognized Dr. Marlin and Beth. As she tried to decide whether to let well enough alone and back out quietly, Dr. Marlin saw her. He quickly released Beth, who gasped when she noticed Lynn.

"Excuse me, I was making rounds," Lynn said. She turned and almost ran into Sheila.

Sheila's eyes flicked over Beth and Barry Marlin, then fixed on Lynn.

"Mr. O'Hara in 518 wants to see you," she said to Lynn.

By the time Lynn was through talking to Mr. O'Hara, it was time for report. She waited until her staff began their assignments before approaching Beth.

"Don't say a word!" Beth told her defiantly. "I'm not doing anything wrong. Barry's separated from his wife."

"I didn't intend to comment on your private life, but I can't have you mixing it with your nursing duties. Okay?"

"I guess." Beth spoke sullenly.

What was Rolfe going to make of this? Lynn wondered. Not that she'd say a word to anyone. But Sheila, a born troublemaker if ever there was one, certainly wouldn't let it rest. She'd pry everything there was to know from Beth, then make certain Rolfe heard. Lynn had no idea how serious a relationship Beth and Rolfe had. Perhaps he couldn't care less what Beth did, or with whom. Lynn suspected, though, that Rolfe, like most men she knew, was possessive.

Like Nick. He felt it was all right for him to look elsewhere, but she shouldn't. She should be happy she'd discovered his weakness before she'd made a real commitment. She'd be far better off with Tim. He was kind, older, stable, and settled. Tim wouldn't ignore her for the first sexy woman who batted her eyelashes at him.

The day went well enough and the apartment was empty when Lynn returned home from work. Renee was probably with Tex. Didn't he work? Lynn shook her head. That was none of her business. Empty suitcases piled in the hall told her the lost luggage had arrived as promised, and that she'd have to find a place to store them. The apartment was really too small for two women to share.

She was ready when Tim arrived at seven. After some thought, she'd decided on casual attire—a burgundy print skirt with a burgundy cotton sweater trimmed in white. She was happy with her choice when she saw his sport jacket and open-collared shirt.

"I'm a little nervous," he said after he handed her into the Cadillac and slid behind the wheel. "I haven't asked a woman on a date in years. I'm afraid I'm out of practice."

"So far you're doing beautifully."

"My wife Margaret and I met each other in college and went together for years before we got married."

"You must miss her."

"I do. She had leukemia, resistant to all treatment, so we both knew she hadn't long to live. It was sadly ironic that she died of her injuries when a car rammed the ambulance taking her to the hospital." He shook his head. "Margaret was an unusual person. Because of her illness, she did her best to prepare Carol for what had to happen. She even told Carol she hoped I'd marry again and that Carol must try to love her new mother. Imagine."

Lynn wasn't quite certain how to take this. Was it a veiled declaration? Was he suggesting if Carol approved of her that she might be asked to be the new Mrs. Brandon? Or was she imagining far too much?

"How is Carol?" she asked.

"Fine. She wants to know when you're coming to visit again. I had a hard time convincing her it wouldn't be tonight." He smiled at Lynn. "She can't understand why I want to be alone with you."

If only he excited her even the least little bit. She liked Tim, no doubt about it, but the extra awareness, the zing was missing. Maybe when she knew him better. . . .

"Would you prefer I didn't ask you about Nick?" he asked.

209

"He—he's just a friend." It bothered her that her voice quivered slightly. "Nothing serious."

"I had the feeling he wasn't happy about tonight."

Maybe Tim did have a flaw—he wanted everything examined and labeled.

"What Nick thinks makes no difference to me," she said sharply.

"Good." Tim reached over and patted her hand.

"I heard Dr. Marlin was separated from his wife," she said, changing the subject.

Tim glanced at her. "Wilma's had problems. Barry's not easy to live with, I'd imagine. They're taking a break from each other, yes. We all hope they'll get back together."

She got the impression there was a lot he wasn't saying. Still, she'd learned that Beth had told her the truth.

"I was married," she said, "so I understand how problems can divide wives and husbands."

"You're divorced?"

"No, my husband died."

"We have more in common than I thought." His sympathetic look made her feel guilty. Her loss was nothing like his.

Feeling it was time to switch the conversation to something less emotionally loaded, Lynn commented on the beautiful evening. The vagaries of California weather kept them going until Tim parked the car at Long Juan's, a Mexican seafood restaurant.

Once inside, she ordered her usual white wine and was delighted to find abalone on the menu. Medical topics kept them away from the personal throughout the meal—until coffee was served. Tim added cream to his and leaned toward her.

"You do understand I'm serious about you," he said.

Taken aback, she said, "Please, let's not go into that."

"I don't mean to push you, to rush you. But I wanted you to know."

I'd rather not, she thought. She didn't know what to do. Maybe she shouldn't have accepted his invitation to dinner.

He kept his word about not rushing her until they stood outside her door. "About this weekend," he said.

"I have my sister-in-law staying with me," Lynn said hastily. "I don't know what her plans are."

"I thought maybe we could take a boat ride on Saturday afternoon. She's welcome."

"No! I mean, well, I think she gets seasick." Lynn had no idea if this was true or not, but she didn't want Renee along.

"I hope you'll decide to come. Carol's looking forward to seeing you."

"If I can arrange it, I will."

He kissed her. His lips were warm, his embrace comforting. She didn't feel repugnance, but neither did he excite her.

Renee wasn't in the apartment but Lynn heard a motorcycle soon after she went to bed. A few minutes later Renee came in. Lynn didn't relax, though, until the cycle roared off. Those three phone calls had convinced her she couldn't trust Renee.

After agonizing over what to do, she'd decided not to mention the calls. Either Renee would deny she'd made them, or she'd accuse Lynn all over again of being responsible for Ray's death . . . or both.

By Friday, Lynn didn't know how much longer she could stand having Renee in her apartment. She looked forward to going to work every morning because it was eight hours without Renee. Solving problems on the unit seemed a snap compared to dealing with her sister-in-law.

When she arrived on Five East Friday morning, Lynn was confronted by a teary, red-eyed Beth and a sullen Rolfe, the two obviously not speaking. Sheila must have spread the news about Beth and Dr. Marlin. Beth appeared so distracted that Lynn asked her if she was able to work.

"I'm all right," Beth insisted. "Just leave me alone."

For a while Lynn worried about whether she should have insisted Beth go home, but then Rolfe called her attention to a swollen, red, and suppurating area on Mr. Franklin's back and she forgot about Beth. Lynn was so certain the lesion was a staph infection that she started isolation procedures before taking a specimen of the drainage for a C&S and notifying the doctor.

Had someone caring for Shaleen broken technique and carried the staph from her room? Or, since the organism could be airborne, was the new case unavoidable? Whatever the reason, Lynn was sure Mrs. Morrin would blame her.

Mr. O'Hara, still under medication for his lung flukes but cured of his symptoms, had gone home. So had Mrs. Lanigan. Mr. O'Hara's bed hadn't been filled by a new patient, cutting down the unit census. With two rooms now in isolation, it was just as well.

When Lynn went in to see Shaleen, she found her standing by the window. "It's sort of like being in prison," Shaleen said, "not being able to leave my room."

"Your infection—" Lynn began.

"I know that. But I'm well enough to walk around and all now. I wish Dr. Dow'd let me leave."

"Where would you go?" Lynn asked.

"Don't *you* start. That social worker won't leave me alone. I told her I'd see the hospital got paid, but she doesn't believe me, I can tell."

"Ms. Ramses is concerned about *you*, Shaleen. And so am I."

Shaleen turned to face her. "I believe you are, I'm not so sure about Ms. Ramses. I want to get out of this place."

The teenager had refused to tell the social worker anything more than she'd told the admitting office. She didn't live with her parents, she insisted, so there was no point in bringing them into it. She herself had no permanent address.

"Dr. Dow said he'd take out the last tube today," Shaleen said. "I'll be glad to get rid of it. Tubes, ugh!"

Lynn left her, feeling uneasy. Though delighted to see her rapid improvement, the girl's restlessness disturbed her. She had to talk to Nick about her, she decided.

She'd been doing her best to avoid Nick, but a patient's welfare came before personal preferences. When he came by to see Shaleen, she'd corner him.

As of noon Nick still hadn't appeared. Lynn returned from lunch and found Beth at the nurses' station, staring forlornly at a chart. She looked so pale that Lynn asked, "Are you all right?"

Beth burst into tears, sobbing hysterically. Lynn took her into the nurses' lounge to calm her down.

"I made a mistake," Beth sobbed.

Lynn handed Beth a box of tissues. "Everyone makes mistakes."

Beth wiped her eyes. "You'll be mad when you hear."

"Your personal life is not my—"

"It's not personal," Beth said. "It was a medication error. On Barry's patient."

213

Lynn stiffened. "You gave the wrong medicine? When?"

"This morning. To Mrs. Adams." She bit her lip. "I tried to call and tell Barry, but I just couldn't."

Lynn stared at Beth. "You mean Dr. Marlin doesn't know?"

Beth shook her head. "I never did call."

"Is Mrs. Adams all right?"

"I—think so."

"What did you give her?"

"It was only partly my fault. I mean, the evening shift discharged Mrs. Lanigan and they forgot to send her meds home with her, so they were still in the drawer. Mrs. Adams was admitted to that same bed. I guess I wasn't paying attention because I set up the pills Mrs. Lanigan used to take and gave them to Mrs. Adams." Beth blew her nose. "I don't know why."

"Don't start crying again. What meds were they?"

"You remember Mrs. Lanigan had a seizure disorder? She was on phenytoin sodium 100 mg. She took 0.25 mg. digoxin for her heart and 10 mg. prednisone, I guess because of her emphysema."

"That's all you gave?"

"Except for the vitamin complex capsule."

"So Mrs. Adams received phenytoin sodium, digoxin, prednisone, and vitamins that were not ordered by Dr. Marlin. Correct?"

Beth nodded.

"I'll check her immediately," Lynn said. "Wash your face and meet me at the desk."

Mrs. Adams, who'd had a cholecystectomy on Tuesday and had been convalescing normally post-op, was sleeping. She roused when Lynn took her blood pressure and checked her pulse. Her vital signs were unremarkable.

"How do you feel?" Lynn asked her.

Mrs. Adams blinked drowsily. "Pretty good. I'm a little tired today."

"Everything seems fine," Lynn told her. "I'll let you rest now."

At the desk, after checking the patient's chart to make certain she didn't have a known sensitivity to any of the drugs Beth had given her, Lynn called Dr. Marlin. While she was waiting for his office nurse to put her through to him, she handed an incident report form to Beth.

"Start filling this out," she ordered.

Beth bit her lip and reached for her pen.

"Dr. Marlin, this is Ms. Holley on Five East at Harper Hills," Lynn said into the phone. "Your patient, Alice Adams, was given four wrong medications at nine this morning." She listed them. "I've checked her chart and she has no known sensitivity to any drug. She claims to be drowsy, but there are no other apparent ill effects. Her pulse is 70 and her blood pressure 140/80."

"What kind of idiots do you have giving meds up there?" he demanded.

Lynn kept her voice expressionless. "I'm sorry this happened, doctor."

"Give me the nurse's name. I want to know who's responsible. And why the hell, if this happened at nine o'clock, am I just being notified?"

"I called you as soon as I learned of the error."

"The name, damn it!"

"Beth Yadon, RN."

Next to Lynn, Beth whimpered.

There was a short silence on the other end of the phone. "What a stupid little fool," he muttered finally. "Keep me posted about Mrs. Adams." He slammed down the receiver.

"What did he say?" Beth asked.

It wouldn't serve any purpose to tell her. Actually, Lynn had the feeling Dr. Marlin would have been considerably nastier if the nurse had been anybody other than Beth.

"He's upset," Lynn said. "Hurry up with your part of that incident report so I can finish it and get it down to Mrs. Morrin as soon as possible. Bring Mrs. Lanigan's meds to me. And be sure you triple-check any other meds you have to give before the end of the shift."

As she turned away from Beth, Lynn noticed Shaleen's chart lying on the desk.

"Is Dr. Dow here?" she asked Connie.

"Come and gone," Connie said.

She'd missed him and she'd be off for the next two days. Was it important enough to call his office? Lynn shook her head. If she'd caught him on the unit, it wouldn't have been a big deal. But since she really had nothing definite to report, if she placed a call to him just to say she felt uneasy, likely as not he'd think she was using it as an excuse to talk to him. She'd tell him Monday.

Lynn took the incident report to Mrs. Morrin herself, since she wanted to notify the DNS there was a possible new staph infection on the unit. Mrs. Morrin wasn't in, so she stopped by Joyce's office.

"Problems?" Joyce asked.

"The C&S isn't back from the lab yet, but I'm almost positive Mr. Franklin has picked up staph. That'll make two cases on the unit. And Beth made a meds error—here's the form."

Joyce glanced at it and raised her eyebrows.

"Beth's distracted today," Lynn said. "I should have sent her home."

"I'll pass this along to Morrin. You know she hates medication errors. What's the matter with Beth anyway?"

"A mixed-up love life."

"Ah, well, haven't we all. Still, most of us manage to leave it at home when we come to work. Do you think she can learn to or not?"

"She's a new grad. Harper Hills is her first real nursing experience."

"It may be her last if she can't shape up. How's Tim Brandon these days?"

Lynn grinned at Joyce. "I left him at home with the rest of my problems."

"Touché. I'll give you a call on Sunday if you're around. Maybe we can take in that art show, okay?"

"Great."

When Lynn returned to the unit, Connie told her she was to call the administrator.

Reluctantly Lynn picked up the phone.

"Ms. Holley?" He spoke briskly. "If you have a few minutes, please report to my office."

What now? she thought as she rode down to the main floor once more.

"I prefer not to discuss this on the phone," he told her when she was seated across the desk from him. He's gained weight, she thought. Unhealthy flab.

"CMC has extended the salary freeze until the last day of June," he told her, "in order to end their fiscal year with no increase in costs. They assure me there'll be no further extensions. My memo's going out today."

"June! The nurses are never going to accept the extension—or CMC's reason."

"I thought perhaps you might be an ambassador of one and try to—"

"No. Even if I agreed with CMC, and I don't, there's not one nurse at Harper Hills who would listen to me."

He shrugged. "What can the nurses do?"

She opened her mouth to tell him they were organizing and realized she didn't want him to know. Sometime in the last month she'd come down squarely on the side of the nurses. "I think CMC is making a mistake," she said. "A *big* mistake. Can't you tell them that?"

"I don't happen to believe it's a mistake. Waiting until July 1 to discuss wage increases makes a lot of sense."

"Not to me."

"I thought you might have some information on what's been going on with the nursing staff." He gazed directly at her for the first time since she'd come into the office. His eyes looked puffy.

She'd made up her mind and she wasn't going to change it. "Nothing I haven't already mentioned."

"I have the feeling you could tell me more."

She shrugged. "I do appreciate getting advance notice about the extension," she said.

"If you change your mind, my office door is always open."

Lynn returned to the unit disturbed and worried about what was ahead for the hospital. Couldn't Conrad see the problems Harper Hills would face if the nurses decided to fight the extension? Even if most of them simply quit and looked for another job, the hospital would be in chaos. Since there was more demand for nurses than supply, he'd be weeks, perhaps months trying to replace them. Without enough nurses, Harper Hills couldn't function.

She had about all she could take today—thank God it was Friday.

On Saturday morning Lynn rose early. She'd discovered

218

the high school track and had been running there since she'd decided to avoid the beach. When she returned to the apartment, Renee, surprisingly, was up and gone. Usually after a late night—she hadn't gotten in until three—Renee slept until noon.

Tim called while Lynn was having coffee and she agreed to meet him at the marina at two-thirty to go boating. Renee came in as she hung up.

"That Nick," she said. "He's such a tease."

Lynn stiffened at the mention of Nick's name. She'd heard the motorcycle last night, so she knew Renee had been with Tex, not Nick. So when had Renee seen Nick?

"Nick came by this morning to ask me if I wanted to have breakfast with him." Renee smiled. "He actually got me out of bed. What a hunk." Widening her eyes at Lynn, she added, "I hope you don't mind me dating him."

"Why should I?"

"I had the feeling there was something between the two of you. I certainly wouldn't want to be the cause of—"

"I told you, Nick and I are friends. Like Tim Brandon and me." Despite her effort to sound casual, Lynn couldn't avoid the stiffness in her voice.

Renee's sly look suggested she wasn't fooled. "Whatever you say," she told Lynn.

I've got to get rid of her, Lynn thought. I can't stand her needling. And how can I bear it if she's going to start seeing Nick?

"You mentioned you were working in a bank in Worcester," she said. "Shouldn't they be sending you a severance check soon?"

"I guess. Those things take time." Renee stretched and yawned. "I've been meaning to tell you—I found some pictures when I unpacked and I want to show them to you.

They're of Ray. I took them when he came to visit me the last time, the last time I ever saw him."

"I'd rather not look at them, thanks."

Renee's mouth drooped. "You can be so cruel. He used to tell me, but I never believed him until you drove him to his death. Cruel, cruel ... you don't even want to see a picture of poor Ray."

Goaded beyond endurance, Lynn snapped. "I believe you have some tape recordings of him as well. Why don't you ask me if I'd like to hear those?"

"I haven't the slightest idea what you're talking about."

"Oh yes you do. Why don't you just leave me alone, Renee? Ray's dead. Whatever you do, you can't bring him back."

"He'd be alive right this minute if he'd never met you!" Renee cried. "You killed him."

"Ray committed suicide. That's the official verdict and the truth."

"It may be the verdict, but it's not the truth. Admit it. What happened was your fault. You're guilty of Ray's death and I'll never rest until you get punished like you deserve."

Chapter 14

"Punishment?" Lynn glared at Renee. "What do you think I went through after Ray's death?"

"You're still alive, aren't you?" Renee demanded. "He isn't. He's—"

The ring of the phone cut into her words, and Lynn, welcoming the interruption, picked it up.

"Thank God you're home!" Sheila's voice shook so badly Lynn scarcely understood her.

"What's the matter, Sheila?"

"It's Justin. He—he's tried to kill me."

Lynn's stomach knotted in apprehension. "Where are you now?"

"At a pay phone. I don't dare go home." Sheila's voice broke. "I don't know what to do."

"The police—"

"No! I can't, I just can't," Sheila sobbed. "You don't understand."

I understand perfectly, Lynn thought. You can't imagine how well I understand. "Tell me where you are," she said. "I'll come by and pick you up."

As she drove away from the apartment, Lynn wondered

221

why Sheila had called her instead of someone else. They certainly weren't close friends. Not even *friends,* really. But she couldn't ignore Sheila's cry for help. When she'd been desperate back in Boston, no one had offered her a helping hand. Would tragedy have been averted if someone had?

Lynn, unfamiliar with the area, had trouble finding the cross streets Sheila'd named, but finally she located Sheila standing on a corner, waving frantically.

"I'm lucky to be alive," Sheila said breathlessly as she slid into the car.

"What happened?"

Sheila's hand flew to her throat. "He got mad because I forgot to buy milk and he wanted some for his coffee. He yelled at me and hit me and then he—he grabbed my throat and squeezed. Just before I blacked out I managed to knee him in the balls. He yelled and let me go. I grabbed my purse and ran. I was scared to death he'd come after me, but I guess he hurt too much." Tears overflowed and ran down her cheeks. "Over a lousy quart of milk."

"Justin's dangerous. *Anything* might set him off."

"All my stuff's in the condo," Sheila wailed. "I'm afraid to go after it. What am I going to do? I have nowhere to turn."

"You can stay with me for the time being." Lynn heard her words with dismay. But what else could she say? "My sister-in-law's in the extra bedroom, so we'll be a bit crowded."

Sheila blew her nose and wiped her eyes. "Thanks. I'll come, even if I can't believe you really want me staying there. What you need is a T-shirt with 'Martyr' printed across the front."

The way she felt at the moment, Lynn decided Sheila

222

was right. The combination of Renee and Sheila might well be more than she could handle.

"I have to get some of my things," Sheila said. "I'm supposed to work tomorrow." She glanced down at her jeans and sweatshirt. "Morrin certainly wouldn't approve of this uniform." She started to laugh, but it changed to a sob. "Oh, Lynn, it was awful. I'm afraid of him, I can't ever go back—"

"If you went to the police—"

"I told you, I can't. They'd put him in jail."

"I don't think so. Not if you explained what happened and said you didn't want to file a complaint, but needed protection to return and collect your belongings. They'd probably send a man with you—"

"No cops. No way. Justin's on something. Not coke or heroin, I think he takes whatever it is from the pharmacy where he works. A cop'd spot he was on something for sure and bust him."

"That might be the best thing that could happen to Justin."

Sheila shook her head.

"Then how are you going to pick up your things?" Lynn asked.

"I thought you might ask Nick to come with me."

"I can't."

"Please, Lynn . . . Nick won't mind."

"Nick and I aren't on the best of terms. Even if we were, I wouldn't—" She paused as an idea struck her. "I may be able to come up with the right man, though. My sister-in-law's friendly with a biker. Tex is pure black-leather macho. Believe me, if anyone can intimidate Justin, Tex is my choice."

Renee was enthusiastic about Tex helping Sheila. Tex,

when she called him, agreed to come over and see what he could do.

"Doesn't Tex work?" Lynn asked, then could have bitten her tongue. It was none of her business.

"He doesn't have regular hours, he's some kind of salesman," Renee said.

Lynn kept her mouth shut. If Tex dealt drugs, as certainly was possible, she didn't want to know. All the same, as she drove to the yacht basin to meet Tim, she found herself worrying over what could happen to Renee if Tex really was involved in drug dealing.

The boat ride with Tim seemed anticlimatic after all the earlier carrying on. Lynn told him about Sheila's problem. "So now I have both Sheila and Renee sharing my apartment," she added.

"Tex sounds like quite a character. And Justin's bad news." Tim shook his head. "I hope you don't get yourself in any trouble on Sheila's account."

"I don't think Justin will bother her now that she's gone. He didn't when she stayed with me before."

"But he's on addictive drugs. I can testify that a man's far from reasonable when he takes any mind-altering medication."

"I'm not worried."

"Perhaps you should be."

She smiled at Tim. "It's nice of you to be concerned. But you did surprise me today. I thought Carol would be with us."

"She had a dancing lesson. Margaret felt a girl needs the discipline ballet provides."

"Does Carol enjoy ballet?"

"Actually, she hates it. But I feel Margaret knew best."

Lynn's strong feeling that Carol ought to have some

choice went unsaid. Her opinion would weigh little against that of Carol's dead mother. Quite possibly that would be the way of it if she ever married Tim, and no one could prevail against the dead.

Not that he'd asked her to marry him. If he did, she wasn't at all sure she'd accept. His kindness and stability might be a plus, but there was no electricity between them ... at least, not on her part. And would it be fair to either of them if she agreed to marry him knowing she wasn't in love with him?

When they said good-bye later that evening, Lynn agreed to have dinner with him again on Wednesday, then had second thoughts. She would have to start being up front with Tim. He had more or less declared his intentions. Either he wanted to marry her or he wanted an affair, and she didn't care for either alternative and would have to say so. If he still asked to date her, at least he knew where she stood.

On the way to her apartment, Lynn, realizing she'd forgotten to pick up the day's mail, unlocked her box and scooped up the contents. When she entered the apartment, she found Sheila's boxes still piled in the foyer and living room.

"I know it's a mess," Sheila said from the couch, "but I couldn't store much in Renee's room. Her stuff takes up most of the space in there."

Lynn nodded, sorting through the mail. The usual Saturday junk, mostly occupant ads except for a letter addressed to Renee from the Worcester Marine Bank. Lynn set it aside and disposed of the rest.

"Tex and Renee went out," Sheila added. "I sort of think, I mean, he did me a favor and all, and she *is* your sister-in-law—" she paused and looked down at her hands. "Maybe I shouldn't say anything."

Lynn sat in the wicker chair next to the couch and waited, aware Sheila wouldn't be able to resist spilling whatever bad news she had.

"I may be wrong, but it looks to me like he's giving her something," Sheila went on.

Lynn blinked. "Drugs, you mean?"

Sheila nodded. "I don't object to the odd toke of pot, but there I draw the line. Maybe she's only on amphetamines, not the really hard stuff. She's got a right to ruin her health, who cares? What worries me is how much of a pusher Tex is. Like, are the cops trailing him to this apartment?"

Lynn grimaced. Trouble always followed Renee. "I suspected Tex, but I didn't realize Renee was taking drugs."

"I could be wrong."

Sheila was probably right. It might explain Renee's outbursts, and those dreadful telephone calls before she flew to California.

"I'll talk to her," Lynn promised.

"I hear you're dating Tim Brandon," Sheila said. "Did you and Nick split up for good?"

Lynn stiffened, then managed a shrug. "I don't date any one man exclusively." She rose. "I think I'll curl up in bed with a book. Goodnight."

"You won't get much satisfaction in bed from a book," Sheila said. "I'd prefer either Nick or Tim."

Lynn turned to look at her. "You might. I've been told my problem is that I have no sense of adventure." Leaving Sheila staring after her, she strode down the hall to her bedroom. Finally, she'd beaten Sheila at her own game. *She'd* gotten in the last word.

Was she too cautious? she asked herself as she undressed. Too much a stiff and proper Bostonian? Remembering the moments in Nick's arms, she sighed. Given the

226

choice, she'd rather have Nick in her bed over a book any day. Maybe she ought to call him up and say so. How surprised he'd be!

But would he respond to her proposition? Lynn closed her eyes, picturing him here with her, in her bed. She and Nick, nothing between them, his hands touching her, caressing her.

She opened her eyes. Yes, and Sheila sleeping on the couch in the living room, and Renee in the other bedroom. No, she could never invite Nick here with them sharing her apartment. Sadly, Lynn shook her head. Even if she was alone in this apartment, she couldn't call him. Maybe she was too proper, but there didn't seem to be anything she could do about it.

On Sunday, knowing Joyce was coming by for her at twelve-thirty, Lynn waited impatiently for Renee to get up. At noon she finally knocked on the bedroom door and went in. Renee raised herself on one elbow, yawning.

"Did you find your letter from the Worcester bank?" Lynn asked.

Renee sat up, her gaze wary. "Yeah."

"Was it a check?"

Renee's eyes widened. "My, aren't we nosy?"

"Was it?"

"Since you insist, yes."

"Good. I know you needed the money. I have another question. Are you taking drugs?"

"My God, what is this? An inquisition?"

"*Are* you?"

"*She* put that idea in your head, I'll bet." Renee nodded toward the door.

"You haven't answered my question."

"No, I don't take drugs!"

"Does that include uppers?"

"What's wrong with popping an upper now and then? They're not really drugs."

"Amphetamines are addictive ... and dangerous. I'd watch it, Renee."

"Thanks for the unsolicited advice. I'm not a child, I know what I'm doing." Renee's voice shook with fury. "If you're finished with the lecture, I'd like to get dressed."

"I have more to say. I told you when you came here that I wanted you out of my apartment as soon as you could afford another place. With your severance pay, I'm sure you can. I'll expect you to leave by Wednesday."

Rage distorted Renee's features. "You bitch!" she snarled.

Lynn stood her ground. "I'm not turning you penniless into the streets. You have money, you have a job. You've done your best to make me miserable ever since you arrived in town. Why shouldn't I ask you to leave?"

"You'll be sorry. I'll go to Nick, that's what I'll do. He offered to help me if ever I needed it. How will you feel when I'm living in his condo with him?"

"Better than I feel with you living with me." Lynn was amazed at how calm she sounded when distaste and anger burned through her like acid. If Nick took Renee in, there was nothing she could do about it except be devastated. But she was damned if she'd change her mind.

"Wednesday," she repeated, then turned and left the room, closing the door behind her. Something thunked against the wood, making her jump. Renee had thrown more than a tantrum.

Sheila, in the kitchen making a fresh pot of coffee, raised her eyebrows. "From what I heard of her shouting, I guess you told Renee to get out. Am I next?"

"Not yet." Lynn was in no mood to be diplomatic.

Sheila half-smiled. "Not if I behave myself, huh, warden?"

"Sheila—"

"Never mind, I don't plan to stick around any longer than I have to, okay? And when I do leave, I promise not to move in with Nick."

Lynn stomped from the apartment, telling herself she would never, ever, no matter how desperate the person might be, take anyone into her home again.

"You look mad enough to spit bullets," Joyce said as Lynn slid into the passenger seat of the Porsche.

"I thought it was nails," Lynn said, momentarily distracted.

Joyce shrugged. "Not these days. What's the matter?"

"Would you believe I have Sheila back with me?"

"Along with your sister-in-law?" Joyce shook her head. "Honey, didn't your mama ever tell you it's all right to say no to girls as well as boys?"

"Justin tried to kill Sheila. She couldn't go home—what could I do?"

"Seems to me you're inviting trouble."

"I don't want to think about either Sheila or Renee for the rest of the day."

"Suits me. Shall we discuss Art with a capital A?"

"Go ahead. I'll listen."

"No way. I'm taking in the art show solely because I like to look at what people paint. Nothing says I have to understand what I see."

Lynn, relaxing as she always did in Joyce's company, glanced at her friend. Sunlight glittered off the metallic threads of Joyce's copper jumpsuit. "The way you look in that jumpsuit ought to distract more than a few art lovers."

Joyce grinned at her. "A girl always hopes."

The outdoor exhibit was at Hillside Park, part of a new development nestled in the hills on the other side of the freeway from El Doblez. They found the parking area crowded, and Joyce had to leave the Porsche some distance from the show. As the two women walked past a large white van, Lynn noted its logo.

"TV coverage, yet," she said, nudging Joyce and nodding at the van.

"Doesn't surprise me Channel 23's picking up on it. I've seen some pretty wild stuff here—artwise, I mean. Who knows if it's good, but it sure attracts attention."

After viewing a dozen paintings, Lynn saw Joyce's point. Color predominated on most canvasses—bold slashes, thick layers, violent contrasts. She stopped by a huge painting, the canvas taller than she was. Gold, copper, rust, and yellow swirled across it in a riot of color.

"This one must have been done with you in mind, Joyce." she said. "You should stand next to the picture in a live display, like those paintings in New York where a person is a part of the art."

"Great idea," a man's voice answered.

Lynn whirled around. A tall, thin man with prematurely gray hair smiled at her. He looked vaguely familiar.

"If you'd introduce me to your friend," he said to Lynn, "I'd ask her to pose with the picture." He motioned to someone Lynn couldn't see.

Lynn glanced at Joyce.

"I don't need to be introduced to you, Mr. Stuart," Joyce told him.

Stuart? Lynn wondered and then recognized him. Of course, he was Hal Stuart, anchorman on Channel 23.

"You have the advantage," Hal told Joyce, bowing slightly.

Still lounging against a wrought-iron fence, Joyce

smiled. "And that happens so seldom," she murmured. "Men usually take advantage."

"Are you a professional model?" he asked, apparently not put off by her reply.

"I'm Joyce Elkins, RN." As she spoke a man pushed through the gathering crowd with a video camera. Other men carrying equipment followed him.

"Will you pose with the picture, Ms. Elkins?" Hal asked. "And give us an interview afterward?"

"Only if you find another painting suitable for my friend to pose with," Joyce said.

Lynn shook her head, but Joyce grinned unrepentantly.

Hal glanced at Lynn, nodded, and turned back to Joyce. "If you'd refused, she'd have been my second choice anyway. It's a deal."

Lynn watched, fascinated, as Hal positioned Joyce in front of the picture so that it appeared for a moment that she was part of the painting. The cameraman moved in as Hal began talking.

"What do you think of the painting, Joyce?" Hal asked after mentioning both the artist's name and hers.

"It swept me off my feet." Joyce said. "Up, up and away."

She responded as easily to his other questions, apparently unperturbed by the camera and the gawking crowd. Later, when Lynn took her turn in front of a picture—a seascape in blues and greens—she tried to emulate Joyce's ease, but found herself unable to act naturally with the camera focused on her and so many eyes staring at her.

"That was fun," Joyce said after the TV crew had left.

"For you, maybe," Lynn countered. "I got uptight."

"Why? If all those couch potatoes out there don't like us, who cares?"

"You're a natural at performing. I'm not."

"Funny—Hal said the same thing. That I was a natural. And what the hell was I doing wasting my time in nursing. And also could he call me."

"Did you give him your number?"

"Why not? Didn't the man tell me I had the advantage?" Joyce's secret smile convinced Lynn her friend wasn't at all adverse to seeing Hal Stuart again. "Anyway, girl, you and me, we were famous for five minutes." Joyce added. "How about that?"

When she arrived at the hospital on Monday, her five minutes of fame behind her, Lynn found a note clipped to her time card. Mrs. Morrin wanted to see her immediately. What a great way to begin the work week.

"I can't understand the delay in reporting this medication error," Mrs. Morrin said. "Can you explain what took so long?"

"I reported it as soon as I was notified. Beth—Ms. Yadon—panicked when she realized what she'd done. She wasn't feeling well, which may have been a factor both in making the error and in her tardy report to me."

"I don't find that an acceptable excuse for the delay."

Lynn added nothing more. What was there to say?

"In your opinion, should I ask Ms. Yadon to leave Harper Hills?" the DNS asked.

The question startled Lynn. "Well, I—no, I don't think so. She came here as a new graduate without much clinical experience. I've found her willing and quick to learn."

"We are not running a nursing school."

Don't respond, Lynn warned herself. Don't get drawn into an argument, she's a past master, she can beat you with one hand tied behind her. Look interested and wait.

"Ms. Yadon, if she stays, will obviously need close supervision," Mrs. Morrin said. "Are you willing to provide this?"

Back in my court, Lynn thought, admiring Mrs. Morrin's expertise. "I'll do my best," she said.

"I hope so. As to the staph infections, if there's a third case of staph on your unit, I'll have to consider quarantine for Five East. That would inconvenience everyone."

In other words, Lynn thought as she left the office, Morrin expected her to stop the spread of staph. She intended to review everyone's isolation technique all over again and make certain the other two shifts followed suit, but Morrin was asking too much. What was Lynn supposed to do about airborne staph? Sterilize the air everyone breathed?

She also wondered why she'd gone to bat for Beth. Beth did master procedures easily enough if she was forced to, but "willing and quick to learn" was stretching the truth. Still, with more experience, she'd make a fair-to-middling nurse. An average nurse. One plus—Beth was honest. She could have kept her mouth shut about the medication error and no one would ever have known.

When Lynn was through with the report and had finished her heart-to-heart talk with Beth, she went in to see Shaleen.

"I'm not staying here much longer," the girl said. "I can't stand it."

"What did Dr. Dow say?"

"This weekend, maybe. If I had a place to go. If I gave him the address and promised to come into the office for a follow-up."

"You don't agree?"

Shaleen scowled. "What's to stop me from just walking out of here?"

"Your own good sense. Dr. Dow doesn't think you're well enough yet, and neither do I."

Shaleen sighed and turned away.

About to leave the room, Lynn stopped. "I want you to write down my home phone number, okay? You can call me any time you need to talk. If I'm not in, leave a message."

After Shaleen had taken the number, Lynn hesitated. "Please don't do anything foolish," she urged. "I care what happens to you, and so does Dr. Dow."

"I know." Shaleen's voice was sullen. "But you don't understand."

Nobody thought she understood. Lynn just wished she understood her own problems half as well as she did other people's. But the problem of Shaleen was as much Nick's as it was hers, and she'd put off talking to him long enough.

She watched for Nick and managed to intercept him before he went in to see Shaleen. "I'm worried about her," she told him. "I'm afraid she may just up and leave when no one's looking. I called the social worker about it and asked her to see Shaleen again, but I don't think Shaleen trusts Ms. Ramses and she may lie to her. You're the one Shaleen has the most confidence in."

"I'll talk to Shaleen, but if she decides to take off, no one can stop her."

"If only she'd tell me what's bothering her!"

"None of us are any too good at that, are we?"

Taken aback, Lynn stared at him.

He shrugged, dismissing it. "I saw you on TV Sunday. Interesting picture."

Pulling herself together, she said, "The seascape? Yes, I liked it."

"Even without you, the painting's not bad."

She couldn't think of a reply. He said nothing more. Yet neither moved. What went wrong? she wanted to ask, fighting her urge to touch him.

Give her a break, Dow, Nick told himself. Tim Brandon's intentions are one hell of a lot more honorable than yours. He needs a wife to take care of that little girl of his, and he'll ask Lynn to marry him. You know damn well you have no such idea in mind.

That didn't stop him from wanting her. Or make it any easier for him to think about Tim touching her, holding her, making love to her.

He'd actually begun to trust Lynn, to believe she was as honest and straightforward as she seemed. No woman was. He should have known better. He didn't know how much of what Renee said he could believe, but she'd dropped enough hints to make him think there'd been something fishy going on in Lynn's marriage. Had she cheated on her husband?

When he'd left for Baja, he'd never thought he'd come back to find Lynn had been dating Brandon while he was gone. It'd been a shock when Lloyd Linnett had told him, and he'd been enraged, both at Brandon and at Lynn. He understood now why a man killed when he found his wife with another man.

But Lynn wasn't his wife. She had never vowed to be true to him and him alone. Never. And he had promised her absolutely nothing. So, okay, Dow, walk away, he told himself.

Instead he said, "We need to talk, Lynn."

"Do we?" Her voice was cool.

He put his hand on her arm, and the feel of her warm skin made him ache to hold her. Her sharp intake of breath told him she wasn't immune to him. She reacted as strongly as he did to the current that flowed between them. Scientists might not be able to measure that intangible flow, but he could testify it damn well existed, whether a man willed it or not.

"Not here," he said. "Not now. When can I call you and not get that damned answering machine?"

"Sheila's at the apartment again. Justin tried to kill her."

"Sheila *and* Renee? Quite a houseful."

"Renee's leaving." For some reason the chill had come back into her voice. "I thought you'd know that by now."

"Why should I?"

Lynn shrugged. "I really must get back to the desk."

"Not until you promise you'll meet me on the beach at dawn tomorrow."

She frowned and his fingers tightened on her arm.

"I'll be there," she said finally.

He let her go and watched her walk away from him. Dow, you're a dog in the manger, he told himself. But no, that wasn't true ... unlike the dog with the hay, he *did* want Lynn. He had to have her, the craving ran marrow-deep. His only problem was that he wasn't going to marry her.

Chapter 15

Lynn glanced from her bedroom window early Tuesday morning to see gray tendrils of mist brushing against the glass as if seeking entrance. Fog wouldn't discourage Nick, and she'd promised to meet him on the beach before she went to work. They'd probably be the only ones crazy enough to attempt jogging on the beach in the fog, so they'd be alone. She couldn't deny how much she looked forward to being alone with him.

She dressed hurriedly and left the apartment. As she neared the ocean, the fog grew steadily thicker until she wondered if she'd be able to find Nick. The dense gray blanket, hiding familiar landmarks from view, made her nervous, and she bit back a startled cry when an indistinct figure appeared in front of her.

"Nick!" she cried. "You scared me."

"I thought I'd better come to meet you so we wouldn't miss each other." He reached for her hand. "Better hold on, I don't want to lose you."

"We can't jog in this," she protested.

"My feeling exactly. If you weren't running a home for wayward girls, we could—"

"Renee moved out last night."

"Oh? Where'd she go?"

"Her biker friend, Tex, borrowed a pickup and helped her with her things. I hope she isn't staying with Tex because I don't trust him." Lynn looked steadily at Nick. "What Renee told me she was going to do is move in with you."

"You've got to be kidding."

Lynn shrugged.

"My place is for me," he said tersely. "I don't take in roomies, male or female."

"You're a real loner."

"Lo, the lonesome Indian. I prefer my way to yours. Sheila's still camping at your apartment, I take it."

"Even if she wasn't, I would have agreed to meet you on neutral territory."

"We could at least get off the sidewalk," he said, pulling her with him as he groped through the grayness. "As I recall, there's a neutral bench over this way."

They found the bench by stumbling against it. "I can't stay long," she reminded him as they sat down.

"You never stay long enough. How serious is this business with Brandon?"

Lynn took a deep breath. "I don't know."

Taking her none too gently by the shoulders, he turned her so she was facing him. "Look at me and tell me you don't know."

"If you mean has he asked me to marry him, no."

"I mean what are you going to say if he does?"

"Why do you think that's any of your business?"

"This is why." He bent his head and kissed her, a hungry, demanding kiss that told her more clearly than words just how much he wanted her.

She knew her response told him as much and more.

Nick pulled her onto his lap, cuddling her up against him. "I'm not going to ask you to marry me," he said, his lips centimeters away from hers, "but we sure as hell have to do something about what's between us." He kissed her again.

"What do we have to do?" she murmured when she could speak. She felt drunk with desire.

"We'll think of something. I know damn well Brandon doesn't make you feel this way."

"Egotist."

He pinched her bottom and she yelped, trying to slide away from him. His kiss stopped her.

"Nick, I'm going to be late for work," she protested breathlessly.

He eased her off his lap and stood up, pulling her to her feet. "I'll walk you home. Tonight's no good, I've got two meetings, one in LA. Tomorrow—"

"I promised Tim I'd have dinner with him tomorrow."

"Unpromise."

"No. But I've made up my mind to tell him I'm not what he's looking for."

He squeezed her hand. "My sweet Lynn, you're exactly what every man is looking for."

"I think Tim wants a wife. I'm not the right person."

"I don't like the idea of you having dinner with him."

Lynn took a deep breath. "Remember the night in the restaurant when I left and you stayed with Renee? I was reminded then that I didn't own you, that you were free to do whatever you wished with whomever you wished. Well, you don't own me either, Nick. I think Tim deserves to hear the the truth from me, and I mean to tell him tomorrow night, when I have dinner with him."

Nick muttered something under his breath. "So Wednesday night's out. Thursday night's too chancy—I'm taking call for Lloyd, and he's got three overdue mamas, one of whom I may have to section. That gets us to Friday." He stopped and grasped her other hand so he was holding both. His dark eyes held hers. "My dear Ms. Holley, will you do me the honor of having dinner at my place on Friday evening?"

Lynn drew in her breath, well aware of what was not being asked but was taken for granted. "Dr. Dow," she said, "I can hardly wait."

He clasped her to him, both of them laughing for no reason at all. His beeper pinged.

Releasing Lynn, he unhooked the beeper and said, "What is it?"

"Call Harper Hills, Five East, *stat.*"

Lynn froze. Shaleen was Nick's only patient on Five East. "We're almost to my apartment," she said. "You can use my phone." They ran the rest of the way through the thinning fog.

"Shaleen took off," Nick said after he hung up the phone. "The night charge checked her at two and she was in bed. At six she wasn't. She isn't anywhere on the unit or, apparently, in the hospital."

Lynn bit her lip. "Ms. Ramses assured me Shaleen had no intention of leaving the hospital until Dr. Dow said she could. I should have suspected Shaleen was lying to her. Nick, that poor girl has nowhere to go!"

"Some guy brought her into the ER, don't forget."

"And dumped her."

"She was sick then. Half-dead. The guy might be willing to help her now that she's on her feet again."

Lynn shook her head. "Shaleen was scared and worried, and she wouldn't say why. I'm afraid something terrible may happen to her."

"I'm upset too, Lynn, but look at it this way ... we

240

tried the best we knew to help her and she wouldn't let us." He kissed her quickly. "I've got to run."

After Nick left, she hastily donned her uniform and ate a croissant with a cup of the coffee she'd left brewing. Sheila, dressed in her uniform, ambled into the kitchen before she finished.

"I know you went to bed alone," she told Lynn, "but I could swear I heard Nick's voice a few minutes ago."

"He got a call on his beeper and came in to use the phone."

"Just happened to be in the neighborhood, I suppose."

"The call was bad news. Shaleen took off and they can't find her." Lynn glanced at her watch. "If you want to ride to work with me, you'd better grab something to eat in a hurry."

Five East was still unsettled because of Shaleen's unscheduled departure, staff and patients alike, and it was after ten before things settled down.

"Do you think the judge came and kidnaped her?" Beth asked Lynn. "I mean, maybe he was afraid she'd tell what he'd done to her and who he really is."

"How would he find her if she wasn't using her real name? Shaleen wasn't kidnaped by the judge or anyone else. She left of her own accord."

"The poor kid. I really feel for her, you know? It's terrible when you have nowhere to turn. It's exactly how I feel sometimes." Her eyes began tearing.

"Stop it!" Lynn ordered. "You'll be making more mistakes if you don't."

Beth's eyes widened at her sharp tone, the tears drying.

"You know Mrs. Morrin won't give you another

241

chance," Lynn pointed out. "Life can be tough sometimes, but save feeling sorry for yourself for your time off."

As she went about her duties, Lynn continued to think about what Beth had said about the judge. She didn't believe for a moment he'd kidnaped his daughter, but Lynn did wonder if Shaleen had feared he might discover where she was if she stayed in one place too long, and that was why she'd fled.

The day passed without any new crises on Five East, or in Lynn's private life, once she was off duty. Though she hoped Shaleen might call her, the phone didn't ring.

Wednesday morning, housekeeping having thoroughly scrubbed and disinfected the private room Shaleen had been in, a new patient was admitted there, Angela McDonald. Lynn thought the unusually attractive brunette looked familiar, but she couldn't place her.

Ms. McDonald, fifty-eight, had suffered a CVA, a cerebrovascular accident or stroke, the day before and was admitted to the ICU for observation. Because the ICU needed her bed and she was stable, she was sent to Five East. She had incomplete hemiparesis of her left side, with slurred speech. Her primary doctor was Tim Brandon, but she had a bevy of consultants listed on the chart—from neurologist to rehab specialist. She also had private nurses around the clock. Lynn thought she'd seen her somewhere before, but with the right side of the patient's face sagging from paralysis, Lynn couldn't be certain.

Sheila had an early lunch and when she came back to the unit she brought the latest report from the grapevine. Angela McDonald was actually Revina Radison, the movie star, and nobody, but nobody, was supposed to know she was a patient at Harper Hills. No wonder she'd looked familiar.

"Everyone's aware of who she is," Lynn told Tim as he leafed through Ms. McDonald's chart at the desk. "You can't keep any secrets from the Harper Hills grapevine. How do you happen to be her doctor?"

"I'm just a flunky, what with all those fast-lane specialists being flown in to see her, but believe it or not, I used to know Angela—that's really her first name—when we both were teenagers. My older brother used to date her in high school. She was the prettiest girl I ever saw."

"She's still a beautiful woman."

"Not in her eyes. Angela's convinced the stroke has turned her into an ugly old witch. She wants to die."

"But she's doing very well," Lynn said. "She can lift her left leg. With therapy she'll be walking again, and the facial paralysis usually improves."

"You try convincing her. *I* can't. Maybe one of the super-specialists will be able to but I doubt it. According to my brother, she was the most stubborn girl he'd ever met and she hasn't changed."

Wednesday evening, Lynn was dressing for her date with Tim when the doorbell rang, peal after peal, as though someone had a finger glued to the button. "Can you get that?" she called to Sheila, hastily buttoning her blouse and tucking it into her shirt.

A moment later she heard the door slam open. Sheila screamed. Lynn dashed out of the bedroom only to duck back as Sheila raced past her to the bathroom. Sheila shut the bathroom door with a bang and clicked the lock. Before Lynn could gather her wits, Justin shoved her aside and began pounding on the bathroom door.

"Open up, you bitch, or I'll kill you!" he shouted.

"Go away, you bastard," Sheila called from the other side of the door. "Get lost!"

Justin responded by kicking the door. A panel splintered under his heavy boots and Sheila shrieked with fear.

"Kill you, I'm gonna kill you," Justin chanted in rhythm with his repeated kicks. More wood splintered.

He means it, Lynn told herself. Jolted, she realized it was up to her to stop him. How? Certainly not by talking. She eased into the kitchen and looked around. Hanging on the wall next to the stove was the small red cylinder that had come with the apartment; a foam fire extinguisher for putting out grease fires. Lynn yanked it off the hook and read the instructions as fast as she could.

By the time she came into the hall again, Justin's kicks had smashed the lower portion of the bathroom door and he was stooping over, reaching through to unlock the door. Lynn ran up behind him.

"Justin!" she shouted, aiming the nozzle of the cylinder.

He whirled around and she pulled the lever releasing the foam. White suds shot out, coating his face and dripping onto the floor. He screamed, clawing at his eyes and staggering away from the bathroom door. Lynn followed him, shooting the foam at his face. Behind her, she heard a scrabbling and hoped it was Sheila freeing herself.

"Lynn!" Tim's voice. "My God!"

"Call the police!" she ordered. "*Hurry.*"

Justin collapsed onto the hall floor, moaning and digging at his eyes.

By the time the police arrived, Tim had belted Justin's hands together behind his back and wiped the foam from his face and was squirting ophthalmic ointment from his emergency kit into Justin's eyes. Lynn was doing her best to calm the hysterically sobbing Sheila.

Since Sheila wasn't able to, Lynn explained to the police what had happened.

"Will you be preferring charges?" the older one asked, looking from Sheila to Lynn.

Lynn nodded.

Sheila turned her tear-stained face toward him. "Yes," she sobbed. "Yes."

They untied a thoroughly subdued Justin and led him away. "He'll be out on bail before morning," Tim predicted. "It's not safe for either of you to stay in this apartment. I suggest you come home with me, at least for tonight. Or longer."

Sheila mopped her wet face and drew a long, shuddering breath. "That's kind of you, Dr. Brandon. I'd be scared to death to stay here."

"I'm not," Lynn said. "There's nothing wrong with the outside door, and it's not flimsy like the room doors. Justin can't get inside unless we let him in."

"I'm afraid," Sheila quavered.

Tim sat beside her on the couch and patted her shoulder. "You'll be safe at my house." Sheila leaned against him and began to cry again. His arm went around her. "I think you'd better come too, Lynn," he said.

She shook her head. "I appreciate the offer, but I'm not Justin's wife; he's not out to get me. I doubt if he'll return tonight anyway. You go ahead and take Sheila with you. I'll pack some of her things."

Tim urged her to reconsider, but nothing he said convinced her she wasn't safe behind her own locked door.

"You're as stubborn as Angela McDonald," he said finally, sounding peeved.

Neither of them remembered their date until Tim was leaving with Sheila.

"We'll take a rain check on that dinner," Tim said.

Lynn nodded.

Alone in the apartment, she wondered if she should have gone with Tim and Sheila. She wasn't actually frightened, but it wasn't exactly pleasant being all alone after what had happened.

She'd call Nick, surprise him.

She got his answering machine and decided not to leave a message. At two in the morning she was still awake. The phone rang and she stumbled into the living room to answer it.

"This is Shaleen."

"Where are you?" Lynn cried. "I've been terribly worried. Are you all right?"

"I'm okay. For now."

"Do you need help?"

"No. Why I'm calling—I used my instant teller bank card. It's really his money—you know who I mean—and I wouldn't touch it, except I figured it's only fair he should pay the hospital and Dr. Dow. I could see Dr. Dow likes you and you like him, so I figured you'd tell him for me that I'm sending him all the money and he can give the rest to the hospital after he takes out what he's owed. Okay?"

"I'll make sure Dr. Dow gets the message. But I wish I knew where you're staying. I'd like to see you."

"I can't take any chances. He's got private detectives looking for me. If they trace where I used the card, they'll come snooping around. I trust you, sort of, but I can't tell you where I am."

"At least promise to keep in touch."

"Okay." Before Lynn could say anything more, Shaleen hung up.

When the alarm buzzed at quarter to six, Lynn felt she hadn't been asleep more than fifteen minutes. She arrived on Five East feeling only half-awake and found the night charge, Laurel Lamont, arguing with Angela McDonald's private duty day nurse about where the patient's medications should be kept.

Lynn entered the fray. "As day charge, I supervise the three shifts on Five East," she said firmly. "At all times, every medication on my unit will be stored on the med carts. Narcotics and other specified drugs will be kept in the locked drawer of the cart."

"But I was told we could keep Ms. McDonald's meds in her room," Bonita Duelle, the private duty nurse, protested.

"Unless I receive a directive from the DNS notifying me otherwise, what I've told you stands," Lynn said. "All medications on the unit med cart, no exceptions. Have you had any problems with Ms. McDonald's meds not being available when needed?"

Ms. Duelle admitted she had not.

"I'm sure our staff nurses are trying their best to cooperate with you," Lynn said. "After all, Ms. McDonald is our patient, too. Please feel free to notify me if you do have any problems."

Rolfe and Beth were still avoiding one another, Lynn noticed. Obviously they hadn't resolved their differences. It was none of her business as long as they didn't fight on duty.

"Let me know when you dress Mr. Franklin's lesion," she told Rolfe. "I'd like to take a look at it."

"Will do." His mock salute didn't irritate her as it would have two weeks ago. Rolfe was Rolfe.

Nick, in maternity greens, his jaw stubbled, came by the desk just before nine.

"Delivery?" she asked.

"Premie twins," he said. "Their mama's kept me up since four. Only five pounds altogether, but they're feisty, they've got a good chance. Aren't you going to ask me why I'm on Five East when I don't have a patient here?"

"Why has Five East been honored with your presence this morning, Dr. Dow?"

"How did the big dinner date go last night?"

Lynn glanced at Connie, apparently oblivious but certainly able to hear. Nick shouldn't be discussing their personal business while she was on duty.

"I'm due for a break. You can ride down with me in the elevator," she told Nick.

"As long as you answer the question."

Lynn waited until the elevator doors closed. "Tim and I had a wonderful time. He arrived just in time to call the police and then he tied up Justin."

"What the hell are you talking about?"

"Justin burst into the apartment and tried to kill Sheila. I sprayed him with flame retardant. Sheila had hysterics and Tim wound up taking her home with him—in case Justin got out on bail. He offered to take me too, but I stayed where I was."

Nick shook his head as they got off the elevator at the first floor. "Never a dull moment at the wayward girls' home."

"That reminds me, I have a message for you from Shaleen." She told him about the phone call.

"How much money is she sending, for God's sake?"

"She didn't say, but I got the impression it was a lot. Have fun counting it."

"Is she all right?"

"She says so. I hope so. She did promise to keep in touch with me."

"That poor kid . . . I wish she'd kept her money."

"The point she made was it's her father's money and she wanted him to pay."

"I'd like to see the bastard pay for what he did to Shaleen—and not with money."

"I'm with you, but we don't even know his name."

Nick stopped at the entrance to the cafeteria. "I'm due in the OR. See you Friday night." There was no question in his voice, but his eyes held hers for a moment, probing, seeking.

Lynn nodded.

When she returned to Five East, she found Rolfe ready to change the dressing on Mr. Franklin's lesion. So far, no other patients on the unit had developed a staph infection.

"Coming in to check on how he's taking care of me, are you?" Mr. Franklin asked her. "It's about time. About time, too, you got rid of all this junk." He waved a hand at the isolation gowns she and Rolfe wore. "Makes a man feel like a leper."

Though still cantankerous, Mr. Franklin was noticeably weaker and more frail.

"I'm hoping it won't be much longer before we can take you out of isolation," Lynn said. "Let's take a look at your lesion."

"The sore on my butt, you mean. Dang thing doesn't seem to want to heal."

He was right. Because of the debilitating effects of the pancreatic cancer, Mr. Franklin's body was losing its ability to heal. The hip ulcer showed very little sign of new tissue formation.

"There's one encouraging change," Lynn told him. "You have almost no drainage, so the infection is clearing up."

"I guess he knows how to do something right, anyway," Mr. Franklin said gruffly.

After they left the room, Lynn said, "That's as close as I've seen Mr. Franklin come to handing a gold star to anyone."

Rolfe shrugged. "He's not such a bad old guy once you get used to him." After glancing up and down the corridor, he said, "She won't listen to me, but someone ought to tell her. Beth, I mean. This Dr. Marlin she's so hot for—he's trouble."

Lynn sighed. "I've done my best to get that point across. She doesn't listen to what she doesn't want to hear. And it's really her business."

"But Beth doesn't *know* anything. It's like she hasn't grown up."

"Rolfe, neither you nor I can protect her. We learned by experience. She's determined to do the same and we can't stop her."

He scowled. "Yeah, but I grew up fast and hard, and you're one tough lady. We learned early how to survive. Beth's as helpless as a newborn kitten."

Lynn wasn't sure whether he meant to compliment her or not. She'd certainly never seen herself as tough, although she was certainly more capable of taking care of herself than Beth.

"I feel the same way about Shaleen McGuire," she told Rolfe. "I wish I could find her, help her, protect her. I can't . . . she won't let me."

"Shaleen got a bad deal but she's a survivor, too. Beth—" He shook his head and walked away.

Tim was at the desk when Lynn returned to the nurses' station. "How's Sheila?" she asked him.

"Still sleeping when I left home. I had to give her a shot of valium. The poor girl's been through hell. She told me I was the first person who's made her feel safe since all this began. I think maybe she ought to stay at my place for a while." He looked at Lynn without meeting her eyes. "Maybe you could pack her things and I'll run by and pick them up on my way home from the office this evening."

"I'll be glad to." Lynn was happy Sheila had found a safe haven, if only temporarily. Or would it prove to be more than temporary? Lynn didn't put much past Sheila. On the other hand, maybe Sheila could give Tim what he wanted and needed.

That was more than she could do, Lynn told herself ruefully.

On Friday, Conrad released his memo about the continuation of the freeze on salaries for another month.

"The shit's hit the fan for sure," Joyce told Lynn at lunch. "I don't know anyone on the nursing staff who isn't upset ... even Morrin. Could be we'll lose some of our best nurses." She slanted a glance at Lynn. "You staying?"

Lynn nodded. "You?"

"I guess."

"You're not sure?"

"Promises, promises. I'm a big girl, I know better than to believe what anyone says. Somehow, though, I keep forgetting. I thought Hal Stuart might call me. He hasn't."

"You don't mean for a date, do you?"

Joyce grimaced. "Yes and no. Oh, hell, forget it ... back to the freeze. Sheila must be rubbing her hands with glee."

"She has other problems at the moment. Justin's in jail, he tried to kill her again. At my place." Lynn told Joyce the rest of the story.

"That won't keep Sheila down long," Joyce predicted. "Monday morning she'll be back stirring up the natives. And this time there could be more than just a few drums being pounded."

Lynn shed her on-duty problems as she drove home from the hospital. By the time she reached her apartment, she was mentally reviewing her wardrobe. Did she have anything appropriate for tonight? What image did she want to project anyway? Maidenly? Sexy?

How did Nick see her? What did he expect? He'd warned her he didn't mean to marry her. Fine. The one time she'd tried marriage, it'd been hell on earth. She wasn't at all sure marriage to Nick wouldn't prove a disaster. But they weren't planning to marry; they only intended to come to terms, as Nick said, with what was between them—that fizzy champagne feeling when they touched, the hot flare of need sizzling in the blood.

She wasn't at all sure she could cope with what was between them, either, but it was past time to try.

While she jogged on the beach, she decided she'd be nervous enough without trying to adapt to a false persona and settled for being herself—casual with a few frills. She had the perfect dress, one she hadn't worn since she'd come to California. Its simple but elegant lines gave her confidence, while the clear, deep rose color set off her hair. She chose heeled white sandals and white silk beads and got everything ready before she stepped into the shower. She was determined that tonight nothing go wrong.

She was washing her hair when the phone rang. Damn, she'd forgotten to flick on the machine. Wrapping a towel around her she dripped her way into the living room.

"This is Nick. I've just gotten a call for help from Renee."

Chapter 16

Lynn, wet and shivering, clutched the towel closer about her as she tried to make sense of Nick's worlds. "Renee called you at your office?" she said into the phone.

"She claimed she needed help," Nick told her. "I've got patients waiting here, I can't leave yet. I told Renee I'd pick you up and come by as soon as I could, but it wouldn't be right away. I figure an hour plus, but I thought I'd better alert you. See you then."

Lynn went back into the bathroom and finished showering. As she blow-dried her hair, she tried to convince herself she wasn't disappointed. Renee might well need help if she was living with Tex, and there was no one else Renee could call on except Nick and Lynn. But why did it have to be tonight?

Lynn hung the rose dress in the closet and pulled out her denim skirt. No point in dressing up to go to Renee's rescue. Too bad she didn't have the "Martyr" shirt Sheila had promised her. At the moment it would suit her mood exactly.

But Renee hadn't asked for her help. It was Nick who included her in the rescue. He didn't fancy riding off alone to slay Renee's dragon. He wanted Lynn with him. He wanted her, not Renee. She had to keep that in mind.

Renee had probably had a fight with Tex. Maybe he'd told her to get out. Her attachments to men never lasted long. Lynn remembered commenting on that to Ray once.

"What do you expect me to do about it?" Ray had demanded. "You find one thing after another to blame me for. I am not responsible for Renee!" His rage over her trivial observation had been frightening.

Lynn shook her head. Tonight she didn't want any reminder of Ray or the past. All the pain and grief was behind her; Nick was ahead of her.

Tonight was to have been Nick's night, hers and Nick's. It'd taken her a long time to decide she wanted Nick in her life, and Renee's call had spoiled what was to have been a perfect evening together, their first. Now nothing would be the same. Lynn chose a shirt at random, no longer caring what she wore. It wouldn't make a difference anyway.

Nick came by in his Kharmann Ghia an hour and a half after he'd called. Lynn, watching for his arrival, quickly left her apartment and slid into the passenger seat.

"A biker can be trouble," he said. "How well did Renee know this guy Tex?"

"She met him while she was waiting at the bus station for me to pick her up."

Nick shook his head. "What'd you think of him?"

"I didn't trust him. Sheila thought he was dealing drugs. I really didn't want him in my apartment."

"Couldn't you have talked some sense into Renee?"

She slanted a look at him. "Renee does exactly as she pleases, always has. She's never paid the slightest attention to what I tell her. She's never liked me."

"I certainly get the impression you don't care for her either."

She turned in the seat to face him. "What do you expect?" she cried. "Every other word Renee's said to me since she arrived in El Doblez has been to blame me for Ray's death. She calls *me* cruel and unfeeling. God!"

Nick didn't respond. After a while he said, "On the phone she told me she was afraid of Tex and she needed a place to stay."

"Take her in if you want to." Lynn's tone was bitter. "I won't—not again. Why did you even bother to come and get me, if that's what you intend to do?"

"Calm down. I didn't say I meant to offer her my extra bedroom."

"What *did* you mean, then?"

"If she's in trouble, don't you think you owe it to your sister-in-law to try to help her?"

"There are hotels. Motels."

"She said she was broke."

"If she is, then she's spent a lot of money somewhere in the past week. I know she had a severance check from the bank she worked for in Worcester—it had to be several hundred dollars, at least."

"You sound like you're calling her a liar."

Lynn's patience, stretched tissue-thin, gave way. "Nick, you know nothing about Renee; I do. I'm tired of listening to this. You've been her knight errant from the beginning—didn't you stay behind with her in the restaurant that time I left? So go ahead with your knight-on-a-white-charger rescue, but first stop at a phone booth and I'll call a cab to take me home."

He shot her a dark look. "The only place you're going is with me. We'll find Renee, get her settled somewhere, and take it from there."

257

It was too late to take it from anywhere as far as she was concerned. Not once had he listened to her side. All he cared about was Renee, Renee, Renee. She withdrew into herself, brooding over Nick's obtuseness, rousing when he stopped the car.

"Here's the phone booth she called from," he said.

There was no sign of Renee.

"Didn't she give you an address?" Lynn asked.

"Yeah, but she said she'd wait here. We'd better go look for her."

A total stranger answered the door at the address Renee had given Nick, an upstairs apartment. Older than Tex, he wore a tattered pair of jeans and nothing else. A large green dragon tattoo curled up his left arm. He didn't offer to let them in.

"Renee?" he said. "She took off with Tex. He borrowed my pickup to tote her junk."

"Do you know where they went?" Nick asked.

The man shrugged.

"Would you tell Tex to ask her to call Nick or Lynn?"

"Yo." The man closed the door, leaving them outside on the landing.

"I don't believe him," Nick muttered, staring at the door.

Lynn, heartily sick of what was going on, turned and started down the steps. Let Nick argue with the Green Dragon if he wanted to, she'd had enough. What had happened was clear enough to her.

Renee had envisioned a cozy twosome, she and Nick together in his condo. When Nick refused to act out her script, saying he'd bring Lynn with him, Renee changed her mind about being rescued by him. It was pointless to tell Nick this—he wouldn't believe her any more than he did the Green Dragon.

"Maybe Tex forced her to go with him," Nick said as he unlocked the car.

"Get real," she snapped. "You've been stood up."

He stared at her. "I'm beginning to wonder if some of the things Renee told me aren't true after all."

"That's your choice. Mine is to go home." She stalked toward the phone booth on the corner.

He caught her arm before she'd gone five steps. "You've walked away from me for the last time. You're getting in the car, damn it, and we're going to talk."

Rather than struggle with him and make a scene, Lynn allowed him to lead her back to the car. There was nothing to talk about, she wouldn't say one word to him except to insist on being taken home.

He started the car and screeched away from the curb. Glancing from the corner of her eye at his profile, she saw that he looked as angry as she felt. She braced herself for a furious fusillade, but he said nothing. He was, though, exceeding the speed limit alarmingly.

"I prefer to arrive in one piece," she said tartly.

He neither responded nor slowed down. He yanked the wheel abruptly, taking a corner so fast the car tilted. She bit her lip to keep from gasping, afraid any reaction from her would only fuel his recklessness. This wasn't the way to her apartment, but at the moment she didn't think it was safe to object.

He skidded around more corners, zoomed up a hill, and finally slowed and stopped. She sighed with relief only to find it was premature as she saw the tennis court to her left. He eased from the car and walked around to her side.

"Get out," he ordered.

"I don't live here."

"I do. Come on, this is no place to talk." He waved an impatient hand at the brightly lit court, filled with players.

259

"Nick," a woman called. "Doubles tomorrow afternoon?"

"Sorry," he called back, not turning to look at who'd spoken, his eyes fixed on Lynn.

No, they couldn't talk here; but then, she had no intention of talking to him, anyway. "Take me home," she ordered.

"Either you walk with me or I carry you, kicking and screaming, to my place. I assure you, these people will think it's a joke and laugh their heads off. You have five seconds to decide."

She knew it wasn't an idle threat. Scowling, she slid from the car and stood beside him. He grasped her unwilling hand and pulled her with him as he strode along a walkway toward the condo complex—square blocks of stuccoed buildings, their stark outlines softened by palm trees and bougainvillea.

He unlocked his door and thrust her inside ahead of him. Lynn looked around, anywhere but at him. She'd never been so mad in her life. Even in her anger, she couldn't help notice how the earth-toned colors warmed the white-walled interior.

"May I offer you a seat?" Nick said, indicating the living room.

She marched into it and sat on the edge of a gold and brown chair. "I'll give you five minutes," she announced coldly, "then I'm leaving."

"No. We'll take whatever time we need to get back on track, and you won't leave until we do."

"Stop issuing orders like some prima donna surgeon."

Nick smiled for the first time that night. "You didn't like being an OR scrub nurse when you were in training?"

"I hated it!"

"If I offer you a drink, will you promise not to throw it at me?"

"I don't want—"

"You haven't had anything to eat and neither have I. I'll pour you a glass of wine. If you don't want to drink it, don't. But I warn you, my guacamole dip is on the hot side."

Nick left the room and it crossed her mind to leave while he was fetching the wine and the dip. She shook her head. In his present macho mood, he'd probably tackle her before she got to the door. Curiosity infiltrated her anger, making her rise and walk around the room searching for clues to what made him tick. A skin drum, the hides brown with age, was displayed on one wall. Chippewa?

A seascape in blues and greens hung on the white stone of the modern, no-mantel fireplace. Lynn drew in her breath sharply when she realized where she'd seen the painting before: it was the one Hal Stuart had posed her in front of at the art show, the one she'd thought of as hers. As she looked at it, her rage flickered and died. She turned around and found Nick watching her.

"Why did you buy it?" she asked.

"I admit I was disappointed the living accessory didn't come with the painting, but you know the old saying— half a loaf is better than none." His eyes searched hers as he took a step toward her. "But I'm a man who wants it all." His voice, low and husky, shivered through her.

Lynn, caught by his intensity and by her own unresolved longings, swayed toward him. Before they touched, she came to her senses and drew back. "I've changed my mind," she said. "I believe I will have a glass of wine."

Lynn had to be the wariest woman he'd ever met, Nick thought as he poured the wine. She was world-class elu-

261

sive. It infuriated him. Hell, he'd given up on her more times than he cared to remember—but he always came back because she fascinated him.

He handed her the wine and offered tortilla chips with the guacomole dip.

"You're right, I'm hungry," she said, helping herself. "Wow!" she added a moment later. "When you say hot you mean *hot*."

"I always say what I mean."

She raised her eyebrows.

"Hey, they don't call me tactless for nothing," he protested.

Her smile persuaded him she'd set aside her hostility and anger, at least for the moment.

"Sit back and sip your wine and listen to me," he told her. "I want to run something past you without you getting your back up. Remember, this isn't anything I said or even necessarily believe, it's what I heard. To clear the air, I have to repeat what I was told."

"I don't think I want to hear it."

"Probably not. But you know how granulation tissue can overgrow in a wound, and unless the growth is healthy, the tissue has to be cut away or the wound will never heal."

Lynn picked up her wineglass and raised it toward him in a gesture of acquiescence. "I guess I can't stop you."

"More than once you've brought up you splitting from that restaurant, and I've never said anything about what happened after you left me with Renee. It's time I did. I worried that you'd gotten sick, but Renee laughed. 'Lynn did this all the time with Ray,' she said. 'You made the mistake of talking a bit too much to me. When Lynn's with a man, she wants his full attention, or else. My poor brother went through hell with her. I think I'd better warn you she's cold and cruel, she has no feelings.' "

Nick heard Lynn's inarticulate protest, but didn't stop. "Renee went on to say, 'If Lynn didn't get her own way, she was vicious. She hated me because, as Ray's twin, I was close to him. Near the end she refused to allow him to see me at all, she cut him off from every friend he had. It's no wonder Ray became desperate enough to take his own life. She killed him as surely as if she'd held a gun to his head and pulled the trigger herself.' "

Nick saw Lynn start to rise from her chair. "Sit still," he ordered, "I'm not through. I'd just met Renee. How could I decide how much of this to believe? All? Some? None? You'd been so reticent about your marriage, I knew very few facts. I wanted to trust my feeling about you, my feelings for you. Medically, of course, I'm well aware no one, not even the best-trained psychiatrist, can keep a person obsessed with suicide from killing himself. But you, Lynn, kept sabotaging my trust with the way you behaved ... or so it seemed. Tonight, for example, you acted as though you really do hate Renee."

"You don't under—"

"Wait. Maybe you *do* hate her, maybe you have good reason to. For God's sake, tell me what it's all about, tell me what happened with Ray and why. Share your past with me so I can understand, that's all I'm asking."

"All?" she cried. "My God!"

"Let go of it, Lynn ... now."

She buried her face in her hands and he longed to go to her, to take her in his arms and hold her. Instead, he waited.

Finally she raised her head. Tears glimmered in her eyes as she looked beyond him. "The person Renee described wasn't me, it was Ray," she said in such a low

263

tone he could hardly hear her. "Ray was possessive. I couldn't so much as smile at another man without being berated later. He needed my entire attention focused on him at all times." A tear trickled down her cheek. "I found that impossible. I knew he needed help and I tried to get him to see a therapist, but he insisted he was a doctor and knew that only oddballs and weirdos chose to specialize in psychiatry."

She closed her eyes and sat back in the chair. "I blame myself for not understanding how depressed he'd become, but by that time I had a problem of my own. I was pregnant. Not on purpose, something went wrong. I was afraid to tell Ray, because I knew he'd insist I have an abortion and I—I wanted to keep the baby. I was four months along when he found out. By this time Ray wouldn't permit anyone in our apartment, not even Renee. I've never felt so alone in all my life."

Lynn fumbled in her skirt pocket and found a tissue. She wiped her eyes. "I assumed I knew what went on in Ray's mind, but I discovered he might as well have been a stranger, for all I understood him. I didn't have the vaguest idea what he was planning. I still haven't come to terms with what he did.

"Boston had an unusual amount of snow that January. One cold night I thought I was having a nightmare about being kidnaped, carried to a car, pushed onto the back seat. But I wasn't dreaming. I only recall bits and pieces of what happened, because Ray had secretly laced my after-supper coffee with barbiturates. I think I must have tried to get out of the car after he backed into a snowbank on a lonely country road, because when they found us, I was on the floor of the back seat with my face pressed to the door, which was slightly ajar.

"I suppose that's why I survived. Ray died of carbon

monoxide poisoning, and so did the baby. I miscarried the next day. Ray wanted to kill us all. He almost succeeded. There were times I felt so guilty, I came close to wishing he had."

Nick fought his urge to hold her close, to kiss her tear-stained face. He longed to comfort her, but he knew touching her would bring a halt to what she was saying. She had to get it all out, she'd been holding her hurt back too long.

"Does Renee know everything?" he asked.

Lynn shook her head. "This is the first time I've ever told anyone exactly what happened. I don't think Renee would believe me anyway. She's convinced I'm to blame for Ray's death. In her eyes, he was perfect—except for marrying me." Her voice broke. "She—before she came here I got three dreadful calls where I picked up the phone and Ray's voice spoke to me."

He frowned. "Ray's voice?"

"On tape, but I was so upset at first, I couldn't think straight, I could only listen to Ray accusing me after death, as he'd done while he was alive. No one except Renee could have the tapes, no one else would've made such horrible calls to me."

Nick, taken aback, stared at her. "You never told me."

"How could I tell anyone? Sheila heard one of the calls on the answering machine, or I might have thought I was going crazy and imagining things."

"Did you confront Renee about the calls?"

Lynn gave him a twisted smile. "She'd only deny making them. Every day she stayed with me, I listened to her accusations. Do you think she'd admit that to anyone? I don't care how heartless you believe I am, I won't have her in my apartment again. I don't even want to see her again."

It was too late to put his arms around her. She'd drawn back to that damned defensive position she was so fond of. After hearing what her crazy bastard of a husband had tried to do to her, he could better understand why she was so reluctant to trust anyone, but he still resented her withdrawal.

He stood and held out his hand. After hesitating, she put her hand in his and he pulled her to her feet. "You've had a bad time and I've made it worse. If I'd known—" He shrugged. "What we both need is food. And don't argue—that's sound medical advice, free of charge. Come into the kitchen and brew some coffee for us while I boil water for the spaghetti."

In the kitchen they worked side-by-side in silence. He had a feeling there wasn't much he could do to salvage the evening other than feed the two of them. She might turn to him for solace and there was nothing wrong with comforting her—he wanted to—but to make love to her under those circumstances could be a mistake. If the chance came, though, he didn't think he'd resist.

Lynn's experience was a shocker; she'd done well to come through it as well as she had. He remembered her anguish in the delivery room the day Elena's dead baby was born—she'd relived her own grief.

As for Renee, he had to admit it, he'd been somewhat attracted to her. Not seriously, because she had come on too strong. Thinking about her behavior, he wondered how he could've missed her being paranoid about Lynn. Fraternal twins often shared as close a bond as identical ones, and Ray and Renee had been twins.

From Renee's point of view, Lynn had separated the two of them; Lynn was the outsider, the enemy. He could understand how Renee might blame Lynn for Ray's death. Those phone calls, though, showed seriously disturbed thinking. It wasn't surprising that Lynn wanted to avoid her. If Renee called him again, he'd suggest she see Phil Vance for some therapy.

"I guess I'm hungrier than I thought," Lynn said. "That spaghetti sauce smells really good."

"It's French, not Italian," he told her. "An old family secret."

"Not Chippewa, anyway. I wondered if the drum on the wall was."

"That's a Mide drum. A medicine drum. After Greatcloud died, Aunt Grace took the drum from his cabin and saved it for me. She said the old shaman told her he had a dream vision about me following in his footsteps and the drum must be mine. He did have certain abilities I've never been able to explain scientifically. I've often wondered if he foresaw that I'd become a doctor. When he knew me as a boy, I seemed much more likely to end up in Marquette State Prison."

"Can you play the drum?"

He shook his head. "I wouldn't dare. Seriously. Those drums weren't made for fooling around. Greatcloud taught by example that truth might be elusive, but truth was there to be found if a man tried in the right way. I think he wanted me to have the Mide drum to remind me of what I learned from him."

"The Chippewa way."

He nodded. "It's easy to lose sight of what's true."

"Sometimes I wonder if I'll ever know." Lynn's voice quavered on the last word.

Nick reached for her, pulling her into his arms. "This is true, it's right," he said fiercely and kissed her.

Some time later, the sizzling of water splattering on the burner as the spaghetti boiled over brought Nick back to awareness.

"That's life, always intervening at the wrong time," he told Lynn as he released her and reached to turn down the heat.

They ate their meal in the living room. When he asked her what music she'd like to hear, she wanted to know if he had anything Indian, so he put on a tape of Lakota chants and dances.

"I met this guy, Pete Bull, in med school," he said. "I don't suppose you know but Chippewa and Sioux are traditional enemies. He was Sioux, Lakota, and we were more or less friendly rivals for four years. He went back to the Rosebud Reservation as a doctor for his people, and once in a while he sends me a Lakota memento. This tape came last year. 'Here's how real bloods do it,' the card with it said.

"Sometimes I feel guilty as hell because I'm not as noble as Pete Bull. Or Paul Salvador. But that was one of the things Greatcloud taught me to face—my own limitations. I'd be miserable on a reservation. I wouldn't be much happier in a migrant worker clinic with Paul. So don't expect too much of me, Lynn."

Lynn gazed at Nick consideringly while Lakota voices chanted rhythmically in the background. *Did* she expect too much? He had a right to decide his own future, and she'd had no business being upset when he spoke of going in with Lloyd Linnett.

She'd expected him to understand her side, to take her part against Renee, even though she'd never, until tonight, told him what she'd gone through with Ray. Had she thought that if he really cared about her, he'd stand up for her no matter what?

In a way, though, he had. He'd insisted on prying the story from her. If he hadn't cared, he'd have accepted Renee's lies and not bothered.

"I shouldn't really expect anything," she said.

He grinned at her. "But you do, and so do I—even though we know better. I wonder if Phil Vance, with his psych background, orders his life any better than us poor deluded peons outside the charmed Freudian circle."

"What do you expect from me?" she asked.

"Do you want the romantic reply—anything you wish to offer is gift enough? Or do you prefer the macho response—more than I've gotten so far?"

Lynn laughed. "I'm not sure either's the right answer."

"Eat your spaghetti like a good girl. I know that's one thing I've done right tonight."

The phone rang and Nick scowled. "I told the answering service to transfer my calls to Lloyd," he said as he strode to pick it up.

Lynn wondered if Renee had his home number.

"Who?" he asked. "Oh, yeah. Just a minute, I'll get her." Nick covered the mouthpiece and said to Lynn, "It's Rolfe Watson."

"I forgot to tell you I put your number on my answering machine in case Shaleen tried to reach me." She took the phone from Nick, wondering what on earth Rolfe could want.

"Lynn, I hate to bother you ... it's Beth. She's been staying at Doc Marlin's place and there's trouble. She's hysterical, wants me to help. I say okay, then after I hang up I say to myself, wait a minute, boy. You're heading for jail, maybe getting shot, you go barging into that house, a black guy invading Doc Marlin's territory."

"What's Beth's problem?"

"Marlin's not home. The doc's wife, ex-wife, whatever, showed up zonked out of her mind. Beth panicked. It's asking a lot, but would you come with me to Marlin's house? With you along I won't be so much of a threat."

"Hold on a minute, Rolfe." She covered the mouthpiece and gave Nick a brief rundown. "I think it's risky for him to go alone," she added, "especially if someone calls the police."

"So Beth's another wayward woman." Nick sighed. "Tell Rolfe we'll meet him at Marlin's."

Nick and Lynn arrived first. Leaving the car in the drive, they hurried to the front door. There was no response when Nick rang the bell and pounded on the door. He turned the knob and found the door unlocked. Raising his eyebrows at Lynn, he stepped inside the foyer. She followed. Every light in the house seemed to be on.

"Beth?" she called.

No answer.

"Barry?" Nick shouted. "Tina!"

No answer.

From the foyer they had a choice of climbing the curving staircase to the second story or turning to the right or the left. "You try one way, I'll try the other," she suggested.

He hesitated, finally nodding. "Be careful."

Left led to the kitchen, a family room and what seemed to be a maid's quarters—bedroom and bath. The bathroom door was ajar, but when Lynn tried to push it open to look inside, she met some resistance. The sour smell of vomit made her grimace. Shoving with all her strength, she opened the door enough to get her head through. She gasped.

A woman lay sprawled on the tiles, blood matting her brown hair.

Chapter 17

As Lynn stood staring at the woman, someone came up behind her.

"What's happened?" Rolfe demanded, apprehension edging his voice.

"It's not Beth," she assured him. "It could be Dr. Marlin's wife. Help me open the door."

With both of them pushing, they widened the space until Lynn was able to slip through. "Find Nick—Dr. Dow—*stat,*" she ordered as she dropped to her knees beside the woman.

"Where's Beth?"

"I don't know. Hurry!"

Lynn found no radial pulse, but located one at the carotid. Respirations were slow, but the woman's airway seemed clear. Blood oozed from a triangular superficial gash in the scalp. A bloodstain on the edge of the sink cabinet indicated the cut was from falling against it.

Because of the expensive clothes and the diamond-encrusted ring on her, Lynn decided the woman must be Barry's wife. According to Nick, the Marlins had a rocky marriage and were separated.

"Tina?" she called. "Tina!"

The woman didn't respond. Lynn heard feet pounding toward her, and seconds later Nick appeared.

"I found a pulse and she's breathing, but she doesn't respond," she told him. "On the phone Beth said Barry's wife was zonked."

"Let me take a look."

She slid out of the tiny room so Nick could take her place. He lifted Tina's eyelid, peered at her eye, shading it from the light with his hand, then abruptly removing his hand, checking on how her pupil reacted. He shook his head. "Call an ambulance."

Lynn picked up the phone in the bedroom and pushed the button. "Address?" she called to Nick as she waited for the dispatcher to answer.

"We're at 1701 Areca," he told her.

Before the ambulance arrived, Nick eased Tina from the bathroom and laid her on the bed. Lynn placed a clean washcloth over the scalp laceration and dampened another to wash the vomit from Tina's face.

"Where's Beth?" Lynn asked.

"She's locked herself in the master bath upstairs. I couldn't persuade her to open up—Rolfe's trying now." Nick took his fingers away from the angle of Tina's jaw. "I still get a pulse, but it's weak. Where the hell's the ambulance?"

As if in answer, they heard the faint wail of a siren. A few minutes later the paramedics had Tina on the stretcher, carrying her to the van.

"We'd better find Barry and tell him about Tina," Nick said as he closed the front door. "Beth must know where he is."

"What do you think Tina's chances are?"

Nick shrugged. "I don't think bumping her head caused

the coma. There's no smell of alcohol, but she could've overdosed on any depressant. Her chances depend on what she took and how much." He strode to the stairs and looked up. "Rolfe!"

"I've got Beth, she's okay," Rolfe called back.

"Bring her down here."

Rolfe appeared at the head of the stairs, carrying Beth, and slowly descended. Nick inclined his head toward the living room and Rolfe followed them into it. When he tried to ease Beth onto the couch, she clung to his neck, refusing to let go. Rolfe finally sat down with Beth on his lap, her face buried against his chest.

"Beth, we need to know where Barry is," Nick said gently.

She whimpered, her face hidden.

"Tell the man," Rolfe urged. "Come on, you can do it."

"B-boat," Beth quavered. She turned to look at Lynn and Nick. "He went sailing this afternoon. I get seasick." Her voice broke and she began to cry. "He never came back. Then *she* showed up. She acted crazy. Called me names. Told me to get out or she'd—she'd kill me. I ran upstairs. There's a phone in the bathroom. I locked myself in and called Rolfe." She clung to him, sobbing.

"Barry must have the *Cut-Up* back in the marina by now," Nick said. "Maybe he decided to spend the night on the boat. Does he do that often?"

Beth wiped her eyes. "He—he says it rocks him to sleep. I get nauseated."

"Lynn and I will go down to the marina," Nick said. "I've been on Barry's boat, I think I remember his slot. Rolfe, maybe you'd better take Beth home."

"No!" she cried. "I'm coming, too. What if that woman murdered poor Barry?"

273

"Beth—" Rolfe began.

"Oh, *please* take me to the marina, Rolfe," she begged. "Please, please. I *have* to make sure Barry's all right."

Rolfe's eyes met Nick's and he shrugged.

By the time they reached the marina it was after midnight. Lynn followed Nick along the plank walkway between the boats. The *Cut-Up* was moored near the end, her sails down, a dim, reddish light showing through the cabin window.

"Looks like he's here," Nick said, heading for the cabin door.

"I'll wait on deck," Lynn told him.

Nick knocked. "Barry!" he called and pushed the door open.

Lynn, walking aft, didn't mean to look in as she passed the cabin window, but a sudden movement caught her eye. To her surprise, she found herself staring at a naked Phil Vance. As she turned away, she saw Barry Marlin, also naked.

As the implications of what she'd seen filtered into her mind, Lynn heard Beth calling her name. She hurried to the rail, hoping to keep Beth away.

"He's here, he's okay," she told Beth, who'd run ahead of Rolfe. "No need to come aboard, I'm just leaving. We can walk back to the—"

"I have to see Barry!" Beth jumped onto the boat. Before Lynn could try to block her, Beth was at the cabin door and ducked inside.

Almost instantly, Nick appeared from inside, one hand clamped on Beth's arm, pulling her with him. He propelled her across the deck and off the boat, Lynn at his heels. Nick thrust Beth at Rolfe, who was waiting on the planking.

"Get her out of here. Take her home," Nick said.

Beth said nothing at all as they returned to the cars. Lynn doubted that Beth had any idea beforehand that Barry Marlin swung both ways.

"Did you know Phil Vance and Barry were seeing each other?" Lynn asked Nick as they drove away from the marina.

"Not for sure. It never crossed my mind that Phil would be on the boat with Barry, or I'd have made certain Beth didn't come anywhere near the boat. Having her burst in on them after I'd just told Barry about his wife—" Nick shook his head. "It's been one hell of a night, hasn't it? Certainly nothing like either of us expected."

"Who *could* expect something like this? What else can go wrong?"

"Don't tempt the gods to show you." He glanced at her. "Tired?"

She nodded. "But I'd like to stop by the hospital on the way to my apartment to find out how Tina Marlin's doing."

Nick pulled up to the ER entrance. Inside, he greeted a middle-aged nurse with blond streaks in her brown hair. "Hi, Fran. This is Lynn Holley, day charge on Five East. How're things going?"

Fran nodded and smiled at Lynn. "Haven't seen much of you lately, Dr. Dow," she said to Nick. "Believe it or not, this is the first time I've sat down tonight. Two fractured hips, a febrile convulsion, one possible bleeding ulcer, and then two ODs rolled in at the same time. We shunted one to ICU, but the other coded and didn't make it. He used to be our pharmacist—Justin Burns."

Lynn stared at Fran. Justin *dead?* "I work with his wife," she said. "Has she been notified?"

Fran nodded. "You'd think a pharmacist would know better than to fool around with drugs."

275

"Tina Marlin's in the ICU, then," Nick said, picking up the phone. He spoke to the nurse on ICU, and when he hung up he shook his head. "Tina's on a respirator."

"We couldn't locate Dr. Marlin," Fran said.

"He knows, he's on his way," Nick assured her.

"How awful for Sheila," Lynn said as they left the ER. "She'll never know whether Justin's OD was accidental or not."

"Not a good night all around for medical personnel," he agreed.

They were quiet as he drove to Lynn's. At her door, Nick put his arms around her and held her for a few moments without speaking. Finally he said, "I'll call you around two tomorrow—no, today, I mean. Goodnight." His kiss was gentle, tender, and comforting.

The phone woke Lynn at eleven. She answered it half-asleep, but when she heard Shaleen's voice, she woke up fast.

"I think he's dying," Shaleen said, her voice thin and taut. "He won't go to the hospital and I don't know what to do to stop his pain."

"Who?" Lynn demanded. "Who's dying?"

"Freddie. I've been taking care of him, and now—" Shaleen's voice quavered but she controlled it. "He's worse. I thought maybe you could help."

"What's wrong with Freddie?"

"He's got AIDS."

Lynn blinked. "That's a serious disease, Shaleen."

"It's fatal. I know that and so does Freddie. He—he wants to stay here, not die in a hospital, and I promised him I'd never send him to one. But he has all this pain, and I—I'm scared."

"If you tell me where you are, I'll come and see if I can help."

There was silence. Then, "I guess I'll have to." Shaleen's words were reluctant. "But promise me you won't tell anyone, not even Dr. Dow, about my call."

Lynn dressed hurriedly. Not knowing how long she'd be with Shaleen, she left a message on the machine for Nick, saying something had come up and she'd call him when she had a chance.

Shaleen was living not in El Doblez but in the next community down the coast. Lynn drove past the center of town and turned onto a road lined with date palms. Arriving at the cross streets Shaleen had specified, Lynn didn't see the young girl at first. Only belatedly did she realize the heavily made-up black-haired woman approaching the car was Shaleen.

"I didn't recognize you!" Lynn exclaimed as the teenager slid into the passenger seat. "You look all of twenty-five. And you've dyed your hair."

Shaleen seemed pleased that her disguise had fooled Lynn. "I have to be careful." She directed Lynn around several corners and along a street. "Stop here and park," she said.

They climbed worn and rickety wooden steps to a studio apartment over a garage. Inside, the one large room smelled of sickness, despite the open windows letting in a sea breeze. Freddie, swathed in blankets, lay on a narrow bed next to one of the windows. A spider plant hung from the ceiling above him, several of the daughter sprouts almost touching him. Lynn crossed to him, sat on the metal chair pulled up beside the bed, and put her hand to his forehead. He was hot.

He opened his sunken eyes at her touch and gazed blankly at her.

277

"I'm Shaleen's friend, a nurse," she told him.

He tried to speak, but instead started coughing, a rasping hack that shuddered through his wasted body. Shaleen reached past Lynn for a bottle of cough syrup on the bedside table.

"Don't try to talk, Freddie," Lynn said when he managed to swallow the syrup. "Just nod or shake your head, okay?"

He nodded.

"You sound to me like you have pneumonia," she went on. "It happens with AIDS."

Freddie nodded again.

"He knows all about AIDS," Shaleen put in. "He watched his friend Richard die with it earlier this year, in a hospital up north. Freddie says none of the nurses wanted to take care of Richard and even the doctor hated to touch him. He tried to go in every day and do what he could, but he had to work, too. He doesn't want to die in a place where people are afraid of him. Right, Freddie?"

He nodded and smiled weakly at Shaleen.

"Freddie helped me when I needed it," she said, "even though he was sick himself. He brought me here and he took me to the hospital when he saw I'd die if he didn't."

"Candy striper," Freddie gasped. "She wasn't afraid of Richard."

"He means me. I was a candy striper on Richard's unit. That's how I met Freddie."

Lynn looked from one to the other. Freddie's age was hard to evaluate because he was so debilitated from his disease, but she figured he wasn't yet thirty. Under all the makeup, Shaleen was only fifteen, too young to understand the danger she was running.

"They could make you more comfortable in the hospital, Freddie," Lynn pointed out.

278

"Still gonna die," he muttered. "Rather be here."

Lynn couldn't deny he was going to die, and soon.

"If you're worried about me," Shaleen said to her, "don't be. We read all this stuff about AIDS and I bought a bunch of disposable gloves I can use when I have to touch anything that might carry the virus. And—" she leaned over and smoothed Freddie's hair—"we're heart friends, not sex friends. The only problem is, I know he's in a lot of pain and I ran out of the codeine pills I saved from when I was at Harper Hills. Even if I hadn't, Freddie can't keep much in his stomach any more. He needs shots for pain, but he won't let me find a dealer and buy heroin."

Good for Freddie, Lynn thought. Shaleen had enough problems without getting involved with illegal drugs. "All narcotics have to be prescribed by a doctor," she said.

Shaleen nodded. "I know that. I thought maybe Dr. Dow would help us. I don't mind taking care of Freddie, but I can't stand to see him hurting."

"You realize I'll have to explain everything to Dr. Dow. He'll want to examine Freddie."

Shaleen bit her lip, looking down at Freddie, who'd closed his eyes again. "I guess maybe I can trust Dr. Dow," she said finally.

"I'm sure you can." Lynn was in sympathy with the idea of dying at home, but with Shaleen involved, she hoped Nick would be able to convince the two of them Freddie would be better off in the hospital.

She called Nick's office from Shaleen's apartment and found him still there.

"What next?" he asked after writing down the address.

As they waited for Nick, Lynn watched Shaleen try to coax Freddie to swallow a few spoonfuls of beef broth. Realizing she'd never actually taken care of an AIDS pa-

279

tient, Lynn wondered if she'd be as reluctant as the dead Richard's nurses had been. She hoped not, but because it was contagious and invariably fatal, AIDS was a frightening disease. Yet here was Shaleen voluntarily caring for Freddie.

What if I had a friend with AIDS? Lynn asked herself. Could I do what Shaleen is doing? Would I?

After Nick arrived and examined Freddie, he shook his head. "You have bilateral pneumonia—both lungs are affected. AIDS-related pneumonia is difficult to treat, but in a hospital—"

"No." Shaleen spoke firmly. "I won't break my promise."

"What do you say, Freddie?" Nick asked.

"Gonna die here," Freddie told him.

"So can't you just prescribe some shots for his pain?" Shaleen asked.

Nick, washing his hands at the kitchen sink, glanced at Lynn, then back at Shaleen. "It'll get worse," he warned.

"I can handle that," Shaleen told him. "I just can't stand watching him hurt."

"I'll give him an injection now." Nick said. "And leave disposable syringes and needles here for you to use with what I'll prescribe. But you have to promise me something, Shaleen."

"What?"

"That you'll come in to my office and let me check you to make certain you're back to normal. Now come over here and watch what I'm doing, because you have to learn how to give a shot properly. First thing you do is put on gloves, because you might accidentally draw blood when you stick the needle in." Nick kept up a running commentary on what he was doing and why as he gave Freddie the injection.

280

"Think you can manage that?" he asked as he pulled off the gloves and washed his hands again.

Shaleen nodded.

He reached in his pocket, pulled out folded bills, and handed them to her. "I checked with the hospital and paid them. This was left over." When she hesitated, he added, "Use it for Freddie."

Shaleen took the money. "We were getting kind of low," she admitted.

"Have you been having any pain around your incision or anyplace else?" he asked her as he took a prescription pad from his bag.

"No. I feel fine. But I promise I'll go to your office when I can . . . if I can. You won't tell anyone about coming here, will you?"

"The only person I'd want to tell is Lynn, and she already knows."

"Has anyone come around asking questions about me?" Shaleen asked.

"Nope."

"Good. Maybe they haven't traced that withdrawal yet."

"Your own father wouldn't know—" Nick stopped abruptly. "Sorry. What I mean is, no one would recognize you in that get-up anyway. I'd have passed you on the street without a second look."

"You mean you've stopped noticing pretty girls?" Lynn put in. "That's hard to believe."

"I realize all the makeup's part of the disguise, but there's too much for my taste," Nick said. "No second look."

Shaleen smiled. "I kind of like it . . . for a change. Look, would you mind staying with Freddie while I go get this medicine for him?"

After she left, Freddie opened his eyes. "Her father—a bastard," he muttered. "Don't let him get her."

"We know about him," Lynn assured Freddie. "We're on Shaleen's side, we're her friends."

"She needs—" Freddie's eyes closed again and he paused for so long, Lynn thought he wasn't going to finish. "Not just friends," he half-whispered. "A big-name friend. To scare him off." He began to cough again.

Once Shaleen was back, Lynn and Nick climbed down the stairs and Nick walked her to her car.

"Do you think Freddie can last more than a week?" she asked.

"Not outside of a hospital. Even in one—" He shrugged.

"At least we know why Shaleen left Harper Hills without notice. She was worried about Freddie being alone." Lynn sighed. "I don't think he's any older than I am. AIDS is a hideous disease."

"Not many teenagers—or older people, for that matter—could face what Shaleen's doing for him," Nick said. "She's a remarkable girl."

"We've got to find way to keep her safe." Lynn's voice was fierce.

"We'll do all we can." Nick opened the door of her car for her. "Did you happen to notice it's a beautiful day?"

"I've come to expect that in southern California."

"Hey, never take good weather or any other good fortune for granted. Enjoy it while it's there, though, as old Greatcloud taught me. So how about the beach?"

"I've been warned the water's still too cold."

"Are you going to turn your back on good fortune?"

282

"Heaven forbid! I'll meet you on the beach near my place in about forty-five minutes."

The water *was* cold. Lynn shrieked when, hand-in-hand, she and Nick plunged into the surf.

"Come on, Boston, don't be chicken," he chided her, pulling her farther out into the breaking waves.

Later, after toweling off and warming themselves in the sun, they ran along the waterline.

"You've got a great tan already," she remarked. "I never really tan, I have to use sunscreen to keep from getting burned."

"I have to confess, it's only half sun. The rest is genetic. If your ancestors had been forward-looking, like mine, they'd have provided you with a few Indian genes to alleviate your problem. Though I admit there's something to be said in favor of those freckles on your nose." He grasped her hand and pulled her to a stop near their towels.

"I promised Lloyd I'd fly to Las Vegas with him," Nick said. "We leave at six. There's an evening meeting with a movie on new techniques in the surgical repair of cystoceles and rectoceles. The conference lasts through Sunday . . . if he was taking Alice—his wife—I'd ask you to come along."

Lynn, who'd taken for granted they'd be together all evening, hid her disappointment. "No gambling?" she teased.

"I'm a sucker for craps, but medicine comes first."

"That's the reason the conference is in Las Vegas, I suppose—because medicine comes first."

"Did I ever tell you you're in danger of becoming a cynic?" Nick leaned over and kissed her lightly. "See you Monday. If Lady Luck smiles on me, I might have enough money to treat you to dinner and, if none of my mothers decide to deliver early, I might even have the time."

"I won't hold my breath."

Lynn was surprised to see Sheila at work on Monday.

"I feel so guilty," Sheila explained. "I'm better off working instead of brooding about how I might have prevented him from killing himself."

"I understand your guilt," Lynn told her. "But in my case there was no doubt my husband committed suicide. Justin might well have accidentally—"

"Not him. No way. He did it on purpose, the bastard. I can almost hear him saying to himself, 'That bitch'll be sorry when she discovers what she drove me to.' He always blamed me. Tim is so understanding—I didn't know there were men like him."

"I like Tim. And Carol—she's a sweetheart."

Sheila smiled. "I went to her ballet lesson with her on Saturday. Surprised the hell out of the teacher when I insisted on going through the routines with the kids, but Carol got a charge out of it. I used to take ballet when I was a little girl. It all comes back, you know? Carol and I are teaching Ramos some of the exercises. He's a neat kid."

Lynn had all but forgotten the Mexican boy who was to have his cleft palate repaired. "How did his surgery go?"

"So far so good. He has to have more operations. I told Tim I didn't think I should stay on at his place, but he insisted. Says he doesn't know how he'd get along without me." Sheila smiled sadly. "I wish I'd met him before I ever laid eyes on Justin. Do you suppose there's some rule that you have to go through hell before anything decent can happen to you?"

Lynn impulsively put an arm around Sheila's shoulders and gave her a brief hug. "I'm glad you and Tim have connected. About Justin—you couldn't have changed what he did. Believe me."

"Yeah, I know. But it still bothers me. Thanks, though, for the good wishes."

Rolfe was working for Beth, Joyce having cleared the trade of days off. "How's Beth?" Lynn asked him.

"Moping around. What she saw on that boat really threw her. She's off Marlin forever. Like I told you, Beth knows things, but doesn't. I mean, she went through college, she learned about gays and bisexuals and all, but it's like she doesn't associate what she learned with anyone she knows. She stayed with me over the weekend, but I'm taking her back to her apartment when I get off today. There's nothing between us now—you know what I mean. Hell, I feel like the woman's my baby sister. She needs looking after, but—" He shrugged.

"As somebody told me once, you're heart friends, not sex friends?"

Rolfe's eyebrow raised. "You got it."

Lynn's estimation of Rolfe rose. He was far more sensitive than she'd given him credit for. A big brother was exactly what Beth needed. It amazed her that Rolfe was willing to take the time and patience to bother.

Bonita Duelle, the private duty nurse, was waiting for Lynn at the desk. "I can't talk Ms. McDonald into having her therapy," she told Lynn. "Dr. Piedmont says she must be forced to go—but how can I do that?"

Dr. Piedmont, Lynn knew, was the rehab specialist from Stanford.

"How can I help?" Lynn asked.

"Since you're the charge nurse, I thought maybe if you insisted Ms. McDonald go to therapy, she might listen."

Lynn shook her head. "I don't agree. I'll go in and discuss this with her, though. In the meantime, you might take a break."

"Oh, I don't need—"

"I think Ms. McDonald and I will do better alone."

"Well, I won't argue." Bonita Duelle stalked off, obviously in a huff.

So much for tact, Lynn thought. I don't know why the woman has her back up. After all, she came and asked me, I didn't go barging in.

"That's a lovely bedjacket you have on," Lynn told Angela when she came into the room. "Peach certainly is your color."

"Do you think so? My couturière says rose is." Angela sounded both patronizing and bored.

Listening, Lynn discarded what she'd planned to say. This was a sophisticated, intelligent woman who'd had it all. Appealing to her pride, mentioning good health, none of the usual was going to work, and Lynn had no idea of how to motivate Angela.

"Why are you staring at me?" Angela demanded.

"I wasn't really seeing you," Lynn said, to her own surprise. "I was thinking of the young girl who was in this room before you were admitted. You remind me of her in some ways . . . you're both unusually attractive, and you both had a catastrophe put an end to your usual way of living."

Angela's right eyebrow raised. "At least you admit what happened to me was a catastrophe. Everyone else speaks of it as a 'slight stroke.' "

"You feel it's the end. Just as fifteen-year-old Shaleen must have when her father raped her and made her pregnant."

Angela gasped. "Should you be telling me this?"

286

"There's worse. Shaleen was desperate, so she found someone to abort her—not a doctor or anyone who knew what to do. She came in here dying. We saved her, but for what? She lives in terror of her father finding her and forcing her to come home, maybe to be raped again and again. Anyway, she thinks so."

"There are laws," Angela said, leaning forward. "The police—"

"Shaleen wouldn't give us her real name, so we don't know her father's. All we know is he's a judge—evidently so highly placed Shaleen doesn't believe anyone can help her."

"That's terrible! It's the worst thing I've ever heard. He should be punished. No one's that highly placed."

"Not from your point of view, maybe. After all, you're a famous actress, an important person yourself. Shaleen's an inexperienced young girl who's been through an experience that's made her trust no one."

Angela gazed at Lynn for long minutes without speaking. "Why did you tell me this story?" she said at last.

"It's true."

"I don't doubt it. Why tell me, though?"

Lynn, who'd begun talking about Shaleen in hopes of making Angela realize others suffered too, suddenly understood how she could use Shaleen to prod Angela to get on with her own life and at the same time help Shaleen.

"Because," she said, "I want to help Shaleen and you're the only one I've met who's famous enough to prove an equal to the judge."

Angela nodded. "You're honest. I like that. But you can see for yourself I'm helpless."

"Temporarily, perhaps."

"Come, you know I've lost my looks, I can't walk, I can't use my left arm—why, I can barely talk intelligibly."

"When you came in, your speech was slurred," Lynn said. "It's improved, you're entirely understandable. As for your left leg, with therapy it'll improve so you'll be able to walk again. Your arm may or may not do as well as your leg—it's too soon to tell. As for your looks—at the moment you have minimal facial sagging which is improving. Even with it, you're still a beautiful woman.

"Think about it. You can decide to stay bedridden or you can learn to retrain your leg so you can get around by yourself. It's your choice. If you don't exercise your arm, you'll never know whether you'll ever move it again. That's your choice as well. Only you can decide."

Chapter 18

At lunch on Monday, Joyce joined Lynn at her table. Lois Johnson from maternity was just leaving, so the two were alone.

"How'd you like to go to Catalina this weekend?" Joyce asked.

Lynn had heard Santa Catalina, the most famous of the islands off the coast of southern California, described as a fabulous resort. "Who wouldn't want to?"

"Be my guest. I've got boat tickets and a reservation at the Pavilion Lodge in Avalon, but something's come up and I won't be able to make it."

"If you let me buy the tickets from you—" Lynn began.

Joyce cut her off. "We can discuss that later. I'm dying to tell you what I *am* doing this weekend. Guess who called me?"

"Hal Stuart."

"You got it. And not just for a date, he's arranged an interview for me with some company up in LA doing TV commercials. What d'you think of that?"

Lynn stared at her. "I'm speechless."

"Seems Hal showed them clips of the art show—you

know, us standing with those pictures—and they're interested in talking to me."

Lynn had often thought Joyce would be a perfect model, but she was somewhat taken aback by Joyce's obvious interest. "Would you really give up nursing?"

"Ask me again after they start talking money," Joyce said. "Who knows, they might not like me in the flesh."

"You'll overwhelm them."

Joyce grinned at her. "I'm too much to take, right?"

"You're gorgeous and you know it."

"So okay, I'll go to LA and you'll go to Catalina. The reservation's for three nights—Thursday, Friday, and Saturday. Any reason you can't take Friday off?"

"The unit's pretty quiet at the moment and I have a day coming to me. I'm sure Rolfe can handle things."

"You sure have changed your mind about him."

"Rolfe is living proof that male nurses aren't all bad." She smiled at Joyce. "Actually, he's damned good."

"I'll arrange for you to take Friday off, then. You'll love Catalina—the island's like nothing else in this world. I like to go there alone to wind down. It's also romantic, in case you have something else in mind."

Lynn hesitated. The idea of Nick being with her was appealing; on the other hand, she needed time to be by herself. With his busy schedule, he probably couldn't arrange to be off on such short notice anyway.

"I think I'd rather go alone," she told Joyce. "It'll be fun to explore the island by myself."

Nick called her just before she went off duty.

"Lloyd's been admitted with a kidney stone stuck in his left ureter," he told Lynn. "I'll be covering his patients as well as mine until he's on his feet again. He has a primipara in labor now, she's about four centimeters dilated. I guess we'd better not plan on dinner or much of anything else until Lloyd gets rid of that stone.''

So it was just as well she hadn't planned on asking Nick to go to Catalina with her, Lynn thought as she hung up. Dr. Linnett could be in the hospital for some time, and until he was released, she wouldn't see much of Nick.

Bonita Duelle came up to Lynn as she waited for the elevator. ''My patient wouldn't go to therapy,'' she said almost triumphantly, as though she was glad Lynn had failed to persuade Angela. ''I think you upset her with whatever you told her, she's hardly said a word all afternoon.''

You can't win 'em all, Lynn told herself as she rode down in the elevator, trying to deny her disappointment. She'd hoped Angela would take an interest in helping Shaleen, thus helping herself. Speaking of helping—without someone to lean on, would Beth be able to recover enough from her traumatic affair with Barry Marlin to return to work? Lynn was doubtful.

But on Tuesday Beth was back, though looking pinched and wan. ''That kid has to toughen up,'' Sheila said to Lynn. ''Nursing'll kill her otherwise. If it doesn't, not being particular whose bed she jumps into will.''

Sheila's words proved that the grapevine was in full blossom.

Later, Beth told Lynn she'd stopped by ICU on her way to work. ''Mrs. Marlin's still critical,'' she said. ''I feel so sorry for her. I'm ashamed I didn't try to help her ... I guess I get scared too easily. Rolfe says I should try to think things through more.''

''That sounds like a good idea,'' Lynn told her.

''If I'd had any idea—I mean, I just didn't know—'' Beth's words trailed off. ''He didn't look like that kind of man.''

Obviously she meant Barry Marlin. "No one wears labels," Lynn said. "That's why it's important to take the time to know people before you get involved with them." My God, she thought, she sounded like a maiden aunt.

"I thought I did know him. How could I tell he was so awful?"

"He isn't awful for being bisexual."

Beth looked at her with disbelief. "I keep thinking maybe he gave me AIDS. What's more awful than that?"

"I admit he should have told you ahead of time, but you can't count on men warning you. You have to take care of yourself."

"That's what Rolfe keeps telling me. He says he doesn't think I'll get AIDS, though, 'cause he figures doctors are careful that way. Anyway, I'll bet Mrs. Marlin didn't like what was going on and that's why she left. It's his fault she ODed."

Lynn decided she didn't have any more time to lecture Beth on responsibility for oneself. In any case, the unit wasn't the place for it.

Remembering her promise to give Mr. Franklin one of her special back rubs, she stopped by his room on her way to the desk. His hip lesion, though not completely healed, was now free of staph, so he was no longer in isolation.

"You do better than most," he admitted when she finished the back rub, "but you don't hold a candle to Watson. Takes a man to really know how."

"He'll be back tomorrow," she said.

"That man gives me a hard time," he grumbled. "Always at me, 'Do this, do that.' Don't he know I'm dying?"

Lynn, washing her hands at the sink, paused for a moment. Mr. Franklin had never before mentioned dying. Did he want to talk about it to her? She dried her hands and came back to the bed.

"Mr. Watson is trying to get you to do what you can for yourself," she said.

"Yeah. Only when a man's dying, seems like other people could take care of him."

"What is it you want Mr. Watson to do for you?"

"He takes so damn much time off."

Lynn blinked in puzzlement, staring at Mr. Franklin. Rolfe took no more than the standard two days a week. After several moments of thought, she realized what the patient meant: he enjoyed arguing with Rolfe, he felt secure when Rolfe took care of him, his real complaint was that Rolfe couldn't be his nurse every day.

She thought of Freddie, dying too, but at home with Shaleen, the person he trusted most. Did Freddie feel more secure about dying than Mr. Franklin, who had no control over his caretakers?

The day went smoothly until the change of shifts. As the evening med nurse counted narcotics with the day shift, Angela McDonald's container of Tylenol with codeine turned up missing.

"I handed it to Bonita for her to take out a pill," Beth said defensively. "I'm sure she put it back on the cart."

"Did you lock the container back into the narcotic drawer right away?" Lynn asked.

"I can't remember. I almost always do, though."

Standard procedure was for Beth to dole out the pill required, or else watch the private duty nurse as she measured the dose, then relock the container into the narcotic drawer.

"I was busy," Beth muttered. "I just can't remember."

Bonita Duelle had already gone off duty and the evening private duty nurse knew nothing about the codeine. She checked Angela's room without finding the container.

"You'll have to write up an incident report," Lynn told Beth.

Beth began to cry. "Mrs. Morrin's going to fire me, I just know she will."

Lynn couldn't reassure her since she knew Beth was very likely right. "I'll help you with the report," she said, that being all the comfort she could give her.

Mrs. Morrin was in her office when Lynn brought the report down on her way home.

"Beth Yadon again?" the DNS asked, raising disapproving eyebrows as she scanned the form.

"The private duty nurse may have inadvertently taken the codeine container," Lynn pointed out.

"That's yet to be determined. Since the narcotic was Ms. Yadon's responsibility, though, the mistake is also hers. I warned her a second medication error warranted dismissal."

"She's been doing better," Lynn said lamely, wishing she could think of something to deter the DNS.

Mrs. Morrin tapped the incident report form on the desk. "This hardly indicates improvement. As you well know, a missing narcotic is a serious matter."

Lynn was willing to swear Beth hadn't taken the codeine, but even if Mrs. Morrin believed her, someone had obviously removed it from the cart. Since Beth had the key to the narcotic drawer, there was no denying she was at fault.

"I have no alternative but to dismiss Ms. Yadon," the DNS said. "Furthermore, the incident must be investigated. I trust the container will be located before we're forced to call in the authorities."

Since codeine was a narcotic, Lynn knew she meant federal authorities.

On Wednesday, Lynn greeted Rolfe with relief, realizing she trusted and depended on him as she'd never trusted Sheila and couldn't depend on Beth.

"Beth's really depressed about the missing codeine," Rolfe said. "I suppose Morrin fired her."

"She told me she was going to." Lynn sighed. "I couldn't do a thing to prevent it since Beth *was* careless."

"Beth didn't take the pills. Who did?"

"Bonita Duelle denies knowing anything about what happened after she took out the one pill for her patient. If Beth left the container on the top of the cart, anyone, including visitors, could have made off with it."

Rolfe shook his head. "I think someone on Five East planned this. This person has been watching and waiting for her chance. Neither Sheila nor I are easily distracted. Beth is, and the one who stole the codeine figured that out. I've got a pretty good idea who she is, and I'm sure as hell going to nail her."

Lynn lowered her voice. "Bonita Duelle?"

He nodded. "I'm going to get her, Lynn. After I do, will you go with me to Morrin to see if we can get Beth reinstated?"

"If we have a case, yes. But speaking of tough ladies—Morrin's the toughest. Besides, you don't know Bonita's guilty. And even if she is, how are you ever going to—?"

Rolfe shook his head. "Believe me, you don't want to know."

He was probably right, Lynn decided. As charge nurse, if she didn't approve of his tactics, she'd have to tell him he couldn't do it, and she had a strong feeling she would definitely not approve. It was better not to know.

Like Rolfe, she was almost certain Bonita had taken the codeine. They could both be wrong, but she didn't think so.

"By the way, you'll be in charge on Friday," she told him. "I'm taking a day off."

His left eyebrow climbed, then he smiled at her. "I guarantee Five East'll still be in one piece when you get back on Monday."

Later that afternoon Mr. Franklin died. Rolfe, who'd been in the room for some time, came out to the desk and told her.

"He knew he was going," Rolfe said, "and he asked me to stay with him. Said he wanted to make sure no one messed up his dying. He'd seen a Code Blue on TV once, and he didn't want that to happen to him." Rolfe blinked and Lynn saw his eyes were shiny with tears. "He was a mean old bastard right up to the end." His tone held admiring affection. "I'm going to miss him."

"He trusted you." Lynn told Rolfe what Mr. Franklin had said to her. "I think he waited to die until you were on duty," she added. "I'll miss him, too."

Before she went off duty she called the ICU. Tina Marlin, she was told, had improved slightly, but her condition was still critical.

Nick called her that evening. "Barry told me Tina might just make it," he said. "He's been haunting ICU. Nothing like almost losing someone to make a man realize."

"Realize what?" she asked tartly. She had never liked Barry Marlin for reasons that had nothing to do with his sexual preferences.

"Who matters to him. Not that I think Barry's going to change a hell of a lot ... but let's assume he'll treat Tina better."

Lynn snorted.

"The cynic speaks," Nick said. "I miss seeing you. I

keep trying to find a patient to admit to Five East, but so far, no luck. And the way this week is going, if I don't see you on duty, it doesn't look like I'll see you at all. I have more bad news. Did you know Renee hasn't shown up for work so far this week? Admissions says they can't reach her at the phone number she listed. Is she usually that irresponsible?"

It hadn't occurred to Lynn to check on Renee, and it gave her a pang to think Nick was interested enough to do so. "I think she worked for that Worcester bank for several years," she said.

"I wonder if she's all right."

"Renee admitted to me she was on uppers, but claimed she had it under control."

"That's what they all say. She could be in a real mess, you know?"

"What do you expect me to do about it?" Lynn couldn't control the sharpness in her tone. "In the first place, I have no idea where she is and I don't plan to challenge the Green Dragon in his lair to see if he knows."

"The Green—" Nick broke off. "Oh yeah, the tattooed pickup owner. If I get time, I'll drop by and see if he's heard from her. No matter how you feel about her, you really wouldn't want anything to happen to Renee."

Lynn sighed. Of course she didn't . . . on the other hand, worrying about Renee wasn't high on her list of priorities. Unlike Nick, evidently. She continued to mull over his continuing interest in Renee while they went on talking, and it wasn't until she hung up that she realized she'd forgotten to tell him she was going to Catalina for the weekend.

After she hung up with Nick, she called Shaleen to ask about Freddie. "He sleeps a lot more," Shaleen said. "I guess it's the pain shots. But he can't eat."

"I hope *you're* eating and getting enough sleep," Lynn cautioned.

"I'm fine, really. Don't worry about me."

Lynn hadn't really counted on Angela McDonald taking an interest in the girl, but she was disappointed that nothing she'd said had been effective either in helping Shaleen or in making Angela want to help herself.

But on Thursday, Lynn was pleasantly surprised when Bonita Duelle wheeled her patient to the desk. Angela had steadfastly refused to leave her room until now.

"I've decided to look over the physical therapy department," she told Lynn.

Lynn nodded, controlling her irreverent impulse to say she hoped the department met with Angela's approval. This was a step in the right direction and she didn't want to do anything to jeopardize it.

After Angela and Bonita had gone, Lynn returned to checking patient care plans, wanting to be certain everything was up to date before Friday. Phone calls from two doctors and one relative interrupted her, then Dr. Anderson, a chest surgeon, needed help changing a dressing on his patient, Mr. Lennox, and Lynn, unable to locate Rolfe, assisted the doctor herself. Mr. Lennox complained to Lynn about the food, and so she called the dietician from his phone and arranged for her to come up and consult with the patient.

As she left his room, Mrs. Duncaster, walking unsteadily down the hall, caught Lynn's attention. Mrs. Duncaster, a post-op hernia repair, was at eighty-six a bit confused and prone to fall. She'd been repeatedly cautioned about getting out of bed without assistance. Approaching her, Lynn said, "I'll walk you back to your room," and offered her arm.

"That's nice of you, dear," Mrs. Duncaster told her,

holding on to Lynn's arm with her arthritic fingers. "I seem to have lost my way."

Lynn helped Mrs. Duncaster to use her bathroom, then settled her in a chair by the window of her room with a large-print book. She was returning to the desk when Rolfe, with Sheila in tow, strode into Angela McDonald's private room. Lynn changed course to follow them. Before she reached the room, she heard Bonita's indignant voice through the open door.

"What do you mean I took it off your cart?" Bonita cried. "You're out of your mind."

Lynn stopped short in the doorway. Angela, back in bed, stared from one to another of the nurses while Rolfe, Sheila beside him, confronted Bonita.

Casting a glance toward the doorway, Rolfe said, "I'm glad you're here, Ms. Holley. Ms. Duelle removed a container of codeine from the med cart and she refuses to give it back to me."

"He's lying!" Bonita insisted.

"I saw you put it in your purse," Rolfe said. "So open the purse and prove me wrong."

"I'll do no such thing."

"Are you certain?" Lynn asked Rolfe.

"I'm positive. She took the codeine. It's in her purse."

"For Christ's sake, Bonita, open the damned purse and get the suspense over with," Angela said.

Bonita, followed by Rolfe, marched to the small chest of drawers in the room and grabbed her purse. She glared at him as she turned around, her hand on the clasp.

"Not here," he ordered. "Over there where Ms. Holley and Mrs. Burns can see."

Bonita, with ill grace, crossed to where Lynn stood with Sheila by Angela's bed. Angela craned her neck to watch, obviously interested in the outcome.

Bonita released the clasp and jerked the purse open. "There!"

'I can't tell if it's there or not," Rolfe said. "Dump the stuff on the overbed table."

Bonita upended the purse. "I hope you're satisfied," she said. "I intend to report you to—" She stopped abruptly, staring.

"That's the codeine, Ms. Holley," Rolfe said, pointing to a green pill-counter container. He made no move to touch it.

As Lynn reached for it, Bonita cried, "No!" and shoved her away. Sheila grabbed Bonita around the waist from the rear, pulling her back. Lynn picked up the container.

"McDonald, Angela," she read. "Tylenol with codeine #3."

"Let me see that, please," Angela said. Lynn moved to hand her the container.

After examining it, Angela gave the container back to Lynn. She looked at her private duty nurse. Sheila had released Bonita, who'd backed up against the chest of drawers, her empty purse in her hand.

"Bonita, why did you take the codeine?" Angela asked.

"I didn't, they're lying, all of them, they plánted it on me, put it in my purse—I swear they did."

"I doubt that," Angela said. "It's totally implausible. Besides, I know Ms. Holley would never countenance anything of the sort. Why not admit the truth?"

"It's not the first time," Rolfe said. "On Tuesday a container of codeine was missing from the med cart after Bonita asked the medicine nurse for a pill for you, Ms. McDonald. No one happened to see—"

"Why, Bonita!" Angela cut in, her voice shocked. "I didn't ask you for a pain pill on Tuesday. I haven't needed one all week. You certainly didn't give me any, either."

300

Lynn had reviewed Angela's chart when making the incident report on Tuesday, so she was certain of the facts. "Ms. Duelle did chart the pill as given to you on Tuesday and she also signed for it in the narcotic book," she told Angela. "There was also a Tylenol with codeine pill signed for and charted as given on Monday." Turning to Bonita, she said. "I think you'd better discuss this matter with our director of nursing services, Mrs. Morrin."

"You're all lying," Bonita muttered.

"*I* certainly am not!" Angela exclaimed. "I may have had a stroke, but it didn't affect my memory. Please gather your belongings and leave, Bonita . . . immediately. I won't have a nurse I can't trust."

Later, after Bonita was gone and calm had been restored, it occurred to Lynn that however guilty Bonita had been in charting codeine that was never given to Angela, she might not have been lying when she said the codeine container in her purse had been planted. Though it could never be proved, Lynn believed Bonita had taken the first container off the med cart when Beth was on duty. But had Bonita really stolen the second container today, or had Rolfe contrived to make it appear she had?

"You don't want to know," he'd told her when she asked how he planned to prove Bonita's guilt. It would be useless to question him—he'd deny everything, whatever he'd done. She'd never know. She'd have to be satisfied that Bonita had been caught charting codeine not given to her patient and had been dismissed.

"I understand why you believe Ms. Duelle was the one who took the codeine container on Tuesday," Mrs. Morrin said when Lynn and Rolfe met with her in her office. "Nevertheless, Ms. Yadon was still at fault for not locking the codeine in the drawer immediately after dispensing the single dose."

"Ma'am," Rolfe said, "I try my best to be careful about narcotics, but Ms. Duelle is clever. She deliberately distracted me today and managed to slide the container into her purse while I was looking the other way. If I hadn't happened to catch her movement from the corner of my eye, I wouldn't have been so positive about what happened. I asked Mrs. Burns to be a witness when I accused Ms. Duelle so it wouldn't be just my word against Ms. Duelle's."

"Commendable." Mrs. Morrin's tone was dry and Lynn wondered if she, too, suspected Rolfe might have set Bonita Duelle up.

"I must point out," Mrs. Morrin went on, "that Ms. Yadon has proven careless on two occasions. How can I be sure this won't happen again?"

Rolfe looked to Lynn to field that question.

"I think reinstating her on Five East would strengthen her self-confidence," Lynn told Mrs. Morrin. "Giving Ms. Yadon another chance would make her realize you think she can be trusted as a nurse. Knowing you trust her, I believe she'd try very hard to prove you right."

The DNS glanced from Lynn to Rolfe. "That she inspires such loyalty in her supervisor and her co-worker is in Ms. Yadon's favor. On the other hand, your positive prejudice may be based not on reasoned judgment, but because you like her. I'll consider the reinstatement over the weekend. If I do decide Ms. Yadon may return, she certainly can't expect any more chances."

"What d'you think?" Rolfe asked Lynn as they rode up to Five East in the elevator.

"With Morrin, who can tell? But I lean toward a yes vote."

"You're right about Beth. If she gets to come back, it'll make her feel a hell of a lot better about herself."

302

"Too bad she can't graft on some of your self-confidence," Lynn said as the elevator door opened and they stepped onto the unit.

"Mine? Lady, you don't know. When I confronted that Duelle chick, I was true and purely scared shitless."

"You mean you weren't sure it'd work?" Lynn asked, her voice as dry as Morrin's had been.

He shot her a quick glance, then grinned. "As an old gambler once told me, the trick is knowing when to make your move." He strode away before she could say anything else.

Lynn decided to let well enough alone. However it'd been brought about, justice had been done. She spent the rest of the shift finishing up paperwork. Before she left, she went in to make sure Angela was all right after the day's confusion.

"I'm glad to be rid of Bonita, if the truth be told," Angela confessed. "There was something about her I didn't like, something sneaky." She shrugged. "Enough of her." Smiling at Lynn, she added, "Congratulating yourself because you succeeded in getting me out of my room?"

"I've been wondering how you liked our PT department."

Angela waved her hand. "I felt right at home. It reminded me of a movie set—some giving orders, others trying to follow directions, lights, camera, action. I asked about the video camera. It seems patients monitor their progress by looking back to see how far they've come. Interesting . . . someone ought to tell them how to use the camera for the best results, though."

Lynn had the feeling Angela would soon be doing just that.

"I haven't forgotten the little girl you told me about—

Shaleen." Angela sighed. "I'm not certain if I can find a way to help her, nothing's come to me yet. Maybe you could arrange for her to come and visit me. Not right away, in a couple of weeks, when I've—progressed."

"Let me know when you're ready."

Angela reached her hand toward Lynn and when Lynn took it, she squeezed briefly and let go. "You deserve an extra day off," she said. "Enjoy Catalina."

Lynn stared. "How did you know—"

"Every place I've ever been has a grapevine. I learned a long time ago how to pick the grapes. Dear departed Bonita told me she heard it from one of your nurses—Sheila, I believe. Ah, Avalon." Angela's eyes grew dreamy. "Such marvelous times. The island ambience works a sea change, turning the most prosaic man into an imaginative and romantic lover." She made a face. "Be warned, though. It doesn't last after you return to the mainland."

Later that afternoon Lynn boarded the Pacific Cruise boat at the Catalina terminal in San Pedro. As she stood at the rail watching the boat churn out of the harbor, she thought of Angela's warning and smiled. No need to worry about sea changes when she was going to Catalina alone.

Chapter 19

As the boat chugged west toward Santa Catalina, the lowering sun turned the clouds to flame and reflected red on the water. Lynn, standing at the rail, felt she was sailing through a sea of fire into the land of the setting sun. Though the ocean breeze was cool against her face, it didn't have the underlying chill of the Atlantic in June. This was a different ocean, a different life.

A different love? No, she couldn't call what she felt for Nick love, that was asking for trouble, inviting pain.

She wouldn't regret he wasn't with her. She'd explore Catalina on her own and discover the island's fascination by herself. She didn't need Nick with her to appreciate a romantic spot.

Santa Catalina, the tourist pamphlet told her, eight miles wide and twenty-one miles long, had been discovered by Juan Cabrillo in 1542. In the early days pirates and smugglers used the sheltered coves on the lee side for their lairs. There must be tales of buried treasure on the island like there were on Cape Cod, where long ago pirates anchored in the many small bays protected by barrier beaches.

The island's only sizeable community was Avalon. A fairy-tale name, conjuring up visions of King Arthur sailing away to the abode of heroes, where the golden apples of the sun grew.

She'd see everything the island had to offer tourists, Lynn decided, from the summer-mansion-turned-museum that William Wrigley, the chewing gum magnate, had built, to the undersea wonders viewed from a glass-bottomed boat. And she'd explore on her own, too—away from the advertised places.

She wouldn't once think of Harper Hills or her patients on Five East. She wouldn't worry about Shaleen or wonder what had happened to Renee. And she wouldn't miss Nick.

Avalon Bay was dotted with small boats anchored in curving rows offshore. Red-tiled houses climbed the steep hills semicircled around the bay, a colorful and exotic sight. As the boat pulled alongside the pier, recorded music tinkled from a loudspeaker with a male vocalist singing "Avalon."

An open car with Pavilion Lodge painted on the sides picked up Lynn and two other passengers. After she'd checked in, she strolled along Crescent Avenue, the street fronting the curve of the bay, until she spotted the small restaurant Joyce had recommended—"Cut of Her Jib." Inside, she discouraged a man with a moustache who wanted to buy her a drink, and ordered fish chowder with tortillas, enjoying every mouthful.

Lynn was annoyed when, on her way back to the lodge, the man with the mustache appeared once more. "Keith's my name," he told her. "What's yours?"

He was a big, hulking fellow—thirtyish, wearing jeans and a corduroy jacket. Lynn wasn't afraid of him, but she didn't go in for casual pickups. She'd already refused him once and to reinforce her total disinterest she didn't answer or look at him.

"No one ought to be alone in Avalon," he said, keeping pace with her.

Because she didn't want him to follow her into the Pavilion, she stopped and faced him. "Look," she said firmly, "when I told you 'no thanks,' in the restaurant, I meant what I said. Stop bothering me. I prefer being alone."

"Honey, I like redheads."

She realized he was too drunk to listen to reason and was likely to prove a real pest. "Get lost," she advised him bluntly and strode briskly toward the motel.

To her dismay, he followed her. She certainly didn't want him trailing her to her room, so she marched into the lobby and told the registration clerk what had happened.

"Sir," the clerk asked Keith, "are you a guest here?"

Keith admitted he wasn't.

"Okay, then buzz off. The lady says you're annoying her." When Keith hesitated, the clerk added. "Want me to call the cops?"

Keith glowered at him, then at Lynn before turning and walking unsteadily from the lobby, muttering as he went. She waited until she was certain he was gone before heading for her room. The encounter, harmless though it had been, had tinged her first night on the island with unpleasantness. Though she'd been considering another walk, she decided not to that night.

By morning she'd all but forgotten Keith as she planned her day. She'd try a glass-bottomed boat ride in the morning and wander around on her own in the afternoon.

As seen through the glass bottom, the seaweed forest under the water fascinated Lynn. She watched a fat gray fish with a pouting mouth weave in and out among the grasses and blinked in amazement at the sight of gigantic goldfish. When she returned to El Doblez, she told herself, she'd learn to snorkle so she could become a part of the underwater world herself.

Coming back into the harbor, she realized why she'd thought Avalon had a foreign flair. The Mediterranean style of the homes, the tiled roofs, the steep pitch of the hills, the bright sun, and the sparkling blue water of the bay combined to make the community unlike anything Lynn had seen anywhere else in America. She wondered then what was beyond Avalon and what the rest of the island looked like.

After lunch she'd explore it, and when the boat docked, she discovered if she hurried, she had time to catch the bus to the Wrigley mansion and be back before noon.

Since she'd expected a huge and ornate place on the order of the eastern mansions she'd toured, Lynn wasn't too impressed with Wrigley's old summerhouse. She found the view of the hills behind Avalon disappointing, too— mostly rocks and grass. Trees, it seemed, might cling to the cliffs around the houses in Avalon, but that was because they'd been planted there and carefully watered. A dearth of water on Catalina not only kept building to a minimum, it meant trees didn't grow on their own on the island.

She decided she'd explore the terrain near the ocean after lunch rather than hike over the barren hills.

"That's a good idea," Michelle, the friendly waitress in Cut Of Her Jib told Lynn. "They say pirates used to hang out along the coast on this side of the island. There's nothing in the hills except a few wild goats. But, hey, I'd go see the casino if I were you. It must've been really fab when you could gamble there, like, you know, back in the twenties and thirties. They say it used to be packed with

308

movie stars—all the old timers like Gloria Swanson and Douglas Fairbanks.''

Michelle's enthusiasm for the casino persuaded Lynn to stop by and see it before she set forth to explore. Old posters inside the picturesque, white-columned, domed building featured the big bands of the forties—Harry James, Tommy Dorsey—and she wondered what it had been like to dance to such music. Gazing at the large ballroom floor, she envisioned herself whirling over the white marble in Nick's arms.

She'd be wearing frothy white chiffon with a skirt that twirled wide when he swung her about. He'd be in a blazer—no, in the forties he'd be in uniform, wouldn't he? A pilot, that's what Nick would have been, a pilot in Air Force blue. Or was it the Army Air Corps then?

Never mind, he'd be in uniform, dark and dangerously handsome. He'd be on leave, shipping out with his squadron the next day. All they'd have was one night together, dancing, and later, being alone under the romantic island stars. . . .

Damn it, she missed Nick.

To distract herself, she looked through the museum inside the Casino and took the guided tour. The afternoon was over by the time she was ready to begin exploring the rest of the island.

She chose a road Michelle had told her led away from Avalon following the water. "There's a sort of horseshoe bay after a couple of miles," Michelle had said, "where they say pirates hid, you know, a treasure chest, like that. No one's ever found anything, though.''

As she walked along, Lynn began thinking about Nick again. She tried with little success to interest herself in rock formations and in watching the seagulls and cormorants. She'd hiked some two miles from the town when a nondescript small brown dog appeared to sniff at her heels, and she bent to pet him. Encouraged, he followed her and she began talking to him.

"I don't know your name so I'll call you Rover, okay?" He wagged his stub of a tail. "I guess you approve. Good. Now that we understand each other, you know the area—why not lead me to a pirate's secret cache? Think of all the bones those pieces of eight could buy you."

As if he knew every word she'd said, Rover plunged into the scant brush alongside the sea side of the road, stopping once to look back as if inviting her to follow. Lynn was certain she hadn't gone far enough to reach the bay Michelle had mentioned, but she shrugged and left the road to go after the dog. He scrambled down and around rocks, Lynn behind him, the swish of the waves growing louder and louder. She lost sight of him and stopped, but then he began to bark and she hurried down the slope toward the sound.

She found Rover on a tiny, pebbly beach beside an ancient half-swamped rowboat. "I can see this boat is old," she told him, "but I doubt it dates back to the pirates."

Looking around the little cove with its narrow ocean entrance, she saw it was much too small for a ship to come into, but the cove certainly was private.

"You think pirates might have found this hidden spot?" she asked the dog. "They could've anchored offshore and rowed in here to bury their loot." Kicking at the pebbles with the toe of her running shoe, she encountered hard rock underneath and shook her head. "Nope, Rover, they couldn't dig here . . . you'll have to do better than this."

Lynn walked along the tiny beach, climbing to the point of land bordering the cove on the Avalon side and found no beach beyond it, just a rocky drop into the ocean. She turned around and tried the other point, the dog at her heels. About to round it, she stopped and stared. A sea cave!

Bending to pet the dog as reward for leading her here, she stopped, listening. Had she heard rocks clattering down the slope below the road? It was hard to tell over the rush of the waves. Lynn bit her lip. It hadn't yet occurred to her that someone might have followed her ... Keith, for instance. She usually wasn't fearful, but she *was* a stranger alone in this isolated place. She eased back far enough to scan the rocky rise she'd scrambled down and saw no one. The dog, sniffing along the waterline, paid no attention to the slope up to the road and Lynn relaxed. Whatever she'd heard hadn't alarmed the dog.

Gingerly, sliding on wet rocks, she approached the cave mouth, above the waterline. When she pulled herself up and looked inside, she saw that there had to be a second opening underwater, for the sea flooded through with every wave. Though some water receded with the ebb of the waves, she couldn't see the bottom of the cave. Heaven only knew how deep it might be down there. A rock ledge ran along the right side of the cave wall, eventually vanishing in the dim interior so she couldn't tell how far back it might extend. The rear of the cave wasn't visible.

"You don't expect me to go inside that cave!" she exclaimed, glancing at the dog who'd come up to watch her, his head cocked to one side. He barked.

"I'm not that crazy about pieces of eight," she told him—and herself as well. The cave was intriguing but could prove dangerous.

To her right, as she faced the cove, a small avalanche of rocks rattled down, several bouncing off the old rowboat. The dog faced toward the cove and growled, hackles rising. Someone *was* coming! Lynn leaned to her left to see what the terrain beyond the cave was and her heart sank . . . another rocky drop into the water. There was no escape that way.

Calm down, she warned herself. Whoever it was might be perfectly harmless. In her mind's eye, though, she saw Keith's ugly scowl as he'd left the motel lobby the night before. But he had been drunk, and probably wouldn't even remember he had met her, she tried to reassure herself.

But what if he did remember and had seen her today and followed her?

Lynn swallowed. Before she realized what she intended to do, she'd drawn herself up and into the mouth of the cave. The ledge was easy to reach and she clambered onto it. The cave was dank and chilly and smelled of seaweed, like iodine. The dog began to bark.

"Shut up, Rover," she muttered, realizing she might have made the worst possible move by entering the cave. If the dog remained where she'd left him and kept barking, whoever climbed down to the cove would easily find the cave. If he looked inside, she was trapped. If the intruder was Keith, he could well be a Catalina native and already know about the cave.

Lynn edged farther along the ledge, away from the mouth of the cave. Fortunately she'd worn navy blue clamdiggers and a shirt to match, and the dark colors would blend into the gloom if she moved back far enough. Rock crumbled under her knee and she froze. A larger chunk broke away from the ledge and splashed into the water below. Before she could retreat to the opening, she felt more of the ledge crumble and scrabbled desperately to solid rock. She lay there, gasping in relief at her narrow escape until it occurred to her to wonder how she was going to get back to the mouth of the cave.

She sat up cautiously, turning to face the opening. "Oh,

no," she moaned. Three or more feet of the ledge had sheered off between her and the cave mouth. She was trapped.

Rover had stopped barking. It must be getting on toward six. Soon it'd be dark ... what if no one found her?

I don't care who he is, she thought, I only hope someone's out there with that damn dog.

"Help!" she shouted. Her cry echoed eerily around the cave, mingling with the gurgle of the water ebbing and flowing. Could she be heard outside the cave?

A voice called faintly. Was it her name? Keith didn't know her name.

"Lynn?" The call came again, a bit louder.

"Help!" she cried, too relieved to wonder who it could be. "I'm in the cave."

Moments later a head thrust into the opening. "What in hell are you doing in there?" a familiar voice demanded.

"Nick!" She'd never been happier to see anyone in her life. "Part of the ledge broke off. I can't get back to the opening."

He levered himself inside, onto the ledge, inched to the broken edge, and thrust his arms toward her. "Crouch on your heels and grab my arms just above the wrists," he ordered.

Lynn obeyed, feeling him grasp her forearms at the same time.

"When I count to three," he said, "jump toward me. I'll pull you onto my part of the ledge. One ... two ... three!"

Lynn, gripping his arms tightly, flung herself into nothingness. Her leap plus his strength carried her so far that she knocked Nick off balance and they sprawled backward, teetering on the brink of the ledge. Nick shifted her toward the safety of the cave wall, and twisting, flung himself at the opening. Clinging to the rocky mouth, he pulled himself up and out. She crawled to the opening and eased herself down beside him. Rover barked excitedly, wagging his tail.

"It's all his fault," Lynn said, pointing a trembling finger at the dog as she leaned against Nick. His arms closed around her and she felt her shuddering ease up. She was safe.

"The dog wasn't dumb enough to go into the cave," Nick murmured into her ear. "Why did you?"

She pulled away a little to look at him. "I just realized you're not supposed to be here."

"Lucky I am, isn't it?" He kissed her, a comforting, reassuring kiss, then released her, and with an arm around her waist, led her to the old boat. "Rest for a couple of minutes before we start back."

Lynn perched on the gunwwale. "What *are* you doing on Catalina?" she asked. "How did you find me?"

"Apparently I was the only one at Harper Hills who didn't know you were off to Catalina," he said.

"I meant to call you—I really did."

He raised an eyebrow, shaking his head. "Joyce told me this morning when I asked her where you were. She also gave me the name of your motel and the restaurant she'd recommended."

"But I thought you were covering for Dr. Linnett. How—"

"Lloyd passed his stone last night and insisted on going home immediately afterward. He's feeling so much better he decided to go into the office today. Neither of us has any babies due for a couple of weeks, so I told him I had an emergency on Catalina and caught an early afternoon boat. As for finding you—I talked to the right waitress at

Cut of Her Jib, Michelle. My curiosity about the barking dog did the rest." Nick tugged one of Rover's ears. "Where did you pick up this dangerous mutt?"

"Rover wouldn't hurt a flea."

"You claimed he led you astray and that ain't easy, as I can testify."

She made a face at him. "They used to have pirates on Catalina . . . and smugglers. I asked Rover if he knew about any buried treasure."

"Being a canine treasure hunter, Rover led you to the cave and then you decided to search for pieces of eight inside, right?"

"He led me here, yes—but credit me with having some intelligence. I wouldn't have entered the cave except that I heard someone coming and I got scared and hid. How was I supposed to know it was you? Or that the ledge would crumble?"

Nick frowned. "It's not like you to be frightened."

"I shouldn't have been. If Keith hadn't followed me last night, I—"

"Stop right there. Who's Keith?"

She shrugged. "Some drunk who tried to pick me up last night and wouldn't take no for an answer. I finally got rid of the guy, but he was angry about my refusing him. So today it occurred to me he might have followed me again. I didn't care to meet up with Keith in an isolated spot like this."

"Didn't it occur to you wandering off on your own might be dangerous with this Keith bastard around?"

Lynn slid off the boat to confront him. "I've stopped spending my life being afraid of what might happen. I've no intention of hiding being locked doors."

"I didn't suggest you should. A little caution—"

"Goes a long way," she finished for him.

315

"Damn it, you've been cautious enough with me."

Lynn smiled. "It was probably the right approach to take with you. They don't call you HHH, the Harper Hills Heartbreaker, for nothing."

Nick stared at her for a long moment before he began to laugh. "My God, who told you that?"

"Who *didn't* would be more to the point."

"You're making this up."

Lynn traced a large cross on her chest with her forefinger. "Cross my heart and hope to die."

"If I've got the name, I guess I'll have to play the game," he told her, pulling her into his arms. His kiss was long and deep, plumbing her secret well of passion.

She clung to him in a daze of desire as his hands slid underneath her T-shirt, warm and provocative against her bare flesh.

Rover began barking.

"Now what?" Nick muttered, pulling away from her to look around.

A man paddling a kayak was gliding into the cove.

"This place is getting entirely too crowded," Nick grumbled, grabbing Lynn's hand and pulling her with him up the slope. "Time to say goodbye to Smuggler's Cave."

She looked back and saw Rover running up and down along the waterline barking excitedly—a welcoming bark, not a threatening one. Could it be his master returning in the kayak? It would explain why the dog favored the cove. When she and Nick reached the road with no sign of Rover following them, she decided she was right.

As they began the hike back to Avalon, she asked Nick how everything was at the hospital.

"Who cares?" he said.

"I don't, not really," she told him. "But I can't help

wondering how Angela McDonald's doing. I tried to get her interested in Shaleen, you know."

"Why?"

Lynn shrugged. "Angela needs to think about someone besides herself."

"I don't think bringing Shaleen into the picture is a good idea. Neither do I think discussing Harper Hills right now is the greatest idea. We're here to forget the place." He squeezed her hand. "Agreed?"

His touch, as always, made her want to forget everything but Nick. She smiled at him. "Okay. I've wiped it from my mind." Seeing that the sun had dipped from sight behind the island hills, she asked, "What time is it? I left my watch at the Pavilion and it must be getting late because I'm hungry."

Nick glanced at his watch. "It's nearly seven. May I have the pleasure of your company at dinner?"

Lynn grew conscious of her dirt-stained pants and T-shirt for the first time. "I'll have to change. Where are you staying?"

He half-smiled. "At the Pavilion, where else?"

"From what Joyce said, I thought reservations were necessary."

"They are. On a summer weekend there isn't a room to be found on the island without one."

Lynn blinked, then her eyes widened as she took in his meaning.

Nick's smile broadened. "Didn't you just tell me you've thrown caution to the winds?"

"I guess I don't have much choice."

He pulled her to a stop and cupped her face with his hands, looking into her eyes. "With me, you always have a choice, Lynn. What will it be?"

She met his gaze, her heart pounding as she fumbled

for the right words. "May I have the pleasure of sharing my room with you?"

He brushed his lips against hers. "I thought you'd never ask."

Once in the room with Nick, Lynn found herself suddenly shy of him, of her own feelings, of changing clothes in front of him. Quickly choosing a white skirt and a gold top, she hurried into the bathroom and closed the door.

Dinner, at Cut Of Her Jib, passed in a dream as far as Lynn was concerned. She ate but couldn't have told whether the food was good or bad to save her life. Nick left such a big tip for Michelle that she came running after him to thank him.

"You've more than earned it," he told her.

"Poor old Rover never even got a bone," Lynn said as they left the restaurant.

"He may have redeemed himself by barking so that I found you," Nick observed, "but since he led you astray to begin with, it comes out even. Now it's my turn."

"Your turn for what?"

"Leading you astray." He put an arm around her waist, fitting her against his side as they walked. "Do you prefer the garden path or the primrose one?"

She slanted her eyes at him. "I won't know until I've tried them both, will I?"

His arm tightened. "Keep looking at me like that and we may never get back to the Pavilion."

"Have you been through the Casino?" she asked. When he nodded, she told him how she'd imagined them dancing to Harry James in the forties. "I couldn't see you as a sailor or a soldier," she added, "So I made you a pilot."

"You think I'm the wild-blue-yonder type? No one else ever has . . . except old Greatcloud. He told me I was born

318

to fly with Eagle, the Thunderbird—I was never sure what he meant."

"He must have sensed you'd free yourself from whatever held you back."

"My parents, my upbringing—or lack of it. Poverty. None of that mattered to Greatcloud ... what was inside a person was all he saw."

"I wish I could have known him."

Nick met her eyes, then looked away. "I think *he* knew *you.*"

Lynn, not understanding, asked him to explain but Nick wouldn't.

"Forget it," he insisted. "I get a little weird sometimes."

The moon had risen, a half-moon, lightly silvering the bay. Lynn waved a hand at the water. "A moonlit path. That's the one I'd like to travel."

They walked to the water's edge. On an anchored boat someone played a Spanish tune on a guitar, the plaintive chords drifting ashore with the lazy waves. Lynn looked at Nick, at his face touched by the moonlight, and a convulsive shiver ran through her. What she felt had nothing to do with desire or with passion, her feeling belonged to the heart.

"Nick," she whispered.

He turned to her but she couldn't find words to fit the intensity of her emotion. Perhaps her feeling was caused by the magic of the moon or by romantic Avalon.

"You saved my life today," she said finally.

"If I hadn't come along, the guy in the kayak would've heard you calling. He'd have rescued you."

"But you *did* come."

"What made you think you could sail off to paradise
319

without me? Tracking comes with the Indian genes. You'll never be able to lose me."

"What if I don't want to?" Her voice was breathless.

"Now you're talking. Those are the words I've been waiting to hear from the woman who always runs away from me."

He crushed her to him and the feel of his body against hers blotted out everything else—moonlight, music, island magic. When she was in Nick's arms, her surroundings didn't matter, he was all she needed.

"It's time to go back to the Pavilion," he said long moments later, his voice husky. "If we don't, I won't be responsible for what happens right here in public."

Chapter 20

"I wanted you on *my* terms," Nick told Lynn, holding her within the circle of his arms after they entered their room at the Pavilion. "In my house, in my bed." He shook his head. "Instead, here we are, on nobody's terms, and it doesn't make the slightest difference."

Their surroundings meant nothing at all to Lynn, it was enough they were alone together in a private place. All that mattered was being with Nick.

He touched her hair, ran a finger lightly along her cheek. "You're beautiful." His hand dropped to the vee of her shirt and he undid the first button, his eyes holding hers.

Slowly, deliberately, he unbuttoned her shirt and slid it from her shoulders. Her lacy camisole was next to go. "Beautiful," he repeated, his breath catching as he looked at her.

Lynn reached for the buttons of his shirt, her pulse racing as she quickly undid them. Nick shrugged from the shirt and she placed her hands flat against his broad, tanned chest, feeling the tiny nipples against her palms.

"Don't stop now," he murmured, bending to put his lips to her throat, traveling in a warm caress to her mouth.

She slid her hands onto his shoulders, stroking the intoxicating aliveness of his skin and arched to him, her breasts pressed against his chest. Desire spiraled deep within her as his kiss caught her up in a dizzying spin of longing.

When he slid off her skirt, her half-slip went with it. He held her away from him to look at her and she could hear his breath rasp in his throat. He hooked a finger under the elastic of her bikini panties and eased them down her legs. "Beautiful," he whispered again.

Lynn could hardly breathe as she unbuckled his belt. He stooped to yank off his shoes and socks and she kicked off her sandals and stepped from her discarded clothes. He stood in front of her, not touching her except with his hungry gaze. She unzipped his pants, her fingers trembling with the urgency of her need.

She wanted to tell him he was beautiful, too, but she was too breathless to speak as she watched him shed the rest of his clothes. His obvious desire triggered an answering ache inside her. He swept her up and carried her to the bed. Pulling aside the covers with one hand, he eased her onto it and stretched out beside her. She turned to him and, with a groan, he crushed her against him.

His lips, warm against her throat, trailed to her breasts. Holding him to her, she stroked the softness of his hair, lost in his caresses. She couldn't remember ever feeling like this before, she never wanted the wonderful sensations to end and at the same time she yearned for more, to possess, to be possessed, to be a part of him.

His hands moved over her, touching, stroking, loving. She gasped with pleasure as he discovered her secrets and she reached to him, wanting to know all of him. He pressed against her hand, then drew away but she persisted, driven by her intense need. He groaned and, after a moment, raised himself above her. She opened in welcome and they came together in a surge of passion that overwhelmed her.

She abandoned herself to sensation—exquisite, demanding, all-consuming. He was a part of her, he always would be. Because she loved him. Loved Nick. She thrashed her head back and forth, wild with the rising crescendo of their lovemaking. She thought she called his name over and over, but she didn't know. She wasn't certain of anything—nothing in her past life had prepared her for the erotic frenzy of their joining.

A fiery throbbing seized her, flaming through her body, and she clutched Nick to her convulsively and heard him cry out. Together they reached a pinnacle of ecstasy.

Lynn lay exhausted in Nick's arms. She'd never believed lovemaking could be so wonderful and she hardly believed it now. She knew Nick was responsible. No other man ever had or could make her feel as he did, because she loved him.

Lynn started. *Love?*

"What's the matter?" Nick asked drowsily.

She couldn't tell him. He'd certainly never mentioned love. "Nothing." She shifted position and her head rested against his chest. Beneath her ear his heart beat strong and steady in a soothing rhythm.

"I don't hear a single murmur," she told him. "No extra systoles, even."

"You should've been listening a little while ago. I'm surprised I didn't go into cardiac arrest." He raised onto one elbow. "Lynn—" He paused.

She looked into his dark eyes and caught her breath at what she thought she saw there.

Nick shook his head. "I can't find any words."

Try "I love you," she wanted to tell him. *Say it. Mean it. What harm can three little words do?*

He brushed his lips across hers. "You're like no one else," he said. "I think I'm still in shock."

Pleasing words, but not what she needed to hear.

"God, you're beautiful," he went on, his hand covering her breast. "Beautiful everywhere."

His touch made her tingle.

"D'you know what I noticed about you first?" he asked.

"My tendency not to mind my own business, I think you once hinted."

"Your legs. Most women have something wrong— knobby knees, thick ankles, a bow. Your legs are perfect ... gorgeous." He ran his hand along her thigh. "All the way up."

Lynn felt herself melting inside. No doubt about it, this man had a magician's touch as far as she was concerned.

"You may be starting something you can't finish," she murmured.

"Who can't finish?" he challenged, sliding closer.

Her eyes widened when she felt his arousal. "Trying to set a record for recovery, Doctor?"

"If I do, you're responsible." He pulled her against him and his mouth sought hers. Once again she was caught in the irresistible current that flowed between them and she knew whether Nick loved her or not, she was committed to him. Not very smart of her, but she'd worry about that later.

Much later.

In the morning, Lynn woke early and found Nick sitting up in bed watching her. She drew the sheet closer around her, feeling inexplicably shy.

"You scared me," he said. "In that cave."

"I wasn't frightened after you came," she told him. "I knew you'd rescue me."

"What if you'd slipped from my grasp?"

"I didn't . . . it never occurred to me I would."

"You trust me that much?"

She nodded.

He closed his eyes and she understood her trust upset him. Why?

Nick slid down in the bed and put a hand to her face. "Lynn, I never want to hurt you. Not in any way."

She waited for him to go on. He didn't. "But?" she asked finally.

"Don't count on me. Don't—oh, hell, how can I say it? You're important to me in a way I never expected . . . but marriage isn't a part of it."

She hadn't gotten as far as thinking of marrying Nick, but if he didn't want to marry her, he didn't really love her.

"Why would I think it was?" she asked. "What has marriage got to do with rescuing me from the cave?"

He grinned at her, reassured. "You know, knights slaying dragons to save a fair maiden and the living-happily ever-after bit."

"Fairy tales belong to childhood. The last thing you make me feel like is a child, Nick."

He nuzzled his face against her neck. "What do I make you feel like?"

"Show or tell?" she asked.

"I'll settle for both."

Lynn sat up. "Assume the prone position then, doctor."

"Sure you don't mean supine?"

"If I wanted you on your back, I'd have said so. On your stomach, Dow, prone position."

He obeyed.

325

Lynn straddled his hips. "All good nurses begin with a back rub," she murmured as she started kneading his shoulder muscles.

"I wonder why they never taught us that in medical school."

She slid down his legs as she worked lower, along the small of his back, then his buttocks. Nick groaned.

"Do you know what you're doing to me?" he demanded.

"I'm showing. You can tell if you want."

He flipped over suddenly, making her fall sideways onto the bed. "Showing's more fun," he said, pulling her against him.

"But I wasn't through," she protested.

"Much more of that and *I* would have been. My turn, now."

His hands moved caressingly over her, touching her everywhere, showing her very clearly how much she wanted him.

"You were right," she said, hearing the hoarseness of passion in her speech. "I did mean supine position."

Nick paused. Turning onto his back, and pulling her with him, he said, "Nurses should never argue with doctors."

His voice was as husky as hers.

She raised herself and slid onto him. He made an inarticulate sound of pleasure, his hands reaching for her breasts. His thumbs brushed back and forth across her erect nipples until she lowered herself so his mouth could replace his hands. Lost in the wild excitement of their joining, she was hardly aware when he flipped them both so he was above her, the two of them locked together in passion so strong and hot and intense that nothing else mattered.

Nick carried her to fantastic peaks of pleasure she'd never dreamed existed—that wouldn't exist except with him. Caught in the spiral of fulfillment, unable to help herself, she cried out his name as she was whirled with him to the top and over.

They were showering together when the phone rang.

"Forget answering it," Nick told her.

"It might be important." Extricating herself from his embrace, she stepped from the warm spray, grabbed a towel, and dripped into the bedroom.

"Lynn Holley," she said into the phone.

"This is Conrad. I want you back at Harper Hills as soon as possible."

Lynn blinked in surprise. "But I—"

"The nurses are going out on strike—today. There's no one to take care of the patients. I desperately need your help, Lynn, and I need it now."

She tried to order her thoughts. The patients were of prime importance. They needed nurses. She didn't see how she could do anything to stop the strike, but she could certainly help take care of the patients.

"I'll catch the first boat, Conrad," she told him.

"I appreciate that."

Lynn hung up and looked around to see Nick standing naked in the bathroom doorway.

"Werth." His voice was flat.

"The Harper Hills nurses have gone on strike," she said hastily. "They've deserted the patients."

"Werth says 'jump' and you still ask how high."

"Nick, can't you understand I'm worried about the patients being left with no nurses to care for them? I *have* to help."

"All I know is he called and you're off and running." Nick's face twisted with anger.

Lynn stared at him. "Why I'm returning has nothing to do with Conrad. I'm a nurse—I *care* about my patients."

"Sure you do. And there never was anything between you and Werth, either."

Rage flooded through her. After what had happened between them last night, how could he possibly think she was Conrad's lover?

"Go to hell!" Lynn told him. She turned away, yanked clothes from her suitcase, and began dressing.

He grabbed her arm and she jerked free. "Don't touch me! Don't even talk to me. I don't want any part of a man who doesn't trust me."

"Maybe Ray *did* have something to complain about," Nick said, his voice cold. "After all, Werth was in Boston before he came here."

Lynn, speechless with pain and anger, flung clothes into her suitcase without looking at Nick. How could he believe such a thing, much less accuse her? Somehow she'd managed to choose another man as paranoid as Ray, with as little cause. It hurt to think she'd convinced herself she was in love with Nick. Wouldn't she ever learn?

By the time she was ready to leave, Nick had shut himself in the bathroom. Lynn stalked from the room, checked out, and was driven by the motel car the few blocks to the dock, where she was lucky enough to catch a departing boat.

Though the trip to Catalina hadn't affected her, she fought the nausea of seasickness all the way to San Pedro. She reached home before eleven and immediately called Joyce to find out what was going on. Joyce's answering machine said she could be reached at the hospital. Deciding not to waste time, Lynn changed into her uniform and drove to Harper Hills.

A picket line of nurses carrying placards with messages like "low pay equals no nurses equals poor patient care," strolled up and down in front of the hospital. When Lynn approached the entrance, Sheila stepped from the strikers' line to confront her. "CMC—The Big Freeze," her placard read.

"Lynn, think about it," Sheila said. "Every nurse who doesn't support the strike weakens our position. Maybe you can afford to work for peanuts, but most of us can't."

"I agree that CMC's been unfair," Lynn told her. "I also think Harper Hills nurses deserve more money. But striking hurts those least able to tolerate it—the patients. Someone has to take care of them."

Sheila scowled. "I might have known you'd be on management's side ... Werth's side."

Lynn, who'd had all she could take of being falsely accused, snapped, "I'm on the *patients'* side," and pushed past her.

Joyce wasn't in her office but Lynn found Mrs. Morrin there.

"I'm here to help," Lynn told the DNS. "Where do you want me to work?"

Mrs. Morrin smiled at her. Was that a first? Lynn wondered briefly. "We certainly need you," the DNS said. "On Five East, Ms. Yadon is coping better than I hoped with Nai Pham's help. I've sent Mr. Watson to Surgical. Ms. Elkins has taken over Pediatrics. Since I haven't been able to locate Ms. Johnson, I'll put you on Maternity for now. I'd appreciate as much time as you feel you can give." A steely glint appeared in Ms. Morrin's eye. "You can be certain I'll fight for overtime for everyone who helps during this crisis. If you need to reach me, call me on the medical unit, I'll be working there."

As she headed for Maternity, Lynn wondered why she was surprised to hear Mrs. Morrin intended to take care of patients. After all, she *was* a nurse. Somehow Lynn had expected Rolfe to be here and she was sure he'd talked Beth into staying on duty. Beth was impressionable and easily led, but she'd listen to him before Sheila.

Lois Johnson, she remembered, had taken five days off. Because of recurring headaches she was scheduled for a CAT scan and her lawyer negotiating the accident settlement had insisted she have the scan done at the same LA hospital, St. Vincent's, where they'd run the first one immediately after the accident.

So it looked as though Lynn would be on Maternity for a few days. She didn't mind except for the fact that she could hardly miss running into Nick. Right now she didn't care if she ever saw him again.

On Maternity, a harried Clovis greeted Lynn with relief. "There's a multipara in labor who's a month from term but dilating fast. Her name's Mrs. Larchmont. Dr. Linnett's on his way. I can handle the rest of what's going on if you take her over."

Lynn hurried into the patient's room.

"I had my first baby two weeks early," Mrs. Larchmont said as Lynn checked her, "but the next was a week late. I never dreamed this one—" She stopped and began breathing deeply as another contraction gripped her.

Lynn saw, to her dismay, that the patient was crowning—the top of the baby's head was visible in the vaginal opening. "Keep up the deep breathing," Lynn told her, keeping her voice calm. "I'm going to wheel you into the delivery room so you'll be all ready for Dr. Linnett."

"Is he here?" Mrs. Larchmont gasped.

Lynn fervently hoped so. She also hoped she'd have time to slide Mrs. Larchmont onto the delivery table before the baby came.

"The doctor's been called and is on his way," Lynn said reassuringly as she wheeled the bed from the labor room and into the corridor. She propped open the delivery room door and pushed the patient inside, pulling the door shut behind them. She positioned the bed next to the table.

"If I help, do you think you can slide over?" she asked.

"I—guess so." Mrs. Larchmont had difficulty getting the words out, since her contractions were now nearly continuous. But she did her best to edge onto the delivery table and finally succeeded.

Lynn hurriedly secured the patient's legs into the stirrups and started prepping the birth area for the delivery. She hadn't finished when the membranes surrounding the baby inside the birth canal ruptured and fluid gushed onto the floor. The baby's hair was now clearly visible in the vaginal opening. Mrs. Larchmont grunted, beginning to push.

Lynn, poised to catch the baby when it emerged, heard Dr. Linnett's voice behind her.

"Just made this one," he said.

Lynn turned and smiled at him, moving out of his way. He hadn't had time to scrub, but he'd put a gown over his street clothes. She opened a pair of sterile gloves and offered them to him. He barely got the gloves on before the baby's head popped through the opening.

Moments later, a tiny girl, screaming lustily, rested atop her mother's abdomen while Dr. Linnett waited to deliver the placenta.

"You have a healthy little girl," he told Mrs. Larchmont, "and I do mean little. We haven't weighed her yet, but she's not much over five pounds, if that." He turned to Lynn and gave her the APGAR rating, the evaluation of the newborn's condition at birth. Baby girl Larchmont scored high, despite her low birth weight.

"My husband isn't going to believe this," Mrs. Larchmont said. Because she'd had no anesthetic, she was completely alert. "I nagged him to go through the birth classes and everything and finally he agreed. Then he never even got to be here. He's at a meeting in LA today."

"You surprised me, too," Dr. Linnett said. "I almost didn't arrive in time."

"I heard you were a patient here yourself," Mrs. Larchmont said.

"Past tense." Dr. Linnett chuckled. "I cured myself, just as a physician's supposed to."

When the cord was cut, Lynn wrapped the baby, laid her in the waiting Isolette, and fastened on the ankle ID. After cleaning up Mrs. Larchmont and returning her to her room, and wheeling the baby to the nursery, Lynn went to the desk where Dr. Linnett was writing on the chart.

"I thought you were in Catalina," he said.

"I returned because I heard about the nurses' strike."

"Nick's back then, too?"

Lynn hesitated. He'd undoubtedly caught the next boat, so he'd probably be home by now. "Yes," she said finally.

Dr. Linnett looked up from his charting. "You don't seem sure."

"We didn't return together." Despite her effort to keep her voice neutral, resentment crept into her words.

The doctor's blue eyes gently probed hers. "Nick's inclined to rashness at times, but it's not a serious flaw."

"That all depends," Lynn said stiffly. If Dr. Linnett

didn't remind her of her father, she'd be inclined to tell him to mind his own damned business.

"I certainly don't mean to interfere . . . but he's a fine young man." Dr. Linnett scrawled his name on the chart and rose. "I'll be home if you need me. Glad to have you back on Maternity, Lynn."

Lynn worked through until the night charge came on at eleven. "Unless you hear otherwise, I'll be back in the morning," she told Mrs. Garcia.

Mrs. Garcia shook her head. "I've got nothing against strikes," she said. "Sometimes it's the only way to get management to listen. God knows I could use more money, but how could I live with myself if I joined the picket line and a patient died because I wasn't on duty?"

Before she left the hospital, Lynn stopped by Mrs. Morrin's office to see if there might be a message for her about tomorrow. The DNS wasn't there, but Conrad was.

"Lynn," he exclaimed. "Why didn't you report to me?"

"I wasn't aware you wanted me to. I came back to take care of the patients."

"I expect you to be on my side, to rally the opposition, to grab the reins from Sheila Burns's hands and work to end this strike. After all, who brought you to Harper Hills in the first place?"

She stared at him in disbelief, deliberately ignoring his implication she was beholden to him. She'd never promised to be his handmaiden. "Even if it were possible for me—or anyone—to do that, I wouldn't. I don't agree with their method, but the striking nurses have a very real grievance and you know it. Why don't you convince CMC to offer the nurses a decent pay raise? An offer like that would end the strike tomorrow."

Conrad flushed, always a sign he was indignant. "Are you saying you're not with me?"

333

"If you oppose a pay raise for the nurses or refuse to demand one from CMC, then I'm certainly not on your side."

"I'm sorry I kept you waiting, Mr. Werth." Mrs. Morrin spoke from behind Lynn, startling her.

"Excuse me," Lynn muttered, turning away.

"You'll be on Maternity again tomorrow, Ms. Holley?" Mrs. Morrin asked.

"Yes."

"Thank you."

Lynn hurried away, wondering how much of the conversation the DNS had overheard. She met Beth in the corridor.

"You're back!" Beth said.

"I heard about the strike. I'll be on Maternity until Lois Johnson comes back, that's if she doesn't decide to join the strikers. I hear you're doing a good job on Five East."

Beth colored. "It doesn't feel that way to me. Nai Pham is a big help. I sure couldn't do it without her. I just never figured I'd have to take charge of a unit. I don't know how you stand the pressure day after day."

Lynn smiled at her. "I'm proud of you, Beth."

Beth bit her lip. "I almost went with the strikers. Sheila made it sound like I'd be a traitor not to. But Rolfe yelled at me and so I came to work instead."

"I'm glad you did. Goodnight."

Beth started to go on, then turned back. "Did you hear Tina Marlin's recovering?"

"That's good news."

"I think so, too. If she'd died, I'd have her on my conscience all my life ... because I didn't try to help her."

334

The picket line was in place when Lynn arrived at Harper Hills on Sunday morning, Sheila in the forefront.

"We're going to be on TV," she called to Lynn. "What d'you think of that?"

Lynn shrugged, not especially surprised. Any controversy was fair game for news broadcasts. Probably they'd get a statement from both sides. She'd hate to be in Conrad's shoes as he tried to explain why CMC refused to consider a raise for the nurses. He'd avoid answering a question like that. Instead he'd concentrate on the patients going without proper care and sidestep the issue.

Conrad had never seemed to be such a weasel when she'd known him in Boston. Had he changed? Or was he simply weak, something that had never before been apparent to her?

Maternity was quiet, no deliveries imminent, all the babies healthy. Though Lynn and Clovis were the only two on duty, it wouldn't be impossible to get through the day unless all hell broke loose. All the mothers could pretty well take care of themselves except for one post-op C-section, and even she was recovering rapidly. Clovis could handle the nursery single-handedly.

Joyce called Lynn at seven-thirty. "I'm planning lunch at eleven-thirty," she said. "Join me?"

Lynn agreed. "How do you like Pediatrics?"

"Let's just say I've cut my projected future family from three children to one. By tomorrow it may be down to none."

Lynn hung up chuckling. Her smile faded when she saw Nick's tall, lean figure disappearing into one of his patients' rooms. She'd fallen asleep quickly last night from sheer exhaustion, but she'd roused near four o'clock and hadn't been able to sleep again because she couldn't stop thinking about him ... because she kept reliving their night together on Catalina.

She rose and left the nurses' station. With luck she might be able to avoid him. Unfortunately, the phone drew her back to the desk.

"What's going on?" Lois Johnson asked. "You know I'm up here in LA visiting my folks this weekend. I heard something on their radio about Harper Hills' nurses being on strike. Is it true?"

Lynn told her the circumstances.

"Would you let Morrin know my doctor says it's okay to work so I'll be back in the morning?" Lois said. "I sympathize with the strikers, but I'd never join them ... not at the patients' expense."

"I'll tell Morrin. And I'm glad you're all right."

Lynn was also happy Lois would be covering Maternity after today. It made it that much less likely she'd have to see or talk to Nick. Now, if she could avoid him this morning. . . .

The phone rang again, Mrs. Morrin checking on how things were going on Maternity. Lynn gave her Lois Johnson's message.

"In that case, would you report to the medical unit tomorrow morning?" Mrs. Morrin asked. "I'll continue to do what I can on Medical but I need some time to coordinate schedules."

Lynn agreed. She put down the phone and stood up ... too late. Nick strode toward the nurses' station. He nodded at her, his face set, and retrieved a chart from the rack.

So we're not speaking, she thought. Suits me. She started to walk away from the desk.

"Ms. Holley," Nick said.

Lynn stopped and turned, her pulse pounding.

"I'm discharging Mrs. Youngblood and son," he told her.

She nodded curtly. As she stalked down the corridor, she blinked back tears. I won't cry over him, she told herself firmly. *Never.*

He looked tired, as though he hadn't slept well. Well, neither had she. He looked upset, unhappy. Lynn turned blindly toward the delivery room, opened the door, and shut herself inside. Clenching her fists, she took deep breaths, fighting her need to give way to tears.

By the time she had gotten herself under control, Nick was gone. Lynn was glad to be kept so busy she didn't have time to think of anything but her work for the rest of the morning.

"Peds is chaos," Joyce told her at lunch. "Not especially because of the strike, either. "It's the nature of kids, even sick ones. I guess Hal is right—I don't belong in nursing."

"How did the conference with those ad people up in LA go?" Lynn asked.

"I got an offer. Hal advised me to refuse what I thought was a small fortune. But he knows the racket, I don't, so I took his advice. He claims they'll dangle more money in front of me. I've got my fingers crossed."

"You said you were serious about leaving nursing, but I didn't really believe you."

"Believe. I don't care what Hal says, I'm grabbing the next offer ... if I survive Peds."

Lynn, despite herself, kept glancing at the entrance for a glimpse of Nick. When she saw the tall, thin figure of Hal Stuart come into the cafeteria, she said, "Speak of the devil."

Joyce turned around to look and immediately waved to Hal. He ambled over to their table.

After nodding at Lynn, he said to Joyce, "Been looking for you. I need a management quote about this strike."

Evidently Sheila had been right about the TV coverage, Lynn thought, though she'd been wrong on who'd be chosen to speak for management. Joyce was certainly better looking than Conrad, and more colorful as well. God only knew what she might say, especially since she'd decided to leave nursing.

"Honey, you came to the only one in this place who'll give you the straight shit," Joyce said. "Only first you've got to tell me what Sheila's been saying."

Hal grinned at her. He hadn't taken his eyes off Joyce since he'd come into the room. He was obviously fascinated by her.

"I'll tell you anything you want me to, baby."

"Yeah, but will it be the truth? Just give me the facts, man."

He glanced at Lynn as though wondering how much he should say in front of her and suddenly his gaze sharpened. "You're the nurse in charge of Five East, aren't you?" he asked.

"Usually, yes," Lynn said, "but—"

"After this strike bit, I want to talk to you, okay? I've got a proposition you won't be able to refuse."

"Don't you listen to him," Joyce advised Lynn. "Whenever a man tells you it's something you can't refuse, that's the time to start running in the opposite direction."

Chapter 21

Returning to Maternity, Lynn passed the nursery windows and was amazed to see Phil Vance inside, seated in the nursery rocking chair feeding a newborn. Intent on the baby, he didn't notice her. Lynn found Clovis at the desk, talking on the phone.

After she hung up, Lynn said to her, "That baby's awfully young to need a psychiatrist."

Clovis smiled. "Phil came by to offer help if I needed any, so I handed him a baby and a bottle. He's really a sweet guy, you know?"

Lynn had liked Phil when she'd met him at Joe King's party. The only other time she'd come across him socially, if it could be called that, was with Barry Marlin, on the boat.

"Don't look so dubious," Clovis said defiantly. "So he's gay, so what?"

"I don't know him well," Lynn said hastily. "I do remember from Joe King's party that he's a great folksinger."

"Phil's a lot of fun and a damn good psychiatrist."

"I don't doubt it. It's nice of him to lend us a hand.

Maybe he'll inspire the rest of the medical staff to help out. Oh, before I forget, we can't miss the Channel 23 News tonight at six. Both sides of the Harper Hills strike are being featured. It's Joyce vs. Sheila."

"Good match," Clovis said. "Who've you got your money on?"

Lynn shook her head. "They're both right, that's the trouble. Sheila wouldn't have so many followers if she didn't have a strong case."

"I figure about forty percent of the nurses are striking. What d'you want to bet Sheila and the rest of them'll be out on their butts when things cool down?"

"CMC ought to have better sense."

"In the person of Conrad Werth? Come on, Lynn, I don't care what the man is to you, he's a creep."

"He used to be a friend," Lynn said, making no attempt to defend Conrad. She feared Clovis was right. If it was left to Conrad, the strikers would be fired.

"I'd better go spell poor Phil," Clovis said. "I'm not too sure he took in my two-second lesson on burping."

"How's the premie doing?"

"Baby Girl Larchmont? She may only weigh four and a half pounds but that kid's the feistiest little peanut I've seen in a long time."

Lynn and Clovis both were working until seven, when the night shift would come in and take over for the next twelve hours, so they watched the six o'clock news on one of the patient's TVs.

Sheila presented the strikers' demands concisely, her voice quivering with emotion. "We care for patients and we care about them," she finished, "but why should nurses be expected not to care about money? We have families, children, and expenses like everyone else. We need decent salaries with cost-of-living increases like other workers.

CMC hasn't kept the promises made to us when the corporation took over Harper Hills. All we want is what we deserve, what we were promised."

Lynn admired the way Sheila handled herself and the topic. The only thing she disapproved of was the strike itself and that was because of the patients.

"Sheila's right, you know," Clovis said. "I'd never desert my newborns, but I sure do resent the way CMC's acted."

Didn't Conrad have any sense? Lynn wondered. If he'd had the guts to force the issue with CMC a month or so ago, the strike never would have happened. How would Joyce present management's side after Sheila's persuasive emotionalism?

Joyce, surrounded by children from Peds, somehow managed to look cool and competent. "I sympathize with the aims of the striking nurses," she began, "but how can I accept the method they've chosen to try to obtain what they want?"

Using the pediatric patients as illustrations of who suffers when nurses strike, Joyce made her point without an elaborate speech. The sight of sick children, in casts, in wheelchairs, some with IVs, spoke for her eloquently.

Clovis spread her hands when the newscast was over. "Joyce is right, too. Hell, all of us nurses are right. It's CMC that's wrong."

Or Conrad, Lynn amended silently. The corporation surely didn't want this kind of publicity. It was Conrad's fault for not alerting CMC sooner, for not letting his superiors know Harper Hills nurses not only deserved more money, but that they intended to fight for their rights. She'd warned Conrad well over a month ago, so he'd certainly been aware of what could happen.

* * *

On Monday morning Lynn was surprised to see only two strikers at the entrance ... Sheila was nowhere in sight. Lynn clocked in and reported to the medical unit only to find Monique Kennedy, the charge nurse, on duty. Monique had been one of the strikers.

"Will you need me here?" Lynn said.

"I don't think so." Monique spoke curtly, barely glancing at Lynn, making it obvious she wasn't going to say any more than she had to. It was no use to ask her what was going on. Uncertain of what to do, Lynn hurried to Mrs. Morrin's office. Joyce was with the DNS.

"Report to Five East for now," Mrs. Morrin told Lynn. "We're still revising the schedule. I'll call if I need to reassign you."

Both Rolfe and Beth were already on the unit and Lynn asked them if they'd heard any more than she had about what was going on.

"It was because of Dr. Brandon's daughter," Beth said. "That's what I heard."

"Carol?" Lynn exclaimed. "Has something happened to Carol?"

"She's doing okay, as far as I know," Rolfe put in. "Emergency appendectomy last night. Sheila's with her, she won't leave the kid." He shrugged. "No Sheila, no strike."

"Practically everyone's come back to work," Beth said. "But they're scared."

"Waiting for the ax to fall," Rolfe added.

Lynn put her worries aside about what might happen to the nurses who'd been on strike and began making patient rounds.

"I've got something to show you," Angela McDonald told her. With effort she raised her left hand several inches from the bed and slowly wiggled her fingers.

342

"Wonderful!" Lynn cried. "When did that happen?"

Angela smiled. "On Friday, in PT. Look what you miss when you take a day off. The nurses go on strike, and I get my hand back."

"Most of the nurses returned to work today," Lynn said.

"I saw Sheila on TV. I must say, she made her points well, but Joyce Elkins eclipsed her. Elkins is a natural actress besides being a beauty. What's she doing in nursing? I know it's a noble profession, but I hate to see God-given talent wasted." Before Lynn could think what to say, Angela went on.

"I've decided I want to meet Shaleen as soon as you can arrange for her to visit me."

"I'll see what I can do," Lynn promised.

Before Lynn went to lunch, Joyce called her.

"Werth's called a meeting with Morrin and me and Dr. Linnett for two o'clock. It'll be to announce he means to fire all the striking nurses, whether they've come back to work or not. What're you going to do about it?"

"What can I do?" Lynn asked.

"A hell of lot more than I can or even Morrin. As for Dr. Linnett, why should the chief of staff care one way or the other? Come on, Lynn, think of something. What Werth's doing isn't fair, even if he did warn the strikers ahead of time that's what would happen. Don't you have any influence over the man?"

What did Joyce expect, a miracle? She couldn't convince Conrad not to fire the nurses. He wouldn't listen to Lynn, no matter what she said. But how could she refuse to try?

"I'll do what I can," she told Joyce.

Who *would* Conrad listen to? Not the DNS or her assistant, according to Joyce. But how about the chief of staff, how about Dr. Linnett? What if the doctor could be convinced the nurses shouldn't be let go? Wouldn't that carry some weight with Conrad? Lynn picked up the phone.

At five minutes to two, Lynn stepped onto the elevator, her stomach churning in apprehension. Dr. Linnett had insisted she attend the meeting in Conrad's office so she'd had no choice but to agree.

"I think the argument would be more effective coming from you," the doctor had said. "You didn't join the strikers, and yet you're willing to speak for them."

Lynn, already nervous, stiffened as she walked into Conrad's office and saw Nick standing next to Dr. Linnett. What was he doing here? She couldn't understand. She only hoped she could concentrate with him watching her, listening to her.

Nick couldn't take his eyes off Lynn. When she'd met his gaze as she entered, it was obvious she hadn't expected to see him in the administrator's office. After looking quickly away, she avoided the slightest glance in his direction. The telltale circles under her eyes told him how hard she'd been working, without enough sleep. Why the hell was she here?

Lloyd had urged him to come to this meeting, but he was damned if he knew why, unless it was for moral support. Lloyd had never seemed to need such support before.

"I believe everyone's here," Werth said. "Will you all please be seated?"

Lynn sat next to Joyce, Nick noticed. Werth, barricaded behind his desk, glanced from one to another of the five of them. Nick thought the man's pale blue eyes were as cold and unfeeling as a Michigan winter sky.

344

"I called this meeting," Werth went on, "to inform the nursing department and the medical staff of my intention to terminate every nurse who participated in any way in the walkout."

"No!" Lynn exclaimed. "That's not fair, Mr. Werth!"

"I understand you remained on duty, Ms. Holley," he said. "This doesn't concern you."

"But it does." Nick couldn't help admiring Lynn's partisanship of her fellow nurses as she went on to explain how she agreed with their every objective, though not with their methods.

"They were driven to this extreme solution because CMC ignored them," she finished. "I can't agree they should be punished. "You, Mr. Werth, are being unfair. You wouldn't listen in the first place, and now you want to penalize the nurses for your *own* failure to take action."

Werth's face flushed blood-red. "I resent that implication!"

"Resent it all you want," Lynn said. "You know very well I warned you what would happen if you ignored the grievances of the nursing staff. I don't believe you ever notified CMC there might be a strike."

Nick applauded silently. That's telling the bastard, he told her in his mind.

"You're here on sufferance, Ms. Holley," Werth warned.

"I'm here because Dr. Linnett asked me," she retorted. "You've made one mistake. Don't compound it by firing the striking nurses."

Werth, in his fury, looked as though he might burst a blood vessel and Nick found himself hoping he would. He couldn't remember when he'd disliked a man more.

"If we may return to my object in calling this meeting," Werth said finally.

"After listening to Ms. Holley," Lloyd said, "I feel it would be a grave error to rush into any punitive action. I invited Dr. Dow to be present to represent the younger staff doctors. What's your opinion, Nick?"

Nick gathered his thoughts. "If I were a nurse, I'd have picketed the place long before this," he said. "CMC's been remiss, why not admit it? Raise nurses' salaries and end the controversy. The last thing the medical staff wants is inadequate patient care. If you fire forty percent of the nurses, that's exactly what we'll be facing. Haven't you heard there's a nursing shortage? Replacements won't be easy to come by. Keep the ones you've got and pay them a decent wage so they'll stay on and be satisfied."

Dr. Linnett nodded. "I couldn't have expressed the situation and the obvious solution better myself. You can take it, Mr. Werth, that I thoroughly agree with my colleague. I doubt if any member of the medical staff will feel differently. We'll stand united against dismissing any member of the nursing staff because of the strike."

"I'm in full support of Dr. Linnett," Mrs. Morrin said. "While I don't approve of nurses going on strike, I feel dismissal is an extreme reaction."

Joyce nodded.

Gotcha, Nick thought, watching Werth. Squirm all you want, you bastard, you've no choice but to back down and you know it.

As he listened to Werth backpedal, Nick glanced at Lynn. It was her doing, and everyone in the room knew it. She'd stood up for what she believed, and to hell with Werth. She didn't have any feeling for the man or she wouldn't have humiliated him in front of all of them. No feeling for him at all.

I was wrong about Lynn and Werth, Nick thought. Hell, I knew I was at the time. I believed there never was anything between them except friendship, just as she said. Lynn isn't the kind to have affairs with married men.

So why did you open your fool mouth on Catalina? he asked himself.

Because you're jealous, an inner voice answered. You want her for yourself. You can't stand the idea she might pay attention to anyone else.

Hey, I've never been the jealous type, he protested to his inner voice.

You are as far as she's concerned. You've been that way about her from the beginning, the voice shot back.

Nick clenched his fists. *That's because she's mine!*

You've given yourself away, friend, the voice advised. "Mine" is possessive, in your case, jealously possessive.

Nick, becoming aware Werth was speaking, brought himself back to what was going on in the room.

"I'll take what you've said under advisement, Dr. Linnett." Werth spoke stiffly.

"I certainly hope so." Lloyd's voice was firm. "The sooner this hospital returns to normal, the better. All of us on the medical staff place the welfare of our patients first, and confusion isn't good for any of them." He paused and smiled thinly. "Or for CMC's corporate image."

Lloyd's uppercut was smoothly delivered, and Nick admired the way the older doctor kept his cool. He, himself, was too hotheaded, and he'd do well to practice stopping to think before he shot off his mouth and made a mess of everything.

Like he'd done in Catalina.

The meeting was over. As Lloyd walked through the door ahead of Nick, he turned and said in a low tone, "Lynn's a fine young woman, Nick. One in a hundred."

Maybe even a thousand, Nick thought ... or more. Hell, she was unique, he didn't need anyone to tell him.

347

"See you later." Lloyd moved off at a rapid pace.

Though he had patients waiting in the office, Nick lingered, waiting for Lynn. She glanced at him as she came through the door.

"Lynn," he said quickly, before she could brush past him, "walk with me. I want to get away from these offices so I can be sure no one overhears us."

She hesitated, as though ready to refuse, but finally shrugged and fell into step beside him.

"Shaleen called me last night when she couldn't reach you." He kept his voice low. "Freddie died. I took care of the details for her, but I think she needs to talk to you."

Lynn sighed. "Poor Shaleen. She must be terribly upset."

"Don't raise your voice," he warned. "I think we're okay at the moment, but Dolly, my receptionist, said a man came by the office this morning when I was in surgery and asked a lot of questions. She knows enough not to tell anything to anybody about any patient so she referred him to me, saying she couldn't help him. He didn't ask about Shaleen by name, but from what Dolly said, it's clear that's who he meant."

Lynn stared at him and then quickly glanced around.

"I figure they got information from the ER somehow," he went on, "and discovered I was the doctor who treated Shaleen. If I'm right, they'll know she was sent to Five East."

"They?"

"The men investigating for the judge. I can't believe he's here in person. Anyway, Dolly described a man who was too young to be Shaleen's father. And I'd be surprised if he was alone. Be careful, Lynn."

"Have you warned Shaleen?"

"I haven't had time."

"I'll do it now."

"Use a pay phone."

Her eyes widened, then she nodded. He caught her arm as she started for the cafeteria pay phone. "Call me tonight and let me know what's going on. No, wait, don't tell me anything on your phone or mine ... we'll meet somewhere. We'd better decide where, so we won't have to name the place on the phone."

"Do you really think our phones are tapped?"

He shrugged. "Our best defense and the best protection for Shaleen is to pretend we know nothing—and suspect nothing. We're better off assuming the phones are bugged. How about meeting in the Dunkin' Donuts a couple of blocks from your place? I should be home by seven for sure, make it seven-thirty. You call me and say you'll be home Wednesday night if I want to come over, okay? Then wait fifteen minutes and walk over to Dunkin' Donuts."

Lynn blinked. "I feel like Mata Hari. Are you sure all this is necessary?"

"No. But it doesn't hurt to be careful."

He watched her walk into the cafeteria. Even with dark circles under her eyes she was beautiful. The only good thing about these bastards snooping around after Shaleen was that he and Lynn would have to keep in close touch. She'd have to forget being mad at him.

He'd tell her how wrong he'd been as soon as he had the chance, when the right time came. When they were alone in a private place. If he could just hold her, everything would solve itself.

As he walked into the lobby, leaving the hospital, Rhonda, the admitting office manager, called to him. He stopped and walked over to her.

"Dr. Dow, weren't you asking a week or so ago about Renee Graham?"

"That's right."

"Well, one of the girls in the office saw her last weekend. You know Milly? She was with her new boyfriend and they went into this bar and there was Renee with a guy Milly said was a real creep. She said Renee was drunk or stoned, and she looked so crummy that Milly didn't want to admit she knew her, so she didn't say hello or anything. Later on she got to thinking that how Renee really looked was sick."

"What's the name of the bar?"

Rhonda made a face. "The Cherry Pit. Some awful name. Milly says it's just off the beach on Modesto Lane. That's not the greatest district in town."

Nick thanked her and left the hospital. He'd have to tell Lynn about Renee. Whether Lynn hated her ex-sister-in-law or not, it sounded as though Renee might need help. First, though, they'd have to figure how to keep Shaleen safe.

"I'll move out of this place right away," Shaleen said to Lynn on the phone. "Did Dr. Dow describe the guy?"

Lynn glanced around the cafeteria as she listened, thinking that even if he was sitting at one of the tables, she wouldn't recognize him. "No. Just that he was too young to be your father."

"He wouldn't show up here."

"I'm really sorry I wasn't home when you called about Freddie," Lynn said.

"He's being cremated and his ashes scattered in the ocean. Freddie arranged all that before, like he did for

Richard." Her voice was flat, without emotion. "Now there's no one left."

The poor kid didn't dare give way to the grief Lynn knew she must be feeling. "You're wrong," she told Shaleen. "Nick and I are your friends. And Angela McDonald wants to be."

"Who's she? I don't want anyone to know—"

"Wait a minute, let me explain." Lynn told her who Angela was and that she was a patient in Shaleen's old room. "She's got money and influence," Lynn added. "Power. And she wants to help you. Think about it . . . you need someone with as much prestige as your father. Angela has that and more. And she's one very sharp lady."

"I've heard of her," Shaleen admitted. "Who hasn't? But what can a movie star do?"

"Protect you."

"I don't know."

"At least meet her."

"With this guy snooping around?"

"So disguise yourself. If I didn't recognize you in that wig and makeup, who will? You can't keep running and hiding all your life. Give Angela a try."

The most Lynn was able to get from Shaleen was a promise to let her know where she was when she settled in a new place, not by calling her at home, but somehow.

Lynn hurried back to Five East where she called Peds to find out how Carol Brandon was doing. Sheila came to the phone.

"Carol's a tough little girl," Sheila said. "I think I was ten times more scared than she was. I worried about her hemorrhaging because of that bleeding problem she has, but it didn't happen. They yanked the appendix at the point of rupture, just in time. She's doing fine, I'm taking her home in a couple of days."

"I'm glad to hear she's on the mend. Tell her I said hello."

"I hear you persuaded Werth not to fire us," Sheila said.

Lynn blinked in surprise. How did information get around so fast? "When the time comes, you can thank Dr. Linnett, not me," she said.

"Ever the modest martyr ... but thanks anyway."

Lynn put down the phone, glancing at her watch. If she hurried she had time, before she went off duty, to bring Angela up to date on Shaleen.

It was close to seven-thirty when Lynn approached the doughnut shop several blocks from her apartment. Through the floor-to-ceiling windows she could see the customers clearly: a teenaged couple and three men. One of the men was in his sixties but the other two were about thirty. It was unreasonable to think either of them might be the man who'd been in Nick's office. He couldn't know they'd be meeting here.

Doing her best to appear casual, she pushed open the door, entered, sat on a stool, and ordered a coconut doughnut and coffee. As the waitress brought the order, Nick slid onto the stool next to Lynn and asked for coffee.

"See anyone you know?" she asked, keeping her voice down and her face turned away from the two men.

He shook his head. "Eat your doughnut," he said, "and we'll take a walk."

"I don't really want it."

"In that case I'll take half." He broke the doughnut in two, took a bite from his portion, and made a face. "Why coconut?"

"I happen to like it."

352

"Then eat."

She managed one bite and drank a few sips of her coffee before Nick was ready to leave.

"This way," he said once they were outside. He steered her across the street and up the block. "Okay, what's going on?"

She told him what Shaleen had said and about Angela.

"You really think Angela McDonald can protect Shaleen?" he asked. "She's had a stroke, and hasn't yet recovered."

"Angela's got the clout you and I don't have. Because of who she is Angela can easily attract media attention. People will listen to her, will believe her. What other choice do we have?"

"I don't like any of this. I'd call the cops if I thought Shaleen would cooperate."

"She's already warned you she won't. Nick, do you think the judge means to kidnap her, to have her brought back by force as Shaleen seems to believe?"

"I don't put anything past a man like him."

"I hope she'll let me introduce her to Angela."

Nick slammed his fist into the cupped palm of his other hand. "Makes me feel so damned helpless."

Lynn put her hand on his arm. "You saved her life."

"But for what?" He covered her hand with his and she pulled hers quickly away.

"About today," he said. "Lloyd claimed he brought me to that meeting to represent the younger doctors, but that's a bunch of crap. He hauled me in there to listen to you." Nick took a deep breath. "I know what you are, what you're like. I didn't need to have you prove it to me today in Werth's office, but evidently Lloyd thought I did." He took a deep breath. "Lynn, I had no business shooting my

353

mouth off in Avalon. The truth is I went out of my head with jealousy."

She looked at him. "I've had more than enough of jealous men."

"Yeah, I know. It's not my style, either ... I was surprised as hell when I figured out what was eating at me. Everything with you is different, like I've never been with a woman before."

What Nick said was so similar to her own feelings in Avalon that Lynn stopped to stare at him. Everything with Nick was different ... *he* was like no one else.

He put his hands on her shoulders. "We have something too good to give up. If I promise to curb the jealousy, can we give it another try?"

Chapter 22

Lynn found herself humming "Avalon" as she drove to work on Tuesday. She made a face but couldn't deny she was happy. Nick's apology had healed the breach between them, and his goodnight kiss had promised that Avalon was just a beginning. She needed Nick and it was time to admit it. When things went wrong between them she was miserable. They were two intelligent adults and should be able to get along without so much emotional seesawing. The ups were cosmic, but the downs were hard to survive. What they needed was a calmer, saner relationship. But staying calm when Nick was around was not easy.

Lynn stepped off the elevator onto Five East and into a maelstrom. "Two admissions since five-thirty," the night charge, Ms. Lamont, said to her, pausing in her rush. "Erle's gone sour, and to top it off, McDonald's private duty nurse got sick and went home after dosing her patient with laxatives. Report's going to be late."

Thank heaven the strike was over, Lynn thought, and most of the nurses back on duty. With CMC guaranteeing their raises retroactive to the first of June, she didn't anticipate any more trouble.

"What can I do to help?" she asked the night charge.

Ms. Lamont frowned. "I just put McDonald onto the john—she refused to use a bedpan—you might check on her."

Lynn hurried toward Angela's room.

"What a night!" Angela exclaimed as Lynn helped her off the toilet and into her wheelchair. "I swear there's nothing left inside me, nothing at all. My God, how I hate bedpans. I wonder what evil spirit invented them."

"I'm sorry your nurse had to leave."

"She certainly picked one hell of time to get sick. And I must tell you I got a very unsettling call about an hour ago. From Shaleen. She was afraid to call you, I gather, because she thought your phone might be tapped."

"What did she say?"

"She apologized for bothering me. The child was obviously scared to death but she remembered her manners, poor thing. She went out to get something to eat last night and when she returned she saw a man on the stairs to her apartment. She decided he'd been sent by her father, so since she was wearing some kind of disguise, she walked past and kept going. After wandering around all night, she finally called me."

"She couldn't know what a bad time she chose. Did she leave a number where she could be reached?"

Angela shook her head. "No need. I told her exactly what to do and she agreed. She's going to be my night private duty nurse. God knows I need a new one."

"But she isn't—I mean, you just can't—"

Angela waved a dismissive hand. "It's a brilliant idea, if I do say so myself. Luckily Shaleen has enough money with her to buy a uniform, a cap, white shoes, and a few other things I mentioned. We've decided her name will be Susan Jones. I plan to tell my day nurse that I asked

Shaleen to come in later this morning to be oriented to the hospital. And now I'm really very tired and I'd like to lie down.''

Lynn helped Angela into her bed. "It could be dangerous to bring Shaleen here," she protested. "What if the man comes to Harper Hills asking questions about her?"

"Surely you've heard of Poe's 'The Purloined Letter.' I've played in several films using the same principle of hiding an object. You put the thing in plain sight in a place where it's logical for it to be. A hospital is certainly the most logical place for a nurse. If Shaleen's dressed as a nurse and working as a nurse, he'll never notice her.''

Knowing it was too late to prevent Shaleen from coming, Lynn said no more. She hadn't thought of a plan to help the girl, but she was dubious about Angela's idea of play-acting. Although it was unlikely, what if someone recognized Shaleen despite the disguise? It was true Angela didn't require complicated nursing procedures and Shaleen *had* taken care of Freddie, but she didn't really know the mechanics of nursing. What if she dropped Angela while transferring her from bed to wheelchair? Lynn shook her head and left Angela to check on Lawrence Erle.

Mr. Erle, forty-three and overweight, had been admitted on Monday with a complaint of crampy upper abdominal pain and nausea. He had a past history of gallstones. His tentative diagnosis was cholecystitis, inflammation of the gall bladder. During the night the pain had become more severe, he'd begun to vomit, and his doctor had been notified.

The diagnosis was changed to mechanical obstruction of the small intestine and Mr. Erle was scheduled for an exploratory laparotomy at ten. He'd had a Levin tube inserted through his nose into his stomach and IV fluids were running into a left-arm vein.

"He's all set for surgery, except for his pre-op meds," Ms. Lamont told Lynn. "Your shift'll have to give those."

"How about the two new admissions?" Lynn asked as they walked back to the desk together.

"Titus Quentin, seventy, congestive heart failure. ICU's full again, so we got him. He has an IV in place, he's hooked up to a portable monitor and seems to be stabilizing. He's pretty deaf. The other's Irma Noyes, fifty, in diabetic coma with a history of alcohol abuse. IV insulin's running, she's got a Foley catheter in and another blood glucose is due in half an hour. She's iffy yet."

Lynn gave Mr. Quentin to Beth and assigned Mrs. Noyes and Mr. Erle to Rolfe.

"If you get hung up caring for Mrs. Noyes," she told Rolfe, "let me know and I'll give the pre-op meds to Mr. Erle."

The assignments given, Lynn began patient rounds. Five East had only two empty beds and, until Sheila returned, they'd be short one nurse ... *if* Sheila returned. Lynn wasn't sure what Mrs. Morrin planned for Sheila.

Beth was at Mr. Quentin's bedside, adjusting his nasal oxygen prongs. "He still has an arrhythmia," Beth said, nodding at the monitor. "But with the IV digitalis, I guess that'll improve, right?"

Mr. Quentin opened his eyes. "Where's Patsy?" he asked in the overloud voice of the deaf. "Is she all right?"

"Isn't that sweet?" Beth asked softly. "He's worrying about his wife." Beth leaned closer to him and said loudly, "Your wife's fine. She went home to rest."

"Didn't ask about her, I want to know about Patsy. My dog."

Beth's startled face made Lynn hide a smile. The younger nurse rallied and assured Mr. Quentin she'd find out about the dog as soon as she could and let him know.

358

"Imagine," she murmured to Lynn as she walked to the door with her. "That's a man for you." She glanced along the corridor to Lynn's left, smiled and waved. Lynn turned and saw Nai Pham waving back.

"She's so sweet," Beth said. "I'm helping her study for her boards and sort of teaching her better English at the same time. It was Rolfe's idea, really. He said I'd be good at it because I'd just passed my own boards. Did you know Nai Pham was married and has a baby? Her husband's mother lives with them and takes care of the little girl. I'm invited for dinner there next Sunday. I'm hardly doing anything, really, but you'd think I'd given her a million dollars, she's so grateful."

"I think your helping Nai Pham is just great, Beth. It may make all the difference in her passing the boards."

Beth flushed. "It's not all that much," she insisted, but Lynn could see she was pleased.

Mr. Quentin's IV line beeped its look-at-me warning and Beth hurried back into the room.

After Mr. Erle was taken to the OR, Lynn sat down at the desk next to Connie to catch up on the paperwork.

"I'm off to PT," Angela said and Lynn looked up. Marie St. Pierre, Angela's private duty day nurse, was pushing the wheelchair. Beside her stood a brown-haired nurse wearing glasses. Lynn stared, her eyes wide.

"This is Susan Jones," Angela told her, obviously enjoying Lynn's reaction. "She's my new night nurse."

Angela introduced Susan to Connie and Lynn. As far as Lynn could tell, Connie didn't recognize Susan at all, and it was no wonder. Shaleen's hair was a nondescript brown and cut quite short. The round frames of the glasses changed the lines of her face, not only making her look older, but also more stolid. Though she was still pretty, her attractiveness had been subdued. The disguise was much more effective than the black wig and the gobs of makeup, since now she didn't attract so much attention. Angela, with her extensive experience before the cameras, must have been responsible for the make-over.

Watching the three of them enter the elevator, Lynn hoped this wouldn't turn into a disaster for either Shaleen or Angela. There'd certainly be no talking Angela out of it, clearly she was having the time of her life.

Just before twelve, Hal called Lynn.

"I'm here to take Joyce to lunch," he said, "but she's been delayed. Mind if I pop up and have a few words with you while I wait for her?"

"If you like," Lynn said, wondering what was on his mind. She felt sure Hal wasn't one for idle conversation.

When he arrived on the unit, Lynn rose and, leading him away from the desk, said, "What can I do for you, Mr. Stuart?"

"It's Hal. And maybe it's what *I* can do for *you*. Has Joyce told you about being offered a contract and turning it down?"

Lynn nodded cautiously.

"They took one look at her on the newscast of the strike and doubled the offer. I mentioned you to them—they saw the cassette I'd made of the art show—and they're definitely interested in you. This outfit does mostly TV commercials, but also—"

"Hal, I don't think I'm interested."

He shook his head. "Don't be hasty. Anyone with your looks is wasted in nursing. As for the money—"

"I don't expect to get rich in nursing, but I like what I do." Lynn eyed him speculatively. "Besides, I have the feeling you have a hidden agenda. Please don't deny it."

Hal shrugged. "I really can get you a very nice offer from this company," he said. "No strings attached. But

360

I'll admit I'd like an interview. Joyce says without your intervention, I haven't a chance in hell of getting one."

"An interview?"

"With—" he lowered his voice—"Revina Radison. I know she's on Five East incognito, so don't bother to try to cover up."

Lynn, accustomed to thinking of her patient as Angela McDonald, took a moment or two to adjust.

"I couldn't," she said. "Even if I could, I wouldn't try to arrange any such interview. My patients are entitled to privacy and I'll do my utmost to see they get it." In her annoyance at Hal, Lynn had failed to hear the elevator door open and she was startled to hear Angela's voice behind her.

"Ms. Jones, wait in my room, would you? Marie, push me closer to Ms. Holley."

Lynn turned, hoping to head Angela off, but she was too late.

"Mr. Stuart, isn't it?" Angela said, extending her hand to Hal. "I'm Angela McDonald. I watched your coverage of the strike. Very effective theater."

"Thank you, Ms.—McDonald."

Angela raised her eyebrows, then smiled. "Perhaps we can strike a bargain, Mr. Stuart." She turned to Marie St. Pierre. "Why don't you go to lunch, Marie? Susan's still around if I need anything." She made a shooing motion with her hand. "Go, go . . . Ms. Holley will see I get back to my room."

When Marie was out of earshot, Angela said to Lynn, "There must be a place where I can speak with Mr. Stuart in private."

Lynn pushed Angela's wheelchair into the treatment room, Hal holding the door open. "I'll be honest with you, Lynn," Angela said once the door was closed. "My discussion will include Shaleen, but you can be sure I'm thinking of her welfare. I know what I'm doing and so does Mr. Stuart. We play by the same rules. Yours are different . . . so I'd rather you left us alone."

What was the bargain Angela spoke of? Lynn wondered as she walked back to the desk. Angela had overhead enough of the conversation between her and Hal to know he wanted an interview with Revina Radison. Apparently she was willing to agree—in return for what? What did Angela expect from Hal? Something to do with Shaleen, she'd hinted, but how could Hal help Shaleen?

When Hal left fifteen minutes later, after pushing Angela back to her room, Lynn was busy with Dr. Verene and couldn't indulge her impulse to confront Angela and ask what was going on. By the time she was finished helping the doctor, Tim Brandon was at the desk.

"How's Carol?" she asked.

"She's doing remarkably well. Sheila's going to take her home in the morning. Carol can be cared for there just as well as here, and she'll be happier . . . she misses Ramos." He glanced around and saw they were temporarily alone at the nurses' station.

"I've been wanting to ask you something," he went on in a lower tone. "You're a friend of Sheila's. As you know, her husband recently died. I suppose it's far too soon to broach the subject to her but Sheila and I—well, we've grown quite close. How do you think she'd feel if I asked her to marry me?"

She'd stop holding her breath for one thing, Lynn had the momentary urge to say, but quickly squelched it. There was no reason to be snide. Tim wanted a mother for Carol and Sheila and his daughter got on well together. Sheila longed for security and she'd said she was fond of Tim.

362

Marriage seemed an ideal situation for all concerned, and Lynn told Tim so.

"That's what I thought, but then I got to wondering if she'd be upset by my asking so soon after—"

"Sheila will understand," Lynn assured him.

"She *is* an understanding person, isn't she?" He beamed at Lynn.

She'd certainly said magic words to Tim as far as he was concerned, Lynn thought. It was one way to make someone happy, telling them what they wanted to hear. Still, she was glad the pieces had fallen into place for the three of them.

Angela was napping when Lynn finally had the chance, as she was going off duty, to stop by her room. "She was very tired," Marie whispered. "She needs the rest."

There was no sign of Susan Jones, though Lynn hadn't seen her leave the unit. She decided it was wiser not to ask Marie anything and she had no intention of waking the patient. She only hoped Angela knew what she was doing.

When Lynn returned to the desk to tell Connie she was leaving, a man stood there waiting.

"This is Ms. Holley," Connie told him.

"I'm Lyle Picard," the man said. He was stocky, in his mid-thirties, with neatly styled brown hair, unremarkable looking except for his assessing hazel eyes. "I'd like to talk to you, Ms. Holley."

"What about?" She hoped she didn't sound too abrupt, but she was sure Mr. Picard would prove to be one of the men looking for Shaleen and she didn't like the idea of having to parry his questions.

He glanced at his watch. "I understand you're off duty. Could I buy you a cup of coffee?"

Whether she wanted to talk to him or not, it'd be better to get off the unit. Lynn walked toward the elevator. "You haven't told me what you want," she said when he followed her.

"It's something I prefer to discuss in private."

If she refused to talk to him at all, wouldn't that make him suspicious? Resigned, Lynn glanced at her own watch and "I can give you a few minutes in the hospital cafeteria."

"Fine."

He followed her out of the elevator and into the dining area.

"I don't expect you to violate professional ethics," he said when they were seated at a table apart from the few others in the room.

"Good."

"A fifteen-year-old girl named Shaleen McGuire was a patient on Five East last month. Do you remember her?"

Lynn decided he must have uncovered some of the basic facts of Shaleen's hospitalization by now, so it would do no harm to admit one or two things he must already know. It might disarm him. "Everyone remembers a patient who leaves without medical consent," she said, her hands shielding the coffee cup.

"Do you recall what Ms. McGuire looked like?"

Lynn frowned. "My problem is I've been distracted lately because the Harper Hills nurses have been involved in a salary dispute and last week went on strike. Maybe you saw it on TV? Anyway, Mr. Picard, I don't believe that I can answer any more of your questions without violating patient privacy."

"I mean Ms. McGuire no harm."

"I have no way of determining that. I suggest you get in touch with the director of the nursing services or the hospital administrator." Lynn rose and nodded her good-bye. He made no move to stop her from leaving.

As she drove to her apartment, she told herself he'd gotten nothing useful from her. If he'd approached her, though, he must be contacting all the Five East personnel. Shaleen, she knew, hadn't been as friendly with anyone on the evening or night shift as she had been with those on days. Rolfe could more than handle himself and would reveal nothing. Connie kept to herself and wasn't likely to talk to a stranger. Nai Pham's English would be a formidable barrier. Sheila wasn't on Five East at present, and Lynn doubted that Tim Brandon would take kindly to an investigator coming to his house where his daughter was convalescing.

And then there was Beth. Without meaning any harm to Shaleen, Beth might very well tell Mr. Picard all she knew. Still, what *did* she know? Enough to identify Shaleen as the daughter of Mr. Picard's employer, but probably no more. Even Beth would be reluctant to reveal any medical details.

But Shaleen would be on Five East tonight as Sharon Jones, and— Lynn's mind conjured up unpleasant scenarios of discovery the rest of the way home.

Nick sized up the man seated in his office. Tall, maybe forty, graying hair, forgettable face. Mencken, he called himself. Private investigator.

"You realize I can tell you nothing without violating patient confidence," Nick said curtly.

"You're listed as Shaleen McGuire's doctor of record at Harper Hills Hospital. You examined her in the emergency room the night she was admitted." Mencken's voice was smooth, his tone neutral.

"You're an experienced investigator, I'm sure you know about the privileged relationship between doctors and patients. I'll answer no questions about any patient of mine."

"She's a minor, her parents are desperately concerned about her, Doctor."

Nick shook his head, afraid if he said a word his anger would betray him. The judge was no fit parent and Shaleen had never mentioned a mother or stepmother.

"Have you seen Ms. McGuire since she left the hospital?"

"Left against medical advice, as you must have discovered," Nick said. "I repeat, I can't and I won't reveal any information about my patients."

After Mencken had gone, Nick took a few minutes to calm down before he made the usual after-hours phone calls to patients who'd asked to talk to him. He hadn't given anything away to Mencken, but the investigator could hardly have expected him to. Was he just going through the motions to satisfy the judge? Or evaluating the possible opposition?

Nick had no doubt the judge was desperate—to keep his role in what had happened to Shaleen hidden from the public. That's why the investigator hadn't threatened a court order to examine Shaleen's records. The judge couldn't take that risk because he didn't know how much Shaleen might have revealed.

When he finished the last of the patient calls, Nick started to punch in Lynn's number, then hesitated. Why not drop by her apartment on the way home? Appearing in person would make it more difficult for her to say no— at least, he hoped it would. He wanted her with him.

Lynn answered the door barefoot, wearing tattered jeans

and an oversize T-shirt. She looked so good to him he reached for her, pulling her into his arms. As usual, touching her made him forget everything else—the judge's henchman, the reason he'd come, how tired he was.

Her lips parted under his and he kissed her deeply, urgently. She fitted against him as if she'd been made for that purpose.

"When you're older, a woman will come," Greatcloud had told preadolescent Nick. "A woman who'll help you soar with Eagle. You'll know her in here." He beat on his chest. "Never mind up here." He touched a finger to his head.

"Made for each other," Nick whispered into Lynn's ear. Her affirmative murmur fired his blood and he swept her up, carrying her into her bedroom and falling with her onto the bed.

Her skin was so soft, so smooth, no other woman had such skin, no other woman felt so good to touch. Her nipples hardened under his caresses and his breath caught in his throat. He delighted in her responsiveness to him.

Her fingers stroked his nape and then slid under his shirt to his back. Impatient with the clothes separating them, he yanked his off, watching her as she tossed her T-shirt aside and squirmed free of her jeans. God, she was beautiful—not only because of the translucent skin that went with her red hair, but with an inner radiance that dazzled him completely.

His fingers traced the gentle curves of her body and she moaned softly, clinging to him. His breath rasped in his throat as he fought his urge to join with her. He needed to savor all of her, he meant to bring her to the edge, to pleasure her past the point of no return. Making love to her was unlike anything in his experience, and he wanted these moments to spin into infinity, to last forever.

367

Lynn's warm hand closed around him and he groaned, intoxicated with desire. This woman made him soar to heights he'd never dreamed existed.

He entered her and she moved with him, Eagle and his mate, flying high, spiraling into the stratosphere. With her he was no longer earthbound. All space was his, was theirs ... they belonged together, he'd never let her go.

He told her that afterward, as she lay in his arms. "I'm never going to let you go."

"Sounds good to me," she murmured. "If you don't care whether or not you starve to death."

He raised his head to look at her. "How did you know I was hungry?"

"Borborygmi," she said, tickling his stomach. "Now *there's* a word I don't get to use often."

"My intestines did *not* rumble."

"The rumbler is always the last to know. I'll bet you haven't had dinner yet."

"I came by to suggest we have it together—dinner, that is." He nuzzled her neck. "We wound up having something very different instead."

"It wasn't my doing."

"Anyone who opens the door looking as ravishing as you did deserves what she gets."

She eyed him incredulously. "Those are my floor-scrubbing jeans. And the T-shirt—"

"—Is sexy as hell."

Lynn shook her head. "You are unbelievable."

His hand moved to cup her breast. "Lady, you ain't seen nothin' yet."

"I thought you were hungry," she protested as his hand slid lower to caress the curve of her hip.

He lifted her, easing her on top of him. "There's all kinds of food in the world, but there's only one of you."

He pulled her head down and kissed her. "Anyone ever tell you how delicious you taste? Golden and sweet—like apricots, only better."

Her teeth nipped his lower lip, sending an erotic message from lip to groin with laser speed. "See what you've done?" he murmured.

"How careless of me." She kissed him again, long and deep and hot, wriggling her hips against him until he groaned.

"You're asking for trouble," he told her, his breath catching in his throat.

"It's no trouble at all." She whispered the words into his ear as she lifted her hips until he fitted into her, taking him beyond rational thought.

He knew he was where he belonged, that he'd never feel the same with anyone else. Only with Lynn did making love transcend mere sensation—their union was far more than simple sensual satisfaction. He wasn't entirely certain what this meant, but he sure as hell didn't mean to give it up.

"Lynn," he whispered, his voice caressing her name as his body caressed hers.

She took him—oh, God how sweetly she took him!—to the moon, past the moon, he was flying into the unknown on a fiery trip for two, he was never going to let her go.

Much later, he said to Lynn in the shower, "I hope your answering machine is on, because you sure as hell aren't leaving to answer the phone if it rings."

"You don't have chest hair," she said, ignoring his comment as she soaped his chest.

"I do. You just aren't looking close enough. There are at least four or five, I forget which."

"The Indian genes?"

"I guess. Native Americans aren't hairy types. Unfortunately, some other ancestor donated the genes for my beard." He ran his hand over his jaw. "Feel the stubble?"

"I don't think there's any part of you I haven't felt."

"I'm willing to let you try again, in case you've missed a spot."

"I refuse to let you die of malnutrition. We're going to get dressed and you're going to have dinner."

As he was toweling himself dry, he remembered what he'd planned to do after he came by and picked up Lynn ... what Rhonda from Admitting had told him about Renee had been bugging him. He'd meant to take Lynn to dinner and then, with her, visit The Cherry Pit to see if Renee was there.

He knew Lynn didn't want to be Renee's keeper. Neither did he, but if she needed help—and it sounded as though she did—Renee had no one but the two of them.

"Don't bother to dress up," he called to Lynn, who'd gone into the bedroom. "We'll grab a quick bite to eat and then we're going slumming."

Chapter 23

Lynn eyed the red neon sign over the entrance to the dingy bar with distaste. "The -herr- -it," she muttered. "I don't trust places that can't be bothered about repairs."

"No one said you had to like it," Nick retorted and she shot him an annoyed look. They'd been on the verge of a quarrel ever since she'd discovered just what he'd meant by "slumming." She didn't understand why was he so interested in Renee.

A man in a black leather jacket emerged from The Cherry Pit accompanied by loud, raucous music. Lynn winced until the closing door cut off the sound.

Nick grinned at her. "The drummer's not bad." He took her arm, led her to the door, and opened it.

Through a smoky haze Lynn saw a once-glossy art deco interior gone to seed. Predictably, cherries were the theme. The smell of beer vied with stale tobacco smoke. A combo—guitar, bass, drums, and sax—blasted out a country western tune with a female singer competing to be heard.

"Ain't seen a good time for a while," she wailed.

Stay in this place and you'll never see one, Lynn thought grimly.

The booths and tables were all taken. Nick steered her toward the bar, red vinyl and black formica, blocking an overweight man who was heading for the only empty stool. Lynn slid onto the cracked vinyl seat reluctantly. Nick stood behind her and ordered a beer for himself and a white wine for her.

Holding her glass but not sipping the wine, Lynn turned on the stool to survey the crowd. Why did so many people come here to suffer smoke-laden air and be assaulted by overloud music? Could she be missing some covert ambience? She enjoyed country western, but she preferred to hear it played at lower decibels, and by talented musicians.

"Do you see her?" Nick asked.

Lynn shook her head. If Renee was here, she must be in one of the back booths, hidden from view.

"Would you mind looking in the john?" Nick said.

She shrugged, set her glass on the bar, and slid off the stool. As she walked toward the bathroom, Lynn tried to prepare herself for what she felt sure would be a disaster area with lewd graffiti, overflowing watebaskets, and a toilet so filthy no woman would use it unless she was in extreme need.

To her surprise, the restroom was reasonably clean, the walls recently painted. Renee wasn't there. As she emerged she noticed a woman, her back to Lynn, using the pay phone at the end of the tiny hall. "Tex, you promised," the woman whined.

Lynn stopped, staring.

"You son-of-a-bitch!" the woman cried and slammed the receiver at the phone, missing the hook so it dangled by the cord. She leaned her head against the wall, her back still to Lynn.

"Renee?" Lynn said tentatively.

The woman whirled and staggered, stumbling against the wall. Lynn started forward to help her, though she wasn't yet certain this was Renee.

Supporting herself with a hand on the wall, the woman threw back her head and faced Lynn.

"Renee?" Lynn asked again, hardly believing what she saw.

Renee's hair hung in greasy tangles around her too-thin face. A black mini-dress hung on her body. Her eyes, shadowed by blue, purple, and silver eye makeup, glittered feverishly. Her cherry-red lip gloss was too bright and garish.

"Are you all right?" Lynn asked, reaching out a steadying hand.

Renee struck at her and missed, almost falling. "Don't *need* help from *you*," she muttered. *"Never."* She began coughing, a deep hacking that shuddered through her body. She slumped against the wall when the spasm finally ended.

"You won't share," the singer complained from the barroom. "You don't care. . . ."

Whether she wanted Lynn's help or not, Renee had to be gotten out of there. Lynn put an arm firmly around Renee's shoulders and led her along the hall and into the barroom. Renee sagged against her, apparently not aware of what was happening. By the time they were halfway across the room, Nick was on Renee's other side, helping to support her. The two of them got her through the door and out onto the sidewalk.

The fresh ocean breeze revived Renee enough so that she recognized Nick. She pulled free of Lynn and flung her arms around him. "Take me home with you," she begged.

He held her away from him. "You're burning with fever, Renee. The best place for you is the hospital."

She stepped back, staggering again. *"Bastard,"* she muttered.

Nick pulled his keys from his pocket and handed them to Lynn. "Unlock the car," he said. He picked Renee up and, carrying her, strode toward the Kharmann Ghia.

Renee swore at him, struggling, and began to cough again. By the time they reached the car she was limp and made no further protest about going with them. When they tried to bring her into the ER, though, Renee had recovered enough to fight back.

"You've got pneumonia," Nick told her flatly. "You'll die if you don't get proper care."

"It's all *your* fault," she shrieked. "And *hers.*" She jabbed a finger toward Lynn. "She kicked me out and you wouldn't take me in. You both think you're so damned superior." Tears streaked her cheeks. "Nobody ever loved me except Ray, and she killed him. She did it, she did it—she killed my Ray." Renee launched herself toward Lynn, her fingers reaching like claws.

Nick caught her from behind and lifted her off her feet, carrying her screaming and kicking into the ER.

"I suspect withdrawal," he told Dr. Buski a few minutes later. "I'm not sure what from ... uppers, probably—don't know that she was on anything else. Plus pneumonia."

Lynn, unable to think of any alternative, listed herself as next-of-kin and promised to pay for Renee's care if no other funds were available. "I hope you won't be admitting her to Five East," she said.

"The way she's acting, she'll wind up in the psych unit for observation," the night admitting clerk told her.

The psych unit was actually part of the medical floor and consisted, Lynn knew, of four private rooms, all with doors that locked from the outside, shut off from medical by another locked door. One of those rooms was little more than a padded cell for violent patients. Renee wasn't that bad, but it saddened Lynn to think of her sister-in-law needing to be locked up for her own good.

I should have tried harder to find Renee before it came to this, Lynn told herself.

"I've asked Phil Vance to see her," Nick told Lynn later, as they were driving to her apartment. "She needs more than antibiotics for the pneumonia, antibiotics won't cure her other problems."

Lynn sighed. "I feel like I failed Renee."

He patted her knee. "It's hard to try to help someone who hates you. Don't blame yourself."

"But I didn't do anything to make her hate me! I tried so hard to get along with her. I wish I could make her understand about Ray."

"We'll hope Phil can help Renee see things more rationally. Don't feel guilty. Remember, you may have saved her life tonight."

"It was entirely your doing. I didn't believe—didn't want to believe—she was that sick, and in need of real help."

"You came with me and we rescued her together. I might not have gone looking for her without you."

Lynn shook her head. "You would've. I think of myself as a caring person, yet I wasn't with Renee."

"You do more than your share. Shaleen's an example of how you—"

"Good grief, I forgot all about Mr. Picard!" Lynn exclaimed. She went on to tell Nick about being questioned.

"A different guy came to my office," he said when she finished. "I claimed doctor–patient privilege."

"Did you know one of them discovered her apartment?" Lynn asked. "Shaleen was afraid to call me or you and wound up contacting Angela McDonald because I'd told her Angela wanted to help. But, my God, such help. You'll never guess where Shaleen's hiding now—at Harper Hills, as Angela's private duty night nurse."

Nick stared at her. "Are all of you crazy?"

"It wasn't *my* idea. Angela claims she's following Poe's formula of hiding something in the most obvious place, in plain sight, and that therefore nobody will find Shaleen. I wish I were more certain she's right."

Nick shook his head.

"I have to admit Angela did improve on Shaleen's disguise," Lynn said. "And in a nurse's uniform, she does blend in. The problem is, Shaleen's not a nurse. What if something happens to Angela because of that?"

"I don't like the set-up."

"You haven't heard the rest. Angela's also making some kind of deal with Hal Stuart that involves Shaleen."

Nick groaned. "Why did you ever tell Angela McDonald about Shaleen in the first place?"

"As I said before, to motivate her. Angela was lying in bed feeling sorry for herself. She wouldn't even go to PT. It seemed like a good idea at the time. How did I know she'd come up with such perilous plans?"

Nick's beeper sounded as he was pulling to the curb near Lynn's apartment complex. He came in with her to use the phone.

"Got a baby on the way," he told Lynn as he hung up. He kissed her quickly and left.

Lynn arrived on Five East the next morning, determined to talk to Angela about Shaleen.

Angela dismissed her worries with a wave of her hand. "We're getting along beautifully," she insisted. "She's a sweet and gentle child. I plan to make damn certain her father never comes near her again, but my plans aren't finalized yet. I'll tell you about it when they are."

"Where does Shaleen go during the day?" Lynn asked.

"You're better off not knowing ... it saves you from lying to those private eyes poking around the place. She told me about Freddie." Tears brightened Angela's eyes. "A dear friend of mine died of AIDS last year and I didn't do a thing to ease his dying ... I didn't even visit him. There's no way to change the past, but I plan to fund a memorial for him that will help other AIDS sufferers. There's so much I want to do that I can hardly wait to be released from Harper Hills."

Lynn decided there was no way of stopping Angela. Once she got motivated, she took hold with a vengeance and plunged ahead without regard for what or who might stand in her way.

Beth was off and a float nurse was covering for her, but despite the several really sick patients, the morning passed without problems. When Joyce called and asked if Lynn could go to lunch, she agreed.

"I accepted the second offer," Joyce told her when they were seated.

"Hal hinted you might."

"I hear you turned down his proposal."

"You're suited for TV—I'm not."

Joyce smiled wryly. "What you mean is you're a more dedicated nurse."

"I'm better at nursing than I would be at TV commercials or any other kind of acting, that's all."

377

"Girl, I'm going to miss you. Honesty is so damned rare. I don't imagine I'll find any of it in this new career I'm taking up."

Lynn smiled. "There's nobody like you, that's for sure. I'll miss you, too. I don't blame you for taking the offer, though. You were made to be appreciated. As Angela McDonald said after seeing you on TV, you're wasted here."

"She really said that?"

Lynn nodded. "She thinks you're a natural actress."

Joyce shrugged. "These people are handing me a plateful of money, so I guess I'd better produce. What about you? Planning to stay on at Harper Hills?"

"I want to take a nurse practitioner course. That's the kind of nursing I'd really like to do."

"San Diego State's offering one. Go for it."

"There's a little problem of money. But I'll take the course as soon as I can afford to."

"And Dr. Dow?"

Lynn sighed and didn't answer. How could she? She might be in love with Nick, but she had no idea what that would lead to, if anything.

Joyce reached across the table and gripped her hand. "Don't let him hurt you. *I* can handle men but *you're* never going to learn, and that's the truth."

"So what's with Hal Stuart?" Lynn asked, hoping to shift the focus from her relationship with Nick.

Joyce frowned. "I've got to admit I'm not dead certain. The man doesn't give much away about himself. But I'm in command and I plan to stay that way. I never think otherwise."

"When are you leaving the hospital?" Lynn asked.

"In two weeks. Morrin's not too happy. I may not be

the greatest assistant DNS in the world, but we do get on together 'cause I don't let her or anyone else intimidate me, and she knows it. That's the only kind of person Morrin respects. Not that she won't try to take advantage of you anyway, so watch it."

"What am I going to do without you?" Lynn asked Joyce.

"Just fine, that's what. And, hey, I'll be checking in with you, never doubt it."

After she left Joyce and returned to Five East, Lynn took a call from Mr. Quentin's sister-in-law, Mrs. Outlander.

"My sister Evelyn had a stroke last night," the woman said tearfully. "She's Titus's wife. Evelyn's unconscious, she doesn't know anything that's going on. I just can't bear to tell him, sick as he is."

"I'm sorry to hear about your sister," Lynn said. "I'll consult with Mr. Quentin's doctor and see what he thinks about telling him. What hospital is Mrs. Quentin in?"

"She was down in La Mesa staying with me, so they took her to Grossmont."

"Please keep in touch with us."

"I'll do that."

"One more thing," Lynn said. "Mr. Quentin keeps asking about his dog Patsy."

"Oh, that dumb dog of his. He cares for the poor old thing like she was a baby. I had to take her to the vet after Evelyn had the stroke because I can't manage a blind and deaf dog that has to be carried outside to do her duty. The vet says Patsy ought to be put away, but I don't like to have it done with them both in the hospital and all. So Patsy's at the vet for now, you can tell him that."

After Lynn got the go-ahead from the doctor to let Mr. Quentin know his wife had suffered a stroke, she walked slowly along the corridor to his room. She hated to be the bearer of bad news and she so often had to be.

Mr. Quentin took it better than Lynn had expected, but when she told him about Patsy, he grew agitated, struggling to sit up in bed.

"Olive never did like Patsy," he said. "She's looking for an excuse to have Patsy put down. I won't have it." His voice quavered and broke.

"Mrs. Outlander said Patsy was under the vet's care," Lynn repeated, "and that she planned to leave your dog there until you were better."

Tears ran down his cheeks. "She's all I've got," he mumbled.

As Lynn reached for his hand and held it, she wasn't certain she wanted to know who he meant.

After leaving Mr. Quentin, Lynn called the psych unit to see how Renee was doing.

"She's resting quietly," the nurse told her. "Dr. Vance plans to transfer her to Medical as soon as they have a bed."

Lynn didn't see Nick at the hospital but he called a few minutes before nine that evening.

"We've been invited to the Linnetts' for dinner two weeks from Saturday," he told her. "Think you can make it?"

"We?"

"You and I, we."

Lynn was silent a moment, trying to come to terms with the invitation. She'd never even met Mrs. Linnett, so why had she been asked?

380

"It's nice of them," she said finally. "I'm surprised, though."

"Yeah, I sort of got the feeling Lloyd was trying to make a point. Whatever the reason, I'd like you to come with me."

"Okay."

"Good, that's settled. I got Tim Brandon to take over Renee for me—pneumonia's a little north of my field of expertise. He says she's not as bad as she sounded—right lobar, bacterial, sensitive to more than one antibiotic."

"I heard she'll be transferred onto the medical unit soon."

"Phil thinks Renee has some paranoid ideation, mostly about you, but she's not psychotic. He'll be following her while she's in the hospital and would like to continue seeing her when she's discharged."

Harper Hills had assigned a social worker to investigate Renee's eligibility for medi-cal, California's medicaid, to cover hospital costs, letting Lynn off the hook if the welfare department approved the case. Once discharged, Renee wouldn't be able to afford Phil's fees as a private patient.

How much can I do for her? Lynn asked herself.

"Money will be a problem," she told Nick.

"Yeah. We'll have to figure out what to do with Renee when she's released. I sure as *hell* don't want her back with you, and I've no intention of taking her in. She'll need help, though."

Lynn sighed. "I know."

"Hey, maybe I should take you in and then Renee could have your apartment."

Lynn's heart leaped at the suggestion. But even if Nick was serious, she couldn't move in with him, wouldn't. "I don't think that's the solution."

"Wait—it'll grow on you. I'd come over and convince you in person, but I'm on Maternity monitoring a probable placenta previa it looks like I'll have to section. So sleep on the idea."

Lynn tossed and turned in bed, wondering how Nick could expect her to sleep after his offhanded suggestion they live together as the solution to finding a place for Renee. She wouldn't do it anyway, but especially not under those circumstances.

And why were Dr. Linnett and his wife inviting her to dinner with Nick? Nick she understood—after all, the doctor wanted him to come in as an associate. But why her? Nick didn't seem too sure himself. What did he mean about Dr. Linnett trying to make a point? What point?

The trouble was, she wasn't sure exactly where Nick was coming from. He'd been frank enough, admitting he had no marriage plans. But did he have any plans for the two of them, or was he content to let their relationship drift any which way?

So you're in love with the man, she scolded herself, but he hasn't called it love. You went into this with your eyes open. Enjoy the present and stop worrying about when it will end.

But she wouldn't move into his condo. It was safer not to. When you were living with a man and he decided it was all over between you it was awkward for him and humiliating for you, to say the least. And with that thought, she drifted off to sleep.

Thursday passed without any new problems and so did Friday, up until three o'clock, when Beth hurried after Lynn into the nurses' lounge.

382

"You never told me she was going to be admitted to Five East," Beth complained.

"Who are you talking about?"

"Mr. Werth's wife. I just heard it from Sheila, she came in to talk to Mrs. Morrin and told me."

"I haven't the slightest idea what you're talking about."

"Sheila? Well, Mrs. Morrin told her she wanted to see her, so—"

"No, I meant about Pat Werth."

"She's coming in on Sunday night for hip surgery on Monday. Dr. Silverman has the case. It's a hip replacement, Sheila said, and Dr. Silverman's—"

"I know he's the best bone man in the area. Are you sure Pat—Mrs. Werth—is being admitted to Five East?"

"That's what Sheila said. She's coming back on Monday, too, did you know? Mrs. Morrin gave her hell about the strike, but said she wasn't going to create a martyr by firing Sheila."

"But why admit Mrs. Werth to Five East?" Lynn spoke as much to herself as to Beth.

"Because we have the only empty private room in the hospital. Sheila said she hopes Mrs. Werth has private duty nurses because she's met her and the lady's a real crab."

Pat was no ray of sunshine, true enough, but that wasn't what bothered Lynn. It'd be bad enough if Renee had been sent to Five East but having Pat Werth here was ten times worse. Conrad's wife hated her. She'd not only blame Lynn for any problems, she'd look for things to complain about.

"I hope Mrs. Werth hires private duty nurses, too," she said fervently.

"I heard something else," Beth said. "Tina Marlin's been sent to that place near Palm Springs to recuperate.

You know, where they dry you out, or whatever. Then she's going back with her husband." Beth shook her head. "If I was her, I couldn't . . . I just couldn't."

"Luckily, you're not her."

"That's what Rolfe says. I introduced this guy I met to Rolfe and they really like each other. His name is Jack Longworth and he commutes to San Diego State from El Doblez. He's into computers and he's teaching me. Jack's a lot of fun."

Lynn wondered how long Beth was going to need Rolfe's approval for everything she did and everyone she met . . . not that it was a bad idea for now—it might save Beth from more mistakes.

"Rolfe's met this gal who works at San Onofre, if you can believe it," Beth went on. "Her name's Laurette and she's a real brain, I guess you'd have to be to work with atomic power. Anyway, Jack and I are double-dating with them this weekend."

"Sounds great."

"We're going deep-sea fishing. I've never been."

"Better take some seasickness meds along," Lynn cautioned.

"Oh, Rolfe's handling all that."

Lynn smiled. She might have known.

Her smile faded as she left the lounge. Her weekend off wouldn't be anywhere near long enough if she had to come back on Monday to Pat Werth as a Five East patient . . . Conrad ought to have more sense.

Checking on Renee before she went home, Lynn discovered she'd been transferred to medical and was in fair condition. She'd decided not to visit Renee until she talked to Phil Vance. The way Renee felt about her, going to see her might be the wrong thing to do.

Marie St. Pierre intercepted Lynn as she started for the

elevator. "Ms. McDonald would like to see you before you leave."

Angela asked Marie to go down to the lobby and buy her a newspaper. Once she was alone with Lynn, she said, "Hal's consulting a lawyer. Once we're certain there's nothing illegal about what we've planned, we'll go full speed ahead. We're going to need you and Shaleen's doctor—Nicolas Dow, isn't it?—to cooperate. Okay?"

"First I'll have to know what you're doing."

Angela waved an impatient hand. "You'll see the script ahead of time. Hal wants to be sure you'll go through with it. After all, this was your idea in the first place."

"*What* was my idea?" Lynn demanded. "I wanted you to help Shaleen, but—"

"How else can we help her permanently, except by exposing her father? And what better medium for doing that than TV?"

My God, Lynn thought, stunned, they want to turn Shaleen's story into a TV special.

"Don't look so shocked," Angela scolded. "What did you think was going on? We're damned lucky to get a pro like Hal Stuart involved. This won't be any schlock presentation."

"But think of the effect on Shaleen!"

"She wants to go ahead. What that bastard did to her was a thousand times worse than exposing his incestuous cruelty on TV. He'll never dare touch her or try to force her to go back home again."

"Do you know who he is?"

Angela nodded, her eyes narrowing. "No wonder the poor kid's so terrified. He's one of the most powerful men in the state. I'd rather not say his name. I promised her I wouldn't until we go public."

Shaleen told Angela but not me, Lynn thought sadly. Why didn't she trust Lynn as she did Angela?

Angela touched her hand. "It isn't a matter of trust," she said, as though Lynn had spoken aloud. "Shaleen knows I can protect her. Not that you wouldn't have tried ... but you knew as well as she did you couldn't, that's why you brought me into this in the first place. As you said then, I have clout. I can make people listen. And I sure as hell intend to."

Chapter 24

Lynn's weekend time with Nick was less than she'd hoped for and included one major disagreement, partly about Shaleen. To Lynn's surprise Nick had been less upset about Angela and Hal's plans than she was.

"If Shaleen agrees, maybe it's just as well to bring the whole mess out into the open," he said over coffee at Mood And Food on Saturday night.

He chose the restaurant because he liked the combo. Lynn enjoyed the dixieland jazz, but not the mahi-mahi she'd ordered. The fish was not fresh, as advertised, and was overcooked besides.

"What Shaleen does is beyond your control, anyway," Nick added.

"But—" she began, then paused. No matter how she felt, he was right about her having no say in whether or not Angela and Hal went ahead with their plans. "So are you agreeing to tell your part of Shaleen's story on TV?" she demanded.

"I haven't decided yet. It depends on how Stuart handles the thing."

Lynn stared at him. She'd never dreamed he'd consider the proposition. "How could you?"

"If Shaleen gives me permission to discuss her diagnosis and treatment, it's not unethical for me to—"

"Sordid!"

He shrugged. "What happened to Shaleen before she came into the Harper Hills ER was. My care of her certainly wasn't. You're overreacting, Lynn. This may be the best way to help Shaleen. It may be the only way."

"All those people watching, knowing—" She shook her head. "What kind of a life will she have afterward?"

"Going public doesn't take any more guts than nursing a dying AIDS patient. Shaleen's a tough kid, she'll survive. In the long run it won't make any difference if she has therapy before or after the TV appearance. I think we both ought to help, providing Stuart doesn't muck up the presentation."

She wished she was sure Nick was right.

"Sorry about your fish," he said. "Two Saturdays from now the food's sure to be better. Lloyd's a fanatic about what he eats, so I can't imagine being served a bad meal at his house."

Lynn, still upset about Shaleen, viewed the mention of the Linnetts like a bull confronted with a matador's red cape.

"Dr. Linnett seems pretty sure of himself, inviting me when he knows I don't approve of your going in with him."

"What does that have to do with being invited to dinner?"

"It's obvious, isn't it? If you're going to be a society doctor, you ought to settle down and get married ... join the country club, buy a yacht. The only thing I don't really understand is why he invited me. He and his wife must know more appropriate women for you to marry, women whose families have status and money."

"You're talking nonsense. I told you I have no plans to get married."

"Did you tell Dr. Linnett?"

"Why in hell would I?"

"So I'm right ... for all I know he's been plying you with eligible candidates and, since you've failed to take the bait, has reluctantly settled for me as a possibility." She gazed defiantly at him.

"I fail to see the point of this."

"Well, it's certainly not that *I* want to marry you. I've had enough of being legally tied to a man. The point is what it's always been. I think you're making a mistake to limit yourself to the type of patients Dr. Linnett attracts." She leaned forward. "There's more to you than that, Nick. You care about people, all kinds of people—including those who can't afford medical care. You won't be happy if you turn your back on what you are."

His dark eyes grew opaque, shutting her out. "I'm aware of my needs. I'm no Paul Salvador, regardless of what you seem to believe. I'm no Lloyd Linnett, either. I admire them both, in different ways, but I'm my own man. I'll do what I think is right for me, whether or not you approve."

Lynn drew back. Placing her napkin on the table, she took a deep breath before starting to speak.

"Don't bother to say it." His voice grated with annoyance. "You do the same thing every time we disagree— you run. Not tonight. You're furious with me, I'm mad at you but damn it, we're not going to fly off in different directions. I'm not taking you home. We're going to go for a walk on the beach and yell at each other until we get tired of fighting."

389

She opened her mouth and closed it again. With Nick's face set in such stubborn lines, she might as well save her breath.

They walked and shouted and fought and made up. She spent the night with Nick. It was a wonderful night. Full of loving words and intimate caresses, Lynn wished it would never end, even though they still disagreed on Nick's commitment to Dr. Linnett.

Sunday began with a delivery and Nick never did get back to his apartment from the hospital what with various emergencies, the worst a pregnant woman injured in a car crash. Lynn had given up in the early afternoon and walked the two miles back to her apartment.

On Monday Lynn went to work knowing Pat Werth was waiting for her on Five East. She'd decided that she'd treat Pat as she would any other patient. No better, no worse. While Pat was on her unit, that's what she was—A patient. Entitled to the best care Lynn could provide, no matter how Pat behaved.

At report, Lynn found that, although Pat had no private duty nurse in attendance at the moment, she'd be covered by them around the clock after she returned from surgery—but only for two days.

Surely Conrad could afford private duty nurses until Pat went home, Lynn thought ... or if *he* couldn't, *Pat* could—the McLeods were wealthy. Thinking about it made her recall Conrad's occasional half-joking complaints about Pat's reluctance to part with money.

"I used to think they were kidding about the Scots being thrifty," he'd said once to her father, "but I guess it comes with the genes. When I married a McLeod, the name should have warned me."

Two days of private duty were better than nothing, Lynn told herself, especially the first two days post-op. In any case, it was none of her business what the Werths chose to do.

She stopped by Pat's room on her rounds and found her sleeping. Lynn saw that the overhead traction frame and the trapeze were in place on the bed. The chart showed that Pat had been shown the use of both and that PT had been working with her, teaching her the use of crutches and demonstrating the type of exercises she'd be required to do post-op.

Relieved not to have to talk to Conrad's wife, Lynn continued on. She'd assigned her to Sheila for the pre-op care and meds. Once Pat was off to the OR for her arthroplasty, they could relax for a couple of days. By then she should be in fair shape, but the real work was just beginning. Because of the traction and abduction splints, hip prosthesis patients required extra nursing care. Though PT did most of the exercising, the unit nurses were involved, too. Lynn hoped Pat would prove cooperative.

The surgery could make all the difference in Pat's ability to walk comfortably and normally, but it was too much to hope improved ambulation would change her personality . . . or the way she felt about Lynn.

Sheila intercepted Lynn before she finished rounds. "Mrs. Noyes' pulse and blood pressure are normal, but I don't like the way she looks. She hasn't been my patient before so I thought maybe, since you know her, you could evaluate her better."

Mrs. Noyes was the diabetic admitted in coma the week before. She'd been doing well, she was ambulatory, her IVs had been discontinued, and her insulin dosage had been adjusted to her food intake. Lynn followed Sheila into the two-bed room. Mrs. Noyes had the bed next to the window. When Lynn called her name, she opened her eyes.

Holding her hand, Lynn asked her how she felt.

"All right." Mrs. Noyes spoke slowly, drawling the words.

Sheila was right, something was wrong with Mrs. Noyes.

"She's been going to the bathroom an awful lot," Mrs. Pantera, the patient in the other bed, volunteered. "She kept me awake with her getting up and down all night."

A bladder infection? Lynn asked herself. Kidney involvement? A gastrointestinal problem?

"I'm going to feel your stomach," she told Mrs. Noyes as Sheila pulled the curtain between the two beds.

Palpation of the abdomen revealed nothing abnormal. Speaking in the same slurred voice, Mrs. Noyes denied having diarrhea or constipation or pain on urination.

Leaning closer, Lynn sniffed, trying to determine if the patient had the fruity-smelling breath of incipient diabetic coma. There was a faint odor—not fruity, but vaguely familiar.

"If I didn't know better," Sheila whispered, "I'd swear she was half-crocked."

Lynn straightened abruptly. Because Mrs. Noyes was a known alcohol abuser, on her doctor's order her belongings were routinely checked by the night shift when they made rounds. But alcoholics usually learned to be very, very clever.

Lynn walked around the curtain and smiled at Mrs. Pantera. "I appreciate the interest you've taken in Mrs. Noyes," she said. "Did you happen to notice if she had any visitors yesterday?"

"Why, yes, she did . . . a gentleman friend." Mrs. Pantera shook her head. "I do wish visitors wouldn't use our bathroom. Isn't there some way you nurses could tell them not to?"

"It's difficult to prevent," Lynn said, everything clicking into place with Mrs. Pantera's words.

Sheila trailed her into the bathroom. Once inside, Lynn looked around. When she saw nothing out of place, she lifted the back off the toilet tank and peered inside. Sheila looked over her shoulder as Lynn lifted a bottle free of the water.

"My God, that's a quart of vodka!" Sheila exclaimed. "And it's half empty. No wonder—" She broke off to glance through the open door at Mrs. Noyes. "I'll call her doctor right away."

At the desk phone, the vodka disposed of, Sheila waited for the doctor to come on the line. "Mrs. Noyes knows diabetics can't drink to excess," she said to Lynn. "She knows it'll kill her. Why does she do it?"

"If I could answer that I'd have a miracle cure for all substance abusers," Lynn said. Immediately, she could have bitten her tongue. "I'm sorry, I didn't think—"

"Don't apologize. Justin knew better ... he thought he was above addiction, that's what his problem was. Renee thought so, too, didn't she?"

Lynn nodded.

"I went to see her yesterday," Sheila said. "I mean, Renee isn't my favorite person, but I sort of felt I had to."

"How is she?"

"Still shaky. Phil's given her the word on the dangers of uppers, but who knows if it'll sink in? The pneumonia's under control, she's coughing up disgusting gunk now. I think—" She broke off and began talking into the phone, explaining Mrs. Noyes's condition to her doctor.

Lynn visited Mr. Quentin later in the afternoon because

he'd seemed depressed during her morning rounds. She'd called Grossmont Hospital and discovered his wife's condition was unchanged—she still hadn't regained consciousness, a bad sign. The longer she stayed in a coma, the less her chances for recovery.

"Olive came to see me yesterday," he told her in his overloud tone.

His wife's sister. She must have told him about his wife.

"Olive says Patsy's no worse, at any rate," he went on. "But I know that vet's going to charge a fortune."

Lynn wondered why he was focusing on the dog while his wife was in such serious condition.

"Evelyn would've taken care of Patsy," he said. "You'd never think Olive was her sister, there's a world of difference between the two of them. My opinion is, Oscar Outlander died young to get away from her."

Lynn decided to mention his wife. "I met your Evelyn before she had the stroke," she said loudly. "She was very concerned about you."

Mr. Quentin blinked and looked away. "I told you she's like that. Olive's the one who doesn't care about anyone except herself. Always been the same. Not much you can do about it. I'm lucky I didn't marry her."

"You're lucky you didn't marry Olive?" Lynn repeated, feeling she might have stumbled on a clue to Mr. Quentin's attitude.

"Met her first, you know," he said. "I can't deny she was a good-looking gal, the kind who turns a man's head." He scowled. "I soon found out she couldn't be trusted. By accident I saw her with Oscar, he used to be a friend of mine. She was canoodling with him, that's what. I never let on that I'd caught 'em. The very next week I proposed to Evelyn." He smiled. "Shocked the poor girl. She never

394

expected any such thing ... didn't stop her from saying yes, though. Evelyn always was practical."

He looked up at Lynn. "Evelyn and me, we went through some hard times. We got Patsy the year our son died." Tears filled his eyes.

Lynn realized then what the old dog represented to Mr. Quentin. Since she could find nothing comforting to say to him, she took his hand and held it between hers.

"You're a good girl," he told her, "to worry about an old man like me."

Tears pricked her eyes. Mr. Quentin's future looked bleak and he knew it. She believed now that he concentrated on the dog's health not only because he loved Patsy but because losing his wife was something he couldn't allow himself to think about.

"Olive thinks she's finally going to get her hooks into me." He shook his head. "If it comes to that, I might just up and die, like Oscar—or I might not. I could let her take me in and then give her a hard time ... that'd fix her."

Lynn blinked, surprised. She didn't understand him as well as she'd thought.

Mr. Quentin smiled at her. "I'm all right, you go tend to someone who needs it more."

Pat Werth was still in the recovery room when Lynn was ready to go off duty. She stuck her head into Angela's room to say good-bye and found Angela sitting by the window in a lounge chair she'd had delivered the week before.

"Where's Marie?" Lynn asked.

"I sent her to buy stamps. Hal got the lawyer's go-ahead, it's all set for Wednesday at four-thirty. Dr. Dow's going to look over the script this evening and show it to you."

"I don't think I can participate."

Angela's eyes narrowed. "What's the matter with you? Are you upset because I took over?"

Lynn shook her head. "I have too many doubts about this going public."

Angela was silent for a few moments. "So you've decided to stop helping Shaleen," she said finally.

"No!"

"That's what it sounds like to me. Your eagerness to do anything you could for her seems to have disappeared now that she has someone else to depend on. Is mama upset because her little girl transferred her allegiance to a new friend?"

Shocked, Lynn stared at Angela. An unreasonable accusation if she'd ever heard one!

Angela shrugged. "I'm no shrink but I've been to enough of them and I've lived longer than you have. Go home and think it over." She turned away from Lynn, ending the conversation.

Nick brought the script by the apartment on his way home from the office.

"I thought maybe you'd play the good samaritan and fix me a sandwich and coffee. I've got a staff meeting in a half hour."

"Grilled cheese on wheat?"

"Sounds fine."

Lynn busied herself in the kitchen, making him a spinach salad with alfalfa sprouts and cubed jicama while the sandwich toasted.

"Think we can talk about Hal's baby?" He waved the script at her.

Surely her apartment hadn't been bugged. Or had it?

"I don't know," she admitted. "Sometimes I think I'm getting as paranoid as Renee."

"How about if you walk me to the car?"

She nodded. When she set the sandwich in front of him, she picked up the script and scanned it.

"Great salad," he said. "Goes good with the cheese." He ate quickly, finishing everything, including a dish of raspberry sherbet.

Once outside the apartment, he said, "What d'you think?"

"How can I tell from such a vague script? 'Angela: Introduction. Shaleen: Tells her story. Dr. Dow: Medical background, surgery, etc. Lynn: Patient care. Hal: Wrap-up.' "

"It wasn't that succinct."

"Almost." She stopped by his car and touched his arm. "Angela accused me of being a jealous mama."

Nick grinned at her. "She could be right."

That wasn't what she expected or wanted to hear from him and she scowled, folding her arms across her chest. "Shaleen told Angela who he was," she muttered.

"That's more than we or the TV audience will know, but so what?" Nick leaned down and brushed her lips with his. "Thanks for feeding me, I'll return the favor soon."

Lynn watched him drive away before she turned and walked slowly back into her apartment. That night she had trouble going to sleep and when she did, she slept restlessly. . . .

Darkness and cold surrounded her. She didn't know where she was or how she'd gotten there. Despite the rhythmic rumble lulling her, she knew she was in danger. From what? From who? Dread clogged her mind.

Lynn tried to run but couldn't move her legs, couldn't move any part of her body. She tried to scream, but she was voiceless. There was no one to help ... she had to help herself. A new terror sliced through her ... not only herself—someone else was in peril because she was here, someone small and helpless. A child. If she didn't escape, neither would the child.

She struggled, fighting her paralysis. The rumble grew louder, menacing now. No, she tried to cry, no, not again. ...

Lynn abruptly sat up, her heart hammering. The only sound was the distant roar of jets, fading as she listened, planes from Miramar, probably, flying one of their night missions from the naval base. She hugged herself, taking deep breaths to dispel the dark, clinging shreds of the dream.

It had been like the nightmares she had had after losing her baby but not quite the same. Intuition told her this dream was related to Shaleen. She slid from the bed and went into the kitchen to warm a mug of milk.

Did she equate Shaleen with her lost baby? If she did, Angela had been on target. How could she bear to lose another child?

But Shaleen wasn't her child to keep or lose. Though she knew it, had known it all along, her heart all too often ignored her head.

At four-thirty on Wednesday, Lynn walked into the Channel 23 studio with Nick. She still wasn't sure she approved of what was going on, but if Shaleen wanted her to help, then help she would. In any case, her contribution was minor, essentially only a corroboration of the hospital part of Shaleen's story.

Hal spent fifteen minutes briefing them on the questions he meant to ask, then Angela's chauffeur wheeled her in, accompanied by Shaleen.

This was the child Lynn remembered as her patient, curly blond hair, no makeup, with wary but vulnerable blue eyes. As she hugged Shaleen, tears blurred Lynn's vision.

Bright lights flicked on. Men adjusted them and moved equipment to focus on Hal.

"This is a Hal Stuart special newscast," he said, "with Ravina Radison."

A video camera panned to Angela, in her wheelchair. She smiled warmly. "As you may have heard, I was recently admitted to a hospital after suffering a cerebral vascular accident, a stroke. Happily, I'm improving. But this is Shaleen's story, not mine." She gestured and a camera followed Shaleen as she came to sit on a low stool next to Angela.

"Shaleen McGuire was a patient in my hospital room before I was admitted there, and her story has no happy ending." Angela stroked Shaleen's shining hair. "As you can see, she's still really a child, she turned fifteen less than six months ago. The story of why she was rushed, dying, to a hospital is more tragic than any film or play I've ever been a part of."

The cameras focused on Shaleen. "What I say is true," she began, "except for my name. I wasn't born Shaleen McGuire, I chose the name to protect myself." Her voice, high and sweet, quavered slightly as she continued. "Maybe some of you will recognize me and understand why."

As Shaleen went on with her story, sometimes her voice broke, forcing her to collect herself before continuing. Lynn felt no one could watch and listen without believing every word the girl uttered.

399

Tears ran down Lynn's cheeks when Shaleen said, "I used to call him Daddy, but after he hurt me, I couldn't say the word any more, so I began calling him the judge."

Shaleen didn't reveal the name of her father. Lynn learned for the first time that Shaleen's mother was an alcoholic who'd been sent two years before to a center specializing in substance-abuse treatment. Shaleen had never been told why her mother hadn't returned.

"I don't ever want to go back," Shaleen finished. "I can't go home. It's not my home, it's his—and I'm afraid of him."

Hal introduced Nick. He asked him questions about Shaleen's condition on admission to the hospital and what had been done for her medically. By the time it was Lynn's turn on camera, she was so emotionally overwrought that she didn't even think of being nervous. She answered Hal's questions, remembering all over again how desperately ill Shaleen had been and recalling the girl's fear as soon as she began to improve.

Then Hal took over. "You've heard Shaleen's story," he said, "the true story of a child who suffered the trauma of being abused by her father and who almost died as a result." He went on to give the statistics of child abuse in California and in the nation. "Sadly, Shaleen is one of many. She, like most abused children, was afraid to tell anyone because she didn't think she'd be believed. Remember Shaleen's story . . . reach out and help any child you suspect is being abused."

"What now?" Nick asked Angela when it was over. "Shaleen can't go on as your night nurse."

Angela waved a hand. "That was only a temporary solution. She's been staying at my house in La Jolla and will continue to do so. Right, Shaleen?" Angela took the girl's hand. "We both need time to decide what comes next, but Shaleen's safe with me. She knows that."

"How do you feel about it?" Lynn asked Shaleen.

"Angela's my friend. I trust her. She won't make me do anything I think is wrong for me." Shaleen's blue eyes shifted from Lynn to Nick and back. "I found out from you two that it's safe to trust some people. Otherwise, I never could have gone through this." She gestured toward Hal and the TV equipment. "Maybe it'll help some other kid. I hope so."

As she was leaving the studio, Angela beckoned Lynn to her side and told her to lean closer. "Watch the papers and TV in the next couple of weeks," she whispered. "There's going to be an announcement that'll knock your socks off."

Lynn raised inquiring eyebrows but Angela shook her head and didn't explain.

Much later, in bed with Lynn, Nick said, "Glad to see you decided Angela was a suitable foster mother."

"I guess it's hard for me to let go of people I love," Lynn told him. "Even though I know you can't put someone in a cage."

"I don't feel the least bit trapped."

"I wasn't aware we were talking about you."

"You mean you don't love me?" Nick's tone was half-mocking, but she thought she heard an underlying seriousness she wasn't ready to deal with.

"Doesn't every woman love the Harper Hills Heartbreaker?" she asked flippantly.

"I swear you made up that name."

"I'm a newcomer here, remember?"

"Boston's loss is El Doblez's gain." He ran a lazy hand along the curve of her hip. "What can I do to convince you never to go back?"

"You're on the right track."

He kissed her, then murmured into her ear. "You realize this would be a hell of a lot easier on both of us if you'd move into my place."

"We Easterners don't believe in doing things the easy way."

"Ah, but you're a Californian now." He pulled her on top of him. "We do things differently here. Let me show you."

Holding her close he kissed her, long and deeply. If she didn't know better, she'd swear his kisses were radioactive, sending hot and dangerous emanations into every cell of her body, making her glow with need.

"You and San Onofre," she murmured against his lips.

"In that case I'd better get on with rearranging your atoms." He flipped her over until she lay on her back and flicked each of her nipples with the tip of his tongue, making them blossom with desire.

He caressed her breasts with his mouth, driving her to distraction. She let her fingers tangle in his hair as she held him to her. His lips, his tongue trailed lower, tasting her until she gasped in mounting pleasure.

"Nick, please," she begged, wanting to share her ultimate fulfillment with him.

"Please what?" He rose above her and waited, his voice grating hoarsely with the passion that gleamed in his dark eyes.

She reached for him, tugging, trying to pull him close. He resisted.

"Please what?" he repeated.

"Love me!" The words burst from her, the wrong words, she knew as soon as she'd said them and she twisted away from him, onto her side. With all the other words available to say what she wanted, why had she chosen those?

Nick pulled her to him, her back against his front, his arousal hard against her buttocks. Holding her gently, he whispered in her ear, "If that's what you want, don't turn away from me."

His warm breath in her ear, his warmth against her, and the insistent throb of his arousal made her quiver with an urgent need. She turned to him, opening her arms as she'd already secretly opened her heart. She wanted what Nick offered her—she always would, even if it was to be lovemaking without love.

When they came together she cried out with the intensity of her pleasure, giving him her love with the joining, giving him all of herself unconditionally.

Much later, Lynn woke when she heard Nick's beeper. He was already out of bed, heading for the phone. After a few minutes he came back into the bedroom, dressed and bent to kiss her. "A gunshot wound to the abdomen, the woman's seven months pregnant. Looks like I won't get back. Better think about what I said."

He wanted her to move in with him. She wanted to. Then why didn't she? Lynn sighed and turned over. He'd clearly told her he had no intention of getting married, so what was the point of moving in with him? Losing Nick was something she didn't want to think about, but at least if she wasn't living with him when it happened, she'd have her own place to hide in, where she could try to survive.

Chapter 25

Lynn had learned the techniques for dealing with hostile patients. No course she'd ever taken, though, had suggested a way to deal with a patient who not only hated her personally but had once actually tried to kill her.

She'd gotten through Pat Werth's two days of private duty nurses without trouble, but once those nurses were gone, Five East was entirely responsible for Pat's care.

Because the patient's operated hip, her left, had to be kept abducted at all times, it required two nurses to turn her until Pat grew accustomed to using the overhead trapeze to help turn herself. Somehow Lynn seemed to be the person most often available when the second nurse was needed and she did her best to maintain a professional attitude. No matter what she said or did, Pat consistently ignored her, though she talked to the other nurses. Pat also ignored any order she didn't care for, no matter whose it might be, including the doctor's. Lynn had come to dread making rounds.

"Good morning, Mrs. Werth," she said on the Monday following Pat's surgery as she walked to the bedside to make certain the hip was properly positioned.

Pat gave no indication she'd heard her.

"Ms. Lamont, the night charge nurse, tells me you threw your pillows on the floor again," Lynn went on. "The two pillows are placed between your legs to keep your hip in the proper position, to prevent dislocation of the prosthesis. It's important you don't remove them at night, because without them in place, a change of position in your sleep could create a real problem."

Lynn knew very well Pat was aware of why the pillows needed to be there. This was the third time she'd told her and she was sure others also had. "We'll be getting you up after breakfast," she added.

Not waiting for a response—Pat never spoke to her—Lynn left the room. At first she'd hesitated to chart Pat's unresponsiveness to her, feeling it was too personal, but she'd changed her mind. Part of her responsibility as charge nurse was to document her patients' conditions, including behavior. She stopped at the desk to make a brief note on the chart about instructing the patient about the pillows and the patient's behavior and continued making rounds.

On Tuesday morning Lynn found the head of Pat's bed raised a good deal higher than a safe 45 degrees. She immediately lowered the bed. "Mrs. Werth, you've been told about the danger of raising the bed too high. An upright sitting position puts a strain on the hip joint and may cause dislocation."

She knew she sounded stiff and formal, but she couldn't help herself. Talking to a patient who never looked at her or gave any indication she heard her was getting to Lynn.

Though it was annoying, she could understand why Pat behaved as she did, childish as it seemed. What made no sense was why the woman endangered her successful surgery by not following orders. They were Dr. Silverman's orders, after all, not Lynn Holley's—and Pat knew it.

On Wednesday, Lynn found a note from Mrs. Morrin on her time card, asking her to come to the office.

"Mrs. Werth was sent back to surgery yesterday evening," the DNS said when Lynn was seated across from her. "Her hip prosthesis became dislocated and had to be repositioned. She insists the dislocation was your fault."

Lynn stiffened "My fault? How so?"

"She says you raised her bed for her afternoon snack and never lowered it. She claims she fell asleep that way and when she roused, she couldn't reach the mechanism for lowering the bed because you'd placed it out of her grasp. When she strained to reach the controls, the prosthesis slipped out."

Lynn was so shocked she almost couldn't speak. "I raised the head of her bed to 45 degrees for the afternoon snack," she said finally. "That much is true. Nothing else Mrs. Werth said about me is. I don't know how the dislocation occurred, but I do know I lowered her bed to a flat position before I went off duty and her hip was properly abducted at that time."

Mrs. Morrin's cold gaze rested on Lynn for some moments. "I hope you can document that."

Lynn shook her head. "I didn't chart it—why would I?"

Mrs. Morrin sighed. "I realize a routine raising and lowering of a bed isn't something normally noted on a patient's chart, but it's too bad you didn't write it down yesterday. Mr. Werth is extremely upset—as is Dr. Silverman."

Lynn said nothing. She'd told the truth, but if Pat persisted with her lies, it would be almost impossible to prove that Lynn wasn't to blame. Still, if anyone knew how Pat hated her, Conrad did. Hadn't it occurred to him that Pat could be lying?

"I'll come up to Five East with you now and review the chart," Mrs. Morrin said.

Pat was back in her room with a private duty nurse in attendance, Lynn noted as she made her morning rounds. She took the report and made the assignment as though nothing had happened, all the while acutely conscious of Mrs. Morrin at the nurses' station poring over Pat Werth's chart.

"The woman's got to be lying," Rolfe muttered to Lynn as she passed him in the corridor. "No way did you do what she claims."

She smiled in thanks for his support and walked on until Sheila popped out of a room to grab her arm. "The old bitch!" she said. "Everyone knows she hates you. You can't let her get away with dumping the blame on you. Hell, we all know you'd never do what she said."

"Thanks," Lynn replied. It was good to discover her staff backed her, even if that wouldn't make any difference to the outcome. No one had been in Pat's room when she lowered the bed. It was Pat's word against hers.

"You hear from Renee?" Sheila asked.

"No—why?"

"She took off on the evening shift—walked away from medical and disappeared."

Lynn stared at her. She couldn't believe that Renee had left the hospital while her pneumonia was still being treated. How could she be so stupid?

"I thought maybe she'd try to con you into letting her stay in your apartment again," Sheila said.

"She doesn't like me well enough."

Sheila smiled wryly. "What's that got to do with it? A bed's a bed."

"Not if it's mine. She doesn't want any part of me."

Sheila shook her head. "You'll never get elevated to sainthood with all these people hating you."

Lynn frowned at her and started to walk away.

"Hey," Sheila called. "Remember I'm on your side."

Later, Nai Pham sidled up to Lynn and murmured, "You no do bad to Mrs. Werth. I know."

Then Connie got her chance to add her opinion after Mrs. Morrin left Five East and they were alone at the desk. "If you ask me," Connie said emphatically, "that woman lied." No name, nothing more, but Lynn knew who she meant and she smiled at the ward clerk.

Unfortunately, those she worked with wouldn't be the ones deciding whether to believe Lynn Holley or Pat Werth.

Conrad arrived on the unit around noon. Lynn didn't want to talk to him, but she knew she had to. Taking a deep breath, she intercepted him before he reached Pat's room.

"I'm sorry about Pat's hip," she said, "but I want you to know she's mistaken when she says I left her bed raised and put the controls out of reach. It's not true."

Conrad looked down his nose at her. "Are you telling me my wife's a liar?"

"She's mistaken," Lynn repeated, refusing to back down.

"We'll see about that in court," he muttered, starting to brush past her.

"Just a minute!" Lynn said sharply, halting him in mid-stride. "You're threatening to sue me? I think you've forgotten the night Pat followed you to my apartment with a gun, the night she tried to shoot me. In front of a witness. I've kept quiet about that night, but if I'm forced to testify in court, I'll make sure it's brought out."

Conrad glowered at her for a long moment, then smiled thinly. "If you do, it'll backfire. Anyone who hears you will be certain you had a grudge against Pat and found a way to avenge yourself."

Lynn was taken aback. What he said could very well be true. At the same time she refused to be intimidated. She was damned if she'd let him know how she cringed at the idea of testifying in court.

Looking him in the eye, she said, "I think you know very well that Pat's judgment about what happened on Five East is as confused as it was about my relationship with you on the night she tried to shoot me. If anyone's set on revenge, it's Pat. And to back her up you'll not only have to sue me, but Harper Hills too, because I'm employed by the hospital. Have you thought over what a mess it's going to be? The media will have a field day."

Without replying, he turned on his heel and stalked away, leaving her staring after him, as upset as she was furious. How could Conrad be so vindictive as to take Pat's accusations to court?

That night she needed Nick, needed to be held and comforted, but he was covering for Dr. Linnett and was too busy to be with her.

The next day Lynn went to work not knowing what to expect. All day, as she went about routine duties, she waited for something to happen. It was, she thought, like having her neck in the slot at the bottom of a guillotine and wondering when the blade would fall.

She went off duty at three-thirty with her head still attached.

That evening Nick came by on his way home from the office. Though he'd already heard about Pat, Lynn told him all over again and he put his arms around her, soothing her with his words and his touch. Unfortunately, he couldn't stay, he had a dinner meeting with the medical records committee.

At the door, Nick took her in his arms again.

"Dr. Linnett won't want me at his dinner table on Saturday," she predicted mournfully.

"He'll be on your side at tomorrow's meeting, wait and see."

Lynn pulled away from him. "What meeting?"

Nick grimaced. "I didn't mean to tell you. I wanted you to get a good night's sleep. Mrs. Morrin asked Lloyd to attend a group meeting with all the Five East charge nurses, Werth, Dr. Silverman, himself, and her. The last I heard, it was planned for tomorrow morning."

"Why wasn't I notified?"

"I suppose because you'll be on duty and available."

"I hate all this. I *hate* it!"

He pulled her close and kissed her. It wasn't until after he'd gone that she realized neither of them had mentioned Renee. Surely Nick must know she'd left the hospital without medical consent.

But she couldn't worry about Renee, now. Not with her own neck in danger.

She hardly slept at all. When she arrived at the hospital, instead of feeling dazed with tiredness, she felt abnormally alert. Predictably, she found a note on her time card telling her to be in Mrs. Morrin's office at eight and was glad Nick had warned her that the others would be present.

The DNS had arranged the seating so two rows of chairs faced her desk. Dr. Silverman was five minutes late, and after he'd closed the door behind himself and taken the last chair, Mrs. Morrin stood up holding a chart in her hand.

"This is Patricia Werth's chart," she said. "I've read

411

every word on every page of it, and I now will quote at length from the nursing notes."

Mrs. Morrin sat down, opened the chart, and began. In her firm, no-nonsense tone, she read what the nurses who'd taken care of Pat had written. Day shift, evening shift, night shift, all documented their continuing difficulty in convincing the patient to follow her doctor's orders.

She finished, closed the chart, and looked at them. When her pale blue eyes met Lynn's they held no warmth. But then, they never did.

"If anyone here doubts that Mrs. Werth often refused to abide by Dr. Silverman's orders," the DNS said, "I'll ask the Five East charge nurses to confirm what's been written on the chart."

"Pat could be difficult," Dr. Silverman admitted.

"The chart mentioned you were notified of your patient's problem on three occasions," Mrs. Morrin said.

He nodded. "I spoke to Pat like a Dutch uncle."

"You refer to such a lecture in the physician notes," Mrs. Morrin agreed. "But I see by the nursing notes Ms. Holley notified you that Mrs. Werth removed her abduction pillows and threw them on the floor the day after you spoke to the patient about her behavior."

He shrugged.

"You agree Mrs. Werth often didn't follow your orders?" Mrs. Morrin persisted.

"I said so, didn't I?" Dr. Silverman snapped.

"Thank you, doctor." Mrs. Morrin turned her attention to Conrad. "Were you aware, Mr. Werth, that from the time of her arrival on Five East, your wife consistently refused to speak to Ms. Holley and also refused to acknowledge anything Ms. Holley said to her?"

"That's nonsense!" Conrad glared at the DNS, but didn't look at Lynn.

"It's documented on the chart. I also have statements from Five East personnel confirming the fact."

"That's damned odd," Dr. Silverman commented, turning to glance at Lynn. "Had a grudge against you, did she?"

"I charted what I observed, doctor," Lynn said carefully. Inwardly she cringed, hoping Pat's jealousy of her wouldn't be dragged into this.

Conrad leaned toward Dr. Silverman. "Look, Henry," he said, "Pat tends to color the facts sometimes. Maybe we've been a bit hasty in taking what she told us at face value."

Dr. Silverman eyed Conrad, then looked at Mrs. Morrin. "It's obvious you called this meeting because you think my patient lied to me about how she dislocated her prosthesis. Since her husband also seems to feel that's the case, why should I believe her?"

He rose and reached for the chart. Mrs. Morrin handed it to him, he flipped it open and, still standing, scribbled something inside. Tossing the chart onto her desk, he turned to Conrad. "My opinion, in writing, is that Pat disobeyed my instructions and suffered the consequences." Without waiting for any comment, he stalked from the room.

Conrad got hastily to his feet and hurried after him. Everyone remaining in the room stood up. Dr. Linnett, who hadn't said a word until now, smiled at Mrs. Morrin. "I can always count on you," he said. He winked at Lynn as he passed her on his way to the door.

The DNS dismissed the other two nurses after thanking them for coming, then asked Lynn to remain.

"I'm grateful for what you've done," Lynn said. "I wasn't sure anyone believed me."

"You document well," Mrs. Morrin said, picking up Pat

413

Werth's chart. "What I read in here convinced me you were telling the truth, though I was inclined to believe you from the beginning." She smiled at Lynn, a genuine, wholehearted smile.

"Thank you," Lynn stammered.

"We've had our differences in the past and no doubt there'll be more in the future, but you're the kind of nurse every hospital needs more of."

Lynn was so startled that she barely managed to repeat her thanks.

Mrs. Morrin handed her the chart. "You may return this to Five East. I consider the matter closed."

For Lynn, though, it wasn't. That evening she brooded about what Conrad's wife had done or tried to do to her, and finally made a decision. She couldn't confront Pat as long as she was a patient on Five East, but when Pat was ready to leave the unit she damn well would.

On Friday Lynn, listening to the early morning newscast as she ate breakfast, paused in raising her mug to take a sip of coffee. ". . . ill health, the judge claims, is his reason for withdrawing from the gubernatorial race. The announcement came as a bombshell not only to his supporters but to. . . ."

Lynn stared at the radio, shocked. Was this what Angela'd told her to watch for? Was this judge Shaleen's father? He must be. My God, no wonder the poor kid had been scared. The papers had been full of his campaign, and according to most he'd been a shoo-in for governor. He'd even been mentioned as a possible presidential candidate four years from now.

Because the judge was so well known, no doubt there'd been quite a few people who'd recognized Shaleen on TV. He'd had no choice but to withdraw. With his political

414

plans so much dust, he'd been punished in a manner Lynn would never have foreseen.

Lynn went to work still musing over the effectiveness of Angela's plan. When she looked in on her, Angela nodded toward the TV. "Serves the bastard right," she muttered, her eyes glued to the screen, where the withdrawal was being discussed in depth.

Just after nine, Connie, talking on the phone, motioned to Lynn as she passed the desk. Lynn stopped, waiting. Connie set down the phone and smiled. "Mrs. Werth's being transferred to Surgical. They finally have a private room available."

Lynn smiled back. Good news. Even though she had a private duty nurse now, Five East would be glad to see the last of Pat.

When the transfer arrangements were completed, Lynn personally took Pat's chart and medications down to the surgical unit. On her return to Five East, she went into Pat's room. The private duty nurse was packing the last few items and Pat lay flat in the bed.

"I'll help you wheel the bed into the elevator," Lynn told the private duty nurse. She then walked to the bedside and looked at Pat. "Do you want your nurse to listen to what I'm going to say or not? If you don't answer me I'll assume you don't care and I'll go ahead."

Pat glared at her for a moment then glanced toward her nurse. "Step outside for a moment, Terri," she muttered.

As soon as the door closed behind Terri, Lynn took a deep breath and let it out slowly, determined to be frank but keep her cool.

"Your behavior on this unit has been self-destructive, to say the least. I hope you see the person you're hurting the most is you. In Boston, I remember admiring your flair for clothes. When did you stop caring what you wore? Or how you looked? That's self-destructive, too. I don't want anything you have, I never did, and I never will.

"You even tried to kill me. How stupid that was! For your sake I didn't tell the police the truth about the shooting, but now I wonder if I shouldn't have. Maybe being booked for attempted homicide might have jolted you into thinking straight. I'm not your worst enemy—you are.

"Stop wasting your time and energy trying to get even with me and use it on yourself. You're still a good-looking woman—prove it!" Knowing better than to wait for any reply, Lynn walked to the door.

"I'm ready to help you move Mrs. Werth to her new room," she said to Terri.

Nick decided the combination of the judge's downfall and Lynn's vindication deserved a first-class celebration, so he planned something special for Friday night at his condo. A mini-disaster in the form of a broken joint in a water connection intervened and, though the plumber finished his repairs before five, the place was a mess.

"So we'll be dining out this evening," Nick told Lynn when he called with the news. "Unless you're into walking barefoot across soggy carpets, it'll have to be your place afterward, but I'll provide the postprandial brandy."

They ate in an old Victorian hotel, The Sea Watch, a few miles up the coast where the surroundings were elegant, the service impeccable, the food *haute cuisine,* and the string trio talented.

As they lingered over coffee, she said, "You keep promising to cook me the perfect meal at your place, but somehow it never happens."

"If you weren't so sexy, maybe I could keep my mind in the kitchen," he said.

"Sure, blame me. Next you'll accuse me of breaking the waterline."

"No, that had to be Manabozo. He delights in spoiling my best-laid plans. He's more trickster than hero where I'm concerned."

"Manabozo comes with the Indian genes, right?"

"Either that, or old Greatcloud sicced him onto me. He mistrusted complacency, and Manabozo certainly prevents a man from being complacent."

She smiled at him. "I think you really do believe in Manabozo."

"Why not? The quickest way to attact his mischief is to pretend he doesn't exist."

"Since I don't have a drop of Chippewa blood, he won't bother me."

"Don't be too sure." He took her hand. "When you're with me, anything might happen."

"And has." She glanced at him from under her lashes. "Frequently."

Her look, touching her, roused him. He raised her fingers to his lips to taste them, pleased to hear her soft intake of breath. It excited him to know she wanted him as much as he wanted her.

"If we don't leave soon," he warned, "who knows what might happen right here?"

When they walked into Lynn's apartment, Nick smiled when he looked at the coffee table in front of the couch and saw three candles—short, medium and tall—in a brass dragon candle holder. Was practical Lynn trying for a romantic mood? As far as he was concerned, the more romantic, the better.

"I like your candle holder," he said as he set the brandy bottle on the counter.

"I found it in a junk shop by the beach," she said. "It reminded me of when we went to the San Diego Zoo, except mine is a mythological flying dragon. I found these there, too." She produced two brandy snifters, one small and green, the other larger and of clear glass.

Nick poured a generous dollop of brandy into each glass, bringing them and the bottle to the coffee table. "Toss me some matches and I'll light the candles," he told her.

By the time he had the candles burning and the lights doused, Lynn had selected an FM station playing classic jazz, the music barely audible. She kicked off her sandals and came to him, her face shadowed in the flickering candlelight so that she seemed a different woman, one he hardly knew, mysterious and alluring.

He wanted her, wanted every part of the woman Lynn was. Since he'd met Lynn, other women didn't exist for him. Sometimes the intensity of his feelings about her scared him.

He reached for her, his arms closing around her. She fitted against him perfectly, her soft warmth igniting a demanding fire in him. The world was reduced to Lynn and Nick and the passion flowing between them. No one else ... nothing else. He lowered his head to kiss her.

As his lips met hers, he thought he heard a noise behind him. Before he could move, a blinding pain streaked through his head and then darkness closed over him.

Lynn staggered as Nick fell against her, losing her balance so she sprawled onto the floor, half under him. She gasped as she saw the dark figure looming over them both and struggled to free herself from his limp weight.

The flickering light turned the face hovering above her into a devil's grinning mask. Lynn rolled free of Nick and tried to twist away as the figure swung its arm down toward her. In the split second before she was stunned by a glancing blow to her temple, she recognized their attacker.

Renee!

Lynn came to awareness hearing a voice calling her name. She opened her eyes. Renee's glittering eyes stared down at her as Lynn fought to remember what had happened. When she tried to get up, she found she couldn't. Her hands were tied together, as were her feet. A cloth gag muffled her involuntary cry.

As the realization of what had happened flooded through her, Lynn strained to catch a glimpse of Nick. He lay beside her, his eyes closed, unconscious, a trickle of blood matting his dark hair. He, too, was bound and gagged. Quickly Lynn shifted her attention back to Renee, wincing as pain stabbed through her head.

Renee held a hammer by the handle, swinging it back and forth as she stared down at Lynn.

"Now you'll listen to me," Renee whispered. "Now you have to listen. You're going to die." Her voice grew louder. "But first he will. Your lover. So you'll know what it is to lose the man who means more to you than anything in the world."

She eased down onto the couch. "I loved Ray. You never did. He loved me, too, before he met you. We were lovers. You didn't know that, did you?"

Lynn felt the bile rise in her throat and she willed herself not to gag and choke. Ray and Renee *lovers?* But they were twins, brother and sister.

"What we had together wasn't wrong, it was beautiful." Tears gleamed in Renee's eyes. "I loved him, but he met you. I went with other men, even though none of them meant anything to me. I tried to make him jealous, but after a while, he wouldn't even see me any more ... be-

419

cause of you." She beat on the coffee table with the hammer and the candle flames danced and flickered. One of the snifters turned over and Lynn smelled the aromatic scent of brandy as it dripped onto the carpet.

"You!" Renee raised the hammer threateningly and half-rose. She shook her head and sank back. "No. Not yet." Her lips stretched in a ghastly travesty of a smile.

Lynn noticed for the first time that Renee was wearing one of her dresses, a soft pink sleeveless cotton. How had she gotten into the apartment? How long had she been hiding here? Lynn had taken Renee's key when she'd moved out, but it was possible she'd had a copy made earlier. For Tex, maybe?

"Ray liked pink," Renee said dreamily, running her hands over the dress that fit her so poorly. "I used to wear pink for him all the time—until he married you. He was mine, you had no right to take him. No right."

Renee's ramblings had a familiar ring. Nausea twisted Lynn's stomach as she realized why. During those last few weeks with Ray before he killed himself and tried to take her with him, he'd told her over and over how she had no right to talk to anyone except him, to smile at any one else. No right.

"I'm going to kill him first," Renee said, gesturing with the hammer toward Nick. Lynn didn't dare take her eyes off Renee to look at Nick.

"Then you'll know how I felt," Renee gloated. "You'll watch me and you won't be able to stop me and he'll die in front of you. You'll see his head all smashed and bloody and know you couldn't save him."

As stealthily as she could, Lynn tired to twist her wrists free of the cord that bound them, but the knot was secure. Her ankles were also tightly bound. But she couldn't lie

420

there and let Renee kill Nick, she thought frantically. She had to do something. But what?

The burning candles!

As carefully as she could, Lynn judged the distance to the coffee table. In a sudden burst of motion, she flung herself sideways and kicked out with her bound feet, slamming them up and under the coffee table. It toppled. Everything on the table scattered onto the floor—glass shattered, the brandy bottle fell on its side, the candles flew from the holder.

Flame leaped from a candle to run along the stream of brandy and up an alcohol-spattered drape. Hitching herself across the rug, Lynn tried to reach the flames, hoping to burn the cord from her wrists.

She was almost to the burning drape when Renee, frozen for a long moment in surprise, jumped up from the couch and, screaming curses, dashed toward Lynn, hammer raised to strike.

Chapter 26

Renee had to skirt Nick's prone figure to reach Lynn. To Lynn's surprise, Nick suddenly rolled against Renee's legs—he must have been playing possum, waiting for his chance. Renee tripped and sprawled onto the carpet, the hammer dropping from her hand. Nick rolled again, and managed to cover the hammer with his body.

Lynn thrust her bound hands against the flaming drapes, biting her lip against the searing pain. If only she could stand it long enough for the cord to burn through. A loud buzzing startled her. The smoke alarm! Would someone hear it and come to check? She couldn't count on it.

Renee, on her knees, clawed at Nick, trying to reach the hammer beneath him. Lynn pulled hard against the cord and felt something give. Coughing from the smoke, she jerked her hands away from the flames and strained as hard as she could. At last the cord parted and freed her hands. She tore off the gag.

Ignoring her still-tied ankles, her eyes tearing from the smoke, she hitched herself across the carpet toward Renee and Nick, grabbing the brass dragon on the way. Renee turned toward her and Lynn raised the candle holder, bringing it down on Renee's head with all her might. Renee slumped across Nick's body. With a violent heave he flung her off and she rolled against the overturned coffee table.

Lynn spotted a sharp sliver of glass from the broken snifter and used it to saw through the cord binding her ankles, then staggered into the kitchen for a knife to free Nick, accidentally kicking the brandy bottle on the way. Knife in hand, she returned to the living room.

To Lynn's horror, she saw that Renee was engulfed in flames. She yanked the afghan from the couch and threw it over Renee, trying to smother the fire. As she hurriedly sliced through the cord on Nick's wrists, she heard a faraway siren.

Once Nick's hands were free, he took the knife from her while she ran into the bedroom for a blanket. Nick, on his knees beside Renee, had plucked away the smoldering afghan by the time Lynn, choking in the smoke-filled room, hurried in with the blanket. They rolled Renee into the blanket and Nick hoisted her over his shoulder as Lynn opened the door.

A fire truck, red lights flashing, pulled to the curb as they came out, and other sirens wailed louder and louder as they approached. Nick and Lynn, still coughing from the smoke, looked at one another.

"Accidental fire?" he muttered.

A better idea than admitting to anyone the terrible truth. She nodded, suddenly conscious of the fiery pain in her wrists and hands. She looked down at them and saw the raw redness and blisters of second-degree burns.

After the ambulance arrived, Nick, Lynn, and Renee were taken to the Harper Hills ER, where they were treated for smoke inhalation. Nick also had his scalp laceration tended to and Lynn's burns were taken care of. Renee, conscious but incoherent, was admitted for further treatment.

"How did she catch on fire?" Lynn asked Nick in a low tone as he, taking over for the nurse, wound Kerlix bandage around her hands and wrists.

"The bottle you kicked splashed brandy over her and the flames followed the brandy. It wasn't your fault, so don't blame yourself."

Lynn closed her eyes.

"I mean to give Phil hell for transferring Renee off the locked unit," Nick went on. "If he can't spot a patient who's so close to a psychotic break, he'd better switch specialties."

He helped Lynn from the gurney and put his arms around her, not saying anything, just holding her close.

While having breakfast on Saturday morning, Lynn found her fingers weren't too badly burned to manage silverware.

"You don't need to cancel for tonight," she told Nick, who'd brought her to his water-soaked condo after they'd left the ER. "If you think the Linnetts won't mind the bandages, I'd really like to have dinner with them. Except I don't have a thing to wear. I imagine everything at my apartment smells of smoke."

"You're sure you don't mind going?"

"I psyched myself up to it last week. Why waste all the energy I used?"

"In that case, I'll take you shopping—on the understanding I get to choose the dress and everything that goes with it."

By unspoken consent, neither of them mentioned Renee

or the horrors of the night before. They'd rehashed what had happened into the early hours of the morning, purging themselves before finally falling asleep, and for now both wanted to forget it all.

When they went shopping, Nick's choice surprised Lynn: it was a deep rose chiffon gown, with long floating sleeves and a high neck.

"You've told me more than once how practical I am," she protested, "and now you want me to wear this totally impractical dress."

"Hey, it hides your bandages, doesn't it?"

"Is that why you chose it?"

"Didn't you look in the mirror when you tried it on?"

She nodded. "I thought it fit well."

He shook his head. "You looked, but you didn't see. I really prefer you with no clothes on at all, but since that'd probably shock the Linnetts, this is the next best thing. Something about the color—or maybe the style, I don't know—suits you perfectly. In it you're every man's dream."

"Bandages and all?" she countered, secretly pleased.

He leered at her. "Doctors have strange fetishes."

The dress wasn't the only purchase. Nick chose everything she wore from the skin out, including pale pink panties and matching bra-slip trimmed with lace, the most frivolous underwear she'd ever owned.

They drove over to her apartment afterward so she could retrieve a few necessities. When she noticed her door was ajar she cried, "Someone's in there!"

"I gave your key to the cleaning and repair service I hired," Nick told her. "They estimate it'll be two weeks before the place can be lived in, what with the repainting and other renovating. They'll bring your clothes and personal belongings to my condo as soon as they have them washed and cleaned."

She gazed at him in astonishment.

He shrugged. "With your burns, you're in no shape to handle any of this yourself. Your insurance ought to cover most of the cost." He grinned at her. "It looks like I'm stuck with you for the next couple of weeks."

That evening Alice Linnett, elegant in silvery blue silk, immediately put both Lynn and Nick at ease with her lively chatter.

"Lloyd's always telling me I talk too much, but then he knew that when he married me, so he can't really complain," she said after they were seated in the dining room and had been served the first course by a middle-aged Oriental woman.

Alice turned to Lynn. "Lloyd tells me you're cool to the idea of Nick coming in with him. I can't for the life of me think why, not when they get on so well together."

Nick, sitting across the table, looked on with some amusement as Lynn, startled, tried to explain. It was her problem. Let her fend for herself.

"Nick has always—I mean, from what I know of him, Nick seems concerned with people who can't afford—that is, poor people." Lynn looked as though she wished she were anywhere but here.

"But what does that have to do with Lloyd?" Alice asked.

"Uh, well, Dr. Linnett—" Lynn paused and glanced desperately at Nick, who smiled encouragingly but didn't say anything.

Lloyd spoke up. "I believe Lynn thinks I won't allow

427

Nick to take on any patient he chooses, that I have a bias against the poor."

"Good heavens!" Alice exclaimed.

By now Lynn's face was almost as deep a pink as her dress. She raised a hand to her cheek and the sleeve fell open to reveal the bandages. The reminder of what had happened the night before twisted Nick's gut. If she hadn't braved the fire to free herself, both of them might have died. If he'd lived and she hadn't, if he'd lost her. . . .

"Lynn," he said, leaning forward, seeing only her. "Lynn, Lloyd and I have worked things out. I'm not going to change, my practice won't change. Our practice, Lloyd's and mine, will broaden instead. I want to work with Lloyd. Try to understand."

Her green eyes darkened as she frowned and, knowing she meant to argue, he leaned closer to her. "Lynn, be fair. You've told me you want to become a nurse practitioner, and you know I don't think much of the idea. In my book, nurses belong at the bedside, taking care of patients. I'm trying to come around to your point of view. God knows, I might not manage to change, but because it's you—" He was forced to break off when, swift as an eagle's swoop, a realization rushed through him.

Lynn. She was the one woman in the world for him, the only woman he'd ever love. If he lost her, he might as well die himself. She was the woman Greatcloud had promised he'd find. He hadn't truly believed the old shaman until this moment. As he gathered his wits, Nick could have sworn he heard a faint sound of distant laughter.

He smiled at Lynn. "We have to understand each other," he said, reaching his hand across the table. "If we don't, we're going to have some terrible fights after we're married."

She stared for a long moment in disbelief, then slowly, hesitantly, her hand crept to meet his.

When their fingers touched, they both knew it was in silent promise.